THE
WHISPER
LEGACY

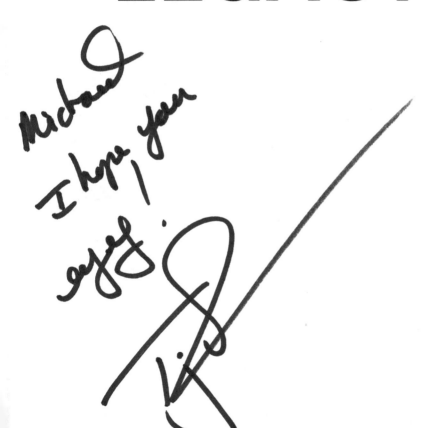

Michael
I hope you
enjoy!

THE
WHISPER
LEGACY

A Pappa Legacy Novel

Tj O'CONNOR

LeVel
BEST BOOKS

Author Photo Credit: Tj O'Connor

First edition

ISBN: 978-1-68512-914-9

Cover art by Level Best Designs

This book was professionally typeset on Reedsy.
Find out more at reedsy.com

For Robert—The real Tommy Astor.
Master Sergeant T If You Please!
Wheeler-dealer, entrepreneur, benefactor, and friend.

Jack—a friendship by chance for 30 years?
Thanks for the laughs, lunches, and support.

And for Nic.
Critic, editor, and longest-running friend.
Thanks for all you do.

Praise for The Whisper Legacy

"O'Connor's *The Whisper Legacy* is an addictive joyride. Sometimes the loudest sound is a whisper when PI/Consultant Marlowe Curran finds himself in the crosshairs as political figures drop. The secrets are buried in the Whisper Legacy."—James L'Etoile, award winning author of River of Lies and the Detective Nathan Parker series

"Former intelligence operative/now down-and-out PI Marlowe 'Lowe' Curran is a fascinating character who takes us on a wild ride through murder, kidnapping, high-ranking political scandal and long-buried secrets in *The Whisper Legacy*. Author Tj O'Connor does a masterful job of providing chills, thrills, excitement, suspense—and lots of fun too—along the way. Highly recommended!"—R.G. Belsky, author of the Clare Carlson series

"Binge read in one sitting! *The Whisper Legacy* has all the makings for a sleep deprived night."—TG Wolff, co-host Mysteries to Die For podcast

"With *The Whisper Legacy's* heart-pounding pace, well-written characters, plot twists, action, and intrigue, TJ O'Connor once again proves why he is a master of the political thriller."—Westley Smith, author of *Some Kind of Truth* and *In The Pale Light*

"Tj O'Connor has a rare gift of combining unique character development with a fast-moving story pace that not only transports you into his world, but also makes you want to stay. From elaborate settings, to plot twists you won't see coming, to larger-than-life but relatable characters, O'Connor's story continues to gain momentum, and I would recommend everyone come along for the ride."—Jay W. Foreman, award-winning author

"Tj O'Connor's spy thriller novel *The Whisper Legacy* is a tour de force that grabs readers by the scruff of the neck, impelling them forward, and it doesn't let go until the last word. Though Lowe Curran is a compelling and humorous protagonist, who endears himself to the reading audience with ease, there are truly spine-tingling moments of terror and horror that he must endure to stay alive and unravel the intricate web of intrigue at the highest echelons of power. The author shows real tradecraft not only in his writing style and character development, but also in his extensive knowledge reservoir of all things spook."—Seth T. Thatcher, award winning author of the epic sci-fi novel *Zendra of the Periphery*

"*The Whisper Legacy* is a powerful and well-written cyber warfare 'take' on the familiar noir tale of criminals needing to keep their stolen records hidden. With some fresh, intriguing twists."—James McCrone, author of the Faithless Elector series and *Bastard Verdict*

Chapter One

Marlowe "Lowe" Curran

G etting old is not for the meek. Especially when, in your youth, you were an adventurer and risk-taker—a man of mystery and worldliness. You know, stuff that made your heart rumba and your pulse sizzle. Having to perform menial, boring deeds in your later years is tough. Especially when you sit around with good bourbon and reminisce about the old days. You tend to drink too much and pine for those glory days and lost adventure. So much that it eats at you. Not that I've ever done that, mind you. Just saying, you know, it happens to *other* people.

For instance, if anyone had told me twenty years ago that one day I'd be standing outside an old, two-story brick Rambler in Leesburg, Virginia, at ten in the evening, wearing old, raggedy pajamas, an ill-fitting robe, and carrying a dog leash—absent the dog—I would have been offended. Such a scenario might have suggested I'd lost my faculties too early in life. Perhaps I'd gone crazy or become homeless. Of course, I'd never seen a homeless person wearing pajamas and a robe at ten in the evening, crazy or not. Still, you get my concern.

I'm Curran. That's *Ker-in*, not *Kuur-an*. It's Irish—not that it matters. But pronunciation is important.

Don't get the wrong idea about me. I don't normally dress up in old PJs and walk neighborhoods with a dog leash. It just seemed like the thing

1

to do tonight. I'm also not that damn old, either. At present, I'm pushing my early-mid-fifties and have a full head of dark, reddish hair, and almost always in need of a shave. It's not that I'm trying to be suave and cool. I'm sorta lazy about shaving. I've been told I look like the dashing Sean Bean. No, not *Mr. Bean*—Sean Bean. Anyway, that's me, and I'll explain more later. For now, my PJs were falling down, and the ratty robe I had on wasn't fitting all too well, either.

My feet were sore from my ambling down a block of crumbling sidewalk in the middle of this beautiful August night. Of course, August in Virginia was hot, humid, and, well, hot. My ensemble was cooler than jeans and sneakers, but it did not include slippers. Barefoot was not accidental. It's for effect.

See, I was going for that crazy old dude persona.

Most concerning to me was my partner. Or lack thereof. Actually, he was my long-time friend and co-conspirator in many such episodes of my life. He's missing. Stevie Keene should have been here an hour ago and running countersurveillance. He should have been watching my back and ensuring I wasn't walking into a gunfight or a pair of handcuffs.

He wasn't.

Stevie hadn't responded to my cell calls. He also wasn't in the van parked across the street from our target like he should be. That was bad. Real bad. I was going in blind.

"Stevie? Where in the flying monkeys are you?" I whispered to his voicemail again. "You're late. I can't wait any longer. If you get here while I'm inside, stay put and watch my escape route. And brother, you better have a good story—like being abducted by aliens."

I peeked at the old Rambler's front windows and dangled the dog leash. I called out as loud as I could, "Rufus? Come on, boy. I've got cookies."

No, I had no dog named Rufus. I also had no cookies. Try to keep up.

The house windows were blacked out—odd even for this part of town. I knew someone was inside. First, a thin sliver of light escaped through a corner of the window. Second, the electric meter around the side was whirling away like a NASA satellite station. Third, and perhaps most important, I'd seen the short, pudgy, receding hairline kid with his embarrassing attempt at a beard slip inside an hour or so ago. He looked like he'd glued stray hair here and there on his cheeks. His eyes were inset, or maybe his fat cheeks hid them.

Billy Piper reminded me of that dumpy loser who tried to smuggle dinosaur eggs off the island in *Jurassic Park*. He got eaten in the first thirty minutes of the movie. Served him right—poor, defenseless dinosaurs.

"Rufus? I've got cookies." I banged loudly on the door and rattled the doorknob. "Don't hide on me, Rufus. Don't be a bad dog."

If Piper was trying to be stealthy, he failed. I heard him approach the door inside before he peeled back the window covering and glared out.

"What are you doing, old dude? Get lost."

As I've already said, I'm not that old. But, given I'd put on a shaggy gray wig and plastered fake beard crap on my face, I give it to him.

A dog barked, then yelped as the face pushed closer to the window. "Shut up, mutt. What good are you? This old fart is almost in the house, and you just noticed?"

Time to play the role.

"You got my Rufus? Give me my dog." I banged on the door again. "Now, before I call the cops. Dog napper."

"It's my dog, old dude," Piper yelled. "Get off my property, or I'll kick your old ugly butt."

I held up the leash and took a step back, turning in a slow circle to appear dazed. Then, I began to cry. It took nearly a full minute before Piper opened the door and stepped cautiously outside.

"What the hell is wrong with you, old dude? My dog isn't Rufus."

I turned to him, reached up to wipe my tearless eyes, and let my bright red identification bracelet show below my pajama sleeve.

"Where am I? Who's Rufus?" I turned in a circle again and let a few more whimpers out. "Who are you? What are you doing in my house?"

At first, Piper turned red-faced with anger. Then, when he saw my medical bracelet, he reached out and grabbed it. "Oh, you're one of those Alzheimer's people. Get the hell out of here. Understand? Go home. Shoo."

Home, indeed. "This is my home. What are you doing here?"

Beside Piper, a brawny black lab trotted into the doorway and barked. Not a threatening bark. More like an obligatory "woof." After two such woofs, he trotted up to me and sat wagging.

"Useless dog. What are you doing inside?" He grabbed the dog by the collar and dragged him past me. He shook him several times, cursing. After berating him again with another smack to his hindquarters, he found a short chain affixed to a big walnut tree in the front yard and clipped it on his collar. "Flippin' mutt. You're supposed to warn me before they get to the door."

"Don't hurt my Rufus," I yelled.

The chain was twisted and wrapped around the tree. The lab only had about two feet of room to move. There was no water bowl and no signs of one anywhere. The wear marks on the grass suggested the dog spent too much time chained to that tree.

What an asshole.

"What are you doing to my Rufus?" I growled. "Where's his food and water?"

"Screw the dog. Maybe now he'll bark when he's supposed to." Piper shoved me sideways and reentered the house. "Get the hell out of here, or I'll call the cops."

"Call? I didn't call you."

"Jesus, I don't have time for this." He squared off on me in the doorway. "Get lost, old dude."

"What about my Rufus?" I shoved Piper back a step. That surprised him. I guess old men with Alzheimer's should be weak and defenseless. "Get out of my house."

Piper reared back to strike me and held his fist in a threat. "I'm gonna put you straight." His smartwatch buzzed wildly and flashed like Dick Tracey was calling. If you don't get the shout-out to Dick, forget it. You're way too young to understand. "Go, dammit."

"Not until I get my Rufus."

His watch signaled him again.

"Ah, shit. No. No. No." Piper shoved me sideways, and I feigned a fall just inside the doorway. He kicked at me and barely connected as I parried with my arm. "Get outta here, old dude. Wander or doddle your way back where you came. I got my own problems." He shoved me out the doorway, swung the door to shut it, and ran down the hallway.

I, not being a confused old geezer, lodged my foot in the door before it closed. With no more than a sore big toe when it hit, I kept the door ajar.

I followed his footfalls to the back of the house. I might be committing a few felonies soon, so I slipped on leather driving gloves to eliminate the chance of any fingerprints. After all, my felony count had just started, and the night was young.

I know cool TV stuff like that.

At the end of the hall, I descended the stairs into a dark basement. There, a small room lay ahead, lighted by a single overhead light that bathed the room in a hazy illumination. There were only a few old boxes stacked around and a bicycle hanging on a wall rack. Ahead was a heavy, steel door, still ajar. A carnival of flickering lights escaped through the opening. Beyond, I heard Piper cursing and babbling in a panicked voice.

I eased inside and found a larger section of the basement. The space was lined with soundproof tiles and heavy industrial carpeting. There was a refrigerator and small stove on one side of the room and cabinets of computers and electronics on the other. Between them was a command console and two gamer's chairs facing a wall of computer monitors and large video screens. The walls not blocked by computer gadgets were covered with movie and book posters of every major spy thriller I'd ever heard of. One was a poster of a pale-faced Alec Guinness wearing oversized, dark-framed glasses—an aged, probably original collector's poster of John Le Carre's *Smiley's People*.

Holy crap, Billy Piper was a wannabe spy.

"Shit, they caught me." Piper stood in front of a shelf of electronics and spun around when I stepped inside. "What the hell, old dude?"

We had to talk about that old dude thing. I was getting there, but really, how rude?

"I told you what would happen if you didn't leave." Piper balled his fist and came toward me. "It's gonna cost you. You should've left to find Rufus."

"Who the hell is Rufus?" I asked.

I don't know if it was my sudden calm, steady voice, or the silenced .22 pistol in my hand—aimed at him—that startled him the most. Either way, I had his attention.

"What the...who are you, old dude?" He stared at the pistol. "You don't have Alzheimer's."

"Nope."

"Who then?" He took a step back as his face tightened and filled with so much anger his cheeks were ablaze. "Ah, shit. Are you with them?"

"Them?" I waved my pistol back and forth to keep his attention. "Explain."

"Screw you." He spun around as his computers began wailing some kind of alarm. "Come on man, I got bigger problems than anything you can bring. If you don't get outta here, those problems are going to be yours, too. Go find Rufus or whatever. Get out."

I aimed the pistol at his head. "I think not, Billy."

He spun back around at me. "You know me? Did they send you?"

"Oh, I know you." Boy, was he slow. "I'm here about money and information. I have no idea who 'they' are. Although, 'they' might be like my clients. You hacked them, and now they want their files and money returned. Right, Chip Magnet?"

"Oh, man. You *are* them." His face blanched, and the tough guy drained away. "Dude, I got money. I can pay. I pay you and you say I wasn't home. Deal?"

Desperation replaced the bravado he'd taunted me with moments ago. "Chip Magnet, are you for real? What a totally bullshit handle, Piper."

He shrugged. "It means—"

"I know what it means, idiot. Look, Billy, you hacked the wrong people— my people. I'm here to fix things. And in the future—if you have one—you might take care who you hack. Some folks out there don't go to the police. They don't hire lawyers or call the credit bureau."

"Huh?" His eyes locked on my pistol as it raised to eye level. "What?"

CHAPTER ONE

"They send me."

Chapter Two

U.C.

The man in the expensive Saville Row suit and Gucci loafers sipped his vodka martini and settled back on his king bed, pillows plumped and perfectly positioned by the staff. He glanced around his Waldorf Astoria suite, feeling very pleased with himself. Never had his accommodation been as nice. Never had his payment been as nice—nor as often—as with this assignment. He wondered how long it would be before it would all end.

The man wore a collarless shirt that fit snugly over ripped muscles. His head was mostly bald but for close-cut, thinning dark hair around the sides and back. His face was narrow and strong, accentuated by a salt and pepper beard that was three days of growth meticulously trimmed for effect—a dangerous, stay-clear effect. In the years he'd operated at the higher end of his profession, he found his persona and image as daunting to his prey as his skills. The million-dollar benefactors he serviced expected a little refinement and image, not to be confused with Hollywood assassins cloaked in black leather feigning brooding personalities. His clients demanded thoughtfulness, the ability to move in any surroundings—Washington dinner clubs or Bangkok brothels.

U.C. had mastered the chameleon persona years before.

The satellite phone on his nightstand vibrated. He scooped it up. The Controller didn't like to wait. Not for the million-dollar price tag for U.C.'s services. Glancing at the screen, the call wasn't from the Controller, but from one of the minions sitting in a lesser hotel room somewhere in the bowels of Alexandria, Virginia.

"Yes?"

The voice was frantic. "U.C., I found him. There's a problem."

"Problem?" U.C.—bestowed upon him many years prior because of his preference to operate against his targets *Up Close*—sipped his drink. "If you found the target trying to hack our servers, just send me the address and—"

"He got through."

"What?" U.C. bolted upright and spilled his drink. "You told me the security was impenetrable."

Silence.

"Well?"

"Someone left some nodes insecure, maybe. I don't know."

U.C.'s mind raced. "An inside job?"

"Maybe."

He closed his eyes. "Sweet Jesus."

"U.C.?" The caller hesitated. "The hacker got all the way into the E-Suite."

He was on his feet now, moving around the room, gathering his things—the most important ones—his shoulder bag, jacket, and silenced pistol.

"Did you hear me?"

U.C. grunted, "Text me the address. Get four men there fast. I'll meet you there."

Hesitation, then, "Orders?"

"Don't be stupid."

U.C. tapped off the call and instantly activated the satellite text program. As he did, the Sat phone concurrently launched an encryption program that NSA would take years to break—another luxury of working for the Controller.

He typed out a simple message—*Urgent. Hack successful. Compromised. I'll contain.*

Miles away, across the Potomac, the Sat Text arrived at the Controller's private office. It took only moments to return a response.

U.C. rarely initiated such calls. Rarely one marked with "Urgent."

The Controller—*Define compromise.*

U.C.—*Total.*

The Controller—*Confidence?*

U.C. finished his text and exited his suite—*Whisper is compromised.*

Chapter Three

Curran

"They send you?" Billy's eyes narrowed as his bravado returned. "For what?"

I wavered the pistol just for giggles. "Guess."

"Come on, man. Don't give me that bullshit." Billy's computer monitor flashed a red warning logo, like he'd just lost communication with his planetary commander. "Who the hell are you?"

"That's complicated." I motioned him away from his computer console. "Why don't you sit? Then, you're gonna recover my client's data."

"Later." He turned back toward his console as beads of sweat consumed his brow. "I back out of this system I'm in, or they'll find me in a few minutes. If I don't..."

Billy Piper, AKA *Chip Magnet*—a silly, juvenile handle like the gamers and hackers love to bestow on themselves—took a step toward his keyboard. He stopped when I fired a silenced round—more a thwack than a bang—that whistled past his head and into the far wall.

"Piper, don't be stupid." I aimed my pistol at his head. "Don't make this worse."

His face blanched as his main computer monitor flashed, *"Trace In Progress."* He spun toward me and thrust an angry finger out, "Do you have any idea what will happen if I get traced? My clients are a nasty bunch. They won't like me getting caught."

"Too late, Piper." His computer continued flashing the end-of-the-world. "Did you ever consider maybe your clients sent me?" I didn't have a clue who his clients were, but I'd heard that line before in many a spy movie. "Now, you're gonna un-hack *my* clients."

The large computer monitor stilled when a single phrase appeared on his screen in big, red font—*Trace Successful.*

Judging from the look on Piper's face, he needed a bathroom.

"Damn you, dude." He raised a fist at me. "They found me. These people won't be playing when they get here. They'll kill me. They'll kill you, too. I'm leaving."

I stepped forward with my pistol chest high, shoved him hard into one of his gaming chairs, and kicked the chair backward into the computer console. He tried to rebound, swinging at me, but my pistol—jammed into his chest now—calmed him.

"First things first. You gotta fix my problem. Then, you can fix your problem. Just don't make your problem my problem."

"You gonna kill me?"

"Depends. All I want is my client's data back, and the release codes for the ransomware lock you put on their system. Easy-peasy. What happens to you depends on how fast you do that. So, hurry the hell up. I'm supposed to be doing something else, and it's important."

"Really?" He gestured toward the refrigerator across the room. "Look, there's twenty-five grand in the safe behind the fridge. Take it. Walk away. Just let me get out of here. Everyone wins."

"Twenty-five grand? Where'd that come from?"

"Who cares? I gotta go."

Who used cash anymore? Old ladies and crooks. Guess which one Billy was? Still, I like cash.

"Take it. I insist."

Well, if he insists. I yanked my cell phone from my rear jammies' pocket and hit the recording button on the voice recorder.

"You insist?"

He nodded.

"For the record, Mr. Piper." I extended the cell phone toward him. "You want me to take twenty-five grand as restitution for your crimes against my clients?"

"Yeah, yeah, that." He grimaced. Thankfully, cell phone recordings don't record facial features. "Call it a gift. Call it restitution. It's yours. Just take it. Come on, old dude. We gotta go."

I tapped off the recording and pocketed my phone. Then, I tossed him a multi-terabyte USB drive from my other pocket. "To speed this along and to make sure I have what I need, transfer any files you stole in the past week onto this drive—it's a special toy that will do it in no time. Then, you'll release your ransomware lock on their systems and give me the codes to each. Got it?"

"Is that all?" His eyes glared hate at me. "I don't have time to fix anything. Their trace was complete. There's no time."

"My problem first. Then you can leave."

"No." His eyes were wild now, darting from the computer screen to me and back several times. "I gotta get out of here. Whatever you want. Take it." He jumped up and started for the door.

"Sit down, Piper." I fired another shot that shattered the gigantic TV screen behind him. "You haven't been excused. Do as I say and you're out of here in ten minutes."

"Ten minutes? I don't have ten minutes." He glanced at his watch, then the shattered monitor. "You don't get it."

"You're wasting time." I gestured to the USB drive. "Get to work on my problem."

"Fine." He returned to his console with me carefully watching him. He inserted the USB I'd given him and stared at the second big monitor—the one without the bullet hole in it. "Jesus. I'm going to die either way."

The monitor in front of him went ballistic with machine code and algorithms uploading into his vast hacking system.

"What the hell is all this?" His eyes glazed over, watching the code streaming across his monitor. "You're hacking *me*?"

Chapter Four

Curran

"You're hacking *me?*" Piper stared at the message flashing across the monitor—*Have a nice day.* "Are you kidding?"

"Why yes, I am. Hacking you, that is. Not kidding. Go ahead and download all the data from the past month—"

"You said a week." His voice strained. "A week. Come on. There's no time."

"A month. Humor me. I'm old, and my short-term memory is bad. Then release the ransom lockouts on those companies and give me the release codes."

He hesitated, looked from me to the pistol, called me something that would make sailors blush, and banged away on the keyboard once again. He sweated and cursed, constantly looking at his watch until the download was done. Finally, he handed me my USB.

"Codes are there in a file. We good?" He stood. "I can go?"

"Damn, Piper. Who's got you all twitchy?" I pointed my pistol toward his refrigerator. "You forget something."

"Yeah. Take the cash. You bastard."

He'd easily rolled the refrigerator from the wall and opened the old-fashioned iron railroad safe. Inside was a large duffle bag.

"Here." He tossed the duffle at my feet. "Tell me you're not going to count it, asshole."

14

"Oh, no. Counting a gift is rude."

"A gift?" His face washed even more angry. "Whatever. Sure, a gift."

"Now you." I waved him backward to the room corner near the door. "What am I gonna do with you?"

"You said I could go." He jutted a steel finger at me again. "I did what you wanted. I gave you money. Don't be a—"

"Zip it." It took me a moment to flex cuff his hands behind his back and prop him against the wall. He fought me at first, but a little tap or two on his head with my pistol calmed him. Okay, a big tap. "We both know you have a backup somewhere. It'll take a few days probably, but you'll be back playing video games and watching porn soon enough. Not hacking, though. And no more ransoms. That's over. You'll notice a new program installed when you load your backups. That's me. If you touch it. If you try to delete it. If you look at it funny, I'll know. That's how I found you, *Chip Magnet*. My clients have been hacked before. There's a tracer in their system files to lead me right to the next bastard who touched their servers with malice aforethought."

Piper struggled against the zip ties. "I'll be dead in a couple hours. They're probably coming here now—any minute."

He cursed so much that I almost wanted to sit and wait with him until whoever or whatever arrived just to see how freaking scary they were. Then again, no. There were things to do, and I didn't want to be here to clean up the mess.

"Sorry, Piper. Hackers are as bad as murderers. You destroy lives nearly as much."

"Screw you and screw them." His ranker was oddly back, given his situation. "I've hacked the best of them—you have no idea. I take what I want and—"

"You destroy people, asshole. You steal bank accounts, retirements, all of it." At least, he did with my client. He raided their business accounts and their employee files. "Ever think of what that does to people?"

"I don't give a shit." He likened me to a goat engaged in unnatural acts. "Let me go. They'll kill me. Both of us."

Billy Piper destroyed people and simply didn't care. That, and he was mean to me—justifiably, perhaps. He was brutal to his dog, and that bothered me the most. I wanted him to feel the fear his poor dog did every minute. That's me, see, a sucker for hard-luck people and dogs. "Don't worry, I'll lock up behind myself."

I went to his hacker-console and found his cell phone there. It was blinking and carrying on like his computer screen.

"Unlock this." I brought the phone to him. "Fast."

"No."

Another bullet struck beside his head convinced him of his error. He rattled off the code, and I tried it in the phone. It didn't work. As I lifted my pistol, this time to eyeball height, he suddenly remembered the real code.

"Good, thanks. I'll be taking this with me to make sure you don't do something silly like call the police. I know you don't have a house phone. After all, you're Chip Magnet—World Hacker Extraordinaire."

"I'm gonna get you, man. I swear." He pulled on the nylon flex cuffs, trying to free himself. "I did what you wanted. You stole my phone, my money—"

"You gifted me the money." My next shot cracked into the wall on the other side of his head and shredded a soundproofing tile, sending him diving onto the floor. "Gifted. Remember?"

"Yeah, right." He rolled up onto his knees. "That God damn dog. Worthless mutt. I got his sorry ass to keep people like you out. If I get out of this, I'll—"

"Where's your bathroom?"

His eyes narrowed. "What?"

"Bathroom. I'm old. I gotta pee."

"Oh, for God's sake." He shook his head. "Hey, there's beer and pizza in the fridge upstairs. Help yourself. You just signed my death warrant—probably yours, too. But after you use my bathroom, have some pizza. By all means."

Death warrant? Wow. Was he being melodramatic or what?

"I'll flush and wash my hands. Getting old sucks, but I still have good

16

hygiene."

"Good for you." Rage filled his eyes. "Thanks to you, I won't be getting old."

"Look, Piper, you stay very quiet and still. I'm sure you're being melodramatic. If anyone has reason to kill you, it's my clients. And see? I'm not going to do that. I'm just leaving—with your generous gift and some pizza. Stay quiet and stop squirming. And Piper, don't come after me. I won't be as nice if I see you again."

"Screw you, old dude."

Minutes later, after using his facilities—yes, I washed my hands—I'd grabbed the pizza and beer from the fridge. Rufus, or whatever his real name was, loved the slice of cold pizza I gave him. All dogs love pizza. It's genetic. I read somewhere that thousands of years ago, wolves braved man's campfires to warm themselves and have pizza. That's how dogs were domesticated.

Tossing the timid Lab another piece of pizza over the seat, he gulped it down like he hadn't eaten in a week. Then, after topping it off with a cold beer—me, not him—we drove from the neighborhood.

There was nothing like cold beer and pizza on a late-night outing.

Chapter Five

Ambassador T. Bradley McKnight (Emeritus)

Eighteen miles east of the old Rambler, an unlisted, private phone sitting atop a grand antique desk rang. The desk was the centerpiece in an extravagant study. The study sat in the rear of an even more extravagant colonial home. The home was tucked away on several acres of land in Northern Virginia's Great Falls enclave.

The aging man, distinguished and more fit than anyone in their mid-seventies could attain, lay sleeping on his overstuffed sofa at the far end of the study. In his deep slumber, he ignored the phone. His aide would get it, and then, only if it were earthshattering, would he be roused.

While it continued to ring, footsteps approached down the wide hall, and the aging man awakened enough to see a fortyish, strapping man in a tieless, white Oxford and khaki slacks enter the study. With a yawn and a casual glance at the grandfather clock across the room—just after midnight—the newcomer lifted the phone.

"Ambassador McKnight's residence," the tired aide de camp, R. Bryan Scott, said with a sharp irritation in his voice. Then, Scott cleared his voice and straightened. "The Ambassador will be on the line shortly."

Scott placed the call on hold and called across the room. "Sir? It's the call. They're waiting."

Ambassador is a title for both the active senior diplomats and those *emeritus* from the State Department of the United States. It is a rare post that is awarded to only the loyal and achieved—both in and out of diplomatic circles. Often, the nomination for an ambassadorship is the reward for support and favor from presidents and secretaries. Other times, the postings are political markers placed on the lands of foreign countries, setting a tone and message from the American leadership. Always, the title demands respect from allies and adversaries, and from both sides of the political aisle.

"Ambassador? Your call—"

"Yes, yes, I'm right here. I hear it, Bryan. How can I not?"

"It's the White House, sir."

"It's after midnight. Doesn't that man ever sleep?"

Scott held the receiver out. "Slightly less than you, sir."

"Right." The Ambassador rose, strode across the room, and took the receiver. "Ambassador McKnight."

"Please hold for the president." A short pause and several mechanical clicks.

"Brad? Are you on?" Christopher R. Cranston, President of the United States, cleared his throat and whispered something to someone nearby. "Brad?"

"I'm here, Mr. President. You caught me napping."

"Napping? You're slipping, Brad." The president laughed. "Well, it's late. Please forgive me. I think you know why I'm calling."

The Ambassador settled back in his chair and let the moment hang. "It would be rude and presumptuous of me, Mr. President."

"Bullshit, Brad," the president cawed. "How long have we known each other? Thirty years? Christ, we just spoke about this last year. The time is coming faster now that the elections are over."

"Sir?" The Ambassador grinned. "Is Vice President St. Croix leaving so soon?"

The president sighed. "We've discussed his future plans, Brad. I have to be nimble and have a lot to do this second term. He's not up for much of it, and whomever I pick will be the ticket leader in a couple years. I wanted you to hear it from me. I'm down to the shortlist. You're on it."

Maintaining lists of key cabinet and leadership posts was a common strategy in politics. The Ambassador knew there were difficulties with Vice President St. Croix, and the president's Chief of Staff had begun planning such a list of replacements even before the first election over four years ago. It was protocol. Although St. Croix had run on the ticket and helped secure the president's reelection, there were signs he was not in it for the long haul of the second term. The insiders knew it was a matter of time before he stepped back. The list of replacements had taken shape—been molded, shortened, and updated. While presidents surround themselves with a critical inner circle deeply more loyal than even his closest cabinet members, a president must always have a list—short or long—of those ready at little notice to assume cabinet posts and other key positions. Not having a list was failure.

From the beginning of his first term, President Cranston's weakest link had been Vice President Grayson St. Croix. St. Croix had risen through the party from a junior Texas congressman to senior party leadership in under thirty years—a fleeting time by political standards. He had helped secure Texas for the president in the last election. Then, he began to falter. He lost focus and often unraveled during trivial sparring matches with the media and political opponents. Even toward the end of the campaign, Grayson St. Croix became more a liability than an asset. Everyone on the campaign knew that. Luckily, the voters ignored it.

Still, President Cranston had returned St. Croix's loyalty with loyalty and support. He spoke highly of him to all. He assigned high visibility tasks and assigned key Cabinet leaders to work with him to offset his dwindling capabilities for the coming year. No one understood the changes in Grayson St. Croix. No one but him.

Simply, Grayson St. Croix was not going to complete his second term tenure as vice president. He'd be lucky to complete another year.

The Ambassador asked, "If I may be so bold, Mr. President—"

"Jesus, Brad," the president laughed again, "it's just you and me. No recordings. No minders. My Secret Service are all in the hall. Call me Chris. Just like the old days."

"Yes, sir, Mr. President." The Ambassador chuckled. "If I may, how short is your shortlist?"

A pause, then, "Well, to tell you the truth, Brad, you're third. That is, if politics go according to plan. I have some concerns about the first two on the list—you know them both, good men but not without flaws."

"Wain and Alvarez. Yes, I know them well." The Ambassador stood and poured himself a congratulatory drink from a crystal decanter nearby. *Midnight be damned.* "Senator Wain is a great candidate. He's got fire. Emilio Alvarez is solid. You'd be wise to go with a Latino this time. No?"

The president hesitated again. "Yes, politics. I hate having to deal with all that race for race and gender for gender. But it's the way things are. You're right; Jameson and Emilio are great choices. That's why you're third and not first. Still, both have resisted my ask. They're just playing it safe and want the job."

"I was under the impression you had a close confidant you were considering. Am I mistaken?"

The president was silent—thinking. "Ah, you mean Doctor Francis Feld. I have plans for Frank. He's my ace in the hole for Middle Eastern Affairs—along with you, of course. But he's finishing up a rather significant assignment for me in the region. And, quite honestly, he's not ready for politics at this level yet. And some of his regional ideas would not play well in Congress at this moment in time. Perhaps next time around."

"Yes, it was Dr. Feld I was thinking of." Dr. Frances Feld—a longtime friend and confidant of the president and the most vocal advocate for Middle East peace using a regional solution. "A shame, really. He's a brilliant man. What about—"

"I'm leaning toward Alvarez. He's tough. His experience as Vice Chairman of Joint Chiefs will be invaluable, and his understanding of the south border countries will be important."

The Ambassador sipped his drink. He knew the answer to the question he was about to ask, but he wanted to hear it, nonetheless. "Who are the other two, Mr. President?"

"Senator Piccolo and Governor Hersh. You top three have to hit some pretty bumpy road for me to go to them."

The Ambassador sighed—it was Alvarez. "Then you've made up your mind. Why call me now?"

"Not so fast, Brad." The president hesitated again. "Truth is, I don't know if Wain or Alvarez can win the presidential election after I'm through here. That's the grand strategy. Wain's been doing some great work in the Senate Intelligence Committee. Emilio will need more time in the public eye. Hell, ninety percent of the country doesn't even know he was Vice Chairman, let alone what *that* is. I doubt I'll have to tap Piccolo or Hersh in either case. They're chomping at the bit for the call either way."

The Ambassador considered that. Third in line was a worthy position for any Cabinet post, let alone the vice presidency. Still, third was third. It was a long climb to first.

"I'll do as you wish. Whomever is your selection, I'll support you one hundred percent, *Chris*."

"There're many posts I'm going to be changing out, Brad. Just sit tight and be ready to say yes."

As was the president's MO, the line clicked off without closure.

The Ambassador sipped at his drink and contemplated the call. He'd expected it earlier in the week. When it hadn't come, he'd summoned allies on the Hill and maneuvered them like a grandmaster assailing the king. His gamesmanship had worked just as it had in years past. With his friends influencing the president, there was no telling where he'd land.

A voice pulled him from his thoughts. It was a soft, lightly accented voice as sweet as the woman who owned it. Over the years, that voice had always been in his ear, in his thoughts, and in his heart.

"Was it the call?" the silk-robed, exotic woman asked from the doorway. "At this hour?"

"It was. The president has me on the shortlist, Abby. Number three."

"Third?" Abby came into the room and slipped into one of the leather wingback chairs facing his desk. "You should be first. After all, he needs you to guide him with the Middle East policies. They have been a shambles for a decade. The country has been bouncing from poor strategy to poor strategy too long. Then there is—"

"Yes, yes," The Ambassador stood and moved around the desk to her. He took her hand and kissed it gently. "I know, my dear. I know. If I were to ascend to the president's side, you would be right there with me, Abby. Right there."

Abigail Angelos rubbed her deep, dark eyes. She was sixty and still as young and beautiful as any woman half her age. She had been his closest confidant, private secretary, and most trusted advisor for decades. They'd first met when he'd been posted in Cairo as an up-and-coming diplomat in the mid-eighties. She'd been a Greek administrative officer at the Hellenic Embassy there. When he'd moved on to Athens, she followed him and joined his staff as a Greek-American liaison. In the past many years, she'd moved from the office outside his door to his bedroom. She was his closest ally. Staunchest supporter. Dearest friend. Only companion.

"I would have liked to listen in, Brad. It's not every day I get a chance to hear a president beg your assistance."

"Stop that, Abby." He kissed her hand again. "Presidents don't beg. They command."

"Of course." She rubbed sleep away from her eyes and stood, enveloping him in a warm embrace and bestowing him a soft kiss on the cheek. "This is far overdue."

"Nonsense." The Ambassador touched her cheek with warm compassion. "How many years, Abigail?"

Without having to think, she said, "Thirty-eight."

"Ah, I see." He laughed as he headed for the door. "You've been counting. I suppose one day—"

"That is nonsense. I need no ring to know your commitment to me. I am here, still in your bed. Aren't I? The public be damned. And if I were counting, I could tell you the months and days, too."

He grinned. "By my side since my youth. I'll let you listen next time. Once it's official."

Abby smiled and yawned. "But ask him to call at a decent hour. A girl needs her beauty sleep if I'm to plot and conquer this world in Washington."

* * *

Ethan Levene

Not many miles away, sitting comfortably in rolling swivel chairs and sipping coffee, two men sat with earbuds surrounded by electronic equipment and computer screens. When the first alert reached them five minutes earlier—that a specific phone number had been activated—the equipment came alive.

So had they.

Listening intently, the younger of the two—a thin, almost gaunt, sandy-haired man barely old enough to understand the impact of his task—grinned widely. His dimples and freckles showed like a schoolboy with a new crush.

"Damn, that was out of left field," the young technician said in a singsong voice. "Not quite the call I expected. Maybe it's something we can use long-term."

Ethan Levene, the older of the two and senior man, was short and plump—but not really fat—and sat close by listening to the same intercept. He shook his head, belched, and reached for another slice of pizza sitting on a small rolling table between them. "We got nothing, junior. Nothing actionable. Not yet."

"He just said—"

"Nothing. The president, putting rich, powerful guys on a list. So what? They didn't talk about money. They didn't talk about favors or promises or quid pro quo. Nothing. Zilch."

"We gotta get something definitive. From someone. Anyone."

Levene stuffed half a slice of mushroom and pepperoni into his mouth, chewed loudly for a few seconds, and dropped the balance of the slice onto a paper plate in front of him. He swiped his thinning red hair behind his ears.

"Patience, junior." A long slug of coffee. "Maybe we just need him to have a crisis land in his lap. Then you'll see how he dances."

Junior, whose real name was Gideon Freedman, frowned. "If we could just figure Whisper out and nail him."

Levene forced a laugh. He'd been in the business for nearly two decades. "You still don't get it, do you, Junior? We don't nail anyone. We listen. We collect. We get information. Someone else does the getting and nailing. Hell, ninety-nine percent of the time, we'll never know what it all means."

"I didn't spend six months training to sit on my butt and watch computers. Neither did you."

"No, but you gotta pay your dues, kid."

"I was top in my class on the range and hand-to-hand. I was second in my class in tradecraft and surveillance."

"So shut up and do your job. Pay your dues. Be patient." Levene stuffed more pizza into his mouth. "Besides, not knowing the outcome of what we do has its perks. If you don't know shit, they can't get worried about you. If they're not worried about you, you might retire one day."

Chapter Six

Curran

As I've said earlier, I'm Curran—Lowe Curran. I'm not really a bad guy. Most of the time, anyway. Okay, bad is subjective. Generally speaking, I'm a good guy who often is forced to do bad things. Forced is also subjective. In time, this too will be apparent.

I was born Marlowe S. Curran to a mother obsessed with Raymond Chandler's tough PI, Philip Marlowe. I loathe the name Marlowe. Actually, my dear mother was more in love with Humphrey Bogart, who played Marlowe in *The Big Sleep*. So, I'm lucky not to be Humphrey. My middle initial is S—yes, for Sam Spade. She also loved Dashiell Hammett. Jeez, can you imagine me as Dashelle Marlowe Curran? I would have been beat up on the playground a lot more in school—by the teachers.

It's a good thing dear old mom is gone, now. No, I didn't kill her for her naming conventions. Although...

Like my namesake, Marlowe, I'm a private investigator and security guru. I prefer private investigator as opposed to all those pulp-fiction monikers like gumshoe and private dick. It's something my mother would have loved to call me. Other than being half PI, my other half is as a private security contractor—a troubleshooter of sorts. Half of me is on retainer for the high-energy client who sent me to retrieve his company's data from Billy Piper and unlock the ransomware holding his business hostage. Working for good ol' Tommy Astor wasn't always much fun. Too often, he gave me some pretty ugly assignments. In the plus column was that his retainer kept me off the unemployment line for the past ten years. Whenever he needed my services, he got the "good buddy discount," and I did his bidding. A lot of the time, I did odd assignments that I didn't know why—dig up intelligence on this person or that company, surveil this or that guy, or the odd, break into this office and get something. He put it all under, "s business venture I'm working. It's all okay. Do it." It worked for both of us, and the money kept me going.

Tommy Astor was truly an acquired taste. Truth is, I'm lucky to know him.

On the ride home, the liberated Rufus The Lab sat in the passenger's front seat. He looked out the window and let his jowls flop in the half-open window like this was his first car ride. That, and my Jeep air conditioner had been broken for months—okay, more than a year—and this beautiful August night was very typically hot and sticky. Did I mention that?

Anyway, the dog occasionally glanced over at me and moaned. Maybe he was wondering if I was going to drop him on the side of the road. Or maybe he wanted a beer. After about twenty minutes, he must have decided he was safe. He straddled the console between us, leaning against me, and gave me a few long, wide tongue licks. That earned him the last slice of pizza.

I'm a soft touch with dogs. And women. And kids. And...oh, forget it.

To be clear, I didn't steal Rufus. He unhooked himself from the nasty chain around the tree and voluntarily followed me into the car. It's a free country. I'm sure he's over twenty-one. Who am I to stop him?

"Rufus?" He didn't even wag. "No. You're not a Rufus."

He moaned and lowered his head in embarrassment.

The first thing was to decide on a new name—like Chip, or maybe Billy. You know, something to remember tonight by. After all, Piper gifted me twenty-five thousand dollars, three-quarters of a pizza, a four-pack of good micro beer, and a very grateful dog. In some cultures, that made us practically family.

On our way home, I stopped at an all-night grocery store and stocked up on some Bogart essentials. Yes, if I'm Marlowe, he's Bogart. Dear old, departed mom would have liked that. She never liked me, but she loved dogs. Dogs and hard-drinking, quick with a punch, fictional PIs.

Bogart it was.

Bogart was terrified when I left him in my beat-up Jeep Wrangler and headed into the store. He howled and scratched at the window. But when I climbed back in with a new collar, six boxes of dog treats, water bowl, food bowl, two twenty-pound bags of dog food, and some dewormer and tick stuff, he sat back in his shotgun seat and played it cool.

He did, however, sneak a few peaks into the bags of Bogart loot.

I had no idea how to care for a dog. So, I got a little—okay, a lot—of everything. I also got some first aid stuff since when I was loading him into my Jeep a block from Piper's house, I noticed some open sores from the chain around his neck.

Suddenly, I didn't feel all that bad about Piper. There are a couple things that will stir me up fast. People who don't tip waiters—er, servers. People who leave trash in their grocery store carts like I live to clean up after them. And yep, people who mistreat dogs. Any animal, really. But dogs especially. And don't be near me when Sarah McLachlan sings that damn song of hers, *Angel*, as the voiceover for the animal rescue commercials. *Damnit, man, I now have the rescue missions on speed dial.*

I'm a little sentimental. That comes with age. I mean, in my younger, more virulent years working around the world doing our government's scrap work, I never shed a tear for anything or anyone. Not once. Of course, back in those days, I never had to stop for a bathroom every hour or quit drinking before nineteen hundred—that's seven pm—so I wasn't up all night peeing. And I definitely didn't grunt and creak when I climbed out of the chair or off the floor after a workout. My joints had been just fine back then. They almost never complained about the abuse I put them through either. Unless there was a bullet hole or piece of frag sticking out of me. Then maybe a little. Who wouldn't? But, today, well, I'm bearing the fruit of my reckless, self-abusing, swashbuckling ways of yesteryear. With that comes sentimentality.

See, it's nature—it's not me.

Note to the younger public—live it up too much when you're young, and you'll pay for it later in spades. Getting old is not for sissies. Here's another tip—when someone older than you whispers in your young ear, "don't do that, dumbass," listen.

Bogart finished half of the first box of cookies before we reached home. I doubt he ever saw a dog treat before. He had his head in the box, trying to finish the last of them when I pulled it off and scolded him. He jumped into the back seat and cowered like I was going to beat him silly. That killed me, and I handed him the box to finish off. He wagged and moaned happily.

Did he just play me?

We turned off Route 50 in southwestern Loudoun County and took a wide county road north. A few miles further in, I eyeballed a long, gravel road called "Cantrell Way" that led to my landlord's farm. I considered driving up and checking on the little fieldstone cottage tucked away on the backside of Cantrell horse farm. My head bounced off the steering wheel a couple times from exhaustion and convinced me I needed sleep instead. Everything else would have to wait.

I drove on another eighth of a mile and turned left into a short dirt drive that led to my loft apartment above the Cantrells' west farm stables. The small, four-room apartment was built above the old barn that hasn't been used for a decade since the Cantrells built a new one closer to the main house. This cozy place has been home for four months. It wasn't the grandest place I'd ever lived, but it was good enough. It came with hot water, a nice bathroom, kitchenette, a few furnishings, and free internet. It also had a sound roof, and the mice *almost* never got into my pantry. Perfect for a guy who had almost nothing to his name and who'd spent a few years bouncing from one economy rental to another. I'm not nomadic, mind you. It just took me some time to find my feet. That and I sucked at money. Spending it, I was a master. Budgeting it for silly things like utilities and rent got in the way of my hobbies. But enough about me.

Bogart sat with his head out the window, snorting the early morning scents of rabbits, deer, horses, and safety.

"We're home, Bogart."

Woof.

Translated, that meant, "I love you, man. Which side of the bed is mine?"

It was just shy of five a.m. by the time I turned off the Jeep and carried all the shopping bags, and my duffle bag of Billy Piper loot up the outside stairs and into the loft. After dropping them onto the kitchenette counter, I considered making a cup of coffee from one of those new pod coffee makers. It would take five minutes to warm up and three minutes to brew a cup. By the time I finished the first cup, the damn machine would be off again. Nope, I'd skip the coffee.

The coffee maker made me feel stupid. Like when I couldn't get it to make coffee. Several times I nearly threw it out the door. But it had been a gift from my landlord, Janey-Lynn Cantrell—spouse to one Charlie Cantrell, old, crusty, rich, and powerful farmer-man. Janey-Lynn was the over-seventy farm lady landlord who owned this quaint, four-room cottage. If she came in and the coffee gadget was shattered in the pasture outside, well, she'd be displeased.

I know what you're thinking. I am not sweet on Janey-Lynn. Truth is, it would be easy to fall smitten if not for her grouchy, much younger, and bitter husband. Janey-Lynn was a sweet, gorgeous, silver-haired woman who could make thirty-year-olds envious. She was a healthy lady—healthy as in curvy and vivacious like Marilyn Monroe. Not that petite, emaciated look that so many women go for these days. If she were ten years younger, and I were a few years older...

Janey-Lynn and I were just good friends. First and foremost, she was my landlord and didn't charge a lot. That meant I had to keep things professional. No ogling her. She was other things, too, but I'll explain another time.

I checked my watch.

My biggest client, the aforementioned Tommy Astor, wouldn't be in his office until at least eight-thirty. That gave me time for some CMA—cover my ass—and maybe catch an hour of sleep.

I needed both.

Starting with my notebook computer, I saw a few dozen alarms from the surveillance cameras at the Cantrell cottage. The cottage was Janey-Lynn's guest house a stone's throw from my barn loft. It was also Charlie's love shack for his many trysts. Trysts he thought Janey-Lynn was unaware of. Did he really think she rented this loft to a private investigator by chance? *Silly man.*

The cottage CCTV cameras had sent me dozens of notifications late last night that I'd missed with all the hullabaloo in Leesburg. Someone had been milling around inside the love shack, too.

Charlie Cantrell was a dog. The alarms said he'd had a wild night. I considered checking last evening's surveillance footage but decided that would have to wait. It wasn't going anywhere, and I was too tired to sit and endure Charlie's X-rated adventures. That, and I planned on running the surveillance a few more nights just to nail down my fees.

Instead, I picked up the USB multi-terabyte drive from Piper's hacking. I copied all the data he'd had downloaded to another similar device. When it was done, I tucked my copy into a Ziploc plastic bag and hid it from everyone except Bogart.

I trusted Bogart. I was his hero and he knew who bought his cookies.

Sometimes, the best protection against unscrupulous adversaries—including clients and the authorities—was having the foresight to create your own get-out-of-jail plan. Having been the victim of backstabbing and duplicitous clients, I was all about CMA. How have I been wronged, you ask? Let me count the ways…I lost my high school girlfriend and my best friend—all in one night. During my junior year, when life should have been grand, said best friend swept said girlfriend off her feet and off my arm. *Ouch.* Not so many years later, I'd lost my fifteen-year career when a mission went south. Afterward, I was blamed for everything except Pearl Harbor and the Huns sacking Rome. It was them, wasn't it? Recently, I lost fifty grand over a high-dollar investigation that cost me six months of my life. The client stiffed me. That client—a high-powered D.C. law firm—had retained me for another secret client. Neither honored our deal. Then, the lawyer I retained to fight the first lawyer stiffed me.

For a moment, my eyes drifted to a silver-framed photo on my mantel. It was a beautiful woman who haunted me nightly. No, Carli was not the high school squeeze who was stolen away. Her loss came after that and before losing my career. Almost thirty years ago, she'd been the love of my life. I've never gotten over losing her. Simply looking at the photo or thinking of Carli was still a gut punch. The pain and tears returned every damn time. Years hadn't soothed the ache.

Loss and loneliness and self-preservation were my life's tenets.

Carli Trevino aside, hiding copies of the data drive makes perfect sense. I mean, if you had my history of getting screwed, you'd hide stuff, too. These days, it wasn't the hiding I worried about. It was remembering where. With age comes a whole new equation—five steps from a room, and you can't remember where you're headed or why. But the painful memories from thirty years ago are as vivid and raw as the moment they happened.

Not fair.

I hid my stash in a small hidey-hole I'd discovered in the loft. It was a loose brick among the footing beneath the kerosene heater tucked into a bricked-up corner of the main living room. Whoever had lived here before me had hollowed out the floorboard beneath the bricks and created a hideaway for valuables. Since I didn't have any real valuables, the data backup was it. After all, Tommy sent me to retrieve it. It was certainly more than accounting files and client records, too. I hoped it was. If not, I might feel bad about Piper later.

Naw, he got what he deserved.

A strange feeling of angst hit me. I retrieved my duffle bag from the table that contained the generous gift from Chip Magnet and Tommy Astor. It was the same gift, of course. But like playing Dirty Santa at Christmas time, you can't steal the same gift more than twice. After that, it's mine. Inside the bag was my silenced .22 pistol which I placed into the hideaway hole, too. Why? Because not only was the silencer illegal, but the pistol was stolen. Oh, not by me. Not really. I'd "found it" during a case I'd worked a couple years back that involved a drug dealer. When I was obtaining evidence on him, I happened upon it and liberated it from his stash. I simply forgot to turn it in to the police afterward. It's a simple mistake. Anyone could make it. Since then, having a throw-away silenced pistol, illegal or not, was often handy.

I pushed Piper from my thoughts and contemplated the overstuffed sofa. I had time for a fast nap and settled in. After all, it had been a tough night.

Bogart stared at me from across the room until I patted the back of the couch and coaxed him over. With a few uneasy starts and stops—I think he wondered if I were entrapping him for a beating—he sneaked onto the couch near my feet, wagging and moaning his appreciation.

Sleep came almost immediately to both of us...

...The smell of charring lamb filtered through the air like a fog settling over the Voula Beach Road. Greeks had many amazing customs. My favorite was Easter, when nearly every household gathered around wood and charcoal firepits and grilled lamb on a spit.

The neighborhood scents and noise sifted over the Villa's tall stone walls. The villa was a grandiose white stone and marble two-story built by one of a thousand Saudi princes and rented out to tourists.

Light and sound swirled around me.

An explosion...pain everywhere.

Angst. Fear. I had to fight.

Blood gushed down my head, my neck, and bathed me.

"Stevie...Stevie!" I grabbed my radio and weapon.

I maneuvered into the hall, searching for targets and friendlies.

My first mistake...the first bullet struck my left leg and spun me around, off balance. My hands flailed for balance.

The second bullet, and my second mistake, struck me and put me down...

...standing over me, the figure raised the gun for the final shot...

...I bolted upright. Sweat drenched me. My shirt was stained from the few moments of memory and dream state—terror and pain.

Bogart stood over me, moaning and licking my hands as they clutched the sides of the couch—white with angst and recollection. My thigh and shoulder tingled with their own version of memory—phantom pain from old wounds.

The dream—the nightmare—had come again.

Chapter Seven

Curran

Regret is an emotion always consumed cold. When it's born, it clings to you. It hides in your subconscious. It stalks you like a monster from your closet. When it manifests, it brings depression, angst, and often wishes that are dangerous and tempting. Those times are hard. Those times can be brought on with one too many drinks, one too many old photographs...one too many sleepless nights.

My life was all of those things. Regret just the lit match that was always too close.

I'd awakened unsettled and jumpy—awakened from short fits of sleep marred by that damn dream. It was always the same whenever the dream found me, and it found me far too often over the past fifteen years. Doctors had called it PTSD—post-traumatic stress disorder. I called it nightmares. Shrinks, hospitals, clinics, and group therapy were not for me. Even after they told me I'd never walk again and that I'd need lifelong nursing care. That I'd never regain all my faculties from the head trauma and blood loss.

I fooled them. It took work and self-therapy.

I know what you're thinking—Jack Daniels. Wrong—most of the time. Often, the best therapy I used was the will to prove them all wrong. This morning's therapy was a good run. I needed exercise to clear my head. There was nothing like a little self-flagellation to clear the cobwebs. So, I slipped on my running shoes and hit the dirt road for a five-mile run. Well, to be perfectly honest, it was more of a five-mile limp.

My limping had many causes. As previously mentioned, I used to be somewhat of a risk-taker. A real adventure junkie. A few of those adventures turned ugly and, well, brought out a weakness of mine—I'm disaster-prone. A few years ago, I cracked an investigation for a nearby airport. Their employees were selling company services and pocketing the proceeds. After paying me a nice fee, they gave me free skydiving lessons. I loved it—something I'd wanted to do since being a kid. I figured Voula Beach didn't kill me, so what the hell. I jumped at the chance to skydive. Pardon the pun. Anyway, on my first solo dive, I overshot the drop zone and got twisted in the wind. Then, I made the ultimate mistake of fixating on a fence I wanted to get over instead of considering the crosswinds. When I awoke, I had face-planted into the side of an airplane on the runway apron. Four broken ribs, a cracked hip, busted lips, and a black eye later, I was released from the hospital on a walker. It took months to heal. But hey, I skydived. One day, I'll go back and finish my certification. They say you have one bad landing every thousand or so jumps. I'm good for another nine-hundred and ninety-nine more—mathematically speaking.

So, yeah, I limp when I run sometimes. It means I've done manly things in my life. That's what I tell people, at least.

For every strong, rhythmic step with my right leg, there were a couple stutter steps and a limp from my left. The old injuries had healed, sure. In their place were scar tissue, ugly knots, and arthritis. Mornings climbing out of bed sounded like the old snap-crackle-pop cereal commercial. Now, tripping along the roadside left me aching and cursing and needing to clear my aches and pains.

It took me nearly fifty-five minutes to return home. Twenty minutes out, and the rest to limp back. The last hundred yards was a flat-out walk—daintily—trying to stay on my feet.

Have I lamented that getting old was not for wussies? Or anyone with bullet holes, shrapnel, or recurring nightmares? If you can't get old without the aforementioned defects, at least marry well and have a bunch of kids to take care of you in your broken-down years.

I never married. I had no children. My future years promised to be grumpy, painful, and lonely. In that order.

Now, at least, I had Bogart.

To be clear, I'm not terribly old. Sort of a mature, seasoned 'older' guy. I'm still reasonably fit. I can run and walk five miles. I work out a few times a week and almost never need more than a handful of pain relievers afterward. I can make it through the night with only one potty break. My hair is only now graying here and there—no, I don't dye it. And to complete my personal visual, I'm a solid five-ten these days. I used to be six feet, but as you age, you shrink. I shrink faster than most. In low light and from people with poor eyesight, I can pass for forty...*ish*.

No, really. I can. My favorite landlord says so.

I succumbed to my needs and attempted the alien coffee maker. Pride swelled when it actually started dripping dark roast into a cup. Not at first. I forgot to put the cup under it, and yes, I made a mess. I'll leave it for the maid.

Regrettably, I have no maid.

On my way to shower, I stood in the hall and contemplated the living room mantel—a heavy timber mounted among the bricked-up corner of the living room where the kerosene stove sat. There were a few items of memorabilia sitting there—some fake Greek pottery, a brass Aladdin's lamp gifted to me by a Saudi Prince years ago, and some other do-dads that always put a smile on my face when I limped down memory lane.

My eyes glistened when I fixed on Carli's picture again. My insides shuttered. She had been the most beautiful and amazing lady I'd ever known. My finger found the glass and traced her cheek. For a moment— a fleeting memory—her smooth, radiant skin warmed my fingertip and caught my breath.

Carli Renae Trevino was a vibrant woman with deep green eyes and flowing dark hair. Her Italian features gave her that exotic, dangerous look that was often betrayed by dancing eyes and a friendly, disarming smile. The photo was taken when we were in New England for a weekend—our last weekend. We were kids then, thirty-one years ago now. I was in the military, and Carli was a few years older and finishing college. She was wiser, and well, more worldly, too. I was so in love.

She should have been my wife. Instead, she was what all men fear the most. She was the one that got away. And I, being a deep-down sentimental fella, never let go. Ever. I had failed her, and she left me. I deserved it, sure, but the pain and loss were still inside. They stabbed and tormented me most sleepless nights.

Like it was yesterday, I felt her touch and heard her infectious giggle as she watched me from the mantel. A more sensual, alluring woman never existed. The loss cut me, and I wiped away an aberrant tear, feeling silly. I'd had those same tears the day she'd disappeared from my life. They were occasional bedfellows still.

I headed for a shower to think manly thoughts and consider what swashbuckling I might do today. Maybe I'd change my oil or give my Jeep a tune-up. Maybe I'd find some tools and repair the loft roof. Except, I didn't know crap-all about engines. If I used a hammer on anything, I'd probably have to call a carpenter to un-fix my repair. The last time I'd changed my oil and rotated my tires, I didn't refill enough oil. The idiot light sent me to a gas station. Good thing, too. My right front tire was falling off. I hadn't tightened the lug nuts properly.

Doing manly things was risky.

The cold water sent more than shivers through me. My teeth chattered, and my limbs wanted to jump from beneath the water. No, this wasn't some shock treatment to get myself going a little faster. The damn hot water heater—a solar gadget dear Janey-Lynn had installed to save money—was on the blink. Or it was that it had rained for three days, and the sun was elsewhere. Either way, the damn well water came from the Arctic.

After showering, I dressed in my best jeans and a maroon dress shirt. After I slipped on my worn-out Kohl Hann loafers with the small round hole in the right sole—no socks, mind you—I drizzled one finger of bourbon into a travel mug of coffee. One finger only. I'm not an alcoholic. Geez.

Lastly, I tucked my Kimber Pro-Carry .45—that's the short-barreled, concealable model—into the holster around my rear waistband and scooped

up the duffle bag of Piper's generous donation to my retirement fund. I next filled a bowl of water and a bowl of food for Bogart and headed for my Jeep.

As I was closing the loft door, Bogart slipped past me and pranced down the outer staircase. At the bottom, he stopped and let out a loud, guttural growl.

A rickety, thirty-year-old Chevy Blazer was parked behind the barn, nearly out of view. Lying on the hood, using its windshield like a bed, was a tall, strong-built man with long, gray hair pulled back in a ponytail. He wore ratty old blue jeans and a seventies rock band tee shirt that was too baggy and too dirty to salvage. His porn-star mustache needed a trim. The round John Lennon sunglasses perched on his nose threatened to slip off with each loud, reverberating snore that passed his lips.

Bogart crept closer, snarling. He wanted none of this guy.

"It's okay, boy." I joined him near the Blazer. "He's one of us. Though, he's a few hours late."

Bogart growled again and slowly stalked closer. When he reached the side of the Blazer, he let out a raucous barking fit and went front-paws-up on the side fender.

Stevie Keene, decades-long friend and brother-in-arms, erupted off the vehicle, rolled sideways, and fell to the ground. He lay there, groaning and coughing.

Bogart was on him. He bounced around the vehicle and landed squarely on Stevie's chest—front paws dug in, eyes wide, teeth bared and threatening.

"Whoa now, doggie. Come on. I'm a good guy." Keene's words slurred from a heavy night of drinking, but he was alert enough to stay down and not resist. "Come on, easy."

"Bogart," I yelled, but since he didn't know his name was Bogart yet, he stayed put. "He's okay, boy. Let the derelict up."

Stevie glanced toward me and smiled. "Oh, hey, Lowe. Can you get your mutt off?"

Bogart did not take kindly to 'mutt' and lowered his head closer so Stevie could inspect his glistening, big teeth.

"Sorry, Bogart. Lowe, please?"

As much fun as this was, I retrieved Bogart by the collar and allowed Stevie to get to his feet. He did, but only with the aid of the Blazer's front bumper. There, he leaned precariously against it to keep from tipping to the ground again.

"Stevie, where were you last night?" I moved up-wind of him from the dank, stale scent of beer. "You were supposed to have my back in Leesburg."

"Last night?" He blinked a few times. Then, he wiped his mouth, finger-combed his hair a couple times, and glanced at his watch. "Crap. I thought that was tonight."

Did I mention Stevie Keene was on the derelict list?

Stevie and I were friends from the way back...*way back in the day, as they say.* We'd been recruited into Dark Creek—a private security firm that lived off government contracts—about the same time and were partners for years. We became the closest of friends—brothers—and rarely took an assignment without the other. Then, it all changed at the Voula Beach Road. Of the entire team there, he and I were the only two to walk away. Well, he walked eventually. He was blown up in the assault and suffered a severe concussion, a few broken ribs, and a broken right leg. Me, I took longer to recover. He was fixed up locally. I was medevacked to Germany.

He came to see me in Germany right before I returned to the States. He didn't seem right then, and I learned he suffered a traumatic brain injury. I could barely walk, and he didn't seem all that stable most of the time—mentally. We drifted apart as both of us took separate paths to healing.

Like all best friends, we drifted back together in time. Five years ago, we reunited—memories and laughs. Or tears as it was for us. He'd been medically retired and set himself up in a tract of land in the West Virginia mountains he'd inherited or something. He turned it into a modern retreat—read that part prepper retreat and part mountain vacation home. Seems hard work and isolation were good therapy for him. When I'd caught up to him, he was a recluse. He'd become an odd, paranoid, heavy drinker, who often disappeared for weeks on end without a word.

It didn't matter. Not to me.

Our brotherhood was odd by any standard. I took the brunt of the physical damage in Voula. He took some, but his penance was deeper. His concussion had cost him memory and cognitive skills—a bad combination of PTSD and the traumatic brain injury that he could never really explain. For that reason, he stayed alone. Since reuniting, I'd toss him a job backing me up on a case. Mostly, it was charity. A grand here or there just to avoid that awkwardness over handing him money for no other reason than friendship. Of all the cognitive loss he'd suffered, pride was not among them.

Last night was why I rarely engaged him for anything serious. In the first few cases, he'd done okay. A little slow responding or understanding his assignments, but he always recovered and executed—mostly. Not true, the past couple years. He'd been unreliable at best. Last night, he was supposed to perform simple counter-surveillance to ensure no cops or other trouble found me while I was dealing with Billy Piper.

Instead, Stevie had found a nearby bar.

Now, he swayed where he leaned on the Blazer. "Oh, shit, bro. I totally blew it again. Didn't I?"

I nodded. "Yeah, Stevie. You did. I got through it. All's good."

"Why do you ever ask me?"

I shrugged. "Because I'd rather have you *maybe* be there than anyone else definitely be there."

He tried to smile but burped and slid to the ground again.

Bogart started to growl, stopped, and looked up at me with a whine.

It took me ten minutes to get Stevie up the outside stairs and onto the living room couch. He was barely on the cushions when he began to snore. I jotted a note for him. Food and coffee were nearby.

I hoped he could handle the alien coffee-pod monster.

"Okay, Bogart," I said, finding him sitting in my leather recliner across the room. "You're in charge. Don't bite him. He's our brother."

Woof.

I started to leave and turned back. "Don't let him throw up on my couch."

Bogart whined and laid his head on his paws, contemplating my longest

41

friend in the world—albeit a drunk and unreliable one. He moaned again.

"Good boy." I piled a half-dozen dog treats at his paws and gave him a head-scratching. Then, I put on some Seger—that's Bob, not Pete. Okay, different spelling. Bogart didn't look like a folk music aficionado. If he were one, our long-term relationship was doomed.

"I won't be late, boy. Keep Stevie safe."

Woof. I tossed him some more dog cookies on my way out.

Note to self—buy more dog cookies.

My cell phone buzzed in my pocket. Janey-Lynn Cantrell.

"Hey, Janey-Lynn, I was just on my way out...slow down. Whoa. I'll be there in five minutes. Don't say another word until I get there."

Chapter Eight

Curran

Some people have the Midas touch. Everything they do leads to wealth. I have the *Sadim* touch. That's Midas spelled backward—I'm a shit magnet.

As I rolled down the gravel road to the Cantrells' main house, my inner shit-magnet started to take hold. At the gravel drive that led to their quaint love shack, the dread arrived. The fieldstone and timber two-story cottage was nestled off the road amidst a stand of Cedars. Behind it was a grand view of the Cantrells' east fields, where their best horses grazed on summer grass and basked in the morning sun. The picturesque cottage belonged on the cover of some country life magazine. Or it would have if it hadn't been marred by the chaos.

Four Loudoun County Sheriff's cruisers awaited—two in the front, one around the side, and the fourth blocked the driveway to the front of the house. There was also an unmarked Explorer parked behind the two cruisers in the front, and a very familiar man leaned against the hood, talking with Janey-Lynn.

A chill ran through me as I realized I'd never reviewed last night's surveillance recordings. I'd been so tired that I'd blown it off. A nagging stab sent a wave of angst behind the chill. I had a very, very bad feeling as my shit magnet vibrated full throttle.

The deputy at the driveway entrance patted the air for me to stop. Then that familiar guy—Special Agent Vernon Evans—called something out, and the deputy waved me through.

Were they expecting me? That was not a comforting feeling.

I parked behind the gaggle of cop mobiles and slipped my Kimber pistol and holster from my belt. Better it should wait for me in the Jeep's console compartment. I climbed out and headed for Janey-Lynn standing near Vern's Explorer. Her face was awash in tears and a pale mask of fear. Her arms were folded, and she swayed from side to side. Those beautiful gray eyes were locked on me, and her mouth was clamped tight and frowning.

"Lowe, thank God." She ran and crushed into me. For a long moment, she clung to me, quivering and enveloped in my arms. Strange, too, because I don't recall her ever being that familiar with me. Not physically, anyway.

"Lowe, thank God." She quickly withdrew and cast an uneasy glance over her shoulder. "It's Charlie. He's dead."

Charlie Cantrell was dead?

Two things struck me like a truck head-on. First, Charlie didn't just die. He was murdered. Hence, the caravan of cop cars. Second, I didn't need to be told that I just joined the list of potential suspects, or as the police like to call us, *Persons of Interest.*

"Janey-Lynn, what happened? Are you all right?" First things first. "Tell me what you can."

Tears flowed, and she trembled down to her toes. She reached out for me to comfort her, but each time, withdrew. "Murdered, Lowe. He and that woman. They're dead."

Did I mention that Janey-Lynn Cantrell wasn't just my landlady, she was also my client? She hired me to prove her lying, cheating, mean-spirited younger husband, Charlie Cantrell, was having an affair. Surely, I alluded to that, didn't I? I mean, I wasn't recording his trysts to sell to cable TV. Hence, Janey-Lynn's comment, "and that woman."

"Lowe, hold it right there," Evans called from his Explorer. He walked up and yanked off his tie to combat the already growing humidity. "We need to talk."

Special Agent Vernon Evans was a short, muscular African American who'd been in the Virginia State Police for fifteen years. He was from Richmond and had worked his way up the lawman food chain the hard way—taking every dirty job and lousy shift no one else wanted. He'd gone to college and earned his bachelor's degree in criminal justice several years ago. Then, he'd aced the BCI exam the next year and joined the BCI as a special agent. BCI was the Virginia Bureau of Criminal Investigation—the Virginia version of the FBI. He was a bachelor these days—a nasty, gut-wrenching, and bank account-emptying divorce caused that. And that, my friends, is how we met. He hired me to prove his then-wife was involved with a local Ecstasy dealer. Said dealer had gotten her hooked, and when her money ran out, she parlayed what little intelligence she could get from Vernon to pay her habit. I found evidence of that fact. When Vernon's soon-to-be ex-wife faced the dealer in family court, she caved. See, I pulled some strings with the correctional system and landed that washed-out Ecstasy dealer a nice deal at a low-security lockup with a few extra privileges. In return, he testified and saved Vernon a bundle. That and I suggested—*suggested,* mind you—that I would leak to the general prison population that said drug dealer was an undercover snitch. I would never do such a thing, of course. But Mr. Dealer saw the light, and Special Agent Vernon Evans won his divorce case.

Now, Evans owed me.

Evans walked over and leaned in close to me, turning his back on Janey-Lynn. "Lowe, tell me you didn't off her husband and his mistress."

Ouch, straight to the point. "I didn't, Vernon. You know better."

"I do?" He laughed dryly. "I know you well enough to know you push boundaries. Sometimes, to the breaking point. I also know you know how to do the deed if need be."

He had me there. All the way around. "I don't murder people."

"Yeah?" He eyed me. "If something bad went down, you know, like you caught Charlie, and he went nuts or something—"

"I did not do this." I patted the air and played my defense cards. "I have the cottage wired with cameras and audio—for Janey-Lynn, Vernon. Soon as Janey-Lynn gives me the go-ahead, I'll give you access. It'll prove whatever happened in there wasn't me."

Evans cocked his head. "How do you know that?"

"Because I didn't do it." Wasn't he listening? I looked over at Janey-Lynn. "Can I give him the recordings? They're evidence. He'll get a warrant anyway."

Her face blanched, and she turned to Evans. "Agent, as I've told you, Lowe works for me and has for a few weeks. This is very delicate. May we have a few moments to confer? I can always call my attorney. I trust Lowe will give me the better advice between them."

Evans narrowed his eyes on her. His gears started smoking. I knew what he was thinking—only guilty people threatened to get attorneys. That was ludicrous, of course, because only stupid people didn't get attorneys. Stupider ones talk with the cops alone.

He looked at the deputies. They were all busy with assignments, and he lowered his voice again. "Okay, Lowe. I owe you, and I know it. You got five minutes. Then I have to take a statement from you. You'll have to get me those surveillance records—all of them."

I nodded. "Thanks, Vernon."

Janey-Lynn grabbed my arm and less than casually walked me back from prying cop ears without appearing to be evacuating me from a combat zone. She failed.

"Lowe, tell me the truth." She lowered her voice and turned so Evans couldn't see her speak. "Where were you last night? You didn't—"

"Me? No." Damn, my own client thought I'd taken her case to the limit. "Janey-Lynn, I was on another case for Tommy. I can't say anything about it, okay? It's very hush-hush. Just know that I didn't kill Charlie."

"You were gone for Tommy? You were supposed to be watching the cottage last night."

"I was." Well, not in person. "There was no point sitting around watching computer cameras when everything's recorded. So, I did a job for Tommy. It was important. Very important." Now, it was also an alibi if push came to shove. Though, if I played that alibi, I might get arrested for the several crimes I committed at Billy Piper's house.

46

See, a shit-magnet.

She sighed. "Agent Evans says he knows you. He wanted to know where you were and what you were doing all night. I told him you've been working for me. He instantly changed his attitude—I'm sure he thinks I killed Charlie or paid someone to. I hope he doesn't think that's you."

Well, Vernon Evans always was a smart lawman. Surely, though, he wouldn't think I did this.

"Janey-Lynn, I can't say what I was doing. It'll lead to more trouble, and I can't involve Tommy. I'm sure I can prove my innocence. Trust me."

She leaned back. "You need an alibi. Evans is already suspicious of us—of me. He asked if your investigation into Charlie led to you and me, you know, to us—"

"Yeah, I get it. There's no 'us.'" I glanced back at Evans, who was staring at me like a hound targeting a fox. "I still can't reveal where I was. I've got the surveillance recordings, though. I'm sure that'll fix this."

"No, they won't."

"Why?"

"They're gone, Lowe." Her face blanched, and her eyes dropped into a crater of trouble. "I used that link you gave me last week to check on your progress. There are no recordings from last night."

No recording?

"Janey-Lynn, are you sure?"

"Dammit, I'm so stupid." She cried openly and looked to the ground again. "I was checking the video like you did for me. I know, I know, you told me not to. But I did. I saw this figure enter the cottage and kill Charlie and that woman. I couldn't see his face or anything. I was terrified it was you, so I deleted everything. I didn't want you to get in trouble, and frankly, I didn't want to be implicated either."

My heart sank. I felt the executioner's needle stick my arm. In Virginia, prisoner executions were by lethal injection. I hate needles. I also hate being executed for something I didn't do. Trouble is, how was I gonna prove my innocence without putting my neck in another noose over Billy Piper? I'd walked a fine line of legality in his basement—okay, I jumped over it into the felony range—and couldn't use that as my alibi without causing Tommy Astor trouble. That trouble might lead to not getting paid, or worse, losing my client altogether.

"Well, crap." I glanced back at Evans again. "Janey-Lynn, I guess you thought you were helping. Truth is, you've made this worse. I'll figure it out. I guess you didn't tell Evans about the recordings?"

"No."

"Damn."

"Lowe, listen." She followed my gaze to Evans and turned back to me as tears welled in her eyes. "I hated the bastard, but this isn't what I wanted. I wanted out. You've been very good to me. I won't cause Tommy any problems, either. Tell Agent Evans you were with me last night. Tell him we were going over your case, and we had a few drinks. You fell asleep on my couch."

Oh, yeah. That's not suspicious. I told her that.

"Do you have anything better?"

Good point. "Okay, but why would you call me over so late?"

She didn't have to think. "I heard something around the house. Charlie was gone, and I called you. You came, checked it out, and stayed waiting on Charlie to come home. As far as Charlie was concerned, you were just another border. We had a couple drinks, things got late, and that was that. You left before dawn and went home."

Wow, really? She came up with this on the fly? She was either the best storyteller I'd ever heard, or she'd already thought it through.

"Janey-Lynn—"

"Yes." Her face reddened. "I thought of this while Agent Evans was questioning me. I don't have an alibi, Lowe. I was home alone all night—alone."

I knew what that meant. "You already told Evans we were together?"

"Yes, dammit, yes." Her eyes filled again. "I thought it was you in the video, Lowe. I did. I thought I was helping. We'll figure this out together. Okay? I'll double your fees."

Something told me helping me might lead to prison. I considered my options—confess to my misdeeds last night with Billy Piper, or throw down a teensy, weensy fib. Be on the hook for a litany of crimes in Leesburg or falsify official statements.

I'll take door number two.

"Double my fees? Okay." Sure, sure, now I sound like a real creep. "But Janey-Lynn, if things get crazy, you zip it and let me talk. Okay?"

She sighed and instantly relaxed. "Lowe, you're the best. Things will work out. You'll see. Just back up my story."

Yep, back up the pretty lady's story seemed easy enough. After all, it was only obstruction of justice and false statements. I hoped her story wasn't the road to a cell and a date with death row. That would really suck.

Charlie Cantrell and his mistress had been murdered. I was on the list of suspects. I wonder, is it double jeopardy if they give you two lethal injections?

Chapter Nine

Curran

Special Agent Evans was no small-town deputy or gumshoe-class investigator. He was smart and cunning. Above all, he was honest. Sure, he honestly didn't ask me how I obtained his freedom in his divorce. You know, pulling strings and coercing the witness and all. Oops. Truth be told, he didn't know how I'd gotten the dirtbag Ecstasy dealer to cooperate. It was all legal, I assure you. Well, legal-ish. I simply asked a favor of one very well-connected Tommy Astor, and poof—a legal, above-board decision was made that should said Ecstasy dealer meet unspecified conditions, he would be granted a lesser correctional institute. Should he not meet those same conditions, his name would appear on a different roster. That roster would list his new roommate, affectionately named Greg the Grinder. Mr. Grinder would receive very detailed information on the "cooperation" said Ecstasy dealer was providing law enforcement. Hypothetically, of course. No money changed hands. No backroom paybacks were made. Most importantly, Evans knew none of it.

So, when he folded his arms and glared in disbelief at me, his "honesty" radar was in the red zone. I swallowed, tried to appear confident, and knew following Janey-Lynn's path placed me in deep excrement.

After a private fifteen-minute interview inside his Explorer, Evans sat sideways in the driver's seat studying me. I'd spent the entire time repeating my alibi as Janey-Lynn had wished. I'd learned from being a private investigator not to align my version of the alibi perfectly with hers. I left a few details hazy, made comments about not believing she'd heard a prowler—though that was the reason I'd gone to her farmhouse. And told him we both knew exactly where her husband was and what he was doing. That conflicted with her story just enough to be believable. Just without holes so big it would cause problems.

"You expect me to believe you spent the night sitting in her living room, drinking and whatever? Neither of you came down to this cottage to confront Charlie?"

I shook my head as a great addition to my alibi struck me. "Why? It was being recorded. Hey, maybe the prowler was the killer. Maybe she wasn't making it up."

"Maybe. Or maybe you're full of shit."

I feigned insult as he thrust a palm up to silence any denial.

"How long have we known each other, Lowe?" He fixed his eyes on mine and drilled through me like a laser. "Five years?"

I nodded.

"How many times have you gotten yourself crossways with LEOS that I bailed you out of?"

Uh, oh. I think he's been counting. "Two or three. But hey, let's be honest. Those were really misunderstandings."

He shook his head. "I'd say closer to five or six *misunderstandings*. Like the time the Warrenton PD caught you coming out that restaurant's back window after starting a riot inside?"

Yeah, there was that. "If I'd gone out the front door, those four guys would have kicked my butt."

"They caught you cloning their cell phones."

"I was on a case."

He shifted in the seat. "And that time you interrogated those two neighbor ladies saying you were a Leesburg cop? They hadn't seen what they told us they saw. You made it look like we lied. You caused the entire prosecution's case to get thrown out."

I didn't remember it that way. "I was working for the defense, remember?

51

I never said I was a cop. I just didn't deny it when they asked. I never said you guys lied—"

His hand flashed up again. "Tell the truth, Lowe. Are you and the foxy Mrs. Cantrell up to something?"

"What?" I put on my best shocked face. "Come on, Vernon. You know me better. I wouldn't put you in a bind like that."

He nodded in rhythm with my lies. "Uh, huh. Look, I don't believe a word of your story. Fact. Either you two were, well, involved all night, or you're both lying, and neither of you has an alibi. Which is it? Did she hire you to dig dirt on her hubby, and it all went wrong?"

Him believing Janey-Lynn and I were *in flagrante delicto* might be a good alibi, but it was a little, well, uncomfortable. Better to play it on the fence. "She hired me. I've been getting plenty of dirt on Charlie. But, Vernon, we're not involved."

He twisted his mouth and stared. Finally, when his gears slowed a bit, he said, "You're full of shit one way or the other. Tell me the flat-out truth here, Lowe. Did you kill her old man?"

Ouch. The question hit me so hard I stuttered trying to find the right denial. Instead, my mouth bobbed around with huhs and hahs and then fell silent.

"Dammit, Lowe," he grumbled. "If I find out you're part of this, I'll tie the rope around your neck myself."

"Virginia is a lethal injection state."

"Screw you." He stabbed the air between us. "You know what I'm saying. Friends and IOUs be damned. This is serious."

Well, I was just trying to be factual. Details matter.

"Vernon, I get where you're coming from. I do." I reached out and touched his shoulder for a man-to-man truth. "I did not kill Charlie and the woman. I don't know who did. I know it wasn't Janey-Lynn. The video recordings will prove it."

He threw me a big curve. "Okay, I got a tablet right here. You say the surveillance stuff is on an IP. Sign in and show me. I'll have a warrant in an hour anyway."

Shit. Shit. Shit. Janey-Lynn deleted the recordings to protect me, whom she believed in her heart, killed her husband. I'm not sure I should be thrilled that she tried to protect me, or concerned she thought I whacked Charlie.

"Let's try it." Better to appear cooperative than obstructive.

As he pulled out his tablet computer, I gave him the URL and waited for him to bring up the site. Then, I took the tablet, turned it away from his prying eyes, and entered my log in and password.

"Here, it'll take a minute to load. There're a lot of files."

And...there weren't.

"What the hell?" Evans and I exchanged glances, and then both zeroed in on the screen. The directory entitled 'Current Images and Videos' was, as I knew, empty. "Let me try this again."

"Yeah, do that."

I did; three times, I logged off and back on, going through the ruse of trying to find the deleted files. There were none, of course. I faked panic well. Truth is, without those videos as an alibi and unable to use my exploits at Billy Piper's as an alibi, I wasn't faking panic.

"Jesus, Vernon. I don't know what to tell you." I handed him back the tablet. "I haven't looked at last night's video yet. I had three weeks of historic videos from a dozen evenings in the folder. Everything's gone."

Evans laid the tablet on a knee and banged away on its digital keyboard. He searched and hunted, cursed and raged, and eventually closed it.

"I swear, Lowe, if you're jerking me around, I'll have your ass in a cell for no less than obstruction. Maybe murder. If you know anything, now's the time."

I knew something all right. As much as I wanted to clear myself, I didn't want to have Janey-Lynn in a cell, either. If things worked in our favor—like the files were recoverable—maybe we'd dodge this bullet yet.

"Okay, look. I'll give you my username and my password." I did. "Get your gee-whiz techs on this. Maybe they can recover it or get with the IP company to recover the data. I'm sure they're backed up."

He eyed me with as much skepticism as concern. He sat watching his deputies working around the cottage. For a bit, I thought he was going to bang his head on the steering wheel. He didn't. Instead, he turned again in the seat, set the tablet on the console, and looked into my soul.

"Lowe, don't think I don't know I owe you." He took a long breath, checked through the window at his men, and continued. "But favors are favors, and obstruction is obstruction. If you're involved in Charlie Cantrell's murder...if you had anything to do with deleting these videos... I'll have no choice. You'll go down for it."

There was sincerity and concern in his voice. Deep and thick. But I made a careful assessment of his words. Nowhere did he say, 'if you know what happened to the video files or do you know who deleted them?' Words matter.

"I get that, Vernon. Let me help us both. Clearly as I can. I did not kill Charlie Cantrell. I did not kill his girlfriend. I did not delete the video files."

He started to reply when a crime scene technician called over, "Agent Evans, we're still searching for the murder weapon. We're sure it's a small caliber, though. Probably a .22 cal."

Ah, what? Was it karma or bad luck that I have a .22 caliber pistol— silenced, too—and had fired it last night at Billy Piper's lair? "Vernon, you should know that Charlie kept a .22 pistol hidden in the bookshelf in the main room."

"Oh, yeah?" He repeated what I'd said to the technician.

"Nope." The tech shook his head. "Already searched the shelves and books. Nothing."

Was that good news or bad? The smart money was on "bad." Assuming they'd believe—rightfully—that we both knew the gun was hidden in the bookshelf, the missing pistol raised us from persons of interest to *suspects*.

Chapter Ten

Curran

Evans left me standing beside his Explorer and went to Janey-Lynn out of my earshot. He spoke with her for several moments, gesturing into the cottage, and watched her reaction. She didn't move her head—didn't give away what she said. Not knowing bothered me. I trusted her, but if she made any mistakes in her answers to Evans, I could be trapped, too.

The game was in its early innings, and I was next at bat. If I fouled out now, we were both in deep trouble. Pardon the baseball metaphor—it's all I could come up with.

Finally, Evans dismissed her and returned to me.

"What about Charlie's gun, Lowe?"

I tried to hide a deep swallow that got stuck halfway down. I'd hoped to get an idea of what Janey-Lynn had told him. That failed. Now, I wanted a clue to what he knew and didn't know. It pained me, but the truth was my best option.

"He kept it there. That's all I know," I said as calmly as I could. Then I sweetened the pot, hoping honesty would trump suspicion. "He kept it hidden behind some books downstairs. Could that be the murder weapon?"

He ignored my question. "How did you know about the gun?"

"Vernon, I've had his place wired for weeks. I've seen him take it out a few times to play with it. He almost shot his own foot one night, waving it around to impress his lady friends."

"Friends? Plural?"

That got his attention. "I've recorded at least three others—not counting the dead one." I rattled off their names. "There's four cottage-queens, but I'd have to check my notes."

He turned and looked across the driveway to her as she sat in a marked cruiser with the door open. "Did she know the gun was in the cottage?"

"Yes, she'd watched the videos of him playing with it a couple times. Though, I don't think I've ever seen her in the place except the day I wired it with surveillance. She was repulsed by it—you know, since Charlie was love-shacking it."

"She said she knew."

Phew. Dodged that bullet.

"Okay." He picked up his leather notebook from my Jeep hood and spent a few minutes writing notes. Finally, he looked up. "I really need those videos, Lowe."

"Not as much as me."

"You replay your statement for my partner, Kershaw, over there." He gestured toward the man on the cottage's front porch. "Then, you can go. You know the drill. Don't leave the area. Stay in touch. Keep your phone handy. If I call, you answer."

That seemed reasonable. "Thanks, Vernon. If we talk again and you haven't recovered those videos, I might get a lawyer."

"Something to hide?" His eyebrow rose. "Now's the time, Lowe. After you leave, it'll look like you concealed something."

Oh? "That's bullshit, and you know it. Anyone who talks to you in my shoes without a lawyer is an idiot. I've been a PI long enough to know that much. I've talked freely so far. But if you don't uncover those videos, I have no defense other than my word."

He nodded the moment I called his bluff. "Okay. Stay in touch."

There's nothing like a good friend wanting to stay close and "in touch." Even if that good friend was a lawman who thinks you might have murdered two people in cold blood.

Chapter Eleven

U.C.

T he big screen television mounted on the wall suddenly turned bright blue, interrupting the telecast from the Senate Well— a permanent channel on North Carolina Senator Wain's cable selections.

U.C. closed the office door behind him and waited for the senator to turn—first to see who had entered his inner sanctum, and second to glance at the breaking news bulletin on the screen...

We interrupt this broadcast of the Senate deliberations for this special news bulletin. Vice President St. Croix was reportedly checked into Walter Reed Hospital earlier today. This comes just weeks after collapsing at a charity breakfast at the John F. Kennedy Center in Washington. Speculation is that this is not a scheduled checkup. No further information on his condition is known.

It has long been reported that Vice President St. Croix has suffered from medical concerns even during the recent campaign. His public performances and appearances have been marred with error and his attendance increasingly unpredictable. While political opponents have been quick to question his competency, others close to the vice president, speaking on a condition of anonymity, have suggested recent health woes are to blame.

Speculation inside Washington circles suggests that President Cranston has been quietly readying a list of potential replacements for St. Croix to fulfill his vice president's term. Insiders agree that among the names on the shortlist are General Emilio H. Alvarez, former Vice-Chairman of the Joint Chiefs of Staff and longtime political ally of the president; Iowa's up-and-coming star, Senator Vincent Piccolo, who crushed his opponent by nearly fifteen points in his reelection last term; Virginia's firebrand Governor R. Felix Hersh; and Senator Jameson L. Wain who...

"Didn't my staff tell you I was busy?" the middle-aged bureaucrat groused, standing when U.C. dropped into the tall-back armchair facing his desk. "Who do you think you are? And how the hell did you get into the building?"

"A mutual benefactor sent me. I've got an appointment."

"Carol?" Wain shot a glance at his secretary. "Who do we have on the schedule this morning?"

Carol, a heavy-set, pretty African American woman in her mid-forties, folded her arms in the doorway. "Only a Howard Cyrus Bell from Trinity Enterprises, sir. I'm sure this, er, gentleman, is not he."

"Trinity?" Senator Wain eyed U.C. with contempt. Then, slowly, his face flushed awkwardly. "Did you say Howard Bell?"

"Yes, sir. Howard Cyrus Bell. He was approved by security just last night. A last-minute—"

"Fine." Wain waved her from the office with a sudden brush of his hand. "That'll be all, Carol. Please shut the door."

Carol shot an irritated frown at U.C. "Sir? This gentleman—"

"He's fine." Another wave from Wain. "That'll be all."

Carol began to leave but turned back at the last moment. "Will you be wanting coffee or tea, sir?"

"No, God dammit. Just go." Wain's sharp retort sent her from the room, and the door banged closed behind her. "Sweet Jesus."

"How good of you to see me, Senator." U.C. crossed his legs and folded his hands on his knee. "I know it's been a long time."

Wain slumped into his chair and leaned back, trying hard to appear relaxed and steady. He failed miserably.

"Mister...er...I didn't catch your name?" Wain asked slowly, forming a perfect politician's faux grin. "You are—"

"In a hurry." U.C. captured Wain's eyes and held them. "We've had some developments that involve you."

"We don't normally take last-minute appointments without considerable cause."

"Whatever." U.C. snorted a laugh. "This appointment was made fifteen years ago, Senator."

"That was a long time ago, Mr.—"

"Doesn't matter. Your first installment is due. You'll have five days to make it."

"Installment?" Wain's voice fumbled the word. "What on earth are you talking about?"

"Whisper."

The word grabbed Wain by the throat and squeezed. "What?"

"Whisper." U.C. smiled a raw, taunting smile and lowered his voice almost inaudibly. "You know what it means. You are over your head, Senator."

Wain's face paled. For a long time, he tried to speak but caught each word as though hot and unable to hold onto them.

U.C. continued. "Your election was expensive. A sizable investment was made. The time value of support is like the market. It always goes up. With Whisper, you've forgotten your responsibilities."

"Whisper? Is that a threat?"

U.C. shrugged.

"What exactly do you want? Money?"

"I don't want anything, Senator. Your benefactor does. He's calling in the first installment." U.C. delivered the pre-approved demand that had been specially prepared earlier by his master. "Five days. Got it?"

"No, I don't 'got it.'" Senator Wain snapped awkwardly forward in his chair and tossed away the ruse of composure. "Do you know what's happening here? I'm on the shortlist for the vice presidency. The shortlist, God dammit.

There's no way in hell I'm agreeing to this."

U.C. sat gazing at him as though he were invisible—unimportant—a mere nuisance.

"You're not getting this." Senator Wain raised his chin. "Do you know who I am? Who I'm about to be? You tell—"

"He said you might be reluctant."

U.C. slid a folded sheaf of papers from his leather jacket and slid them across the desk. "Page one. That's all you'll need."

U.C. was right, of course. That's all it took to send Wain into a panic, flipping through the few pages in the sheaf. "What the hell? This is not even extortion. It's damn near treason. Do you know what you're asking? Do you know what could happen to me? The president will want an explanation. The press will be digging around. Do you—"

"Yes, I do. Do you?" U.C. stood, retrieved the papers, and placed them into his jacket again. "A deal was made. You received your request. We kept our promise. Now it's time *you* kept yours."

"Screw you." Wain jumped up and sliced the air between them with his hands. "Who the hell do you think you are? The flipping Godfather? You don't look like Charlton Heston."

"Marlon Brando, Senator. The Godfather was Marlon Brando."

Wain's flailing right hand knocked over his coffee cup beside his phone. Steaming coffee flooded his desk. "Dammit. Brando, Heston. Who gives a shit? I'm not doing this. That deal was a long time ago. No one will believe you now."

U.C. took out his cell phone, tapped a video program, and let the image begin to play. He turned the phone around and showed the video to Wain.

"Senator, you'll recall this meeting in West Virginia. No?"

Wain's eyes narrowed on the phone's screen. As they did, they closed slightly—shame.

U.C. watched him. "Just you, an emissary from our mutual friend, and this hidden camera. Did you really think we'd not have proof?"

"Screw you. I still won't—"

The video played for a few more seconds before a call came in. U.C.

tapped the call and showed Wain the sending number.

"No. You wouldn't," Wain cried, barely able to form the words. "She's not part of this. She's in college—just a kid. She doesn't have any connection to me or this. She barely knows me."

U.C. pocketed the phone. "Five days, Senator. If you act appropriately, your second installment might not be for a long time. Understand, however—your debt is due."

Chapter Twelve

Curran

A few minutes and a thousand bumps down the back roads later, I emerged onto Route 50 and headed east. As luck would have it, and as Northern Virginia was known for, traffic along 50 and all surrounding arteries was dense and obnoxious. I'm sure there was a time of the day that Loudoun streets weren't packed like a four-year-old's sandbox full of Matchbox cars, but I'd never discovered when.

It took me a while to reach TAE Inc.'s two-story, brown brick building tucked away in a Dulles business development. That would be Tommy Astor Enterprises, Incorporated.

The building was a nondescript industrial build set back off Route 28 in Northern Virginia. It was one among dozens of similar structures that consumed ninety percent of the once-farmland of Loudoun County.

TAE was strategically located in Dulles, Virginia, for three reasons. First, it was close to Route 66, a main thoroughfare in and out of Washington, D.C. Second, it was just a couple miles north of Dulles International Airport, where Tommy kept his private jet. And third, it was only five miles from Tommy's rambling estate. He once told me it sat on his daddy's land bought in the fifties. I figured Tommy built the place to ensure his enemies' bodies would never be uncovered.

Tommy's family lore was a little dark.

My head was spinning during the drive. In one evening, I'd committed a few misdemeanors and a felony or two at Billy Piper's ransomware cave, lost a good-paying case because my target had been murdered along with his lover, and the crème de la crème, I was a murder suspect.

I thought dodging bullets for the government had been risky.

I wheeled my old Jeep into my private parking space, oddly titled "K. Astor, Chief Operating Officer," and not "Lowe Curran, Executive Security Grand Poobah." I slid out and shook the wrinkles from my rumbled blazer that had been lying on the backseat. I slipped it on, adjusted my holster, and checked my pocket for the computer drive I'd liberated from Chip Magnet.

Duffle of cash in hand, I headed inside.

As I passed through TAE's glass double-door entrance, I glanced back to see a sporty Mercedes convertible screech to a halt right behind my Jeep. Had she not glanced up from her cell phone in time, she might have slammed into it. Then she really would have been pissed.

The woman at the wheel was a lovely creature. Forty-something, with long blond hair and sparkling blue eyes. She had an hourglass figure that, under other circumstances, might have made me lose my scruples—assuming I had scruples. But, knowing her as I did, the only thing I feared was losing my, er, man parts.

Chief Operating Officer Katelyn Astor—yep, Tommy's daughter—turned toward the entrance and flipped me the bird. Twice, she pointed at my old Jeep and gestured, rather rudely, for me to move it. She might have gestured a third time, but I didn't see. I was inside and headed for Tommy's second-floor office.

Tommy had no secretary. He liked giving orders himself—directly. The Office Manager took his calls, messages, and made his appointments. Otherwise, Tommy was a one-captain fleet.

So, without the hindrance of a guard-secretary outside his office, I knocked once and strolled in. I found him sitting with his feet on his desk, talking on his cell phone. I dropped the duffle onto a round conference table and meandered to a chair across from his desk.

He waved me to a coffee pot and put a finger to his lips.

Tommy's office was more a shrine than an office. He had a complete fascination with all things golf. That passion filled every nook and cranny in the room and threatened to escape into the outer office and out the windows. He had dozens of golf clubs stacked around the room, boxes of balls, hundreds of autographed photographs of famous and unknown golfers—many posing with him. I recognized a few faces. In the side of the room, he had a specially made putting green that he'd removed the office wall into the outer office to install it. That adjacent office was the overflow for his golfing memorabilia.

His executive desk was stacked a foot-high with notebooks, sheaves of papers, mail, magazines, a box of Cuban cigars, a bottle of unopened Dom Pérignon, and a stack of Virginia peanut canisters he gave away for holiday gifts. He also had a stainless steel .357 Magnum Colt Python sitting atop an outcropping of opened mail. The gun was probably unloaded and I doubt he could hit anything. Hopefully, not even me across the desk. It had been a gift from some British client and Tommy used it as a paperweight. I'd hate to see what he used for a doorstop at home.

I found a cup of coffee—yes, another pod-pot. I swear they're extraterrestrial pod-people taking over the world. Careful not to be beamed aboard its mothership, I made a cup that I nearly fell asleep waiting for to brew. Finally, I returned to my seat as Tommy tapped off his call.

"Pappa, did you get it?" he boomed loud enough for the office building across the street to hear. "Did you?"

Sweet Jesus. "Don't call me that, Tommy. You know I don't like it."

"Get over yourself, Pappa. Did you get it?"

Tommy was a colorful character and powerbroker. He was also what many might call my Godfather. No, not the type of Godfather that has you kiss his ring and swear loyalty in blood. Close. Several years ago, when I began this struggling career as a private investigator and security consultant, Tommy took a liking to me. I'd answered a call from his lawyer one day, and the next, I was bailing Tommy out of some embarrassing situation. One of his senior managers had embezzled tons of money. Embarrassing because, for years, Tommy had let this little shithead run the company virtually unsupervised. Tommy had considered this crook family for the longest time. Well, it took only a few days to trace the losses to little-sticky-fingers at the General Manager's desk. I invited him to seek unemployment or go to jail. Restitution would cost the little twerp decades to repay. At first, Tommy didn't believe it could be his loyal subject so devoted to him. Surely, I was wrong. Surely, he needed to fire someone else. His confidence in his "people radar" outweighed my evidence. Until the stupid bastard—the crooked General Manager, not Tommy—slipped up and asked if Tommy would accept a credit card to pay some of his ill-gotten gains.

Tommy became my benefactor.

Since then, he liked me to be nearby—in his building—and often engaged me on investigations and fixes involving his businesses. While his monthly retainer wasn't much, when he needed help, he paid well on top of it. Which was also often, since Tommy had the propensity to get himself into, *er*, binds. Over the years, we became more than friends and not quite family. He was always there when I was down and out. That paradigm had befallen me often back in the old days. After saving his bacon from a wrongful death wrap—long story—I was still not making it on my own. Tommy then granted me a monthly retainer to cover most of my living expenses. I needed to advertise and purchase surveillance equipment and office gear to be able to take on other cases. Being the guy he was, Tommy loaned me cash. Sure, sure, the interest rate was obscene, and I had to fork over some personal capital as collateral—my kidney, liver, and manhood—but he threw me a rope when I needed it most. To say that I owed Tommy my second life since the Voula Beach Road was as much an understatement as saying politicians are dishonest. No, really. It's true—they are.

My loyalty to Tommy Astor ran as deep as any emotion I had. Probably deeper.

"Tommy, what did you do this morning?" I asked lightly. Before he could answer, I continued. "Me? Oh, the usual. I became a prime suspect in Charlie Cantrell's murder."

"What?" He snapped to his feet. "Charlie's dead?"

I nodded. "Yep. Him and his latest concubine were shot sometime last night."

65

"Is Janey-Lynn all right?"

"Yes."

"Lowe?" He moved around his desk, closer to me. He cast a glance at his office door and asked, "Did you kill him?"

What the hell? "No, Tommy. I did not kill *them*."

"You sure? He had it coming." He watched my face contort and stepped back, a big grin consuming him. "Oh, come on, Lowe. I know you didn't. I mean, you—"

"No, Tommy. I didn't." I told him everything I knew. "If Evans can recover those erased videos, Janey-Lynn and I should be clear."

He returned to his desk. "Will he?"

"He should be able to."

"If he does, is Janey-Lynn clear, too?"

That was a funny thing to ask. Or was it? "Sure, I guess. I trust her, Tommy. So do you. After all, you referred me to her. Why would she let me put all those cameras in her cottage and then murder him while I was watching?"

He thought about that. "Good point. Only a crazy person would make a mistake like that."

Yeah, a crazy person—or a very, very devious one. Was Janey-Lynn that shrewd?

"Bastard deserved it. That's why I referred you." Tommy broke my paranoia. "So, Lowe, did you get it or not?"

"Yes, Tommy." I was happy to change topics. I tossed him the computer drive, grinning like I'd just pulled an inside straight. "I have the ransomware unlock codes, too. The data he stole is on that drive. Your IT guys should have you back online in an hour."

"Pappa, you da man. You banged him good." I hated it when Tommy tried to talk gangsta. I hated it almost as much as when he called me my old call sign—Pappa—from the dark old days. "Do I need to worry about him in the future?"

"I don't think so. Piper felt very bad about stealing from you, Tommy." I gestured to the black duffle on his conference table. "He offered a cash settlement in exchange for us not going to the police."

Tommy's eyes went big. "You stole his money?"

Stole? Me? "He gave it to me. Honest."

"How much?"

I thought quickly. No reason to be *too* honest—I have bills. "Twelve thousand."

"So, really more like twenty or thirty?" Tommy was quicker with math than me. He also knew how the game was played. "He gave it to you?"

"We called it a gift. He begged me to take it. I have it recorded for your records."

Tommy walked to the duffle on the table, opened it, and whistled. "Very generous of Mr. Piper."

"And his dog."

Tommy's brow furrowed. "His dog was generous?"

"No, he gave me his dog." Was I speaking Greek? "Everything's good. All you need is on the drive. I did this rush, Tommy. And while I hate to ask, I need—"

"Your fees."

I nodded. "Rent's due."

"You don't pay much rent."

"My car payment's due."

"You bought it used. You paid cash, and it's a piece of shit." He eyed me and lowered his voice as though there were spies under his desk. "What about, er, *him*?"

"Piper won't be bothering you again. I promise."

"I won't ask." He cocked his head. "Not like Charlie. I mean—"

"Tommy, I didn't kill Charlie." I should get a sign around my neck. "I left Piper alive and well. Not happy. But alive and well."

Tommy hesitated, then said, "Ole buddy, you know you can't ever tell anyone—and I mean anyone—about what you did last night. I mean, I never sent you. We never talked about it. You were never there."

"Yeah, I get it. Hush, hush, secret, secret."

"You have no idea, Lowe. None. The people I provide services to are serious people. The information you retrieved is highly sensitive. If anyone found out..."

"I get it, Tommy. I can't tell anyone. Super-secret. Your reputation and God knows what else is at stake. Got it. Though the truth about what I was doing is my real alibi for Charlie Cantrell's murder."

He shook his head. "Find another one."

"Curran," a voice boomed from behind me. "You bastard."

On cue, that beautiful blond with the amazing, animated hands burst into Tommy's office.

"Curran, get that piece of scrap metal out of my parking spot. Now."

Tommy quickly zipped the duffle closed. "Relax, Katelyn, Lowe's leaving shortly. Park in visitor until he does. Okay, my precious?"

"My precious?" Katelyn's face exploded red. "You want *me* to park in visitor? Why doesn't he?"

"I'm family, sis." I winked.

Big mistake.

She stormed deeper into the room, kicked the side of my chair, nearly sent me out of it, and jabbed a hard, pointing finger at me.

"Curran, I have no idea what my dad sees in you. Now, get that junk out of my spot before I have it towed. You have five minutes."

She loves me. You can tell.

Tommy started to speak, but Katelyn shot him a look that froze fire. He was a brilliant entrepreneur and a consummate business gamesman. He was smart and cunning. And he knew his daughter. Silence was his best defense.

"I'm going." I stood and gestured to the computer drive I'd given him. "You better get that to your IT guy, Tommy. Problem solved."

"What? Already?" Katelyn asked. "You got our data back?"

I winked again. She loves that. "And the ransomware unlock codes. It's all there."

She lifted her chin and glanced from me to the computer drive and back. Then, she looked at Tommy. "Well, I guess he has some value after all."

"Katie, I think you owe him an apology," Tommy said. "He hit a home run for us."

"Five minutes, Curran, then I'll tow it." She spun on her thousand-dollar heels and went in search of more victims.

Tommy lifted the black duffle off his conference table and tossed it to me. "Spoils of war, my friend. We'll call it an unreported bonus."

Either Tommy was still feeling guilty about introducing me to the pond-scum D.C. attorney who stiffed me for fifty-K, or he was feeling magnanimous. Something about that was unsettling. Like a free ticket on the Hindenburg.

"Ah, Tommy. I don't think—"

"Go on, Lowe, take it."

I could use it. Especially if I needed a good criminal lawyer over Charlie Cantrell's murder. Dog cookies were expensive, too. "That's a lot of money."

"Yes." He laughed and returned to his desk. "I don't want to have to explain that cash to Katie any more than you want to report it on your taxes. Besides, you'll owe me for this. You will be doing me a special favor soon."

I will? *Gulp.* "Thanks."

"Just remember, if anything comes of this from the authorities, you never showed me that money."

I shrugged. "What money?"

The landline on Tommy's desk buzzed, and he lifted the receiver. He listened for only a few seconds. When he hung up, his face was tight, and his eyes locked onto the duffle in my hand.

"Lowe, have you told me everything about last night? Charlie Cantrell or about the hacker?"

"Nothing about the hacker. Why?"

"Anything else? You know, like anything *bad*?"

"Other than being a murder suspect?"

"Yeah, like that." He walked to his window overlooking the front entrance. "Because the FBI is downstairs."

Chapter Thirteen

Curran

For normal people, having the FBI at your front door would be scary. For me, well, it was no big thing. Not because the FBI made a habit of seeking me out. Not because I expected the FBI to come calling because Billy Piper gifted me twenty-five thousand bucks. And not because I was the newest face on Post Office's walls for the murder of Charlie Cantrell, either. It was because the FBI didn't impress me—they didn't scare me. Many people's philosophy is if you're innocent, then don't worry. That, of course, is just stupid. Innocent people go to jail way too often. Courtrooms are not always about the truth or evidence. It's about whose lawyer can dance the best. It's show and tell. No, my philosophy keeps me calm in moments like this—distance and shielding.

If the FBI can't grab me, they can't scare me.

"Tommy, I'm going out your private entrance." I headed for the oak door to the right of his credenza. "I'll call later."

"No, you're not." Tommy thrust up a hand and stopped me. "We'll meet them in the conference room. Better we know what's happening than to act guilty."

Well, maybe better for him. Guilt was not always the reason people went to jail. It was often a matter of not being able to prove your innocence—beyond a reasonable doubt—that caused the problems. I had such a dilemma. I lied to Agent Evans about being with Janey-Lynn last night. I couldn't very well tell him what I was doing at Billy Piper's Leesburg crime operation center. The combination of lying and what I was really doing all night was tantamount to a long stay with the chain gang.

"Come on, Lowe." Tommy headed for the stairwell. "Let's see what the fuss is before we pee ourselves."

I didn't believe in coincidences. I already knew what the fuss was about. Or at least, one of the fusses. I hoped it wasn't too late to *not* pee myself.

When we walked into Tommy's conference room in the rear of the first floor, the first thing that struck me was that the FBI was establishing a field office there. There were five suits—stern-faced and stiff agents—and one muscular guy dressed in jeans, a golf shirt, hiking boots, and a leather jacket.

Five uptight Feebies and a DIY guy. Which of these didn't belong?

I felt drawn in a weird, familiar way to Mr. Leather Jacket. He was suave, with dark eyes and hair. His young physique—maybe thirtyish—said he worked out and took the physical part of his job seriously. That was something I used to do when I was younger and had less scar tissue in me. There was something about him—something eerily familiar. More to the point, Mr. Leather Jacket had his radar locked onto me, too, and had been watching me from the moment I'd walked into the room. He hadn't taken his eyes off me for a moment. Now, those eyes were dissecting me inch-by-inch.

Jesus, what was it?

"Good morning, gentlemen." Tommy strutted over to the conference table like he owned the place. Okay, he did own the place, but he loved an entrance. "I'm Tommy Astor—of Tommy Astor Enterprises. What's this about?"

One of the suited men, a broad-shouldered older man with gray temples and deep-set, gray eyes, walked around the conference room table with a cup of coffee in his hand—yup, one of those alien pod coffees the receptionist made him.

"Astor, I'm Special Agent Curto—"

"It's Mr. Astor. Surely, Quantico had a course on manners."

Score the first hit for Tommy.

Agent Curto's jaw tightened. He was a big guy, at least six feet and some change. His gray hair and bulk told me he wasn't used to being bested by someone like Tommy—not for a long time, anyway.

"Fine, *Mr.* Astor, we're FBI. We've come to discuss your computer system and a report that your firm was the victim of a recent widespread ransomware attack."

Phew, at least it wasn't about Charlie Cantrell. Not that my involvement with Cantrell was harder than Piper's mess, but at least my alibi was holding. I'll take my victories where I can.

"My computers?" Tommy eyed me as he put on his best used-car salesman smile. "We have no such problem here, gentlemen. I assure you."

The other suited agents exchanged their own telepathic glances before Agent Curto opened a notebook he was carrying. "You haven't been the victim of a recent ransomware attack?"

Tommy must have gone to acting school. "No, we're just dandy. Why?"

"We're looking into a pretty sophisticated series of cyber-attacks. The UNSUB—that's Unknown Subject—"

"Yeah, I watch TV, too," Tommy quipped.

"Of course." Agent Curto nodded. "The UNSUB launches a Spear Phishing prob—that's where the UNSUB sends random emails to your employees that appear innocent. They trick them into hitting a link, like with a request for an email response, or some form of verification of information that has imbedded code. The employee hits the link and unknowingly launches a RAT into your system that allows the UNSUB to insert malware code like a ransomware lock on your accounts—"

Tommy threw up a hand. "Hold it, hold it. You're saying a rat did what?"

For his part, Tommy was as gifted an actor as he was a businessman. He was playing the dumb, southern rich guy very well. And from the look on Curto's face, he was selling it.

"Remote Access Trojan—RAT," Curto said, eyeing Tommy. "It's a cyber attack that implants malicious code into your computer network to give the UNSUB the ability to manipulate your systems. In the cases we're investigating, it seizes control of your entire network, security systems, everything IT, and locks you out. Then, for a big payoff, they'll release you. Of course, they'll just come back again for more unless your own cyber people can find and scrub the RAT first."

Tommy stabbed the air at Curto. "All this because somebody's employees opened an 'oops' email they weren't supposed to?"

Curto nodded.

"Phew," Tommy said, grinning. "Good thing we don't have stupid employees like that. We maintain strict rules here, Agent Curto. So you can relax."

"Really? Our information is that you've been off-line for a couple days." Agent Curto eyed him with malice aforethought. He waited a moment trying to gauge Tommy in some kind of telepathic lie detector. "Our information is you were the subject of such an attack."

"Where did that information come from?" I asked and realized it was a bad idea as soon as the Fed Brigade turned toward me.

"Excuse me?" Mr. Leather Jacket stepped forward and eyed me with dark Italian eyes. "Who are you?"

Yes, dumbass, who is it who can't keep his mouth shut? I faced him, and that *déjà vu* washed over me like spring rain. It had my attention and kept me from answering. Instead, my brain was replaying my life looking desperately for the connection. It was there, somewhere, just out of reach. *Who—*

"I asked you a question," Leather Jacket repeated in a less-than-friendly tone. "Who are you?"

I shook myself out of it. "Chief of Security. Since you're the one who's barging in making accusations, I think we have a right to know the details. Don't you?" There, I told him.

Not.

"I asked who you are." Leather jacket had a big attitude. "I didn't ask your position."

He had a point. "Lowe Curran. You are?"

"We ask the questions." Then, a reverse *déjà vu* came over his face, too.

His eyes narrowed and zeroed in on me, one eyeball at a time. He studied my face and then cocked his head like he was trying to recall me from some wanted poster. "Marlowe Curran?"

Uh, oh. I hope he guessed at Marlowe and not because he'd already seen my name on the NCIC under Murder Suspects. "Do I know you?"

"No." Mr. Leather Jacket looked quickly to the floor and shook his head. "We don't know each other. But we're gonna."

Tommy folded his arms. "Then introduce yourself, sonny-boy. After all, you're standing in my building." He waved a hand toward the other agents. "In fact, let's all get acquainted, shall we? That or I call Shelly Rawlins."

Agent Curto scrunched up his face. "Look, Astor—"

"Now see, there it is again." Tommy took a step forward, and the used car salesman's smile vanished into a killer shark's grin. "It's Mr. Astor. Clearly, you didn't recognize the important people I just mentioned. Shelly and I are golfing buddies three or four times a year. We also have dinner in D.C. whenever he has time—at the Army Navy Club."

Agent Curto showed no recognition.

Tommy was exaggerating. He golfed with Shelly only twice a year and maybe had dinner as often. Sure, sure, it was at the Arlington Army Navy Club—a swank who's who club for the rich, powerful, and political—but he was stretching the truth a little.

Leather jacket jabbed the air. "Look, I want to know—"

"I call him Shelly, you know." Tommy cut him off like he hadn't been speaking. "I'm sure, Agent Curto, you'll recognize him as the Honorable Shelton V. Rawlins, US Federal Judge of the Eastern District." Tommy waited as the air was sucked from the room. "Yes, sir, Shelly and I go way back to our college days. And let me tell you, he cheats at golf. I let him. You don't want to piss off a federal judge. Do you, Agent Curto?"

I have to tell you. If you've never heard the sound of five sphincters snapping closed all at the same time, you're not living right. I looked from pale face to pale face around the room and enjoyed the moment. After the boy's anal muscles began to relax, you could hear a pin drop on a rubber mat. That and the sound of churning stomachs.

"Right." Agent Curto looked at Leather Jacket and then at the other agents. He stepped forward and extended his hand to Tommy. "I was rude, Mr. Astor. We've had a complicated case land, and things have been hectic. We're from the WFO, that's the—"

"Washington Field Office," I said. "We're not uneducated hillbillies out here, Curto. You guys in suits are FBI. This fella isn't." I gestured to Mr. Leather Jacket. "Who are you?"

The suave, Italian complected, Mr. Leather Jacket sent death threats from his eyes to mine. Still, he behaved himself. "Deputy United States Marshal Gallo."

A quick search of my memory came up blank. *Gallo....* Nope. Nadda. Not even a blip on the gray matter radar. Why a US Marshal? This just got weirder than the time Tommy sent me to find his college roommate in Boston and get him out of some trouble he was in with the Irish mob. Tommy's guy, then Stephan Berkowitz, was now Stephanie-Anne Berkowitz, and she owed fifty grand to her Irish mob pimp for back rent and "taxes" on her "alternate sex enthusiasts" business. Long story. Maybe later.

"What's the Marshal Service have to do with hackers and ransomware?"

"None of your business," Gallo snapped. "I draw the line—"

"Ah, right." Tommy cut him off again with his hand waving like a conductor toward the other feds. "And these gentlemen?"

Agent Curto rattled off the other FBI agent's names...Temple, Fasel, Regan, and Plunkett. Then, he turned back to Tommy. "I'm afraid I can't tell you how we know, Mr. Astor. Can you tell us the status of your ransomware attack?"

"Absolutely. By God, Agent Curto, there isn't one," Tommy said. "We're just fine."

"Did you pay the ransom? Is that what you're telling me? We don't recommend paying these people. It'll lead to future attacks and escalating ransoms."

I forced a laugh. "Then why don't you stop them before they do it? I read about this crap every day. You guys can't stop it and almost never catch anyone. Private companies have to fend for themselves. Unless you're a government contractor. Then look out, you guys are all over it like..."

I almost dropped the "cops on donuts" cliche but caught myself. I had nothing but respect for cops—not so much the feds—but *real* cops. Unless they had pulled me over at three in the morning for weaving the roadway after I'd had too much wine. Then, well, not so much. But that almost never happened to me.

Gallo looked at me. "You *were* hacked. You paid?"

"Nope." Huh, he wasn't so dumb. "We're good."

"I don't believe you." Gallo pushed again. "Does the name 'Piper' mean anything—William Piper?"

"No," Tommy said as the conference room door opening turned him around. "I can honestly say I've never heard the name William Piper before."

Of course not. Neither have I. We have, however, heard the name Billy Piper. But then, they didn't ask about Billy Piper, did they? Specificity is important.

"Dad, what's this about?" Katie Astor strode in with the authority of Madeleine Albright. "Why's the FBI here?" Her eyes went immediately to me like I was on the Ten Most Wanted list. "Curran?"

If she only knew. "Oh, come on, Katie. Really?"

"Good, Katie, you're here." Tommy held up a hand. "Agent Curto, this is my daughter and my COO. She'll explain. We have not been hacked, and we never heard of William Piper. We have not been attacked by any ransomware. We're just fine."

For a long moment—too long for my nerves—Katie glanced around at the feds standing there, hanging on her response. Then, she looked at me, frowned, and turned back to Tommy.

"No, Dad, we're fine. We had a system outage the past two days as you know. But things are back up and running fine. Who said we were hacked?"

Agent Curto squared off on her. "Are you certain, Ms. Astor? Lying to a Federal Agent—"

"Lying?" Her arms snapped folded in a pre-attack position. "Lying? Really?"

Oh shit, Curto did it now. I took a step away so the blood splatter wouldn't get on me.

Katie stepped up to Agent Curto—about a foot away—and let her eyes explain the ways of powerful women who didn't take shit from anyone—*ever*. "Lying under oath is a federal crime. Lying to obstruct is a federal crime. Telling you bozos that our computers are just fine and showing you the door is not a crime. It's an honest response to boorish, arrogant accusations by bureaucratic misogynists who think they can bully everyone. Do you want to measure anything, gentlemen? I can go first."

Damn. I'm sure they'd lose, too.

"No, ma'am," Agent Curto said. "We're just—"

"Do you have a warrant?" she demanded.

"Not yet," Gallo said, "but we can get one."

"Do it," she snapped. When lionesses defend their pride, they focus on the enemy and don't take their attention away until she kills them. "We have no ransomware problem here. If you come back with a warrant, plan to sit in the parking lot for a very long time. I will personally send our private jet for Uncle Shelly. He's in Richmond this afternoon. We can have him here within an hour."

Damn, Tommy had nothing on name-dropping compared to sweet Katie.

Marshal Gallo wasn't sure what to say or who to say it to. So, he did the only smart thing he could. He shut up and looked to Agent Curto for their next move.

Damn, where did I know Gallo from?

"Ms. Astor, we don't need to go to those lengths," Agent Curto said. "We're simply trying to verify the companies our source tells us were the subject of a ransomware attack. We're trying to get to the bottom of a much larger case. Any information you can give us would help us tremendously."

Tommy reared back and whooped up a big, raucous laugh. "Why, Agent Curto, why didn't you just say that? On your way out, my receptionist can give you the number of my attorney. You'll recognize his name, too—the Honorable Jay Thomas Carello. Yes, that's right, the former Chief White House Counsel for the last administration. I'll let him know you'll be calling.

You can chat with him about your questions."

It's fun being in the company of titans. Tommy may not have been a true titan, but he hung out with titans. And I hung out with Tommy. Who you know matters.

"Gentlemen, have a nice day." I gestured to the conference room door. "Come again when you can't stay as long."

Agent Curto, Marshal Gallo, and their well-dressed entourage filed out with muttered, "Thank you and have a good day" to Tommy and Katie.

I got crickets.

Katie followed them out. Probably to kill off the slowest of the pack to set an example. As soon as she was out the conference room door, I shut it and faced Tommy.

"Tommy, what aren't you telling me about those computer files?"

Chapter Fourteen

U.C.

Generael Emilio H. Alvarez, retired Vice Chairman of the Joint Chiefs of Staff, was the first high school graduate in his family. He was also the only member of his high school class to escape the Watts conviction of teenage youth. It was saying something that he reached the rank of Lieutenant General and had continued to climb to extraordinary success after his Pentagon retirement.

U.C. watched from behind the draped bay window in General Alvarez's den as the General parked his Mercedes in front of his Georgetown estate. He grinned as the General waved his groundskeeper to the car, and as the Latino approached him, the General unleashed a tirade, pointed to the flowerbeds, and ranted. When General Alvarez completed his harangue and reached his front door, it opened. His staff was ready, waiting for his arrival.

U.C. observed his routine, first from the window and then the partially opened den door. As the General entered the Tudor home, he readied himself for any sudden change in plan.

The General ignored the housekeeper at the door. He paused a moment to admire his dozens of Command Flags displayed in the grand foyer—mementos of his thirty-five years in the Army, commemorating his rocket-like rise from West Point to the Joint Chiefs.

The General lingered there, basking in his own glory.

Finally complete with his self-adoration, the General dropped his windbreaker on the chair inside the foyer for the housekeeper to hang and headed for his den.

Finally. U.C. backed from the den door and tucked himself into the corner of the room.

Inside, the General paused in the den doorway as though making a grand entrance to some military gala in his honor. He stood there, admiring the trappings of power and achievement hanging on the walls and positioned strategically on shelves. Antiques and military souvenirs from battles around the world—Anzio, Omaha Beach, Antietam, the Argonne, even El Alamein and Leningrad. He'd fought in none of them.

In the short time U.C. had sequestered himself in the den, he'd admired the collection of relics. He'd made mental notes of the General's achievements— more for his own amusement than any professional trigger.

The private den was the General's Fortress of Solitude. It was his self. His ego. His memories. U.C. knew that the General allowed few to stay more than a few moments to bask in his greatness. Often, the great are humbled in their willingness to keep private their greatness from others. Or, perhaps, it's pure condescension.

Abruptly, the General realized *he* was there. Now. Uninvited. An interloper.

"Who are you? What the hell are you doing here?" General Alvarez commanded. "Who let you in?"

"No one, General. Relax. I've only come to make life easy for you."

General Alverez stepped farther into the den but left the doors open behind him. He glanced cautiously around and settled on U.C. eye to eye.

"What do you want?"

"I'm an admirer, General." U.C. waved his hand around the room. "I come with a message from very important people. I was here for a bit and must apologize. I was lost in your museum. I've never been in the company of such personal history before. Tell me, what is this one here?" He moved to a bookshelf laden with large, historic editions and pointed to a bronze cast of an ancient Greek warrior.

"Ares," General Alvarez said, still eyeing U.C. with contempt, "Greek God of War. I served in Athens—"

"Yes, you did."

The General swelled up now. "Who sent you? What message are you talking about, and from whom does it come?"

U.C. ignored him. "Have you read all these books? Impressive. I have to say, your foyer is breathtaking, too. The president never said."

General Alvarez blinked several times. A faint, almost imperceivable smile cracked the corners of his mouth—more from flattery than any veiled deception. "The president didn't send you. Did Senator—"

"Whisper."

General Alvarez's words froze on his lips. His eyes didn't blink. His throat went dry. His face blanched ever so noticeably. "Excuse me?"

U.C. picked up the Ares bronze and tossed it across the room to the general, who stood statue-still and missed it. The piece hit him in the belly and fell to the floor at his feet.

"Whisper," U.C. repeated. "It's time to pay the piper. Please, spare me the 'do you know who I'm about to be' speech. I've heard it all before."

Chapter Fifteen

Curran

I followed Tommy back to his office. As soon as his door shut, I asked, "Exactly what have you got me into, Tommy?"

The old fox sat at his paper-strewn desk, hands steepled on his chest, grinning. No, he didn't, and I doubt I was going to get it out of him.

"A hint?"

He shook his head. "It's best you believe it was our financial data. Trust me."

Whenever someone told me to trust them, I didn't. Even if it was my best benefactor. "Tell me, Tommy. Why—"

"Because I wanted to ensure we got something back and it never happens again." Tommy picked up the Colt Python on his desk and played with the cylinder like a game of roulette was about to begin. "If you're worried about the assignment, you should have asked more questions before you went."

Yeah, no kidding. But cash money was something I needed. Lots of it. I leaned back against the windowsill across his office. "Tommy, forgive me, but I really need to understand how much trouble I could be in."

"Like being a homicide suspect?"

I nodded.

He held up a finger to make a point that irritated me as soon as he did. "Ah, but I already warned those nice FBI agents about my lawyer and good ole buddy, Shelly."

"Yes, but they're your friends. They never heard of me."

"You don't think I'd take care of you?"

Would he? Tommy was a consummate businessman and a shrewd chess player—figuratively. I shrugged, and he laughed out loud.

"Ye of little faith, my friend." His desk phone buzzed. He hit speaker. "Yes?"

Katelyn's voice boomed and instantly gave me a headache. "Dad, the tow truck is on its way. If you're done with Curran, tell him to get out of my parking space."

"Katie, I think you love that parking space more than me," I quipped. "Call off your tow truck. I'm headed down now."

She slammed the phone down so hard I heard it all the way from the first floor.

"She's in a bad mood, Tommy. Maybe buy her a nice lunch."

"You buying?" He aimed a finger at my black duffle of cash. "After all, you just made twenty-five grand that won't get reported as income. Maybe you buy and leave a big tip. We'll call it your parking fee. There will be plenty left for your defense lawyer."

"Parking fee it is." I pushed myself off the windowsill, praying I didn't need a lawyer. "I know you're hoping that me and Katelyn get together. This will be goodwill."

"You two?" Tommy threw his head back and laughed, slapping the desk when he lurched forward and stood. "You do know that tigers eat their mates."

No, Tommy, they don't. "I think it's the praying mantis' who eat their mates, Tommy."

"You get my point."

I did, but what a way to go.

Chapter Sixteen

Deputy US Marshal Terry Gallo

G allo sat in his four-by-four across the boulevard from TAE. He flipped another pistachio into his mouth, worked the shell off with his front teeth, and spit it into a cup like a cowboy spitting chew.

He'd been waiting on his target to emerge since leaving TAE earlier that morning. He'd already gone through a half-bag of pistachios—his only vice in an otherwise 'my body is my temple' lifestyle. Now, he was getting thirsty. He hadn't geared up for surveillance, or his kit would have included a thermos of coffee and real food. He'd skipped breakfast after two hours at the gym after he'd received the call from the Marshal's D.C. Headquarters about their discovery in Leesburg.

Billy "Chip Magnet" Piper had just caused his career to get red-flagged.

Piper was his responsibility. His. He'd last seen him last month. Last spoken by phone two weeks ago. This was after constant monitoring and communications for a year. A year keeping Piper under the radar and out of sight from the Los Angeles field office of the *rossíyskaya máfiya*—Russian organized crime.

Billy, whose real name had been Stacey Thomas Lane, had been a world-recognized hacker, known in every established dark web hell hole as 'Chip Magnet.' One evening, two years ago, Billy had hacked into an offshore account of one Vladimir Dmitriy Semenov, known affectionately as Vlad the Impaler. Not for his love of Bram Stoker or the enigmatic Romanian Vlad Dracula, either. His methods of maintaining good order in his business empire involved long poles and dead bodies.

Although Billy—Stacy Thomas Lane, of course—was a salty, irritating pain in the ass—he hadn't counted on the Russians. By the time he'd realized that the five million dollars and thousands of files he'd stolen were from Russian organized crime, it was too late. Lane, AKA Piper, tried to put it back and cover his tracks. Time didn't permit him. Moments before Vlad the Impaler found him in his beachfront condo, bags in hand and heading for the airport, so did the FBI.

Piper/Lane became the biggest prize in the anti-Russian RICO—Racketeer Influenced and Corrupt Organizations—Justice Department probe in history. The information Piper had stolen was a treasure trove. All the FBI had to do was keep him alive long enough to put the spear into Semenov's heart.

Six months later, they had. Semenov was doing life in Colorado's ADX Florence supermax prison. Piper/Lane had been put into protective custody and spirited away to the East Coast. Gallo had tucked him in, all snug, safe, and sound, in his two-bedroom apartment at the Arlington Arms apartments. That was some forty minutes away from this mysterious Leesburg residence.

Gallo had been assigned his handler since day one. It was a gravy assignment until earlier that morning. For the past year, Piper had been a model WITSEC—Witness Security Program—protected. So much so that Gallo had been re-directed and only checked in on him periodically. The last check-in was two weeks ago. Things seemed fine. Piper reported toeing the line as a protectee, and despite his loathsome personality, nothing raised suspicion.

Obviously, Piper had played them. Played *him*.

In hindsight, there had been signals he'd missed. First, Piper stopped complaining and seemed too reticent. Gallo chalked it up to accepting his fate. Then, Gallo had become concerned when Piper had bought an expensive gift for an elderly neighbor down the hall in Arlington. His ward had denied he'd returned to his prior profession and claimed he'd saved up his spending money to honor the old veteran. Again, Gallo dismissed the situation as his own paranoia. Unfortunately, Gallo's superiors put him onto two other key WITSEC protectees. Digging into Billy's situation was delayed. After all, surely Billy wasn't stupid enough to hack the Russians again.

What Piper had been doing in that seedy, Leesburg rambler was evidence. A cataclysmic problem. He'd missed it. Piper had accumulated the money and the means to rent the place. He hadn't done this overnight. Clearly, he'd returned to his old ways—hacking, identity theft, fraud, and God knows what else.

Piper had been hacking all the wrong people again. Earlier that morning, unbeknownst to him, the FBI computer crimes squad raided the seedy Leesburg rambler. Their target was an unidentified hacker responsible for ransomware attacks on five US Government defense contractors, three Congressmen, and countless other high-profile businesses in the D.C. area. He'd also reportedly raided several retirement accounts at small businesses around the Beltway. The hacker had made off with nearly five hundred thousand in stolen funds and countless more in ransom before the FBI had been notified.

When the Bureau swooped in, what they found was more than just a teenage computer wizard that they expected to find. It didn't take long to identify the man behind the ransomware attacks—Piper had left a stack of overdue credit card bills behind. Despite his clever cyber skills, he'd failed to protect himself from the old-school giveaways—his name and address on the mailing labels.

The hunt began.

Piper's Justice Department files had been earmarked such that the FBI should have known he was in WITSEC. That cowboy Curto had simply ignored it and launched the raid anyway. Their crime scene team had included the Leesburg PD, but oddly left out the US Marshal Service. Once the scene had been secured, Curto had summoned him.

It had been all downhill since.

By the time Gallo arrived, Curto had the names of Piper's previously unknown targets. Each had been the victim of ransomware attacks in Washington, D.C. The crime scene team hadn't found the master files of these attacks, but what data they'd retrieved had only been research Piper had kept about his victims. Aside from the US Government targets and elderly retirement accounts, there was a Chinese Bank, the Virginia Lottery office, and his favorite, a fast-growing information brokerage firm making its millions off political lobbyists, TAE, Inc.

To build a better case would require finding all of Piper's victims. One of them had apparently entered the rundown Leesburg Rambler before the FBI had arrived. The Russians and the Chinese were on top of that list. Next were powerful deal brokers.

TAE was on top of that list.

Earlier, the FBI's visit with Tommy Astor had been the first wave. Stop in, rattle their cage, and find out if Piper had actually hacked them. It should have been a simple matter had FBI Special Agent Curto not gone in like gangbusters, pounding his chest and demanding the spotlight.

They'd learned nothing.

That wasn't what had Gallo riled up, though. Curto had been Curto. He'd worked with him before and knew the FBI man's ego was in play the moment he'd pushed through TAE's front door. None of that bothered him. It had been *him...*

Marlowe Curran. He knew the face as soon as the conference room door had opened. The name was seared in his mind. The years hadn't been necessarily kind to Curran. He was graying and moved like a cowboy who'd busted too many broncos. Still, after looking beyond first impressions, he knew. It was him.

"You bastard. Show me what you got, old man." Gallo spit another few pistachio shells into the cup. "I want a piece of you. I want every piece. One at a time."

Chapter Seventeen

Curran

I arrived at my barn loft apartment at nearly two in the afternoon. I'd stopped along the way and picked up a bucket of fried chicken for Stevie and me, and more dog treats for Bogart. I'd already eaten three pieces of it by the time I shut off my Jeep—the chicken, not the dog cookies.

Stevie's Blazer was gone. A barely-legible note, scrawled on the backside of an old pizza box, was duct taped to the loft stair banister—*Hey, brother, sorry about last night. I screwed up again. I'll make it up. Going home to crash for a day or so. I'll call you. I owe you, as always.*

The note, nearly identical to the fifty previously scrawled by Stevie after similar episodes, went into the trash before I ascended the stairs.

I knew something was wrong the moment I reached the upper landing. Bogart was nowhere.

My front door was open. No big, friendly rescue dog was inside or out. I'd promised him cookies, and he was smart enough to know I was good for them. Yet, he was absent.

Considering Charlie Cantrell's murder, I wasn't taking chances. I slipped my .45 from behind my back. I took a careful peek around the loft doorframe, scanning the main room inside.

Papers were strewn everywhere on the floor—some shredded and others helter-skelter about. The three-bulb floor lamp near my leather recliner was on its side in the middle of the braided wool rug in front of the fireplace.

The cushion of my leather chair was beside the lamp and shredded.

Following my gun sites deeper inside, I checked the kitchen and bedrooms only to find the same carnage. My bed was disheveled, with the blankets askew on the floor. Both pillows were shredded, and stuffing lay everywhere. The kitchen was the least assaulted, though the cabinet drawers were all open, and contents littered the countertops.

Someone had been searching for something.

Had the cops already executed a search warrant? I've seen them trash places on searches, but never like this. I went outside and checked around the door, then returned inside and searched again. If they'd raided my place under a warrant, they'd have to leave a copy either stapled to the door or inside where I could see it.

No warrant. Was that good or bad?

"Damnit."

I rushed over to the edge of the kerosene heater and found the loose brick just touching the footer. Kneeling down made my knees cry out in anger, but I got there. Twice chipping a nail, I slipped the brick out and dug beneath it. Still where I'd hidden it earlier, was the copy of the USB drive I'd liberated for Tommy Astor—my CMA stash.

Whoever had been in my place hadn't found it. Though, it hadn't been for lack of searching.

What about Bogart?

I holstered my pistol.

I know what you're thinking. No, Stevie Keene did not ransack my place. Why would he? If he wanted anything, he knew just to ask. Also, if he had, why leave a nice "I'm sorry" note behind. He'd know that if he lost his mind and trashed my place, I'd know it was him. So, a triple negative—he didn't need to, he wouldn't do it, and if he did, he'd know I'd know. Nope, Stevie was a lot of things, but he was no traitor.

Simple logic. Try to keep up.

I grabbed the duffle. It wasn't going to fit in the secret hiding hole beneath the heater. Instead, I secured it in the second safest place in the apartment—at the bottom of my highly piled laundry bin in the bathroom. Then, I went to look for Bogart.

He could be anywhere and he didn't know his surroundings. I hope he hadn't tried to run home to that bastard, Piper, out of some misplaced puppy-dog loyalty. I've heard of dogs doing that—travelling thousands of miles, through forests and deserts and across the ocean to find their rightful masters. Okay, maybe not oceans.

No, he hadn't run away. It was much, much worse.

In the distance, oh, maybe a quarter of a mile, I heard a dog howling in terror. That would put him just about in Janey-Lynn's front yard. Bogart was there. The question was, was the trouble that had trashed my apartment responsible for his fear now?

Not wanting to alert any bad guys of my approach, I jogged the distance through the trees to Janey-Lynn's. Once at the Y-shaped driveway that separated her farmhouse from the main barn complex, I took a position beside a stone pump house near the barns.

Bogart let out a lonesome, terrified howl that sent ice needles through me. It took all I could muster not to charge in to save him. Before I set one more foot closer to trouble, I had to know what I was up against. I'd learned that the hard way in Voula.

It could get me killed—for good.

"Hold on, boy," I muttered. "I'm coming."

A strange car was parked in front of the house. Very strange. It reminded me of a hooptie from one of those Charles Bronson gangbanger movies in the seventies or eighties. It was about twenty years old, looked like the remains of an old red and rust import, and was on its last leg. How the hell it got all the way to Janey-Lynn's house without breaking down—from wherever—was a miracle. Yet, here it was, parked almost touching Janey-Lynn's black Mercedes SUV.

The old junker clashed with Janey-Lynn's style, like oil and water. She was a classy lady with generally classy friends—well, except for me. She liked things neat and orderly. Even the farm equipment was always in top shape. This junker looked like her Mercedes defecated, and this car came out.

Who could this be?

Bogart's howls and deep, agitated barking erupted again from behind the farmhouse.

I couldn't wait any longer.

With my .45 out, I moved slower in my stalking dance I'd learned in the military. Easing ahead and following Bogart's cries into the farmhouse's back yard, I moved around the gray clapboard, two-story. I took a position at the farmhouse's corner, where her wraparound front porch met her rear patio.

Sweet Jesus, Bogart?

He let out a long, terror-induced howl. That stopped me in my tracks and sent chills deep inside like lightning bolts of ice. Bogart was tethered on two sides to the rear patio railing. He was covered in suds as Janey-Lynn assaulted him with a garden hose. When he caught my scent, he wrenched his head sideways, locked his big, brown eyes on me, and let out a long, lonesome plea for help.

"What the hell are you doing to my dog, Janey-Lynn?"

She snapped upright and spun toward me. Her eyes froze on my pistol. "Sonny-boy, you best put that pop gun away before I turn this hose on you."

Bogart woofed—*run for your life*.

"Oh, yeah, sorry." I holstered my Kimber. "Now—"

"He smells. He's got fleas." She let him have it with another burst from the hose. "He's a big baby to boot. He's been carrying on like I was torturing him."

Bogart moaned and pleaded for rescue.

"What's going on?" I slipped onto one of the patio chairs and watched Janey-Lynn scrubbing him vigorously with a sponge full of suds. "My place is trashed. Was it the cops? Did they leave you a warrant?"

"The cops left a little bit ago." She hosed Bogart down, pulled a big bath towel from the nearby table, and began towel-drying him. He liked that. "You owe me two throw pillows and a leather chair cushion."

I did? "Why?"

"Him." She poked Bogart in the belly as she toweled him off. "He ate them."

Bogart lowered his head and whimpered. Guilt was an amazing thing.

"What about the rest of the mess? Looks like Bogart went on a tear. I guess he doesn't like being alone."

"Nope." She finished toweling him, unclipped the two tethers holding him in place, and stood, facing me. "Wasn't your dog or that house guest of yours, either—you know, the dodgy one."

"House guest?" Dodgy? Stevie? I asked her.

"Don't recall his name. He left a little bit after the cops and the others."

"The others? What others, Janey-Lynn? What happened?"

She began wiping the suds and water off her. "Nothing much. They took my statement here, so I didn't have to go into the station. Your copper friend, Evans, is a good one. I think he believes us."

"He doesn't." She needed to know. "He saw right through that 'we were together' story, Janey-Lynn. I'm sure of it. Pray they're able to recover the deleted video."

Her eyes teared. "I hated the bastard, Lowe. But I wouldn't wish this on him. I just wanted out and a safety net. Who killed him? Why?"

From what I knew about Charlie Cantrell, that list was going to be long and convoluted. Ex-husbands. Current husbands. Current, jealous lovers. Former jilted lovers. Bookies. Loan sharks. That's all I could think of without checking my notes.

I told her all that. "Janey-Lynn, get yourself a lawyer. They're going to come at you. Soon."

Chapter Eighteen

Curran

"Come at me?" Janey-Lynn's face puzzled up. "Are things that bad?"

"Most murders are committed by close friends and family, like a spouse. Charlie is rich, and his death makes it all yours. Add jealousy and revenge, and you're prime suspect number one. I'm a close second. Pray those videos are recovered."

Janey-Lynn looked at me like something was simmering. "I called a friend this morning. He's got a good lawyer for me. I was going to call Tommy but didn't want to involve him."

"He wouldn't mind." I told her about my morning with Tommy and the FBI. "He's probably already lining you up with a winner. Don't worry."

She came to me and clutched me close as she sniffed back tears. I didn't resist. Having a beautiful woman do this was a curse. It happens all the time to me. Okay, now and then. Well, this was the first time in many years. But hey, Janey-Lynn made up for my dry spell.

We stood there, embracing and not saying a word. She was an amazing woman—strong, intelligent, and easy to talk to. We'd spent many lunches or evening cocktails doing just that. Charlie was never around, and I lived alone. Company was the catalyst for our friendship. But in the weeks I'd known her, it had become something more. Not physical. Not any deep, torrid thing. Comfortable like the friend you'd hadn't seen since high school and after decades, showed up like they were always there. Warm.

Trusting. More.

Finally, she kissed my cheek in a deep, comforting show of affection.

"I'm so glad you're here, Lowe."

Gulp.

"Janey-Lynn, I'll dig into Charlie's murder as soon as we know if the videos are recovered. Between Evans and me, we'll find the killer. It might take time. The list of those wanting revenge on Charlie is long. That's in our favor."

Her embrace lasted a little longer. When she released me, her face was tear-streaked and red. "Thank you, Lowe. I know I can count on you."

"You can."

She held me at arm's length. "You still owe me the cushions."

Of course, I did. "Janey-Lynn, who owns that junk car out front?"

"Junk car?" Her face twisted a little. "Oh, that. it belongs to my stepson, Randy."

Stepson? When did Janey-Lynn get a stepson? In all the meetings and discussions on her case—my surveilling Charlie, not any murder plot, I assure you—she never mentioned a stepson. In fact, she'd more than once inferred that she and Charlie were both childless.

"Janey-Lynn, you never mentioned any stepson."

She glanced over her shoulder. I felt her angst building.

"He's not been around for years, Lowe." Her voice was low and strained. "I'll explain later. It's a long story and not a good one."

That didn't sound good at all. Odd that this mysterious stepson arrived on the heels of Charlie Cantrell's murder. I took her hands in mine and tried hard to show confidence. I also wanted her to be thinking like I was—everyone else was a suspect. Trust no one but me.

"Charlie and his lover were murdered last night. Where has your stepson been? Don't you think—"

"Don't go there, Lowe. He said the cops called him this morning. He showed up just an hour ago." Her face paled as she watched the house. "You worry about you and those men."

Oh, yeah, the 'others.' "The others—right. Tell me."

94

"Two suits showed up an hour ago. Came here first. They thought you lived here. I straightened them out fast. I thought they were Agent Evans' men. They weren't."

"Describe them to me." She did, and they didn't ring any bells—especially any young, leather-jacketed Italian-complexed guy. "They weren't cops. Maybe feds. I had a visit with them earlier."

"They didn't act like feds, Lowe." She looked over at Bogart, still rolling in the grass, and cursed at him. "I rescued Bogart when they left the cottage. He was carrying on and on. That's when I saw your friend leave."

"Rescue Bogart? From what?"

"The boogeyman, I guess." She shot him a nasty glance as he rolled again and came up dirty on his butt. "I heard his bellyaching all the way here. I went down and saw your friend driving off. Then, I found Bogart tearing the crap out of my chair cushion. I guess he was lonely, or you hid his treats in the stupidest places. You should have asked before you got him."

"Yeah, sorry." Now was not the time to tell her the story of Billy Piper and Bogart's rescue. "I'll get the stuff fixed. Finish telling me the rest."

"Stop that." She cursed at Bogart as he rolled a little more. "They asked a bunch of questions I couldn't answer—and if I could have, I wouldn't have. They asked what you do for a living and for who, how much, and on and on—about your past. Seems like they knew more than me, too."

Maybe.

"They started getting too personal. I demanded to see badges and IDs. That sent them packing." She faced me with a stern, parental glare. "What do they want, Lowe? Something tells me they weren't cops. Are you in other trouble again?"

No, not cops...wait, other trouble *again*?

Janey-Lynn reminded me of Helen Mirren. Finely aged, sexy, well put together, and bright. She had penetrating, intelligent eyes that didn't seem to miss anything—including a look into your mind now and then—like a mystic seeking the answers to the universe inside your head. I wondered what she found in mine. Couldn't be good. She was without a doubt a lovely and vivacious lady. She also had Helen's directness and demeanor she often portrayed in her roles—a tiger lady with a biting personality. Now, she unleashed on me without a second thought.

"Did you think I'd move you into my loft apartment without checking you out, Boy Scout? Just because Tommy said you were okay?" She watched Bogart running like a crazy dog through the yard. "Stupid dog is going to need another bath."

She'd checked me out? She couldn't have found much. Especially since my fiasco on the Voula Beach Road. After all, I'd signed a non-disclosure agreement that made the Ten Commandments look simple. Only Stevie and Tommy Astor knew anything important. And Tommy knew no details. Just the aftermath.

"I'm talking history, Lowe. Before you became a PI. You got twisted up with the government. That's true, isn't it?" She cast a sideways glance at me. "You totally screwed up. Afterward, you were persona non grata."

Did I mention that Janey-Lynn was not a shy woman? "Yeah, you could say that. You still hired me and put me up here, though. My past didn't scare you?"

"Maybe a little." She shrugged. "Tell me your side of the story. Or, I have to go by what I was told."

"Told by who?"

"Does it matter?"

It did, and I said so.

"Lowe, or should I call you *Pappa*?"

Oh, crap. She knew more than I thought and far more than I'd hoped. "Please don't call me that."

She grinned a devilish grin that was half-sexy and half-I'll do what I please. "You don't own a couple thousand acres of prime real estate in this county without having friends. I was told you got tossed out on your ass by the government after some big screw-up overseas a few years back. Kabul or Baghdad?"

"Voula. In Greece." Geography is important. "It wasn't my screw-up. At least, I don't see it that way. That mission almost killed me. I was in the hospital for a year. They tossed me after I recovered. They needed to blame someone."

"They always do." Janey-Lynn threw a thumb toward the house. "You can tell me over a beer."

Damn, she transitioned like she lived—fast and directly.

"Janey-Lynn, it's barely two-thirty."

"Oh, yeah, right." She waved me toward the wicker lawn furniture. "I'll be right back."

A few moments later, she returned with a pot of coffee and a decanter of bourbon. Bourbon, she informed me, was the pre-five o'clock drink of the refined.

"Janey-Lynn, if you know everything, what's there to say?"

"The truth is always somewhere between. This morning, I thought you killed my husband. I know that's silly. To protect you, I erased those videos and lied to the police. I wouldn't do that for just anyone, Lowe. In fact, I can't think of anyone else."

Hold on now. "Janey-Lynn, I didn't ask you to do any of that. You never should have suspected me."

"Perhaps. But I knew what happened to you overseas. That told me a lot."

"Like what?"

"You know how to kill. You've done it before. You're good at it."

Ugh. True. Guilty. "It's not the same."

She folded her arms. "Then tell me your side of that mess. Tell me so I know it's different. Tell me so I know I didn't give you an alibi when you didn't deserve one."

Ouch. Deep down, Janey-Lynn wasn't sure I hadn't killed Charlie; not so deep down, she wanted to be. A moment ago, she was in my arms, holding on for dear life just for comfort. Now, she was, well, I don't know what she was doing.

Fair was fair. She had acted to protect me. I owed her.

I sat in a wicker chair and told her the condensed version of how I got three round scars, an occasional limp, and a pink slip from my former employer.

Telling the story was hard. Damn hard. The bourbon helped.

It all started on the Voula Beach Road. Truth was, it damn near ended there, too. At least, for me.

Chapter Nineteen

Curran

Fifteen years ago, I'd been a different man. Not just younger and more agile and less grumpy, either. Bigger differences. I'd been a Dark Creek operative—a private contractor living off government work. Dark Creek was created to fill the void of US Military Forces leaving the Middle East and other rough spots around the world. It was filled with former special ops folks, intel-types, and people like me. We all had a history. We all had a price tag. When a country had a problem somewhere the US Forces didn't want to engage in, say, Baghdad or Kabul, the US Government graciously opened the door for Dark Creek. Often, we worked with the State Department and Defense Intelligence Agency—DIA—the CIA's defense counterpart. As private contractors, the US Government retained plausible deniability for the occasional *oops*.

I'd been assigned a DIA protection unit. We were based in good ole Virginia and deployed wherever needed. Our mission was simple. We located valuable assets DIA's spies found and protected them while they were spilling their guts to DIA's intelligence officers. In civilian terms, we protected foreign spies and turncoats who were selling out their respective countries to us. Over the years, I'd played a role in successfully retrieving and protecting Russian operatives, Syrian military guerrillas, a few Taliban who'd seen the light—read that money and living in resorts and not caves— senior Pakistani military officers, and yes, a long list of others who decided the West wasn't all that bad. When DIA made a deal with a turncoat, it always included lots of cash and protection. Uncle Sam provided the cash. Dark Creek provided the protection. Simple.

My team did it often. We did it well. We'd never lost an asset.

Until the Voula Beach Road.

Fifteen years ago, DIA had recruited Khaled Hafez Kalani—a senior general in the Hezbollah terrorist organization. Fact is, calling Hezbollah a terror organization is a misnomer in part. It's a damn army. A huge army. Primarily headquarters in Lebanon, it got its working capital and many resources from Iran. That's because they share a very important distinction in the region—they are Shia. So are the Iranians. Saudis, Iran's enemy, are Sunnis. Shias and Sunnis. Both Muslim, both hate each other. The only people they hate more than each other were the Israelis and the West. I could give you the history and the big issues, but I'd be lying if I said I understood them all. After thousands of years, anyone who says they do is lying.

Anyway, Hezbollah has terror units all over the world. Kalani promised to give up everything we wanted to know about Hezbollah operations. That and his soul. For a price, that is. At first, he lived in Beirut and passed intelligence on Hezbollah's contacts with the Iranians and cell activity inside the Israeli West Bank—Hezbollah's primary target. He gave up pending attacks that had saved Americans throughout other parts of the Middle East, too. He was the biggest intelligence coup in years in that part of the world. A part where American operatives had short life spans.

Kalani was happy. We were happy. Everything seemed fine.

Then, something went horribly wrong—Kalani hit the panic button and cried for help. An Army Special Forces team spirited him out of Beirut to Greece—the closest friendly port where DIA had resources large enough to protect him. My team went to Athens to babysit until DIA could sort out his problems. That took one meeting. Hezbollah was onto him in Beirut. They wanted to filet him and put his head on a spike. Unfortunately, they got his family before anyone knew he was compromised. Their heads were found in the courtyard of his West Beirut villa when the Green Berets arrived to extract him.

Enter Dark Creek. By Dark Creek, I mean me and my team. I was at the helm, and Stevie Keene was my number two—a steadfast guard dog if there ever was one.

We secured a private estate from a local Saudi Prince—names aren't important as there are hundreds of Saudi princes. Prince somebody's estate was along the Voula Beach Road—a swanky road along the nicest beachfront in Southeast Greece. The villa was surrounded by ten-feet-high stone walls. It had a hardened steel entry and rear gate. CCTV and alarms. Even a rooftop defense battery. All this for a twenty-five-year-old twenty-fifth removed Arab prince. But he had a cool pad, and we paid handsomely for it. Oh, and we promised not to tell the royal family about his heroin habit, too.

All was well.

We hunkered down with fifteen highly trained, highly motivated, and highly paid operatives. I had former Navy Seals and Special Forces and even a couple of British SAS. Me, I'm a former somebody, too, but that doesn't matter. My credentials at that time trumped their former credentials. So, poof, I was the boss—the oldest, still alive-est, best paid-est Dark Creek contractor in country.

As a result of that nomenclature—age mostly—I was nicknamed *Pappa*.

Our mission had been simple. Babysit Kalani until DIA senior intelligence chiefs arrived from D.C. Once they were on the scene, we'd transfer Kalani to another safe house in the Peloponnese peninsula, and DIA would assume responsibility. When they were done sucking his brain dry, Kalani would be whisked away to some far-off new life. Like maybe a bagel shop in Detroit.

Except things didn't work out so good for Kalani, or my team—and certainly not for me.

It was early evening. One of my team—I can remember his face like it was yesterday, but his name has been lost in the cobwebs of physical therapy and coma—was making dinner in the well-stocked kitchen on the Villa's first floor. I was in the command room on the second floor that was wired with cameras, alarm monitors, and all manner of spook-stuff. We had teams on the perimeter and in the rooftop defense station. Counter-surveillance teams were positioned outside the villa nearby to alert us if trouble approached.

What could go wrong?

As I told Janey-Lynn the story, I closed my eyes to hide what was coming back to me...

* * *

...The smell of charring lamb filtered through the air like a fog settling over the Voula Beach Road. Greeks had many amazing customs. My favorite had been Easter, when nearly every household grilled lamb over wood and charcoal firepits. The neighborhood scents and noises flowed over the Villa walls and played a part in dulling our senses.

I was in the command room watching the perimeter CCTV monitors with two other operators. This wasn't my post—I roamed about keeping my finger on the pulse of everyone and everything. The Villa cameras showed me every square inch of our inner and outer perimeter. If anyone came calling, we'd have a few precious moments to see, identify, and prepare should we not like their intent. Unless it was the mailman, any unknown visitor meant trouble.

It was beautiful spring weather in Voula. High eighties, balmy, with a nice Aegean Sea breeze blowing into our open, barred windows. The roads were busy with tourists, and locals headed south toward Vouliagmeni and the many tavernas and nightlife there. All seemed at peace on the Voula Beach Road.

I stood and stretched. As I downed the last of my coffee, the CCTV cameras all went dark. "Rogue three, eyes blind. Check it out."

The radio burped in my earbud. "Roger."

The sudden contrail from an RPG—rocket-propelled grenade—erupted from a neighbor's yard. It hit the rooftop position overhead before my brain translated the threat. The explosion was cacophonous and shook the villa to its foundation. It toppled me over the monitors, into the wall, and down onto my ass in the middle of the room.

A second RPG hit somewhere along the villa wall and rocked the air with a thunderous explosion.

The early evening erupted outside into the blasphemy of gunfire.

My right ear earwig gushed voices from the perimeter security team— gunmen were breaching the Villa from all sides. The second RPG had shredded the rear gate, and fighters were swarming in.

We were under siege.

As I grabbed my radio to call in our emergency response team stationed two blocks away, the third explosion knocked me off my feet again.

The radio went silent. Not even static.

I stood, grabbed a Heckler and Kock MP-5 subgun from the rack along the wall, and bolted for the balcony overlooking the downstairs entry.

A fourth explosion.

The percussion spun me around, careened me into the wall, and sent me tumbling to the marble floor. My head struck the wall and then the floor. Blood gushed from my head, my neck, and soaked me. The pain invaded and kept me down for precious seconds.

More gunfire. Frenzied voices—English and...*Arabic*.

Hezbollah was here.

I crawled to the stairs, fell more than walked down, and used one hand to steady myself from collapse—my other hand hefted the subgun as I surveyed the entrance hall looking for targets.

The heavy, grand oak front door was open three feet.

Biting my lip to stave off the pain, trying desperately to pull me into shock, I pivoted from the stairs and cleared the lower hall.

Clear. Safe.

Gunfire. Two more explosions shook the outer courtyard. The Arabic voices were everywhere. The English voices were silent—gone.

"Stevie," I called into my headset, "Rogue two, report."

Nothing.

"Rogue three—four—report."

Silence.

"Rodriquez, White...Volesky, report! Conner? Report dammit. Who's out there?"

Silence meant bad things.

I reached the main hall, checked it—clear—and pivoted back to the front door, pressing myself against the wall beside it.

I began the peeking game around the half-closed front door. I leaned around to see past the heavy wood, quickly taking visual snapshots and retracting to the faux safety of the wall.

That was my first mistake.

What is half-closed is also half-open. I failed to consider this physics maxim as I made my second "peek" around the half-closed door. As I did, a Hezbollah terrorist outside in the courtyard shot me through the half-open side.

The pain was instant and devastating. The bullet hit my shoulder and sent me backward onto the cool marble. The impact rattled my brain for the third time. The light around me began to ooze in and out as consciousness threatened to abandon me. As I fought for control, I looked up.

Standing in the doorway was a man. He wore dark jeans and a black shirt common with local street wear. His face was obscured beneath a checkered keffiyeh wrapped around his head. Only his dark eyes showed—and they were staring hatred at me.

Our eyes met, and he lifted his AK-47 for the kill shot...

* * *

...Janey-Lynn stared open-mouthed with a very tall bourbon stalled halfway to her lips. She hung on to that description, waiting for my next memory.

I couldn't.

Not that I didn't want to, though I truly didn't. No, it was that I didn't know. My memories ended there. The next images were a medevac aircraft bouncing over the Alps en route to Frankfurt, Germany. There, waiting for me, was a super-smart trauma surgeon who'd perfected his craft on war-wounded US forces out of Iraq and Afghanistan. He and a team of equally brilliant war-docs put me back together. It took nearly a year—eight surgeries and so many therapy sessions—physical and mental—I couldn't count. There were three bullet holes in me. One nearly took my heart out. One that ripped deep into my shoulder and nearly exsanguinated me. One that left a gnarly gaping wound in my left thigh. And there were broken bones, cracked this and that. Percussion damage. Other...

How the second and third bullets had happened were a guess. My best one was the short, stocky guerrilla with the checkered keffiyeh had gifted them. Evidence at the scene suggested I'd killed him before he put a fourth bullet in me. How, I had no idea. Luck, most likely. Or his remorse over hurting me brought him to suicide. I wasn't putting any bets on that.

"That was that." My hands trembled. She noticed and politely looked away. "Total mission failure. Kalani was killed in his room. One of my men, Liam Conner, an SAS guy I'd hired, died trying to protect him in the first wave of attack. When it was all over, I had thirteen dead. Only Stevie Keene and I made it. The Greek Ministry went nuts, and a storm of shit hit us. DIA blamed me, of course. It took nearly a year to recover enough to head home. I got fired and branded a failure. I was unemployable after that."

Her eyes were glossy and fearful. "A year? How did you—"

"Let's just say I was pretty near my end." I didn't want to go into any more details. "Docs didn't think I'd walk, let alone function outside a nursing home. Fooled the shit out of them, though. Luck."

"No." She stood and walked to me, knelt beside my chair, and put a warm, comforting hand on my cheek. "Divine intervention."

Not for me. Nope. "Luck. One bullet a half inch to the right would have shredded my heart. Another quarter inch left, and I'd be drinking dinner through a straw and drooling on myself for life. Luck."

Now, she patted my cheek as she stood again. "That's not luck, Lowe. Trust me."

I shrugged. "I got a year's severance pay, the contents of my IRA I'd been stashing away for ten years prior, and a 'don't call us' email. Oh, and a thirty-page non-disclosure agreement that I have now just violated. So, I got that going for me."

"What happened to your friend, Stevie?"

Ah, yes, Stevie. "He got hit in his legs and an arm. A bad concussion, too. Real bad. He's been, well, suffering that for years." I tapped my temple. "Bad stuff. PTSD and traumatic brain injury. You saw him at my place earlier."

Her eyes dissected me. "Is that why you stay close?"

"Yeah, that too. He was older than me by a few years, and he had retirement options. I didn't." I patted her arm and took her hand. "He works for me now and then. You know, when I need my ass covered. Truth is, he can't do much. He never fully recovered."

"Oh, I see." She squeezed hand. "You're a good friend, Lowe Curran."

Her eyes bathed me in uncomfortable light. "I owe him, Janey-Lynn. They said he dragged me clear and covered me until our backup team arrived. All the while, he was messed up bad himself."

Janey-Lynn emptied her bourbon and returned to her chair. Then, she refilled her glass and topped mine off to the rim. She sat there, staring and slowly shaking her head. Bogart had leaned against her as she mindlessly stroked his head.

"I'll never tell, Lowe," she managed in a croaking voice. "Those bastards. What they did to you. Your story is safe with me. Your friend is welcome here anytime."

Yes, those bastards. The question was, which ones? Hezbollah? The Saudis for maybe ratting us out at the villa? Or our bastards? After all, someone ratted us out. Hezbollah's attack had been well-planned, well-executed, and well-concealed. That took one thing they shouldn't have had—inside intelligence. Where'd they get it? From friend or foe? These days, and then, too, it's hard to distinguish the difference. Those days fifteen years ago hadn't been any different.

"You're right, Janey-Lynn. Those bastards." I winked at her. "Now, do you believe that I didn't kill Charlie? I've come clean. Not sure it proves my innocence. Are we good?"

"Yes, we're good." She gulped back her bourbon and refilled her glass yet again. "I guess the stories I heard were true. Here I've been thinking you were fired for banging the boss's wife."

Chapter Twenty

U.C.

U.C. watched his sat phone, waiting for the Controller to respond. Finally, after a long and concerning silence, the phone buzzed.

The Controller—*You have an update? Have you spoken with Wain and that tin-soldier?*

U.C.—*Yes, both. They were resistant to your requests.*

The Controller—*I hope you explained that it was no request.*

U.C.—*Of course I did. Jesus, give me some credit. It's not my first mission.*

The Controller—*You know who you have to visit next, correct?*

U.C.—*Yes, of course.*

The Controller—*Anything further?*

U.C.—*We identified the hacker. His name is William Piper. We traced him to Leesburg. Crazy bastard built a security system throughout his house and recorded everything inside and out. I have copies of the video files.*

The Controller—*That's your job.*

Without hearing the Controller's voice, he knew there was an edge to the text. Still, the words were condescending as always, and he expected nothing less. He was almost delighted in giving him the next news.

U.C.—*It's worse than we anticipated. Much worse.*

The Controller—*You said you had it contained. Explain.*

U.C.—*We contained the breach on that end. My man inside the Leesburg PD has been helpful, but it's not enough.*

No response.

U.C.—*Someone got to Piper before we did. He beat us there by an hour last night. He got everything.*

The Controller—*Everything?*

Not so condescending now, eh?

U.C.—*The someone took all Piper's hacked files. That includes Whisper.*

U.C. knew the mention of Whisper sent The Controller into a rage. The silence was telling.

The Controller—*How could you let this happen? You have to recover, contain... eliminate all risks.*

U.C.—*I know my job.*

A long emptiness.

Finally, The Controller—*That is worse than previously considered. We can still recover. It might get a little complicated.*

U.C.—*More complicated than Wain?* He was not easily convinced. *Then there's the other threat.*

The Controller—*What other threat?*

U.C. smiled. He knew the new threat was no laughing matter. Still, it would send a lightning bolt up The Controller's arrogant ass.

U.C. took a long breath—*Not 'what' but 'who.' Piper was a paranoid schizo. He literally filmed this old guy talking his way into his place last night. I wasn't sure at first, now I am. I watched the video five times. It's someone from our past. He's back in the middle again.*

The Controller—*Explain.*

U.C. tapped away on his sat phone keypad and waited until the message flashed SEND Complete—*I've sent a short video clip to you. It's him—Voula Beach.*

Nothing again. U.C. knew The Controller was absorbing the images, watching the video clip multiple times.

U.C.—*Do you recognize the man beneath the old man disguise?*

The Controller—*No. It's impossible. He was dealt with—twice. It cannot be him.*

U.C.—*It can, and it is. It's Lowe Curran. Pappa has the Whisper files.*

Chapter Twenty-One

Curran

Sitting there, trying not to let the darkness of reminiscence overtake me, I realized that had Stevie Keene showed up last night, I wouldn't have had to lie to Evans. Stevie would have been my alibi. A damn good one. Having missed his assignment and with his condition this morning, he was useless. For the short term, Janey-Lynn was it.

She watched me over her bourbon glass. Her eyes locked onto me with a strange, half-pity, half-disbelieving look. I wasn't sure which one she'd settle on, so I interrupted the awkward silence.

"It's okay, Janey-Lynn. Really. I got lucky. Docs said I'd be totally screwed for the rest of my life. I beat the odds. But it cost me in ways that surgery couldn't fix."

"Like?"

I felt my face drain from the memories I kept deep.

Her eyes softened. She reached out and touched my hand with a warmness that melted me yet again. "Who was she, Lowe?"

Damn her. "Doesn't matter, Janey-Lynn. It's a long time ago."

"Not for you. I can see it in your face." She leaned back and studied me. "That lovely lady on your mantel?"

I shook my head and sipped my bourbon. This was not the time or the place to toddle down memory lane any further than I already had. I'd rather go back and take the bullets on the Voula Beach Road than reminisce about lost loves and a lonely life.

Janey-Lynn's cell phone vibrated on the table beside her, and a strange, ping-ping-ping chirped from it. She glanced awkwardly at me and scooped it up, looked at the screen for a moment, and then looked at me.

"I've got to take this." She looked away. Embarrassment? "It's that lawyer."

"No problem. I'll grab Bogart and go home. I'll call you later." I stood and waved for the Lab, who was almost asleep at her feet. "Come on, you big baby, let's go. You're embarrassing."

"Lowe," she said, cupping her hand over the phone. "I don't like what happened to you back in Greece. I don't like what's happening now. I won't do anything to hurt you. No matter what. You have my word."

Damn, if she wasn't getting sentimental with me.

"Yes, ma'am. Back at you." I gestured to the phone and winked. "Better take your call. The lawyer is probably charging you a thousand bucks while he's on hold."

Before things got too gooey, Bogart and I headed for my loft apartment. On our way to the shortcut through the woods, I stopped to take notice of the junker behind her Mercedes SUV. I made a mental note of the Maryland license plate, and the hair stood on my neck. Bogart didn't like the vibe, either. He crouched low and began to growl, staring at the farmhouse.

Instinct sent my hand to my Kimber. Common sense kept it in the holster.

Standing in the farmhouse's front door was an average height, shifty-looking guy watching us. He wore no shirt, jeans, and tattoos covered most of his arms and shoulders. He was thin and with a scruffy beard like he'd not seen a barber or a razor for months. The thing that made me release my Kimber's grip and snort a laugh was his dark hair pulled back into a manbun on top of his head.

Now, a manbun wasn't really a bad thing—say, for a twenty-something millennial. The younger generation finds them cool and hip. If hip's still a thing. But this guy had to be in his forties. The straggly beard, gaunt body, skinny-pants half-way down his ass, and manbun looked, well, ridiculous. I'd call this urban grunge. Maybe he was trying out for a part in an urban version of Shogun.

Am I judging too much?

Was this Randy Cantrell? No wonder Janey-Lynn never spoke of him. He looked like one of those relatives you keep in the basement and only bring out on Halloween.

Sorry, that was harsh. True, but harsh. I'll pay penance later by dropping a tenner in the next homeless person's bucket, I see. Although I will check to make sure it's not Randy.

I waved, but it wasn't returned.

I snorted again. "Let's go, Bogart. I bought cookies."

Woof. Snort. Growl.

Even Bogart didn't like his manbun.

As much as I wanted to introduce myself to Randy, I needed to regroup and try to sort out my next moves. I'd never been a murder suspect before. Sure, Evans called me a 'person of interest.' Either way, I needed a plan to prove my innocence should those videos Janey-Lynn deleted not be recovered.

The moment we got within sniffing distance of my loft, my new faithful companion growled low and steady—more so than at Randy Cantrell's manbun. The hair went up on his back—Bogart's, not Randy's.

"Good boy, Bogart. You have the makings of a great detective." He ruined it by slipping behind me and peeking around my legs. "Or not."

We slipped behind the barn to approach where no window would give us away. As we emerged along the opposite side of the barn, I drew my pistol and eased toward the stairs. In seconds, I was on the landing.

My front door was ajar, and there was movement inside—the creek of old floorboards, the opening of a drawer. Footsteps. Someone mumbling and milling around.

Peeking through the open door sent a wave of *deja vu* over me— *what is half-closed is also half-open.* I shook it off. The intruder stood near the kerosene stove, examining several knickknacks. He focused on Carli's photograph on my mantel. He meticulously replaced everything, straightened them in an attempt to hide his presence, and turned around. He knelt and lifted my black duffle bag containing my twice-gifted twenty-five thousand bucks and grasped the zipper.

So much for hiding stuff in my dirty laundry.

I stepped inside. My Kimber was waist high, pointing generally at him—generally at his chest. The look on his face wasn't surprise or concern. It was, well, indifference. He glanced at me and then the pistol as his hand moved easily to his belt and touched his own sidearm holstered beneath his leather coat.

"Pulling a gun on a US Marshal is a serious offense, Curran," Gallo said. He gestured for me to lower my gun. "Not as serious as shooting me. Put it down."

I grunted a laugh but kept the gun up. "I have this gun because an intruder broke in. An intruder who illegally entered my apartment without a warrant and who failed to identify himself. Should you decide to pull that Glock, self-defense against an armed illegal intruder trying to shoot me might be messy—considering you're a Marshal—but justified."

That wasn't exactly true, mind you. As a current murder suspect, if I shot Gallo, the cops would dispense with silly things like the Fourth, Fifth, and Sixth Amendments. They'd walk me out back and stick the needle in my arm themselves. Maybe Gallo didn't realize that, though.

He watched me with a strange, quizzical expression. His fingers rested on his pistol, but they didn't close around the butt. After a long moment of contemplation, he moved his hand away from the gun and patted the air.

"Okay, Curran. Put it away. I'm here on official business. Let's talk."

"Really?" My Kimber didn't move. "We have nothing to talk about. I think Tommy and Katelyn Astor explained that. What do you want?"

"Answers." Gallo glanced down at the duffle at his feet. "What's in the bag?"

"Laundry."

"Laundry? Like a pair of old, ratty pajamas and a bathrobe too big for you? Let's see."

Shit, he knew. "No. I'm shy about my dirty undies. Kick the bag away. No warrant, no underwear party."

"Cute." He looked down at the bag, back to me, and grinned. He gave the duffle a shove and rolled it a couple feet away. "You have heavy socks."

I did. About two and a half pounds of green Andrew Jackson socks.

"Nice place." He lazily waved a hand around the room. "Quiet. Secluded. Very rural Americana. Not quite like your Athens or D.C. digs years ago."

My, my, wasn't he well-informed? He's been busy checking me out since our first meeting this morning. "You didn't answer my question."

"Tell me about yourself, Curran. You can skip the part where you're a murder suspect. I already know that."

Good news always travels fast. "It's *Mr.* Curran, Marshal. I'm probably twice your age. If you can't respect your betters, at least respect your elders."

"My betters?" He laughed and wandered toward the kitchen. "You know nothing about me, Curran."

"Ditto. Unless those government computers have been snitching on me again."

"Again?" He faced me. "I know what the computer told me. I want to know what *you* can tell me. You know, the juicy stuff."

Something told me Deputy US Marshal Gallo knew everything he needed to know. Maybe not what he wanted to know. Once he was in my apartment—illegally—he knew twice as much as I wanted him to know. To quote a master gamesman, *two plus two plus one plus...*oh, you get it.

"I've been checking you out, Curran. Life's been tough since you got booted from that silly-ass black ops group. Hasn't it? What was it called, Deep Swamp or something?"

"Dark Creek." Funny guy, this Marshal.

He grinned. "Yeah, those guys. You went from being a hotshot protective agent to a lonely, reclusive PI who might have murdered his client's husband—among others."

Others? *What the hell was he talking about?*

"I'm not reclusive. I'm not lonely. I'm also not a murderer. Time will prove that one."

"Sure, sure." His odd glare unnerved me. "You never married, why?"

Wow, he was veering around like a drunk on a sobriety test. "None of your business."

"I've made it my business." He cocked his head—his intensity palpable. "You have trouble with women, don't you? I guess professional failure is just a symptom of bigger failures. Maybe you killed Charlie Cantrell because of that? He had what you couldn't?"

"What the hell do you want?" I had to fight the urge to shoot him in the balls. "You're digging into things that don't concern you or the Marshals. I have nothing you want. Nothing you need. And nothing to say. Time to leave, Gallo. Out."

His face tightened. "Not until I get some answers."

"I haven't heard any coherent questions." The heat tightened my face, and I could feel my finger itching to squeeze the trigger. "You're illegally here. So, either get the hell out or tell me what you want."

"William Piper," he said flatly.

Oh, shit. Here we go again. "I told you. Neither TAE nor I ever heard that name."

He closed the short distance between us so fast I didn't have time to lift the Kimber and warn him back.

"I think you have, Curran. I think you were there last night—in his Leesburg house."

Uh, oh. Was this a guess? He'd already commented on my PJs and robe. Had Piper had a hidden security system at his house? What kind of hacker recorded himself? *Shit. Shit. Shit. Shit.*

He leaned in close—inches close. "You know what, *Marlowe S. Curran*? I think you murdered him."

Chapter Twenty-Two

Curran

Murdered? Well, crap, he knew I was there in my PJs and robe. So, I guess there were hidden cameras in Piper's house. If so, then he knew I left the little bastard, Piper, zip-tied in the basement.

"Where'd you find this Piper guy?" Oh, crap. The connection between this US Marshal, Billy Piper, and now me, smacked me in the face like a hot chick in a bar I'd just asked if she were a hooker. I've never done that, mind you, just drawing a picture. Billy Piper was in Witness Protection. And I screwed with him good. "How was he killed? And—"

"You can't think I'll answer those questions. Do you? You're no LEO."

I considered that and shook my head. "Just trying to help. But, if you really think I killed someone, you'd have a warrant."

I didn't know what made me feel worse, that I'd hunted down a US Marshal Service WITSEC protectee, or that I was the prime suspect in his murder. Well, maybe the prime suspect in two murders. I can't forget about good ole' Charlie Cantrell and his mistress. After all, Charlie came first. At least, I think he did. Oh, shit. That would make me a prime suspect in three murders.

How do I get myself into these things?

Wait. How is it that a Marshal's witness was running a hacking scheme? Did Gallo not know he was bilking hundreds of thousands of dollars from people like TAE? What was that all about? Was Gallo in on Piper's scheme? Is that why he was gunning for me—solo and warrantless? Was Piper's twenty-five grand to me meant for him? Remember, that was a gift.

Maybe that gift was originally meant for Gallo. Payment to look the other way. *Hmmm.*

Good questions, all. I'd kill for some answers. Well, not kill…

Piper had been terrified of someone coming. I'd dismissed it last night as a stall tactic. Maybe he wasn't stalling. Maybe he was terrified of Gallo—his presence here made a lot of sense. He was acting like a dirty ex-partner with his hand in the till when the drawer was slammed closed.

"I don't know what you're talking about, Marshal. I have nothing to do with your dead WITSEC guy. It does sound like you and he were up to something, though."

It was his turn to talk stupidly. "Who said Piper was WITSEC? Who said he was dead? How do you know about WITSEC anyway?"

Oh, please.

"You just accused me of murdering him. I kinda think you'd only do that if he were dead. If a Marshal is involved, he was WITSEC. I mean, come on, I watch cable."

"Bullshit." Gallo's face reddened, and he retreated to the mantel. "You're involved, Curran."

Yes, I was. But I didn't kill him. I poked the bear. "Is it true, Deputy, that the Marshal Service has never lost a witness? Until yours, I mean—"

"Screw you, Curran." He spun back around and split the air with an angry finger. "Where were you last night? Hell, where had you been for the past twenty-four hours?"

As much as I wanted to poke Gallo's smoldering fire, I stayed quiet now. Blurting out anything at this point would look contrived. Especially since I had him dead to rights violating a half-dozen laws. Better to play shocked and innocent.

"Curran? Are you going to answer me?" He demanded. "Let's have you identify every firearm you own—legally and illegally. And hand over that one in your hand."

Nope. "Not without a warrant, Marshal." I tapped the side of my leg with my Kimber. "Or at least a really good reason. Hating me doesn't count. That much I learned on CSI."

"You have no alibi for last night. Do you? You were at the scene, and we both know that."

Now, a smart man would have given him a great alibi—like the same one Janey-Lynn gave Evans for us. A smarter man would cop for a lawyer and send him packing. Me, well, having neither a true, great alibi nor a good lawyer—the last one screwed me twice in one week, remember? I decided to wing it.

"Marshal, I was with Janey-Lynn Cantrell. I work for her. She's my landlord and client. But you already know that."

His cheeks reddened. Points to me.

I went on. "As for my firearms, I'm sure you looked all that up on your computers. After all, you've been peeking. Haven't you?"

The redness spread like a rash across his face.

"I'm a private investigator and security consultant. I legally own and carry weapons." I lifted the Kimber again. "Like this one."

"Hold that thought." His eyes brightened, and he pounced. "You're not licensed as a PI. Any PI work you do is illegal. You don't have any credentials anywhere as a security agent. Pesky Virginia laws and all."

Oh yeah, I forgot. "I work for TAE where I—"

"So you claim. Where were you the last twenty-four hours?"

Very good question. One I'd been repeatedly asked recently. I guess he didn't believe I was with Janey-Lynn. He and Evans had that in common—that and they both thought me a candidate for a Virginia needle.

"Where, Curran?"

"I was with Janey-Lynn." This winging-it strategy was working great. "She'll confirm that."

Jesus, I hope she still would after talking with her lawyer. Lawyers have a wonderful way of using me as chum in shark-infested waters. If the lawyer told her to drop my alibi, I was toast in two murder investigations.

"How's that?" Gallo asked. "Don't tell me you're sleeping with that ninety-year-old widow?"

"I should be so lucky." I put on my best disgusted face. "Janey-Lynn is not ninety. And no, she's far too classy for me. You're late to the party, asking us for an alibi. We have one—each other. You have nothing on me. She'll confirm where I was."

"We'll see." Gallo's eyes darted around the room and eventually returned to me. "I'll just check with her then, Curran. Bet on that."

I would, and I hoped my horse would come in.

"Anything else, Marshal?" I prayed he didn't have any real evidence because I was running short on bullshit. "Or will you be leaving now?"

He considered me for a long time. I wasn't sure if he was thinking of another battery of questions or sizing me for a cell. I would not do well in a cell.

He brushed past me and slammed my shoulder like a high school bully in the locker room. At the door, he turned around, stabbed the air at me again, and left. Oddly enough, he didn't turn his big black SUV left at the entrance and head to Janey-Lynn's. Instead, he went right and headed for the main road.

As I shut the apartment door, I wondered if Janey-Lynn was still my best gal.

My cell phone rang. Guess who?

"You can take me to dinner tonight, Lowe. There's a new Bistro in Upperville. Quiet. Expensive. Alibis don't come cheap. Neither do lawyers. And Lowe, I'll be wanting to talk more over dessert...at my house."

'Dessert,' said the spider to the fly.

Chapter Twenty-Three

Curran

After Marshal Gallo left me wondering how deep in crap I was, I found a new hiding place for my duffle bag. No, I didn't hide all the stacks of Jacksons in my freezer. I didn't hide them in a pirate chest in the back yard, either, although the thought did occur to me. And I didn't secret them into any new floorboards or false ceiling panels.

I'd seen all those movies and if my dirty laundry basket wasn't safe, neither were they.

Luckily, Piper had the decency to leave the bills in their original violet banking bands—a hundred bills per strap, two thousand bucks each. That was twelve and a half straps of rainy-day money to hide. The storm clouds were building, and it was ugly out there.

It's not that I don't trust banks. I do with other people's money. It's that I understand the banking laws. If you walk into your bank with a deposit over ten grand, the IRS requires you to fill out a nifty form under the Currency and Foreign Transaction Reporting Act. The government calls that preventative criminal investigation. I call it none-of-their-damn-business.

I, however, being a mere puny citizen and not a government aficionado or banking czar, have no say. So, my large cash transactions—few and far between as they are—go into the Marlowe S. Curran safety deposit system. I hide them. I'm like a dog with his favorite bones or a pirate with his treasure. I have a couple hiding places for my booty, and not much booty at all. When you have nothing, hiding it is easy.

This stack of purple-banded bucks went into my favorite spot only recently required by a swindling lawyer previously mentioned. A year ago, I'd stashed some emergency cash from a good-paying detective gig in an old set of encyclopedias. It took me hours to carve all the volume's pages into cavities to hide a band of money or two. I'd hidden forty grand. That stash was long gone. I had to live on it for a year after previously said lawyer screwed me out of my fees.

Am I being petty? Repetitive?

Anyway, the old encyclopedias were a great twenty-six volumes of hiding space. I was able to stuff two bands of twenties in the first twelve books and one in the thirteenth. The volumes sat on the bottom shelf of a five-shelf bookcase in the rear spare room. Bric-a-brac hid them, as did the reading lamp in front of the case. Since nobody used encyclopedias any longer, I figured they were safe.

Afterward, I dropped onto my nice, comfy bed and caught up on a few hours of needed sleep. Stalking computer hackers by night and dodging federal agents by day was tiring work. Let's not even talk about being a murder suspect.

My sleep was restless, and I dreamt as I always did. In nightmare vignettes...

...The smell of charring lamb...

I was back on the Voula Beach Road.

The safe house was quiet. Two operatives were just down the street providing countersurveillance and early threat detection. Two were on post inside the walls. One in the front near the steel entry gate and one at the rear of the house near a back entrance.

From my vigil inside the villa's makeshift command post on the second floor, I watched the monitors—a row of six small, closed-circuit television monitors that viewed every square inch of compound.

The me aside from the dream knew what was about to happen. I felt it coming.

Knew it moment-by-moment. Dream-me was unaware.

As I stood and stretched, downing the last of my coffee, it began.

The CCTV monitors flashed black.

The early Easter evening erupted into a blasphemy of gunfire from all directors outside.

The earwig in my right ear gushed from the perimeter security team—gunmen from all sides of the villa were breaching our compound.

We were under siege.

The first explosion rocked me off my feet and slammed me over the monitors into the wall and down to the floor—stunned.

Light and sound swirled everywhere.

An explosion...pain everywhere.

Angst. Fear. Fight back, Curran, fight...

Blood gushed down my head, my neck, and bathed me.

Mistakes, mistakes.

...the smell of smoke and explosives...pain everywhere, blood flowing from me...I was down and fading in and out...the keffiyehed man stood over me, his rifle settled on...those eyes—his eyes—

The knock on my loft door saved me.

Sweat dampened my face, stung my eyes, soaked the sheet beneath me. Fear and danger are strange bedfellows. When you live with them, you can conquer them in your fight for survival. When forced to relive them over and over, they conquer you.

The knocking persisted, and I climbed to my feet.

Whoever was at my door better be young, gorgeous, funny, rich, and available. Or Ed McMahon with my ten million dollars. Did Ed still do that?

I made my way to the door in just my old ratty jeans. I didn't bother to put on a shirt. I wasn't trying to be sexy or anything, and I doubted Ed would care. Whoever was hammering on my door was impatient and I think all my clean shirts were in the laundry basket Gallo dumped on the floor.

It wasn't Ed McMahon, my ten mill, or someone selling car warrantees.

Janey-Lynn gave me a very provocative once-over as she strode into the living room. She wore jeans and her customary tight blouse, trying to ensure anyone interested noticed her buxom physique.

I did and told her so. Purely to be polite, mind you, and help her dwindling self-confidence.

Her face deleted that provocative ogle and turned into a scowl.

"Dinner will have to wait, Lowe." She stomped over to my makeshift bar near the window. "Gallo came back."

Yeah, that would irritate her a bit. Not as bad as it would irritate me. I'd hoped he took my alibi lie and swallowed it. The look on her face said he didn't.

"And?"

She retrieved a bottle of mediocre bourbon from the bar, ignored the dust on a cheap plastic coffee cup nearby, and poured a few fingers—a fist full, actually. She poured half of it into her. Then, turned to me with fire in her eyes like Lucifer readying for battle.

"That little bastard played word games trying to get me to say we're lying."

Of course, he did. "Well, we are, Janey-Lynn."

"That's beside the point." Another finger of bourbon down. "He was an ass. But I stuck to it. Just like we rehearsed."

Well, we never rehearsed anything. That would be illegal. Sure, lying about the alibi was already illegal. Rehearsing it was worse. At least, I think so.

She lifted the cup toward me. "I told that little tin-star shit that I was with you all night. Same as I told Evans. Except when he made comments about what we were doing, I didn't answer. I told him it was none of his business."

Great. She deepened the lie and not in a good way. Is repeating the lie over and over separate counts of perjury? "Janey-Lynn, you might have made this worse. We told Evans I went there because you heard something when Charlie was out. Remember?"

She grunted a yes.

"Letting Gallo think we had a fling isn't good. It contradicts our other story. It makes me look like a liar."

"I didn't say we were fooling around. I didn't say we weren't." She finished her drink. "This bourbon sucks, Lowe. We should take this up at my place. I've got a bottle of Pappy. Let's face it, Evans and that Marshal think we're hooking up. Better you look embarrassed to be spending the night with a sweet, beautiful, more mature woman like myself than them thinking we killed my husband."

Well, damn if that didn't make sense.

"Has Evans reached out about the video files?"

"No." She dropped the coffee cup on the bar and walked over to me. "Won't that take time? I mean, it's been a few hours."

"Yeah, it will. They're moving too slow. I have to do this myself. I need to find Charlie's killer."

"No, first you need to get that Marshal off our backs. He's trouble. He's acting like he's out for blood—yours." She handed me a piece of paper. Her eyes grabbed mine, and her voice was low and conspiratorial. "It's time to go on the offense. Screw that little tin-star shit, Gallo. Two can play the 'I got a secret' game."

Chapter Twenty-Four

Ambassador McKnight

The Ambassador sipped his afternoon gin and tonic and pushed his plate of fruit and cheese into the middle of the wrought iron table. He reached for the cigar still smoldering in the ashtray aside his lunch tray. He stoked it and sat back, contemplating his future.

The Cuban had barely touched his lips when a guttural cry came from the outer hallway. A second later, his aide, R. Bryan Scott, was propelled through the French patio doors and onto the sunporch floor. His face was swollen, and blood dripped from the corner of his mouth. The aide hit hard and rolled sideways, glaring back through the doors but remaining still.

"Bryan?" The Ambassador jumped to his feet. "What's happening?"

Following Scott into the sunporch was an average-built man. He was nearly bald with a strong, square jaw framed in a neatly trimmed salt-and-pepper stubble. He wore a silver Saville Row suit. He smoothed his ruffled sleeves down and stood over Scott.

"Good afternoon, Ambassador," the man said in a low, smooth, and confident voice. "I'd like a word."

Scott tried to get to his feet, but the intruder put an expensive Italian loafer on his shoulder and shoved him back down onto the marble. There, he lay still, alternating panicked glances from the Ambassador to the intruder.

The Ambassador stepped around the table and confronted the intruder. "What right do you have—"

"I have a message, Ambassador."

Scott croaked, "Sir, do as he says."

"I'd listen to him, Ambassador," the intruder said. "My benefactor is high in the food chain and thinks you should stay *emeritus*. There's no place for you near the White House. Do you understand?"

"Screw you," Scott yelled, and climbed to one knee. "You're committing a dozen federal offenses just now. You and whoever sent you. I can guess— Piccolo? Tell him to kiss our asses."

The Ambassador didn't budge. "Is that it? Piccolo? Is the good senator from Iowa flexing his muscle? I have to say, I'm shocked."

"It's him or that hillbilly, Hersh." Scott yanked his cell phone from his pocket. "I've recorded it all, you're—"

The intruder struck Scott in the temple with a lightning-fast kick, knocked his head sharply backward, and sent him backward onto the sunporch floor. In one smooth, controlled movement, he landed his foot atop the cell phone, stomped it into unrecognizable pieces, and ground the remainder into dust.

Scott went limp.

The Ambassador shoved him away and knelt over Scott. He thrust two fingers against his neck and waited. Finally, a pulse. Relieved, he stood and turned around. Anger filled his cheeks.

When he looked up, the intruder was gone.

"Abby," he shouted. "Abby, come here."

Footsteps descended the steps and across the hall. A moment later, Abby eased open the door, holding a short-barreled pistol in her hand.

"Bradley?" She swept the gun in a semi-circle, surveying the sunporch and outside area. "I heard the commotion and Bryan cry out. Is he—"

* * *

126

US Embassy, Athens, Greece—15 Years Ago…

The tight-jawed defense department lawyer closed the folder on the table before him. He shoved himself back into his chair, his face taut and angry.

"Gentlemen, I don't like this deal one bit. Kalani may be valuable, but no one is this valuable. He's killed hundreds of our allies. God only knows how many of our own people."

"I do not disagree, Jameson." Ambassador McKnight lowered his voice. "But facts are facts. He has value more than any other we've found in years. You must sign off on the deal."

"I will not." Jameson L. Wain, Department of Defense Assistant General Counsel, Embassy Athens, abruptly stood and strode from the room.

"Ambassador," a low, youthful voice said from the back of the embassy conference room. "Might I make a suggestion?"

McKnight turned and, for the first time, noticed Wain's aide, a handsome, strapping young man in his mid-twenties—R. Bryan Scott. The young legal aide had been in the meeting the entire morning, passing notes to Wain and receiving nothing but a stiff hand each time.

"Scott, is it?"

"Yes, Scott." Abby Angelos cleared her throat from beside Scott. "Bradley, I think you should hear him out." When the Ambassador narrowed his eyes on her, she realized she had been too familiar with him in public. "I mean, Ambassador McKnight. Please."

"Go ahead, young man. What is it?"

Scott stood and approached the table, sliding his cell phone in front of the ambassador. "Take a moment for the video to play."

"I don't see—"

"Bradley, please." Abby ignored his raised eyebrows this time. "Watch it."

Ambassador McKnight did—twice. At first, he was unsure of what he was seeing. By the third time, he sat back, slid the phone back to Scott, and folded his hands on his lap.

"So, Mr. Scott, our legal friend, enjoys young women. What of it?"

Scott grinned and leaned against the conference table facing him. "Mr.

127

Wain is married, Ambassador. And not to that sixteen-year-old young girl, either. I've been with Wain since college, and this is not the only proclivity he enjoys."

"I see," the ambassador said, eyeing him. "What do you suggest?"

"Leverage, Mr. Ambassador." Scott glanced at Abby and then back to the ambassador. "Kalani is very valuable. Ms. Angelos has shown me the files and information we should expect from. A coup for whomever ally he makes a deal with."

Ambassador McKnight nodded. "I know that, young man. Get to the point."

"It should be us. Mr. Wain will sign off on that deal with the right encouragement."

"Encouragement?" Ambassador McKnight looked at Scott's cell phone sitting on the table. "I think I understand. If you were to motivate such a change in Wain's position, what is in it for you?"

Scott smiled now, slipping the phone into his pocket. "Oh, I think we can reach an arrangement, Ambassador."

"Leave that to me, Bradley," Abby said, moving beside Scott. "I already have a very good idea."

McKnight stood. "Do it."

"Excellent suggestion." Scott shook his hand and turned to Abby. "Shall we stay and negotiate, Ms. Angelos?"

* * *

"No, he's alive." The Ambassador gestured for her to lower the gun. "We need an ambulance, my dear. Quickly."

She brushed back her onyx hair and rushed to Scott's side. "No. Let me see. An ambulance will bring too much bad publicity. Whatever happened needs to be contained. I'll check him."

The Ambassador stood and watched her perform a rapid triage over Scott. "Yes, yes. I see your point. How is he?"

She ran her hands across Scott's neck and head a third time. "Nothing broken. Just a couple bad gashes. He'll be fine with ice and a whiskey or two. Who was that man I saw running out?"

"I don't know." The Ambassador dropped into the patio chair in front of his drink. "But I will soon. Trust me. I'll know soon."

Chapter Twenty-Five

Curran

I've had a lot of crazy cases in my life, especially since leaving—okay, fired from—Dark Creek. Like working for corporate bigwigs and high-net-worth types. Cases that revolved around going places I wasn't supposed to be, doing things that I wasn't supposed to do, and performing services that I should've had my head examined for doing. Okay, we'll call it what it was—industrial espionage and dirty tricks. Sure, I'm normally billed out as a private investigator and security consultant. I don't bill out as a dirty trickster. It's true, now and then I provide a teensy-weensy, itsy bitsy, number of said dirty tricks. Particularly when Tommy Astor requested them. To be clear, I never performed those dirty tricks for Tommy. Well, other than last night at Billy Piper's residence. No, typically, Tommy was a broker for much more politically and economically positioned people who required those services. Read that as the rich and powerful. Tommy was a man who knew everyone. Everyone loved Tommy. Tommy liked to get things done for them. Favors begot power. Tommy knew me. Voila, I did stupid shit for Tommy's friends.

There was an upside, though. It paid well. Most of the time. Unless it was that sniveling bottom-feeding lawyer I mentioned earlier who stiffed me on my fees. Tommy was still a good client.

Still, I digress.

I sat in my Jeep and watched the Reston residential street lined with small, single-family homes and commuter cars. It was starting to get dark and I checked my watch—twenty-oh-five.

That's five after eight p.m. In five minutes, the owner of the fourth house on the left would receive an urgent call. Within minutes, unless I misjudged the mature and devious Janey-Lynn Cantrell, said homeowner would exit his house, jump in his fed-mobile, and head to the urgent rendezvous. If the plan—Janey-Lynn's 'I've got a secret' plan—worked, I'd have about an hour to surreptitiously enter the home and find something worth the risk I was taking.

Okay, in plain English. I'd break into Deputy US Marshal Gallo's house, search for something I could use to get him off my back, and be gone. No, I was not talking about blackmailing him. Not really. Although if that works, I'm in.

Sometimes, I walk on the other side of the ethics line. Okay, I walked over there a lot. Okay, okay. I jumped across the line and stomped around. A lot.

Phew, confession is good for the soul.

Anyway…

My cell phone buzzed. The text message read—*I've got a date, big boy. Not as cute as you, though.* Okay, the 'not as cute as you' might have been my imagination. The text meant Janey-Lynn had Gallo on the hook.

When Gallo didn't emerge from the two-story Colonial, nerves got me. As I was about to call Janey-Lynn, a thin figure walked down the sidewalk, crossed the street, and entered Gallo's home. When the figure passed beneath the front porch light, I saw it was a teenage girl, perhaps seventeen or eighteen. A moment later, Gallo emerged, climbed into his government SUV, and headed south toward the Dulles Access Road. He drove away from me as I'd planned, toward his urgent rendezvous with Janey-Lynn, who had something salacious to confess to him.

What was this teenager doing at Gallo's house? Oh, shit, a dog?

As I climbed out of my Jeep to reconnoiter, Gallo's front door opened, and the girl emerged with a small dog on a leash. She walked him around the small front yard, out to the streetside mailbox, and returned inside.

Phew, a dog sitter. A little, non-dangerous dog.

A few moments later, a loud motorcycle pulled up to the front drive. The teenage girl emerged again, climbed on behind the rider, and they sped off past me.

My badly counterfeited Rolex said I now had only fifty minutes at best, so I hustled to Gallo's and rang the doorbell.

I know that sounds stupid—starting a break-in by ringing the front doorbell. It's not. Someone like a lonely girlfriend or roommate might still be home. Dog sitter or not. Strategically, it was better to meet them at the front door with some BS story about looking for your lost dog than to meet them in their kitchen after slithering through their back window. Explaining that would be easy. And, let's face it, I'm the master of the lost dog ploy.

Twice, I rang the bell. Twice, nobody answered.

My counterfeit Rolex now said forty-five minutes remained. I left the front porch and moved around back. Luckily, the rear patio door was unlocked—odd for a federal cop—and I went inside.

The little dog, a Pug, I think, was nowhere to be seen. I moved as quietly as I could, hoping he didn't have a big brother Doberman who didn't need to use the bathroom earlier.

Obviously, Deputy US Marshal's pay was much better than mine. Gallo lived quite comfortably. Nothing outrageously expensive, but nicer than I could afford. The furniture, bookshelves, and artwork all looked like big box store stuff. The main hall was decorated with photographs of famous places—obviously places he'd worked or travelled to—including the Grand Canyon, Disney, Paris, London, and even Istanbul. The living room had a large screen TV, nice video equipment, including a huge gaming system, and wall-to-wall bookshelves with an impressive array of classics, law books, and modern fiction. There were also lots of photos everywhere of a young child through the years, starting at birth. That teenager was no dog sitter. She was the child in the photos, of course.

Time was ticking, so I began searching the kitchen, looking for anything I could use—secret rooms with hostages, a printing press with a fresh batch of counterfeit twenties nearby, or diabolical plans to overthrow the government. You know, the standard stuff. After admiring the contents of his pantry, I walked into the living room.

A voice spun me around, and I yanked my Kimber for combat.

Oh, crapola. How had I misread the room so badly?

Standing on the stairwell landing was my demise. One I never saw coming and failed to find in the background investigation I'd run on Gallo earlier today.

Like the Grinch stuffing a Christmas Tree up the chimney, I was had.

Betty Lou Who stood staring at me with wide eyes and a small, pretty face. She wore a long, silk Scooby Doo nightie and slippers. She had dark hair that was long and pretty—freshly brushed I think—and her eyes were green, bright, and friendly. I didn't know kids' ages well since I never had any, but I'd guess she was somewhere between eight and twelve. In her arms was the little tan Pug, glaring at me with a low, protective growl.

"Mister, what are you doing in our house?"

Chapter Twenty-Six

Curran

Yes, Mister, what are you doing in her house?

"Mister?" the little girl asked again. "Who are you?"

Gulp.

Damn, I wished I'd watched *The Grinch* a few more times. If I had, I'd have a clue what to tell this grade-schooler standing across the room, probably as terrified of me as I was of her. It wasn't Christmas, so the old "fixing your tree" thing was out.

New plan.

First, I holstered my pistol. Second, I grinned my best grin and thought of a lie, and I thought one up quick.

"Hi, sweetie. Is your...er...is Marshal Gallo home?" Lame, but it was something.

"Who are you?" she asked in an emboldened voice, her eyes now strong and focused on me with no fear showing. She clutched the Pug for safety as he bared his teeth. "Do you work with my daddy?"

Daddy? Hmmm...*Paydirt.*

"Not yet, sweetie." I smiled my Uncle Curran smile. "I just got into town and came by to introduce myself. My name is...ah, Peter Gunn. What's yours?"

"Peter Gunn?" Her eyes went wide like a lie detector needle on crack. "Like that old T.V. show?"

She knew Peter Gunn? "Yep, just like that old show. Do you like it?"

She shrugged. "My daddy watches all that old stuff on TV. I think it's boring."

"It's not that bad." Maybe Gallo wasn't such a bad guy. "What's your name, sweetie?"

"Madison." She smiled a big, enchanting smile. "Everyone calls me Madi. I'm almost ten. I like Madison better."

I hope it didn't get around to Tommy Astor that I got caught by an almost-ten-year-old who watched Peter Gunn reruns. I prayed she wasn't a *Columbo* fan, too, or she'd figure me out quick.

"What are you doing here alone, Madison?"

"Um…" She glanced toward the front door and then down at her feet, thinking. Finally, she looked up. "Patty went out real fast with Sam for ice cream."

The old Sam and Patty trick, eh. Hmmmm… Patty, the babysitter, ditched Madison, her protectee, for a motorcycle ride with her boyfriend, Sam, the moment Daddy left. That sucked. How often did this happen? Worse yet, how long would little Madison be alone when it did?

"Does Patty do that a lot, Madison—leave you here alone?" I didn't need her to deny it—as she did—to know Patty was a little-shit, self-centered teenager. "Are you afraid to be here alone?"

"No." She shook her head but looked away as her eyes glistened in a fearful, sad way that said she was embarrassed. In those tears, there was the truth. "I'm okay. Really. She's never gone too long. Well, almost never."

Almost never?

"Besides, I've got Goliath with me." She held up the little Pug. He tried to hide when he got too close to me. She beamed a little smile that melted me. "He's tough. He told me you were down here. I'm not afraid."

Wow. This little kid was amazing. I knew someone like her once—back in the day, as they say. As that pretty Italian face flashed in my memories, I felt my old man's heartstrings play a wee little bit. I'm not getting soft. I'm just using strategy here. Really.

"Hey, I'll wait for your daddy for a little while if that's okay." I didn't just say that, did I? "What games do you like to play?" Yep, I did. *Dumbass*.

Her smile spread across her face and pushed away any fear that might be hiding there. "I like checkers. Do you play checkers?"

"Yes, I do. Do you have a checkerboard?"

She nodded and ran up the stairs, leaving Goliath on the floor to face off with me.

He stood there, casting a nervous glance in her wake. So much for being a watchdog.

"Easy boy," I said, "Bro code. Okay? You don't tell on me, and I won't tell Madison you're scared shitless."

He wagged his little pug butt. An agreement was reached. Had I known, I would've brought dog cookies.

Five games of checkers, two diet sodas, and a bag of microwave popcorn later, Madison had won the thirty dollars in my wallet. She played me good, too. First, she beat me handily -twice, then playfully taunted me until I bet her money that I could win the next three games.

The thirty dollars was hers. Clearly, she cheated.

"Okay, kiddo, you win." I stood and downed the last of my soda. "As soon as Patty gets back, I gotta go."

"Oh, no. Really?"

As I leaned back and watched her, a strange, comforting familiarity settled over me. Madison Gallo had connected with me like no one ever had. She was never afraid. Never intimidated. She simply pulled me into her orbit and poof, we were friends.

How is that?

"Mr. Don't go." She sat at the kitchen table, eyeing the dollar bills in front of her and the empty bowl of popcorn. "Do you want ice cream? Daddy has good ice cream."

"I thought Patty went out for ice cream?" The disgusted look on her face told me she was wise for her years. "Oh, okay. I get it."

She folded her arms and glanced at the ceiling in a melodramatic huff. "Patty went to kiss her boyfriend. She'll come home and give me ice cream from the frig and tell me she bought it at the store. She doesn't fool *me*."

Patty better be careful. Pretty soon, those ice cream runs with Sam were going to start costing her real hush money.

I checked my watch—ninety minutes since I entered Gallo's house. I was late getting out. I hadn't sent Janey-Lynn our secret 'all clear' code—"Kiss your date goodnight." Absent the code, she'd find reasons to schmooze Gallo and buy me time.

"Okay, Madison, why don't you go up to bed and—"

Outside, a motorcycle came to a stop. A few seconds later, the front door opened and closed.

I winked at Madison. "Okay, kid, go on up to bed."

"Oh, please?" She shook her head and reached across, taking my hand with a comforting squeeze. "I want to be here when Daddy gets home."

I didn't. But that little girl's hand holding mine was like an anchor holding me at the table. "Get cleaned up for bed, then. I'll talk to Patty. I'll see you again soon, I promise."

"Promise?" Her face flourished into a smile. "Good, I can win more money."

Great.

Patty walked into the kitchen and nearly crapped herself when she saw me. "Who are you?"

"I'm Marshal Gallo's new partner, Patty." I stood and gave her the angry eyeball. "You're busted."

"Ah, shit." She dropped into one of the kitchen chairs. "I never did this before. Honest."

"Liar." I threw a thumb over my shoulder toward the door. "When Marshal Gallo gets back, you're gonna explain how you leave Madison alone all the time. If you don't, I will."

Her face fell, and she begged Madison's forgiveness. Instead, Madison slid off the chair and came around the table. She threw herself against me, gave me a bear hug like I'd never had before, and looked up at me with eyes that melted any indifferent veneer I'd mustered.

"Mr. Gunn, thanks for playing games with me. I can't wait to tell Daddy."

Yeah, me either. He'll be so surprised.

"Mr. Gunn?" She gestured for me to lower my head—which I did—and she kissed my cheek. "I hope you come back and play with me again soon. You don't let me beat you like Daddy does. But I still beat you."

Ouch.

Chapter Twenty-Seven

Curran

After learning from Madi—*er*, Madison—that I was horrible at checkers, I exited stage left. First, though, I cautioned the derelict, Patty, that her future as a babysitter might be over unless she came clean with Marshal Gallo. Then, I hot-footed it out.

I didn't want to be standing in Gallo's kitchen when he returned. I don't have life insurance, after all.

Just shy of an hour later, I pulled up in front of my barn loft apartment and slipped out of the Jeep, suddenly feeling very stupid. I must have been really tired, because I'd missed all the obvious signals that my night just got weird. Er, weirder.

No, it wasn't the billions of lightning bugs lighting up the surrounding trees like it was Christmas. It wasn't the sultry night air or the occasional bat that whizzed by me from the barn, either.

No, the missed signals were the two big, black SUVs beside the barn. They lit me up with their high beams like an ice skater doing a solo at the Olympics. Except I couldn't skate. Which was okay because there was no ice. And there was no crowd to yell and clap and ooh and ah.

Then, I heard SUV doors open—four of them—and realized I'd just stepped into an old spy movie's secret rendezvous. This one was only missing a guy wearing a trench coat and smoking a cigarette. Oh, and lots of fog. Then, the movie plot changed in my brain—it felt like an ambush—

mine.

"Relax, Curran," I said to myself. "Don't be melodramatic. You'll get out of this. Janey-Lynn and Bogart need you. Be smart."

The SUV headlights blinded me. I felt like a fox tethered to a tree, waiting for the hounds to arrive.

Pay attention, Curran. Your life might depend on it.

Two figures moved away from the SUVs and flanked me on both sides. Two others moved between the SUV headlights like two space aliens about to invite me up for a probe. One silhouette in the headlights spoke.

"Good evening, Mr. Curran. I've been looking forward to meeting you."

A knot formed in my throat, my stomach, and my sphincter.

"Who are you?"

"Nobody."

"Nobody? Clever." Nerves took hold and refused to allow my brain to keep my mouth shut. "Who are you?"

The voice was whimsical. "Nobody. Everybody. Names aren't important."

"Yet, you know mine." If I was going to die in an ambush, I wasn't going out quietly. "What's this—"

"Just listen, Curran." The other figure on the left stepped forward for me to see he was carrying a long gun aimed in my direction. If I were a betting man, I'd say it was an M4 carbine—the small, close-quarter combat version of the M16 rifle. "Be quiet until you're told to speak."

His at-the-ready M4 trumped my holstered Kimber. I nodded and did as I was told. Cooperation is important.

"Mr. Curran," Mr. Nobody said casually in a voice nowhere in my memory banks, "I have a job for you. A very difficult but well-paying job. Extremely well-paying. More than you make in several years."

Well, as far as opening lines go, his wasn't bad. Except most of the time, when you're offered tons of money as the opening bid, it means very bad things.

I decided to get my rules to live by spelled out. Life rules are important.

"I'm no hitman, bank robber, kidnapper, or other felon. Other than that, I'm potentially interested."

"Good." Mr. Nobody laughed. "That leaves a lot in the spectrum, Mr. Curran. Good for you."

Yeah, I guess it did. "There're other things I won't do, but in good faith, I'll consider all offers. Anything that gets me home without holes in me is a starting point."

He laughed again. "There is someone I need you to find. Someone incredibly valuable. Very valuable to many other players, too. I am one player in a very complicated game. I wish to find this person before anyone else. Once found, I wish you to protect him until I say otherwise. It could be a week or six months."

So far, nothing really bad. Except, of course, for all the white space between his players, the game, the person, the timeframe, the months, etc. So no, nothing really bad.

"I need some details—"

"Two hundred thousand if you successfully locate him and secure him before anyone else intervenes."

Details just like that. "That's a lot of money for locating someone. Tell me why I have to find him and what the threat is."

Mr. Nobody waved into the light. "Those are perfectly acceptable questions. I would not wish to engage you if you weren't a careful man. The threat assessment is high, Mr. Curran—very high. There are at least two other parties—we'll call them the "others"—searching for this asset besides me. Perhaps more."

I held up my hand. "Wait, you're Mr. Nobody and you're telling me of the "Others?" Have I stepped into a thriller-movie marathon?"

He chuckled or maybe cursed my humor. "This asset possesses something extremely important, including the knowledge of how the 'something' was compromised in the first place. Most importantly, *why* and for *whom*. What he might know or have seen is life changing—and life ending. I wish him found and protected. The others wish him dead."

Well, other than the dead part, that was clear as mud. I said as much.

"Mr. Curran, once you agree to our terms—and you will—you will be provided all the details necessary."

This all seemed very questionable and slimy to me. Not that questionable and slimy bothered me—I've done both before…often. I just wanted to know the lay of the land. For two-hundred grand, even the lay of the land wasn't a deal breaker. But, since I was a murder suspect, I needed to be careful who I dealt with—like Mr. Nobody.

"Why not get the cops involved? You sound like a man who has them at your disposal."

He chuckled again. "Very astute, Mr. Curran. Yes, I certainly do. Except, the authorities want this person, too. Some of those authorities might well be compromised and that is potentially disastrous for me. Others, if they learned this asset's value, could compromise persons under my umbrella. It could lead to some very messy situations."

His umbrella? Messy situations? Well, damn, why didn't he say so in the beginning.

"How about a few hints to help me make up my mind?"

"Two hundred thousand dollars, Mr. Curran. And a bonus for speed."

Wow, he hinted really, really well.

He went on. "For that, I want this person located quickly. I want what he has and what he knows. I want him protected. I want it all first, last, and only. I am told you are the right person for this job."

"I always wanted to be 'the only man for the job.'"

"You're not, but you are local and available."

Ouch. "You do know I'm just a private investigator these days? I'm not—"

"Yes, of course, I know," he said. "But you have acquired some very valuable skills and knowledge over your career. All of that is necessary. That, and you're not, how to say this delicately, *anybody*. No one will see you coming because no one has heard of you. You're simply not a player."

I'm glad he put it delicately. "So, I am not that guy I was in the old days."

"No, you're not *Pappa* anymore."

Oh, come on now. How'd he know about that?

I tapped the side of my leg for effect. "Look, my bones creak. My knees don't want to move sometimes. And I forget why I went into the bathroom now and then."

"It's difficult to get old, no Mr. Curran?" he said lightheartedly. "I'm a little farther down that road than you. Still—"

"One last thing. That's a lot of money. I want to be honest with you—"

"The Charlie Cantrell matter. I know all about that."

Damn, if he wasn't read-in well. "Yeah, I didn't murder him."

"I don't care." He held up his hand. "I came to you for three reasons. First, you're extremely loyal. Second, you are apolitical. And third, you will do almost anything for money."

He really nailed me. Maybe those things should be on my resume.

"Okay, Mister. Fair."

His delivery hardened. "Understand, Mr. Curran, that there are three rules when working for me."

He sure liked the number three, didn't he?

"First, you can tell no one now or ever about this contract. To do so is a major violation of our agreement."

"Check."

He stepped a little forward, almost enough for me to see him clearly, but realized it and stepped back. "Second, you will be in some danger from the others. While you are authorized to respond as required. Further, you have no sanction from me should you be arrested. I never heard of you. Attempting to connect me to any untoward actions is a major violation of our agreement.

"Check and check."

Mr. Nobody stepped back farther where he was just a voice in the bright lights again. "Lastly, once you engage with me, you are engaged until the end. No withdrawal. Days, weeks, or months. All in. That is the contract."

"I counted four rules. You said three. I can't tell anyone. I can't mention you. I can't attempt to contact you if I'm in a jam. And the fourth—in for a penny, in for a pound."

He sighed. "Yes, there are four rules. Very good. Any violation of those is a breach of our agreement."

I took a step forward and drew movement from my flanks. "Any violation is a breach of our agreement. Got it. Check. I'm sure I know what the breach means, too."

"Any questions?"

Oh, so many questions. "Two hundred grand if I grab him. How much in operating expenses and how much if I don't find him?"

The silence was disturbing. Finally, Mr. Nobody spoke again. "Two hundred is the finder's fee, Mr. Curran. Three thousand a day—ten in cash as a retainer—to hunt him. You may work for up to ten days."

"What's magical about ten days?"

"Do the math." The armed man on the left stepped out of the light toward me. "In ten days, if you don't have him, he'll be dead."

Ah, duh. "Why's this guy so important?"

"That is the real issue, isn't it?" Mr. Nobody said. "As I have said, you will only be informed if we have a deal. Time to decide. Yes or no."

"I really want to do this for you. I do." I did since the money was great, but the risks made my belly churn. "It's what you're not telling me that's scaring the crap out of me."

"It is what it is, Lowe." Tommy Astor walked around Mr. Nobody and stepped through the light enough for me to make him out. "There's big risk and a big reward."

"Tommy?" I cawed. "If you're behind this, all you had to do was call me. Why all the Casablanca skullduggery?"

"I'm not behind anything, Lowe." His voice was not as friendly as usual. "I referred you. I warned you earlier I'd call in a favor. This is it. It's a whopper, ole boy."

He did warn me. That twenty-five grand looked so good this morning that I totally missed the nuance of his gesture. Silly me.

As I've explained before, Tommy Astor was as close to family as I had these days—and had been—for over ten years. I owed him almost everything. He knew that. He knew I was loyal. So, if he wanted me in, I was in—twenty-five grand bonus or not.

"Is this legit, Tommy?" I hated asking, but Tommy or not, tossing me tons of money with no facts was insane. "I'm not helping execute a coup against our country or an assassination that'll get me killed. I'm not hunting down a mob witness so someone can whack him. That's all true, right?"

"Of course." Tommy backed into the light. "I wouldn't do that to you. Are you in?"

Another few seconds of paranoia flowed through me. Then, "Sure, Tommy. For you. Not them. You. I'm in."

"Good. But, Lowe," he vanished behind Mr. Nobody. "You work for them. Not me. After tonight, I'm out."

I didn't like the sound of that. I did, however, like the sound of two-hundred-K.

"Good, Mr. Curran." Mr. Nobody said.

An armed bodyguard tossed a soft-shelled leather shoulder bag onto the ground between us. "Don't lose it."

"What's 'it?'"

"Mr. Curran," Mr. Nobody said whimsically, "pick up the bag. Get to work. You begin immediately."

"One last thing." I eased forward and grabbed the bag. "If everyone is after this guy, how do I know he's still kicking? Maybe he's been caught by the feds or someone else. I don't want to spin my wheels, and then you stiff me because someone else already got him. I don't mean to offend, but I've been screwed before."

"No offense taken, Mr. Curran," Mr. Nobody said. "However, if that were so and this asset was already gone, I would know. Of that, you can be assured."

"Got it." The leather bag was lighter than my imagination thought it should be. I wondered if it was empty and if this was some kind of test. "You know, all this cloak and dagger wasn't necessary. All you had to do was call and tell me Tommy sent you."

"Oh, it is." Mr. Nobody's voice sharpened. "No one sends me anywhere, Mr. Curran. I do the sending. Just like I'm sending you on this assignment. Tommy was simply a conduit to you. A matchmaker."

I guess my debt to Tommy was mounting again. "All right, if Tommy says it's all good, I trust him. Who am I hunting?"

"You've already met him, Mr. Curran. You found him once. You can find him again. Bring me Billy Piper."

Billy Piper? "Him? Finding him the first time and grabbing his computer files was for you?"

Mr. Nobody said nothing and retreated to the SUV.

"You know, the US Marshals think he's dead." I raised my voice so there was no fear they wouldn't hear me. "In fact, they think I killed him."

Mr. Nobody's voice came through the lights. "That would be unfortunate, Mr. Curran. However, I would certainly know if he were dead."

Well, that's a relief. "Why didn't you just have me grab him in the first place?"

"Why indeed." Mr. Nobody's door closed, and the bodyguards climbed into their respective vehicles. "Good night, Mr. Curran."

Before I could rethink my decision, Mr. Nobody, Tommy Astor, and their armed militia drove away. I wondered if I'd just signed up for long-term disability—or a burial plot.

My insides stirred, and I jogged up the outside stairwell to my apartment. I suddenly had to get to my bathroom. A great man had once said, "A man should know his limitations." I know mine, and I'm at the end of them.

Getting old is not for the meek—and definitely not for anyone with a small bladder.

Chapter Twenty-Eight

Curran

Billy Piper. Clearly alive and well. Everybody wanted him—first me, then the feds and Marshal Gallo. Now, the mysterious Mr. Nobody. What had Piper done to piss off all these people? Other than hacking, that is. Hacking into people's computers is sort of a bad thing these days. But this had to be something else.

It was a little after midnight, and I was beat. I'd barely made it to the bathroom, and I wanted to chill. Bogart was not around, so I assumed he was curled up with the suddenly dog-friendly Janey-Lynn. He was probably snoring up a storm, snuggled on a pillow, or tucked into her bed beside her.

Bogart had that suave, dog-of-the-world kinda thing.

Standing in my living room, I had the weirdest sensation that I wasn't alone. And by not alone, I didn't mean Bogart was hiding beneath my bedcovers, either.

No, it was something else—*someone* else.

Was I paranoid after the *Meeting At Midnight* thing outside?

I headed for the kitchen to beg the alien machine to make a cup of coffee and ease my pinging brain.

I made it three steps when the creak of a floorboard stopped me. It seemed rather cliché. I mean, a creaking floorboard? It was so cliché that I snorted a laugh, dismissed it to my imagination, crazy night, and no sleep.

I took another step.

"Who the hell are you, old dude?" a voice yelled across my apartment. "Take another step, and I'll kick your ass."

My pistol was in hand before I realized it. I pivoted, lifted my Kimber to eye level, and aimed at my bedroom's open door. There, standing just inside, looking at me, was Randy Cantrell and his manbun.

"Randy?" I lowered my pistol. "I'm Curran. I'm sure you're mom—"

"She ain't my mom, old dude." He stepped into the living room and folded his arms, trying to flex and intimidate. He failed. "I don't give a shit who you are."

What was it about millennials that everyone older was "old dude?" Not in the mood for crap from anyone—especially a skinny, manbun urban grunger like him—I said, "What are you doing here, Randy?"

He stepped closer. "Whoa now, old dude. What the hell are *you* doing here? I'll kick your ass if you don't get outta here fast."

There were three things very wrong with this situation. First, disrespect oozed from his mouth with "ain't my mom." Second, he called me "old dude" again, and coming from a mid-forties guy wearing a manbun who still said "dude" every other word, that was rude. But mostly, it was number three. He was standing in *my* apartment, had been in *my* bedroom, and threatened to kick *my* ass. Unless his manbun was awarded him instead of a blackbelt, I doubted his tattooed, skinny-ass wannabe gangsta-self was up to the task. Though, truth be told, I was sorta an old dude and might slip a disc or throw a hip kicking *his* ass. But still—respect is important.

"Randy, I rent this apartment from Janey-Lynn. What are you doing here?"

"None of your business, old dude." He stood in the middle of the living room. "How you paying the rent? Huh? You screwing—"

I stepped forward and my pistol raised all on its own. "I'd let that one go, Randy. It's got ugly written all over it."

"Whatever." He tried to hold my eyes but couldn't. "Mommy dearest didn't say much about you. I can see why. Not much to tell."

What an asshole.

Under normal circumstances, I might have punched manbun in the face and tossed him out of the apartment. But something tickled my brain and I remembered how Janey-Lynn was upset when she mentioned him. Something wasn't quite right. He was a piece of work—or something—for sure, but there was more troubling her than his darling personality and lack of hygiene.

"My business arrangements with Janey-Lynn are between us. If you want details, ask her."

He tried to flex his biceps again to project a badass persona. He looked like a peacock with gout. "I will."

Oh, brother. "Whatever you want isn't here. There's no reason for you to be here. How about you leave? It's late."

"Curran, you said?" Randy's face tightened, and he cocked his head with a weird, cynical frown. "You're that private eye dick, aren't you? Like Mannix? Harry-O? Dick Tracy?" He cracked himself up. Only himself. "I'm thinking Scooby Doo."

How flattering. Scooby was my hero. As for the others, I had to give him points. He was only in his forties. Knowing those fictional detective names was impressive. Mannix and Harry O were from the late sixties and early seventies. I was just a kid. Dick Tracy was forties stuff, I think. I'd only seen reruns on video.

I gestured to the front door. "It's late. Early. One of those. Time to go."

"You're that asshole who killed my father." He flexed his scrawny arms again and swaggered side-to-side like a gangbanger getting ready to bust a move. He pulled off a scarecrow, trying to fend off the crows, nibbling at his straw head. "We got lots to talk about, old dude."

The heat rose in my face. To ensure I didn't shoot him, I holstered my Kimber. "Let's get a couple things straight, *dude*. I didn't touch your father. I don't know who did. Second, *dude*, we have nothing to talk about. Nothing. The sheriff and BCI are investigating it. If you have questions, take them up with Special Agent Evans, *dude*."

"Bullshit, private eye man." He followed me into the kitchen and stopped right behind me, jabbing the air as I turned around. "You're going to answer some—"

Nope.

I stepped in close—danger close—eye-to-eye with him. I rarely, if ever, try to do badass characters or tough guy moves like on television. Maybe back in my heyday, but not after all the surgery, stitches, plastic, and screws in me. Certainly not after receiving my first AARP invitation, either. Pulling off the tough guy routine might get my ass kicked. Though, I'm sure Randy was a different story. He looked and acted like some wannabe thug who was all peacock and no bear.

"We're done here, *dude.*" I leaned in close, and he inched back, trying to maintain his swagger. "Get your ass outta here before I forget that you're Janey-Lynn's stepson."

"I...you can't—"

"Now."

He smeared a greasy, cocky grin across his face and retreated a fast couple steps. His hands rose into a feeble fighting stance, imitating some Bruce Lee moves.

"Stop, you're scaring me." I laughed. "Let me guess, you learned that from Don Knotts."

His face screwed up.

"You know, the 'Ghost and Mr. Chicken?'"

He wavered his karate hands at me. "Old dude, I could whip your ass. But, fine. Another time. I'll be back, and you'll be gone. See you real soon, Grandpa."

I stepped toward him, but he pirouetted and escaped through the front door.

What a shit.

Randy Cantrell and I were not going to be friends. Although I did enjoy The Ghost and Mr. Chicken. He and Don Knotts really nailed those mail-order karate moves.

Chapter Twenty-Nine

Curran

Piled on my small dinette table were the contents of Mr. Nobody's shoulder bag. What a nice surprise it all was, too.

There were three items inside. The most important was a manila mailing envelope containing ten thousand dollars—all twenties. There was also an expensive satellite phone with a charger. The thing that surprised me most was the Kimber .45 semi-automatic pistol. Funny, they knew my brand and upgraded it with a suppressor screwed onto the barrel—much better than my chintzy .22 pistol hidden away.

Mr. Nobody was a thoughtful guy.

I counted the money twice. In the past day, I'd been gifted thirty-five grand—twenty-five from Billy Piper and now ten from Mr. Nobody. I hadn't been given so much as a birthday present in decades. Suddenly, I was cash-rich. Thirty-five grand wasn't a fortune by any means. But it was worth fifty grand if I had to pay taxes. Which, of course, might slip my mind. That's not illegal. I read on the internet that if someone gifts you cash, you don't have to declare it for taxes. It's called the 'goodwill clause.' It had to be true.

I considered stashing the cash in the encyclopedias with the twenty-five grand. Instead, I stuffed a couple hundred in my wallet. I placed the remainder into my black, ballistic nylon backpack from the closest—my go-bag.

A go-bag was something I used in my Dark Creek days. Most intelligence folks and operators—that's Special Forces types—always keep one within arm's reach, twenty-four-seven. It is as essential as socks and underwear. A go-bag is an emergency kit for those unforeseen events that smack you in the face when you're not prepared. So, you pre-prepare. Everyone outfitted them differently. Some guys kept a spare gun and ammo, cash, and emergency food bars. Others added small tools like lockpicks and such, a change of clothes, and the keys to secret stashes of bigger toys—cars, guns, more cash, and changes of identity. A go-bag was only limited by your imagination and the size of the bag you were willing to schlep around.

Mine was basic. I wasn't working in Dark Creek any longer and didn't expect to go up against Hezbollah or the Spetsnaz.

I had some basics already inside. So, I added four loaded magazines for my Kimber and a change of clothes.

Next, I turned on my new satellite phone. It was fully charged. After tapping here and there, I found its number and committed it to memory. To my surprise, there was already a text message waiting—*Mr. Curran, respond to this text every four hours. If you have nothing to report, cite NOTHING. Keep this phone close. It will be your only communication with us.*

Very James Bond. I liked it.

I already had a lot of intelligence on Piper. Finding him again should be easy. Assuming, of course, he wasn't dead like Marshal Gallo thought. Except, the offer of two hundred thousand bucks and three grand a day didn't sound easy. It didn't sound legal, either. But hey, like I have said all along, I walk on the wild side now and then. For this kind of payday, I'd stomp, run, hop, and breakdance on that side. Still, I knew my limits in this case. I just hoped I wouldn't reach them any time soon.

What were my limits, you might ask? Well, those limits were squishy. Two-hundred-K bought a lot of squishy.

Billy Piper. What an enigma. Marshal Gallo had accused me of murdering him. The joke was on him. I believed Mr. Nobody—Billy was alive. I couldn't be a murder suspect any longer—well, not Piper's murder suspect. There was still Charlie Cantrell and his mistress. Mr. Nobody was a details-kinda-guy. One who didn't get those details wrong very often. No, Piper was alive and well.

Sure, Piper could be buried in a deep grave somewhere and word hadn't leaked out yet. I doubted that. Billy Piper was simply missing.

Gallo had played word games with me about whether he knew Piper was dead or not. He was trying to make me squirm and give up anything I knew. The big questions nagged at me. Was he really in the dark about Piper's hacking business? Might he be part of it? Whoever Billy Piper was, he was not just some hacker in WITSEC. There was something else going on. Nothing I knew about him would give me any clues as to where he'd run to after I'd left him last night. He was terrified of someone, that was certain.

Where would he go?

I brought out my notebook computer and logged onto the internet. I did what I hadn't done after tracing his hack on TAE—when he'd returned to hack TAE hem the second time, I'd been waiting for him with my own IT geek—a close associate of Tommy Astor—who traced him. One thing led to another, and I'd located his secret lair in Leesburg. I'd never bothered to finish running a full background on him.

Would someone as tech-savvy as Piper actually leave an internet footprint?

The only way I'd know was to look.

With old, not-so-nibble fingers, I checked social media, my PI database, and a few other tricks I knew.

Nothing.

Wait, there was something else I could try. When I'd left Piper's basement, I grabbed his cell phone. That phone was in my kitchen drawer. While I had a bad memory, I did remember his passcode. He'd given it to me, fearing for his life. I have no idea why.

Bingo—I was in.

Nearly every night, sometimes twice a day, he'd called one particular number. With a fast check of my PI database, I found the address at the Arlington Arms Apartments, yep, in Arlington, Virginia. I ran a few more quick PI checks and located one William Piper, Apartment 3-F, Arlington

Arms. Wow, hiding in plain sight.

Surely, he wouldn't be stupid enough to go there. Would he?

* * *

Levene

"Levene, I got something." The thin, sandy-haired Freedman said, staring at his computer. "Somebody just web-searched Piper. They're accessing all kinds of database portals. I don't think they got anything, though."

Levene yawned and sat up from his cot across the room. "Who, Junior?"

"I don't know. I tried to trace them, but they got off too fast."

"I thought you were a computer whiz?"

"I am. I didn't see it fast enough." Freedman shot a part angry, part embarrassed glance sideways at Levene. "I was doing my own search when I tripped into this one."

Levene stood and sauntered over to Freedman's workstation. "Can you find him? I want to know who's looking for Piper besides us."

"I'll try." Freedman's fingers hovered over the keyboard. "Not much to go on."

Levene was already on his secure satellite phone. "Sir, it's Yankee 2. We've got another player snooping around. We're tracing."

Freedman finished entering the commands in his program, turned, and froze at the expression on Levene's face. "Levene?"

"Yes, sir. I understand." Levene's face was ash as he tapped off the call. He dropped into a chair beside Freedman. "Skywalker One."

"What?" Freedman felt his face blanch, and he pushed away from the computer console. "No way."

"Yes, way. Do it."

Freedman shook his head. "I've never done one before."

"Time to learn, Junior."

"You said we don't nail anyone." Freedman stood and walked to the rear of the small listening post. "You said someone else does that stuff."

"I thought you wanted to get your hands dirty. What about all your training and bullshit you were yapping about before?" Levene spun in his chair and thrust an angry finger at him. "I said ninety-nine percent of the time, someone else does it. We were just ordered into the one percent."

Chapter Thirty

Billy Piper

B illy Piper stood amidst a stand of trees across from the Arlington Arms Apartments—home. His real home. It was late, sometime after midnight, and there was no one around. An occasional car passed along the boulevard, but even those were sparse at the late hour. At least if anyone hunting him approached, he'd have a chance of seeing them coming and escaping.

Perhaps. Maybe. He hoped.

The evening air was sticky and thick—a product of the eighty-five degrees and nearly one hundred percent humidity.

Billy's clothes were sweat-stained and damp. His forehead was pasty. Each vehicle's lights that passed by glistened on his cheeks and made him look away—partly from the glare and partly concern to be recognized.

He'd lurked near the apartments for an hour, now. Earlier, he'd made his way—by Uber and three commuter buses—from the seedy beltway hotel in Tysons Corner, where he'd been holed up since his escape from Leesburg and that crazy old man. This move—an obvious blunder in any manhunt—was either a brilliant masterstroke or the last move he would make.

No one, not the Marshals nor others hunting him, would believe him stupid enough to return home. His Leesburg basement had already been compromised by that odd old man last night. Anyone hunting him would think he would contemplate a return here. No one would think him that stupid.

It was so obvious that it was brilliant.

Twice in the past hour, an odd passerby appeared on the sidewalk nearby. Both times, he'd reached behind his back for the .38 revolver he'd tucked into his waistband gangster-style. Both times, he'd overreacted. He'd felt stupid afterward and relieved. He wasn't sure he could actually kill another person. Not even if it was in self-defense. Hacking was one thing—stealing millions in corporate loot and retirement funds wasn't life-threatening. It was a victimless crime—just an insurance matter for his targets.

At least, that's the way he saw it. The way he needed to see it.

The safety of hacking was his style. He was anonymous. No one could see you, could attack or react fast enough to catch you. He could do what he pleased and never worry about anyone lashing out in self-defense. No hacker needed a gun. No hacker needed to run and hide. No hacker need worry about escape.

That's the way it used to be—until he'd double-crossed the wrong people.

Now, he was terrified of those hunting him. He was carrying a gun—an aged Smith and Wesson .38 revolver he'd purchased at a gun show months ago. He didn't even know if it would fire. He was running and hiding. He was focused on escape. He was experiencing all those things he believed no hacker ever did.

All because he played the wrong people. Whoever *they* were.

Last night, it hadn't taken him long to cut the ties the old man who busted into his place had bound him with. He'd used a trick he'd seen on the internet to break loose the zip ties. Time had been mounting against him the moment that old man had forced him to download the hacked business files. One of his targets began a trace for him—a masterful piece of anti-spyware he'd failed to detect during one of his penetrations. Thankfully, the old geezer had been in a hurry and hadn't tightened the zip ties around his wrists well enough. He'd been out of the plastic restraints before the old man left his house. He'd grabbed the .38 revolver and dumped the remainder of the extra rounds from a box into his pocket. Then, he grabbed a stack of cash from a second hidden stash and fled—fast.

No sooner had he escaped and other men arrived in a large, black SUV. Four of them. They didn't waste time with niceties. They kicked in his front door and charged in.

Had he still been in that basement…

A shiver ran through him as he sipped his coffee and scanned the boulevard.

No one. Not even a car.

Time to move.

Hoping none of his hunters would expect his return home, he moved from the trees onto the sideway and walked away from the apartment complex, surveying the parking area as he went.

He really had no choice. He had no idea how the old man had found him in Leesburg. The other men had found him much easier. They already knew where he lived and had made that clear during their initial contact. Why hadn't he just done what they asked and not pushed the envelope and double-crossed them? His hubris was thinking he was smarter than they were. How wrong he'd been. They had caught him the first time—caught him so badly he was in WITSEC. Why hadn't he considered they'd catch him again?

Since then, he'd protected himself the best he could. He'd erased his life. Erased his past. Erased his future. Still, it would only take a little time before they'd find his trail again. It was as inevitable as it was unthinkable.

In his haste to escape his Leesburg basement, he'd left his wallet. A dumb mistake, though its contents were worthless anyway. He couldn't use his credit or debit cards. They'd identify his location in seconds. His death would be mere minutes later.

He'd loved—devoured old spy movies. *Smiley's People*, *The Spy Who Came In From The Cold*, all things MacLean. He'd studied them. Learned the craft. Readied himself. He was one of them.

Now, he moved slowly through the dark, turning away whenever a car passed by. He walked by the Arlington Arms apartment complex again, navigated a side street to view the back of the complex, and double-backed again—twice.

Finally, he went inside.

One thing he hadn't forgotten was his apartment keys. Luckily, they'd been in his pocket even as the old geezer zip-tied his hands. Now, he rode the elevator to the third floor. He carefully checked both stairwells at the ends of the hall to ensure there were no assassins waiting. Then, slowly, he crept down the hall to apartment 3-F.

He listened at his door. Nothing. Surely, if anyone were waiting inside, they wouldn't be laughing and joking and making noise.

He touched his key to 3-F's lock...

A door creaked open down the hall behind him. He tried to tug his revolver free, but it had slipped lower in his waistband, and the hammer caught on his belt loop.

Every synapse in his body screamed at once—*they found you.*

Chapter Thirty-One

Billy Piper

"Billy?" A barely audible voice beckoned from down the hall. "Billy?" His heart nearly exploded from his chest as he whirled around, struggling to free the revolver.

"Easy, boy. It's me." A head and shoulders leaned out an apartment on the left. It was old Mr. Culpepper. "Get in here, boy. Quick."

The aged, retired bookkeeper—a dear friend from two doors down—beckoned him frantically. His face was ashen, and his normally bright, cheery eyes were dark and narrow, darting around the hall as nervously as Billy's.

"Mr. Culpepper?"

The old man waved again. "Come here, boy. Be quiet."

Billy hesitated. Seeing the angst in the man's face worried him. He tiptoed down the hall, and as he approached, Mr. Culpepper eased open the door, grabbed his arm, and pulled him inside. The door closed behind them, and three deadbolts were quickly engaged.

"Don't go home, boy," Mr. Culpepper said. "Real bad men came here earlier. They said they were feds. I'm not so sure. They flashed some IDs and wanted to know all about you—especially where you might be."

Billy's face blanched. His breath threatened to cease in his chest. It took him several moments to calm. When he did, Mr. Culpepper had already brought him a cup of steaming tea.

"Tell me what's happening, Billy." Mr. Culpepper sat in an overstuffed recliner facing him. "What have you done?"

"Nothing, Mr. C." Billy considered telling his story but realized that might place Mr. Culpepper in danger. Since entering Witness Protection with the Marshals, he hadn't had any friends but this old man. Truth was, before WITSEC, he hadn't had many friends either. Not real ones. Online somebodies here and there, but none he'd ever spent any time in person...in real life. "Nothing."

For the years they'd been neighbors, Marvin Culpepper had befriended him. How and why, he really didn't know. Mr. Culpepper had been his only friend—real friend—in a decade. That was by choice. Deep down, Billy loathed most people. That's why his keyboard and computer monitor were his closest friends. Yet, somehow, Mr. Culpepper had broken through that façade.

First, Mr. Culpepper recruited him to help carry his shopping from the taxi or Uber—he'd long ago given up driving and didn't own a car. That turned into helping him do his shopping. Over a few more months, it grew into the occasional lunch before shopping. Then it became Sunday dinner. The old man couldn't cook, but Billy could—at least a little. They'd bonded a friendship separated by nearly forty years. Mr. C was the perfect neighbor, though. He never complained, always had good gossip about the other tenants, and loved the same old spy movies and British mysteries on television that Billy did. Often, he'd sleep through most of them. Billy was sure it was the company, not the plot, which kept the old man returning.

Despite Billy's distaste for people, he truly liked and cared for Mr. C.

Mr. C leaned forward and stabbed the air with his finger. "Billy Piper, you tell me, boy. You're in serious trouble. Let me help. Lord knows you've helped me enough."

"No, sir. I can't. They're really bad men. They think I did something, or they want me to do something, oh hell, I don't know. They want to kill—"

"Kill you?" Mr. Culpepper's eyes went wide, and he slid back into the chair. "Why, Billy? What have you done?"

"It doesn't matter, Mr. C." If he told him the truth, it would put him in the target hairs, too. "I'll deal with it."

"It's that damn computer stuff you do. Isn't it?"

The old man was sharp. "You know about that?"

"You're always on that computer." Mr. Culpepper shrugged. "You always try to hide what you're doing. Either you're watching porn and not sharing, or you're up to something."

"Well, yeah, okay. I did some dumb stuff." He'd done it now, and he couldn't take it back. "You might not like it."

He swallowed hard, took a long mouthful of the tea, and told the old man everything—*everything*. Well, almost everything. He didn't admit to being a serial hacker or mastermind internet thief. He admitted to just a few hacks here and there, and that was sufficient. He glossed over his hacking the Russian mafia, the straw that had sent him into Witness Protection. He'd suggested that was a one-time oops. If he'd denied any wrongdoing Mr. Culpepper wouldn't believe him anyway.

Mr. Culpepper listened. He asked no questions while Billy spoke. He nodded along, stopping and closing his eyes when Billy told him about witness protection and how the boredom drove him back to the keyboard. He skipped the details of last night's encounter with the strange old man who took his cash and his dog. Not that he missed that damn mutt. His story concluded with his narrow escape before the armed men stormed his Leesburg hideout to kill him.

When Billy was done, he stood and paced the room. He stopped and turned to Mr. Culpepper as though about to impart some vital solution or strategic plan. Each time, returning to his pacing.

"Billy, do you know what they want?" Mr. Culpepper asked. "They believe you stole information from their computers."

"I did." Billy shrugged. "I was bouncing around several companies. You know, trying to find my way in—"

"What were you looking for?"

Billy hesitated. He didn't want to explain that he'd been paid handsomely to hack certain systems. He didn't want to admit that he'd not even checked out who paid him. He'd only been concerned with the fifty thousand dollars he'd been paid—or rather, allowed to keep in return for his skills. The assignment had seemed so simple—child's play. Never did he consider that anyone willing to pay him that much might be willing to kill him to keep it secret. That was a mistake that might now get him killed.

"I was just cruising around their systems, Mr. C. Their firewalls and security were too easy. I got carried away."

"I don't understand all that firewall stuff. In my day, it was paper and typewriters. File cabinets and safes." The retired accountant grinned. "Why didn't they just call the police? Why send someone to kill you?"

"I don't know," Billy lied. "I'm screwed. I gotta get some things from my place. Then I gotta find somewhere to hide and figure this all out."

"You've been in Witness Protection all this time?"

Billy shrugged. That was one thing he really didn't want to tell Mr. C. When he did, he felt dirty and ashamed. Not for being in WITSEC. He didn't want Culpepper hating him for his past or for lying to him all these years. Now, it was inevitable. Oddly enough, he rarely cared what anyone thought of it. With this retired old accountant, he cared too much.

Mr. Culpepper didn't seem phased. "Can't you just call the Marshals and have them protect you like before?"

"No. When the Marshals find out I've been, er, back in business, it'll void my protection contract. They'll kick me out on my own. Probably even prosecute me. Then, the Russians will find me. I'll be dead."

"Boy, Billy. You sure screwed up." Mr. Culpepper eyed him. "Tonight, you'll stay here. Get some sleep. We'll figure this out in the morning."

"Morning? What about those two guys who came here? You said they were FBI?"

"They said that," Mr. Culpepper grunted. "What they say is not necessarily true."

"If they were FBI, I'm in deep shit enough. If they aren't FBI, they're the guys hunting for me. They'll kill me. Them or the Russians."

"We'll figure it out."

"There's no 'we,' Mr. C. I gotta do this alone." Billy stood and walked to the door. "I can't stay here. It might be dangerous for you. I hope I haven't already got you in trouble."

"Nonsense, boy." Mr. Culpepper motioned him to sit again, went to the kitchen, and returned with the pot of tea. "Have more tea. It helps you think. Wait here."

Mr. Culpepper disappeared into a back room. He was gone several moments and returned with an armload of clothes, an old army rucksack, and other things. He dumped the load onto the couch and gestured to Billy.

"You stay away from your place, Billy. They're probably waiting for you. When they left here, I saw them through my peephole at your door. I never saw them leave. Can't say if they're still there, but maybe."

"Jesus, Mr. C., you could have said that earlier."

The old man grinned. "I guess I should have. You could have told me you were a computer hacker being hunted by the Russian mob, too."

Billy lowered his head. "Touché."

"Forget it." Mr. Culpepper pointed to the couch. "These are my youngest son's old things. Some clothes he kept here when he'd visit years ago. I just never got rid of them once he stopped staying over. It's been, ah, it's been twenty years or more, I guess. Take them. Some might not fit, though—he was bigger than you. Maybe an inch or so taller, too. Put them all in my old Nam rucksack. It'll save you from buying anything. These bastards can probably trace you by your credit card like they do in the movies."

"Yeah, they can." Billy's face fell. "I left my wallet in Leesburg anyway."

"That's probably better. You gotta disappear." Mr. Culpepper cocked his head. "How much cash do you have?"

Billy shrugged and pulled a wad of bills from his pocket. "A couple hundred, I guess."

Mr. Culpepper went into the kitchen and returned with a freezer bag frosted over. He tried to hand the bag to Billy, but he refused it.

"There's five grand in there, Billy. Take it."

"No." Billy shook his head. He never gave a second thought to raiding old folk's retirement accounts. Yet now, taking this small few thousand made him almost sick. "I can't, Mr. C. I just can't."

Mr. Culpepper stuffed the bag into his hands. "You take it. Pay me back when this is over. I got plenty more in the bank. I keep that in the freezer for emergencies. What good is a bunch of emergency money if I can't use it for an emergency? Besides, what emergency could I have? Slip and fall? Break my hip? Cash won't help me there. Take it."

"But...yeah, okay." Billy took the bag, considered it for a long time, and stuffed it beneath his jacket. Then, he shook the old man's hand, went to the couch, and packed the clothes. "Thank you, Mr. C. I'll pay you back. With interest."

"Just don't hack some bank to do that." The old man laughed. "Wish I had a car to give you. I don't. Got a phone?"

Billy shook his head. "Nope. That crazy old man took it last night."

Mr. Culpepper tossed him his cell phone from atop the lamp table beside his recliner. "Take mine until you get one of those burner things. Then toss mine. I'll get a new one tomorrow. Call me on the house phone and leave your new number."

Billy nodded. "For somebody who doesn't know about computers and the internet, you sure got all this figured out."

"It's all those movies we watched." Mr. Culpepper reached into a small drawer on the lamp table. He withdrew a .45 semi-automatic Colt pistol. "Take this, too, Billy. You need it more than me. It saved me in the Tet Offensive in the Nam. My rifle jammed, and this was all I had. Shot my way out of a lot of shit."

Damn, Mr. C. was a real badass back in the day.

"Nope. I got one." Billy slid the .38 revolver from behind his back. "Kept one in Leesburg just in case."

"Good." Mr. C motioned him toward the door. "Go if you're gonna go. Call me tomorrow. Got it? If you need anything, you tell me. Money. This pistol. Anything. If you do, I'll find a way to get it to you secretly and all."

"Yes, sir." Billy tucked the phone into his pants pocket, hefted the rucksack, and headed for the door. "I can't thank you enough. I'll pay you back."

"Just be safe."

Mr. Culpepper locked the apartment door behind him.

Billy edged down the hall toward the stairwell. Two steps before the steel fire door, he heard Mr. Culpepper's door open behind him again.

What did he want now?

"Run, Billy," Mr. Culpepper yelled. "Run, boy."

A gunshot split the air just as Billy glanced back.

Two men had stepped out of his apartment. Both had guns.

Mr. Culpepper leaned out his door with his .45.

"Run, boy!"

Two bullets slammed into the fire door just ahead, barely missing him. He tugged on his revolver just as Mr. Culpepper fired two cannon-like shots at the men.

They returned fire.

Billy Piper did the unexpected—a movie moment he'd thought about many times. He spun around, fired two shots at the men down the hall, and backpedaled through the stairwell door.

Damn, I did it.

The last thing he saw before the door closed behind him was one of the men lying on the hall floor. As he descended the stairs, two more shots thundered from the hall behind him. He bound down, three steps at a time. He turned the corner on the second floor and headed for the red-lighted exit sign.

Mr. Culpepper was on his own.

Two more gunshots. The gunfight was still on.

Silence.

Chapter Thirty-Two

Curran

During my sleep to blow the cobwebs out, I dreamt of hundred-dollar bills—all two hundred thousand worth—dancing around me. I would have slept more, but the Voula Beach Road crept into my fantasy and had my heart racing again. Oddly, Carli was there, too. A strange addition that wasn't real. Wasn't true. Couldn't be true. She was never there. Still, she was there in my dream and standing nearby as I lay near death in the villa. Just before my dream state ended, she waved goodbye.

I woke and got to my feet.

A few minutes later, with a cup of coffee in hand, I took out my cellphone and started to dial Janey-Lynn's number. I wanted to ensure she was okay, and, yes, that Bogart was okay, too.

Before I hit the second digit, the phone rang—Special Agent Evans.

Gulp. Now, what? Maybe there was another murder they wanted to hang around my neck.

"Vernon, you know it's barely after six am?" Sipping my coffee, I wondered if prison coffee was made with those alien peapods, too. "I hope this is good news."

"Well, it depends." He hesitated, but when I didn't ask, he continued. "My techs got the original data from your IP server. They recovered the videos. We saw the murder go down, Lowe. I'm fairly sure it wasn't either of you."

Fairly sure? Throw a guy a rope and yank it away. "Of course, it wasn't us. Why—"

"The killer went in and took the pistol from the bookcase where you told us Charlie kept it. He shot Charlie and his girlfriend. Then, he did something really weird—but I'll keep that to myself."

"Oh, come on, Vernon. Just a hint? Whoever killed Charlie could be trying to frame Janey-Lynn and me. It looks bad for us. Well, mostly her."

"Maybe," Evans grunted. "Or she's behind it and wants to look bad."

Wow, last night, I was in a Charlie Chan movie. This morning, it's Alfred Hitchcock.

"Come on, Vernon. You can't believe that."

"Yes, I can." He sighed. "I have to consider you, too, Lowe."

Gulp. "Where's this leave me and Janey-Lynn?"

"It's not a woman in the video. We're sure. As for you, the perp doesn't move like you and is taller. You're what, five-seven?"

"Five ten."

"Not according to your driver's license."

"I shrunk. Old age does that."

He chuckled. "Well, it works in your favor, Lowe. I'm estimating the perp was nearly six feet. We're sending the videos to our main lab in Richmond. They'll get more."

I thought about all that. "So, for now, I'm good?"

"For now. Anything you want to tell me, Lowe? I mean, want to update your alibi or hand over the murder weapon?"

How rude. I know he figured I'd lied a little. Still, no idiot would pick this moment to admit to lying. "Nope. I'm good."

He was silent for a moment. A moment too long.

"What aren't you saying, Vernon?"

"Lowe, we're friends." He cleared his throat. "So, I'm gonna say this with your best interests in mind. No malice. Okay?"

"What?"

"What do you really know about her? I mean, *really* know?" He didn't wait on an answer and plunged into his soliloquy. "Well, I did some digging around—mostly what the local cops knew and had on file. Did you know she was on like her third marriage or close to that when she met Charlie Cantrell?"

I didn't, but didn't care. "Okay, she's not exactly in her thirties, Vernon."

"No, she's not. She didn't have much to her name other than a few bucks and jewelry from a previous marriage. Charlie's farm and all the trimmings came with marrying him. Not a bad deal marrying up, is it? Oldest motive in the world, Lowe."

I didn't really know Janey-Lynn's history much, but I knew her well enough to know she was no gold digger. I told him that.

"Maybe not, but convenient, isn't it? And then there's that wild-ass son of Charlie's—Randy. Charlie and him never quite got along. Charlie wanted him to work the farm and work damn hard. Randy wanted a free ride, to smoke dope, and God knows what else. Sheriff's boys knew him on site and all too often, too. He was in and out of jail more times than Charlie knew. And for more bad shit than he would have tolerated, too."

"I'm shocked, I tell you, shocked. But get to the point, Vernon. What's this got to do with me?"

His voice was almost conspiratorial. "Not long after Janey-Lynn married Charlie, she claims Randy stole a lot of her jewelry. Stole lots of cash from Charlie, too. Well, guess what—Charlie kicked him out, took him out of that rather sizable will, and cut off all contact. They got into quite a few fights, and the sheriff had to pull him out of that place a few times thereafter. Charlie just wanted him gone. Randy blamed Janey-Lynn."

"And..."

"Lots of people do, too, Lowe. She gets a boatload of money without any strings—or philandering Charlie—attached. Doesn't take a genius to see how this looks."

No, and it doesn't take a genius to see Randy as the killer, either. "Are you saying she's guilty because people gossip, or are you saying Randy is because he's a piece of shit with a long criminal past? Pick one."

Evans sighed and stayed quiet for a long time. Then, "It's odd that Janey-Lynn rents a room to you. Then, she hires you to investigate her husband.

Then he's murdered. It's all too *convenient*."

If only Vernon knew, convenient wouldn't be the word he'd use. He'd use 'planned.' Tommy Astor had sent me to the Cantrell farm to rent this apartment. In hindsight, that wasn't a coincidence either. Tommy wanted me to help her out with the libido-raging Charlie Cantrell. He put me in the right place at the right time under the right circumstances.

I said, "What's convenient about it? Other than I'm a PI of sorts, and Charlie was into other women and vice three at a time? Did you ever think I rented the room there because of the case?"

"Maybe." He hesitated—too long again. "Convenient that on a night you're unaccounted for—and don't give me that bullshit about being with her—Charlie and his plus one get murdered. Murdered on cameras *you* installed. Convenient that somebody wipes them."

"Wipes?" Crap, crap, triple-decker crap. He knew. "What's—"

"Come on, Lowe," his voice hardened. "My techs have the logins and the timestamps. Someone logged in with your password and deleted all the folders. Amateur stuff, considering there're backups. You understand that. I doubt she does."

As it sank in, I didn't like the goo it created. "You think Janey-Lynn set me up?"

Silence. A grunt. "The perp wasn't either of you. Look, Lowe, I feel sorry for Janey-Lynn, given Charlie and that shit stepson of hers. So she hired you. She could hire someone else."

"No way." Way? My guts churned. "Look, you analyze those videos and let me know anything you can. I'm on another case right now, but I'm gonna find the killer if you don't first. It won't be Janey-Lynn Cantrell."

At least, I hoped not.

Chapter Thirty-Three

Curran

Evans' theory was ugly. I truly liked Janey-Lynn. I trusted her, too. In my gut, I think she likes and trusts me, as well. Or she just finds me dashingly handsome, rugged, and desirable.

No, really. That could be it.

After downing another cup of coffee, I walked out onto my stair landing and into the August early morning sun. The birds were chirping, the sky was a deep, cloudless blue, and the world looked peaceful and inviting.

Except for the angry, fiery eyes of Marshal Gallo staring at me from the landing.

The moment I locked onto him, seasoned instinct made me step back and increase the distance his hate-filled glare scorched between us.

His hand snapped out, and he jammed a steel finger into my chest, pushing forward, closing in closer, and pushing me against the wall beside my door.

"You sonofabitch." His eyes burned through me. His face contorted between hate and an unsuccessful attempt to control his rage. His finger drilled into me like a steel spike, searching for my spine.

I didn't move. Couldn't breathe. I made no attempt at communication, worried he'd pull his Marshal pistol and shoot me if I said, 'good morning.' For the longest, most heated moments I'd had in a while, he stared at me and I at him. As he drilled his finger deeper into my chest, I wondered if it were still a crime if a US Marshal carved out your heart with his finger and offered it as a sacrifice to the LEO gods? Is there such a thing as Marshal brutality?

"Curran, I'll kill you if you come near my daughter again." I guess I should have known why he was here. "Who the hell do you think you are?"

I wiped the stardust from my eyes and carefully touched his hand, moving it away from my chest so I could breathe.

"I think there's a misunderstanding. Honest." There, that'll work. "Marshal brutality is a crime. And I bruise easily."

He jutted his finger at me again. His face was twisted and angry like a tornado about to touch down. Exactly how long had he been waiting outside for me? He'd been simmering long enough to build into a boil that was overflowing on me now.

"Stay away from my house. Stay—"

"I don't know what you're talking about." Uh, oh. I should have lost more money to Madison and paid off the babysitter for their silence. Hindsight is always clearest when bad decisions place you in precarious situations. "I think I know why you're upset—"

"You're damn right I'm upset." He stepped back and took a heavy breath. "Madi told me you were there. She told me everything."

"She prefers Madison." The look on his face suggested I should not be so clever. "Okay, okay. Look, you should thank me and fire Patty. Her hormones are raging too much. I'm sure she explained to you her wayward ways last night. She left Madison alone, and I happened by."

His face twisted again as he tried to hide the fact he knew I was right. Truth be told, dads don't care about facts and reason when it comes to their children. Especially daughters. At least, that's what I've been told. Not having any kids, especially daughters, I could only learn from those around me. Gallo was teaching me that very lesson right now.

I backed from the landing into the loft to put more space between us should he lunge at me or draw his Glock. I might get a few steps to escape. "Look, Marshal, I went looking for you last night to talk. That's all. I found Madison alone and felt bad for her. Honest. Ask her."

"Yeah, yeah, yeah." He dropped his hands and seemed to cool. "My sitter told me about you. I didn't know you'd joined the Marshals, Curran. Funny story there, I'm sure. My neighbor's security cameras caught you on the sidewalk. So it was easy to figure who the jackass was breaking into my house."

So much for my reconnoitering *his* place. I should have reconnoitered his nosy neighbor's, too.

"I didn't break in." Well, technically, I guess I did. Surely, no neighborhood camera caught me going through his back door. If it had, I suspect I'd be in handcuffs. Although, the day was young. "Look—"

"What were you doing in my house?"

"Babysitting." I regretted the barb but didn't leave it be. "Someone had to."

"Mind your own business."

I patted the air. "Honest, I went there to talk. I saw the babysitter leaving and figured you were home. Madison was alone and scared. That little dog wasn't going to protect her. I stayed and waited for your sitter to get back. Ask Madison, she'll alibi me."

Gallo considered that. He cocked his head to listen—a good sign. "Keep going."

"You owe me thirty bucks." I extended my hand, palm up. "She says you let her win at checkers. I think she cheats. Thirty bucks. I lost big."

He actually laughed and glanced around as though embarrassed. "Okay, okay. But don't ever come to my house again, Curran. Ever."

Dads and their daughters. Didn't I mention that?

"Look, Gallo, I really did feel bad for her. She's a great kid."

"I know." He backed up to the top of the stairs. "What did you want to talk about? Want to confess to killing Piper?"

"We both know I didn't kill him."

"We do?"

"Yes." I threw bait into the water. "Because he's not dead."

"Oh, no? Then what was so urgent you came to my house and—"

"Babysat your daughter?" My grin blunted his anger a little more. Time to open the lion's cage and peek in. "You've been all over me since you showed up with the Feebies at TAE. I want to clear my name and get you off my back."

Now he grinned. "If you're innocent, you have nothing to worry about."

That's the third biggest lie in the world. "We both know that's BS, Gallo. I'm sorta guessing you have something that links me to Piper. You're pulling that string so hard because you have no other leads. He's obviously disappeared. You want to find him and don't care if it screws me over or not. Me, I want to find him, too, to prove I didn't kill him and get out of your crosshairs. Sounds like we should be on the same team."

Gallo's grin faded and his eyes narrowed on me like he was contemplating which eye to shoot. "We'll never be on the same team, Curran. Never. As I said before, stay away from my house and my daughter. That's a warning. The only one you'll get."

Actually, that was the fourth or fifth one since he punctured my chest cavity. "Right. Got it. What about my thirty bucks?"

He snorted, turned on his heels, and headed down the stairs to his Explorer. When he got to his vehicle, he turned back and looked up to eye me for a long time.

"You know, Curran, you're nothing that I expected. She had you all wrong. That's your loss."

Chapter Thirty-Four

Curran

"She had me all wrong?" I rubbed my chest where Gallo's fingerhole was. "Who had me all wrong?"

No answers came, so I grabbed my go bag, left a big bowl of food and a huge bucket of water for Bogart just inside the open barn door, and locked up my loft. You know, just in case some rogue US Marshal decided to visit and ransack my encyclopedia collection.

After I climbed into the Jeep, I sent a text to Mr. Nobody as directed—*Nothing so far.* That would buy me four hours before I had to report in again. Then, I headed out to find the elusive Billy Piper. I'd start in the only place I could figure out—his Arlington Arms Apartment. I might get lucky and find someone who knew him or had an idea where he'd go. I'm sure Gallo had the same idea, too. With no other leads, Arlington, here I come.

As I rolled onto the county road, I dialed Janey-Lynn. She didn't pick up and I left her a brief message about what Evans had told me. I left out the part where he considered her behind the killing and setting me up. I finished the call with a thanks for taking care of Bogart, where his food and water were located, and a promise of another call later.

It was just after seven a.m. when I hit Route 66 and headed east. The drive took over an hour and a half fighting commuter traffic headed to D.C. We've already discussed life on Virginia streets, right? I mean, Virginia may be for lovers, monuments, and tourists. But it was also for insurance companies, tow trucks, and speeding tickets. I wanted none of that, so I maneuvered carefully to Arlington.

When I pulled into the Arlington Arms Apartments, a cop car was sitting at the end of the parking area with a uniformed officer inside. He was drinking coffee and talking on his cell phone. He didn't seem interested in much other than that.

Was he there for Billy Piper, or just wasting a little time? Gallo and the FBI had intimated Piper was on their BOLO list—that's cop talk for Be On The Look Out, or the old-fashioned Dragnet APB. The FBI wanted him for hacking computers and general ethernet skullduggery. Gallo wanted him even more. After all, the Marshals didn't like misplacing one of their protectees. It was bad form and a little embarrassing.

I drove around the side of the apartment complex and found a parking spot to watch the cop and wait for an opportunity to slip inside unnoticed. Caution kept me there, wishing for a cup of coffee and a bagel.

What kind of PI was I? I should've stopped for breakfast before coming here.

Luck was on my side, strange as that was. The cop started his cruiser, did a drive-around the building without giving me a second glance, and drove off into Arlington.

Phew. One problem down. A thousand to go.

After a few minutes surveilling the area, the most sinister thing I saw was a brown delivery van off-loading a handcart full of boxes. Though I wasn't in the Jelly of the Month Club, they might just solve one problem for me.

As the crew reached the rear complex door, they buzzed an apartment from the call button panel alongside the door and waited.

I headed for them.

Most residents of apartment buildings, especially in the city, are security conscious. They kept their doors locked and didn't fall for the TV gimmick of buzzing all the apartments until someone gets irritated and simply lets you in remotely. But there was always that one or two who couldn't care less.

Timing was everything, and I reached the entrance just as a young twenty-something millennial—sagging pants, grody tee shirt, and sandals—walked through the lobby and exited the front door. He brushed past the delivery guys like they weren't there. I held the door for them as they juggled their handcart through and to the elevator. Once we were all snuggly onboard, they exited on the fourth floor. I continued to the fifth.

The movies, not special elevator training, taught me the best way to arrive at my target location. First, don't get off on the right floor. Standing on the inside when the doors open can lead to surprises—bad ones. In the movies, the elevator doors always open into an ambush by the bad guys. Like when Don Victor Stracci gets blasted in the elevator by one of Don Corleone's boys in The Godfather. Not that Stracci was a good guy, and well, neither was Corleone or his guys, but I rooted for Don Corleone. In fact, there weren't any real good guys in The Godfather. Maybe there was hope for me after all.

If the cops or anyone else were watching Piper's apartment—number 3-F—they'd expect any unwanted visitors or troublemakers like me to be coming from the ground up.

Me, I'd do the reverse—top down. Clever, aren't I?

I exited the elevator on the fourth floor and scanned around. Nothing. I continued to my real destination, the third floor—apartment 3-F—via the stairs. Once out of the stairwell, I waited near the exit, chatting with no one on my cell and laughing up a deeply humorous account of a wild and crazy night that I never had and wouldn't be caught dead doing. Cell phones were good for many things, and a cover for surveillance was one of them. Ordering pizza was also pretty important.

As I surveyed the third floor, I saw the remnants of a crime scene.

Apartment 3-F was halfway down the hall—Billy Piper's apartment. Two doors down on the opposite side of the hall, yellow crime scene tape was stretched across the doorway of apartment 3-H. As I approached Piper's apartment, I found a three-foot square cut out of the cheap carpet. The carpet had been cut away to the wood flooring beneath. Adjacent to the missing carpet, about waist high, were two holes in the wall.

I bet the missing carpet had blood stains on it. I'm a trained PI, mind you, and I watch a lot of *Columbo* reruns.

Before I went into Billy's apartment, I maneuvered down the hall, looking for more clues of what had happened. I found two more bullet holes in the door of apartment 3-H. There were also two indentations in the steel emergency door leading to the opposite stairwell. They were assuredly made by bullets.

There had been a gunfight.

At least one of the shooters had been hit near Piper's apartment. Someone else had escaped. The bullet marks in the stairwell door suggested that someone bailed through that door with bullets chasing them. My best guess, based on hours of training under *Columbo*, *Starsky & Hutch*, and *Law & Order*, was that Billy had been ambushed. He'd returned fire and escaped. He'd hit his assailant.

It could have been the other way around, and that would be bad.

"What you doing out here, mister?" a voice croaked from behind me. "You with the police?"

I turned and found an elderly African American woman in her late seventies leaning out her apartment doorway two doors down. I smiled and said, "No. Why?"

"Because they been here all night long. Big shootout last night. Right here. Could have killed me or any one of my neighbors. Never had this kind of goings on here before. Never."

"Well, ma'am, I'm glad you're okay." I walked to her, smiling and trying to appear as innocent as I could. "What happened?"

"Poor Mr. Culpepper right here next door." She glanced down the hall toward the stairwell. "I guess somebody tried to break in. He's a tough old bird. Tough like me. He wasn't taking any of their shit, you know? He shot it out with them. Hit one, too, I'm told."

Well, no mention of Billy Piper. Good.

"Ma'am, was anyone else involved? I mean, I hope no one else was hurt."

"Don't you 'ma'am' me, fella, I'm Mrs. Joleen Adams. Widowed now, but still a Mrs. if you understand." Joleen shook her head and jutted an arthritic finger toward Piper's apartment beside me. "That young man there, Mr.

Piper, he was involved. I saw him going in Mr. Culpepper's place a little while before the shooting started. Never saw him come out, but you know, when the shooting started, I hid in the back room."

Piper was here. "Smart thing, ma'am—er, Mrs. Adams. What about Mr. Piper? Know where he might be?"

She thought about that. "He and Mr. Culpepper are buddies. Real close. Maybe the hospital, I'd guess."

"The hospital?"

"Old Mr. Culpepper got shot, and they ambulanced him out early this morning." She wagged her finger at me. "Who are you, mister? Why you asking all these questions?"

Ah, right, Curran. What's your story?

I thought one up fast. "Sorry, Mrs. Adams. I'm thinking of renting an apartment here. Now, I'm not so sure. Mr. Piper's name was given to me as a reference by the rental people."

She scoffed and waved at me, easing her suspicion a bit. "Oh, sure you do. Nice place. This was the first bad thing that's happened since I moved in. I've lived here twenty years, give or take. Anyway, I gotta get back in. My shows are on, and I'm making tea." She abruptly shut the door.

Three locks clicked into place.

I waited a few seconds before returning to Piper's apartment. There, I performed some magic with a lockpick kit I never left home without. In Virginia, like most states, such a kit was legal when used by a properly trained, licensed, and bonded professional locksmith. I was not one of those—though, it was just a technicality. As I felt the lock give to my talents, I glanced back at apartment 3-H as the crime scene tape, typically secured across a scene, fell away. Odd since it was normally securely fastened so that didn't happen. As I started through Piper's door, two clunks came from behind me. I turned, half expecting to see Mrs. Adams in the hall watching me again. Instead, a third clunk made apartment 3-H's door shutter.

I went to check it out.

The crime scene tape was not the only oddity on the apartment door. The light plastic security seal, affixed by the crime scene people, had been pulled free and haphazardly replaced. The cops wouldn't have done that. They would have replaced the seal entirely.

Now, there were two possibilities inside apartment 3-H. Possibility one was that the cops were inside continuing their investigation and had not yet fixed the crime scene seal. Possibility two was that someone else was inside and up to no good.

I was betting on possibility two.

I slipped my Kimber out, and, as quietly as possible, opened the apartment door less than a foot. It hit something and blocked me from opening it wider.

Winner, winner. Chicken dinner.

Chapter Thirty-Five

Curran

J ust inside the door of apartment 3-H, a handcart with several boxes still stacked on it blocked the door. Across the room, a man dressed in a brown delivery uniform was rooting through a bookcase, taking books off, fanning through them, and tossing them behind him onto the floor. He was a short, heavy-set guy losing his hair. Earlier, he and his partner hauled the handcart from their delivery truck into the apartment complex. I'd even held the door. They'd fooled me then, but not now.

You see, most delivery guys don't carry silenced pistols. The heavy-set guy had his sitting on a shelf within arm's reach.

What can Brown do for you? Kill you. That's what.

Footsteps crossed the room, and the second not-a-deliveryman came into view. He mumbled something to the heavy guy and started across the room.

As I tried to silently close the door and make a stealthy retreat, it happened. Like every thriller movie I'd ever seen—including those stupid slasher films—the door did what it hadn't done when I opened it. It squeaked.

"Levene, someone's here," the second man called out, turning toward me. "Get him, Freedman."

Too late. I slammed the door and bolted down the hall. There wasn't enough time to make the stairs or the elevator, so I slipped into Billy Piper's apartment just as 3-H's door banged open behind me. Luckily, the handcart

181

had slowed Freedman and Levene's pursuit or I might have taken a couple bullets in the back. Silenced bullets, mind you, but they hurt just as much.

"Where'd he go?" Freedman called out. "He's not at the stairs."

Footsteps outside Piper's door.

The second voice—Levene, I think—said, "He has to be in here."

"What if it's the cops?"

Levene was the thinker of the two, obviously. "They wouldn't run away."

"Oh, yeah."

Silently, I locked the apartment door lock and engaged the two deadbolts above it. As long as they didn't start shooting, I had a few minutes to find a way out without sprouting wings. If they started shooting, I was in trouble.

The door rattled, first quietly, and then with force and anger. Two shots rang out, and the doorknob blew inside and fell to the floor in pieces.

Time for wings.

Two more bullets penetrated the door, searching for the deadbolt locks. One of the deadbolts succumbed and followed the doorknob to the floor. The second survived by a misplaced shot an inch too far to the right.

I returned fire—two quick shots spaced wide enough they'd miss the men outside. Well, hopefully. Unsure of who they were—confident they weren't cops or feds themselves—I still didn't want to be another murder suspect.

"Damn," Levene yelled. "Get back."

Frantically, I looked for a way out and found a possibility on Piper's small twenty by eight-foot balcony. Unfortunately, there was no fire escape or trees to climb down to safety two floors below. No, that would have been too easy.

So much for old movie scripts.

Another bullet went through the door and convinced me I had to take a chance and free climb down.

To recap, I'm getting a little old in the bones for a young man's foolery and action-hero crap. Of course, that didn't stop me from wanting the two hundred grand for this case. Though, at that moment, I wish I'd considered the risks before taking this assignment. Right then, I realized that this was not only a young man's game, it was a *much* younger man's game.

Note to self—consider risks in the future.

From this third-floor balcony to the grass below me was nearly thirty feet, give or take. In my younger days, I could dangle over the railing doing the spider drop and safely make it down to the second floor. Then repeat, stick a rolling landing, wave to the adoring crowd, and run my butt away. Thirty feet would have been a cakewalk. Now, however, there was precarious, bone-jarring pain looming. Or a broken something. Or both.

There had to be a better way.

In the corner of the balcony, Piper had one of those cotton rope hammocks strung up. With age comes ingenuity. After holstering my pistol, I unhooked the hammock from the wall and dropped it over the side. It dangled three-quarters of the way to the second-floor balcony below.

Three-quarters was good enough.

Over the side I went just as Piper's last deadbolt took a bullet in the heart and died. Another shot followed, and the front door crashed open.

Using the hammock as a rope ladder, I went hand-under-hand to the second-floor balcony railing and got my feet under me. As I did, that balcony door slid open, and a seven-hundred-pound Rottweiler charged out, gnashing his teeth and salivating for my flesh.

Okay, so it was a fifty-pound mutt yapping like an idiot. Sue me.

Before Cujo could sink his little teeth into my ass, I dropped down, grasped the balcony railing, and continued down toward the first floor below.

Not in time.

Cujo got a mouthful of my left-hand fingers. Then, Levene or Freedman— whoever the worst shot was—let fly another shot that missed me by a foot. Except the combination of the mutt's assault and flying lead loosened my grip. I plummeted the remaining six feet and crashed into a Chaise lounge. I hit it feet first, crumpled, and bounced as much as fell out onto the grass.

Ouch. Ouch. Bloody hell ouch.

Stunned, I opened my eyes, rolled on my side, and locked onto the older, balding delivery man—Levene—lining up my kill shot.

Somehow, I yanked my pistol and jerked off two rounds in his general direction. Not waiting to see if I hit anything but the ceiling fan over his head, I tried to roll away, but the pain in my aging bones ordered me to stay put a few more moments and recover. Moments I didn't have.

Freedman poked his head over the railing again, and I sent him back with a shot that whizzed past his head and slammed into the roof overhang. He blindly jutted his gun over the railing and returned fire. Thankfully, those shots missed.

We played two more rounds of 'who's the worst shot' until my body approved my escape. I got to my feet and squeezed off another wide shot to make my getaway. Limping like the wounded, old dude I was, I reached the side of the building where my new buddies couldn't get a clear shot. I headed for my Jeep.

There, I checked my six and so far, no bullets. It wasn't until four streets and three green lights later that I eased. I did a fast accounting to ensure I had no more orifices than I was born with.

Nope. All holes accounted for. Thankfully, those two assassins were worse shots than me.

Chapter Thirty-Six

Deputy US Marshal Terry Gallo

Terry Gallo sipped his steaming coffee and tapped away on his cell phone. He'd been tracking Curran since he'd left his farm loft apartment after their early morning encounter. Gallo had stopped for a fresh cup three blocks behind Curran and made a morning phone call to check in with his office. He wasn't concerned with losing his nemesis in the metro traffic. He knew right where he was. The little blip on his cell phone map program gave him that information. Earlier, before confronting Curran, he'd planted a tracking device on his Jeep. Since leaving there, he'd followed that blip all the way to Arlington. He knew exactly where he was going. When the signal stopped down the boulevard at Piper's address, Gallo wheeled into the convenience store and sought his breakfast.

One large coffee, an egg and cheese bagel, and a large bag of pistachios later, and he slipped back into his SUV. Ten minutes passed before he decided to confront Curran again. Despite denials, Curran was involved in Piper's disappearance. Involved up to his neck. Why else would he have made a beeline for Piper's apartment?

He wheeled into the Arlington Arms Apartments and looked for a secluded parking spot where he could observe the building and catch Curran leaving the building. He'd checked up on Billy Piper dozens of times just like this. Each time, Billy had checked out. No signs of trouble. No signs of being up to trouble. No signs of anything to be concerned about. Except he'd missed it all. Billy had been up to his old bad habits in Leesburg. How had he missed that? He didn't have to guess what his Marshal superiors were thinking. He was thinking the same things. He'd failed. He'd totally missed it all. Now, Piper was in the wind.

The Chief Marshal allowed him to continue searching for Piper. They wanted him to clean up his mess. If he found him, they'd assign another Marshal. They might even kick Billy out of WITSEC. If he didn't find him, his career was over—if it weren't already.

To make things worse, from out of the blue, Lowe Curran was smack in the middle of it all.

He found Curran's Jeep parked in the rear lot, and Gallo positioned himself on the front corner near the exit. He could observe the Jeep and the front entrance easily. Curran would have to drive past him to leave, but there was still enough cover among several other vehicles to conceal him. Not that anonymity was vital any longer. If Curran spotted him, it didn't matter.

He rolled down his window, took a long slug of coffee, and leaned back to wait.

The first gunshots were faint. At first, he wasn't entirely sure what he'd heard. Still, this was Piper's building. Curran was inside. There were no coincidences.

Curran. Jesus Christ, it's you, isn't it?

He grabbed his cell, dialed 9-1-1, and gave a brief explanation to the emergency dispatcher, ending with his identification. Then, he jumped from his SUV, tugged his Glock from his belt holster, and ran to the front entrance. He followed his pistol into the building, through the lobby, and to the stairs. Curran would be on the third floor—Piper's floor—so he started up, easing up the stairs, one at a time, peering over his pistol sights into the stairwell above.

More shots, loud now, one more floor up.

At the third-floor landing, he stopped to assess what might be waiting. The shooting was coming from down the hall—too faint to be right outside the steel stairwell door. It had to be within one of the apartments. That might make it difficult to find quickly. He didn't relish clearing the floor by himself, but with Curran involved, he wanted to catch him in the act.

Easing the steel stairwell door open, he first noticed the gunshot stippling on its outer shell. Then he saw crime scene tape dangling from a doorway where the apartment door was ajar. Farther down the hall, Billy Piper's apartment door was open.

More gunshots—inside Piper's apartment.

He moved quickly, Glock up and arms partially extended, ready to shoot if needed.

He'd been trained for this. Trained well. Still, angst began to flow. He began to sweat. Adrenalin fought to take over, but he willed it back, steadying himself and getting control over his surging emotions.

He was ready.

Piper's apartment door had been broken through. The door was riddled with bullet holes, and the doorknob and two security locks literally shot off.

Another shot. Two. Both from an inner room.

He tried peering around the open front door to find the shooters. The door, only partially opened, blocked his view and forced him to slip behind it to get a look deeper into the room.

"US Marshal, drop your weapons and…"

Something slammed violently against the inside of the door and propelled him sideways into the doorframe. The door knocked his pistol from his hands onto the floor. Before he could recover, the door crashed into him again. Then, a third time, this time with tremendous force. As he began to fall, stunned hurting, someone grabbed his head, yanked it downward, and crushed a knee into his face.

Darkness consumed him.

Chapter Thirty-Seven

Deputy US Marshal Terry Gallo

"M arshal?"

The voice called him from somewhere beyond the darkness. He tried to awaken—to find the voice.

"Marshal Gallo?"

His eyes fluttered, and light seeped into his vision. His thoughts stopped swirling, settled, and allowed him to open his eyes. After a few blinks to steady his focus, he found the voice calling him.

An older police officer dressed in a dark blue uniform knelt beside him. He had a round, strong face and deep, blue eyes. The officer—Danker on his uniform nameplate—spoke into his radio microphone tethered to his shirt epaulet. He informed the dispatcher that his victim was awake.

"Marshal, can you stand?" Danker asked. "You might have a good headache, but I think you're in one piece."

Gallo blinked several times and sat back against the doorframe. "Yeah, yeah, I'm good. Some bastard bulldozed me and clipped me good on my way down. Did you grab him? An asshole named Marlowe Curran?"

"Nope." Danker stood and looked at his partner—a thin, tall man much younger than he. "Any other witnesses, McGregor?"

McGregor shook his head. "None. But this is the same place as last night's shooting. Just two doors down from 3-H. Must involve that old man and that Piper guy again."

"Piper? An old man?" Gallo steadied himself and climbed to his feet, using the doorframe for balance. "Are you talking about Old Culpepper and William Piper?"

"Yeah, that's them," Danker said. "You know them?"

"I don't know Culpepper personally." Gallo rubbed his head. "I Piper. He lives in this flat."

"Then you know Piper is a person of interest in the shootings here last night." Danker stepped back and watched him closely. "Before we get into that, Marshal, how about walking us through what happened here."

"Give me a minute."

"Sure." Danker guided him to a straight chair nearby. "For the record. start with what you're doing here."

"Looking for Piper," he said and explained to the two officers a sketch of how he came to be unconscious on Apartment 3-F's floor. He skipped details on Curran. Instead, he began the story saying he simply was looking for Piper, whom he dubbed a potential witness to a case he was working. He also avoided any mention of WITSEC. He ended with being taken by surprise and knocked out. "You mentioned something about last night. What happened?"

"Right here, Marshal, big shoot out. Marvin Culpepper, Piper's friend, got into it with an unidentified perp. Somebody got hit but made it out. Our boys got here minutes later. Culpepper was lying in his doorway, shot and blood all over the hall by his apartment doorway. You might have noticed the carpet out in the hall—crime techs cut it up for evidence."

"No, I was busy getting my brains bashed." Gallo rubbed his face and eyes again. His nose ached, and he felt dizzy and sore, but he didn't think it was broken. "Any signs of Lowe Curran? I watched him come in here right before the shooting started."

"Curran?" Danker exchanges sideways glances with McGregor. "Who's he?"

Gallo waved the question off. "Is that a 'no?'"

"Never heard of him. We'll make a note if you give me particulars. Tell us why you're so eager to put him here."

Gallo eyed them. "He's a person of interest in one of my cases—same one involving Piper. I followed Curran here this morning. By the time I parked, I heard gunfire and came in. He was here."

McGregor was taking notes. "Did you see him shooting?"

He shook his head.

"Getting shot at?"

Another headshake denial.

"How about last night," Danker pressed. "If you were tracking this Curran guy, was he in the area? Say, around midnight?"

Gallo thought about that. Curran was at his house playing board games with Madi until early evening—something the little girl hadn't stopped talking about. Where he went afterward, he didn't know. This morning, when he'd confronted him at his barn apartment, he hadn't given any impression he'd been involved. Though, the Lowe Curran he knew about was very possibly a great actor.

"I don't know for sure, Danker. Though, truthfully, I doubt it. I followed him here this morning. I can't put him in the gunfight or even on this floor for certain. But he was involved. Trust me."

McGregor jotted more notes. "Why do you think he's involved? Just because he was here?"

He nodded. "I know him. At least a little. He's always in trouble. I don't believe in coincidence when two persons of interest collide. Do you?"

"Nope. I don't. Does Curran have a record?" Danker asked. "What's his story?"

Gallo hesitated, then shook his head again. "No conviction record worth mentioning. Yet."

"Yet?" McGregor said, waiting for a nod from Danker. "Look, the downstairs neighbor said some guy climbed down the outside balconies from this one. This neighbor's dog intercepted the guy, and he more or less fell to the last floor. Then there was a bunch of shooting."

"What did he look like?" Gallo asked. "Young? Old? White? African American? Asian. What?"

McGregor laughed. "He looked like Spider-Man, Marshal. What the

190

heck do you think? All kinds of shooting and some guy climbing the walls. Scared the shit out of everybody. Ground floor resident said she heard the shooting, looked out her patio doors a minute or two later, and this dude falls onto her lawn chair and almost kills himself. He just lay there. Then more shooting, and this fallen guy is in a gunfight with someone on the upper floors."

"Sounds like my man," Gallo asked. "What else?"

Danker continued. "Witness says somebody was trying to shoot him. He was trying to shoot them. Eventually, he got up and limped off. Must have hurt like hell falling like that. That and the dog getting a bite or two."

Gallo walked to the balcony and looked out, noting the hammock tied off on the railing. "Looks like he tried to climb down first. Did you check all that for prints yet?"

"Marshal, tell us more about Curran," Danker said. "We'll need to interview him. If it's him like you said, he's a person of interest in *our* cases, too."

"I can't go into details right now. But I'd appreciate anything you can give me on this mess today and last night—crime scene tech findings, too. I know that old shit is involved somehow."

Danker shook his head and forced a guttural laugh. "Yeah, of course. Typical fed. Can't tell us shit but wants everything we got. I'll give you this. The old Nam vet, Culpepper, is in critical condition at The Virginia Hospital Center here in town. We don't know much more than that. This apartment renter, William Piper, is a person of interest. Your Curran boy, too. You got POIs, and we got POIs—how wonderful they're the same. When you get around to it, we can share. As in two ways."

Gallo patted the air. "Look, I get it, guys. I just can't share info without permission. That's Marshal protocol." He stood, wiped some blood from his mouth and nose, and pointed to his Glock lying across the floor. "Can I take my piece?"

"Nope." Danker shook his head with a wry grin. "You're an incidental to the crime scene. Until the techies and my sergeant clear your gun, it's ours. You can check headquarters later to see if they'll release it."

"I never fired a shot."

"Oh, yeah?" McGregor snorted. "We only have your word on that. I mean, we can't share crime scene information or release evidence without permission. That's *our* protocol, Marshal. You get that, don't you?"

Oh yeah, he got that. Tit for tat.

A uniformed officer from the hallway called Danker and McGregor into the doorway. They spoke in hushed voices for several minutes. Danker asked questions and nodded his head. McGregor jotted notes as rapidly as he could. Finally, Danker threw a thumb out the door and sent the uniformed officer away.

He and McGregor returned to him.

"Well, looks like your man Curran might have been here after all," Danker said. "Lady down the hall—Mrs. Joleen Adams—spoke with him just minutes before all the shooting started. Seems he was asking a lot of questions about Piper and Culpepper. He was real interested in what had happened last night and where they might be. Mrs. Adams said he was nosy but a nice, polite young guy. Just pushy. Sound like your boy?"

"Yes, except he's not young," Gallo said.

McGregor shrugged. "She's almost ninety. Young is relative."

Gallo considered that. "It's got to be him. What else? Give me the details."

"Sure, sure. It'll be in my report to my sergeant." Danker looked at McGregor. "We'll make sure it's all dotted and crossed and nice and neat later."

McGregor laughed. "Exactly. Because that's our protocol."

Shit. More games. "Look, I've told you everything I know. Can I go?"

Danker shook his head again. "Not until my sergeant gets here. Then, maybe. After a proper statement. You might want to get comfortable, Marshal. It's been a busy morning, and our sergeant is running late."

Chapter Thirty-Eight

Billy Piper

B illy glanced at his watch for the tenth time in five minutes. It was just after nine-thirty a.m. He'd stayed in the house too long. He should have left before dawn, but exhaustion and the safety of the empty house was too comforting. He'd needed to think. To rest. To sort out what to do next. Last night, he'd been confident the house was empty. Now, however, someone could arrive at any moment.

Discovery could lead to the police. The police would lead to jail. Discovery might also bring a bullet.

He hefted the .38 revolver he'd held all night and chanced a peek out the front windows. He'd barely slept. Each nightbird or passing car seemed a threat. Every noise in the empty rooms had brought him to his feet.

He was in trouble. The worst he'd ever been in. He'd spent the night in this small single-story house a dozen blocks from his apartment. It had taken him an hour last night to find this place—an Under Contract sign gave him hope. He'd spent thirty minutes snooping around—praying no one would see him—peeking in windows to ensure it was unoccupied. Luck held, and it was—not even any packing boxes or furniture—so he climbed through a rear window and slept in the empty living room on the thick-pile carpet.

Slept was the wrong word. He'd dozed sporadically. Mostly between the panicked recreations of the gunfight at Mr. Culpepper's house. He'd barely made it out alive, and he wasn't sure about Mr. C.

He had to be okay. He'd hate himself the rest of his life—however long that might be—if anything happened to that old man. He'd rarely had friends throughout his life, and losing the first one he truly cared for would destroy him. Going forward, he'd never allow anyone to get close to him again.

Were those gunmen from his former client? Mr. C. had said they claimed to be federal agents but didn't believe them. When they came out of his apartment and found him in the hall, they didn't show badges or try to arrest him. They started shooting. Had his client sent hitmen for him? Had the government sent federal agents to silence him? He understood that Si-Int was a powerful, secretive Beltway bandit. Surely, they had resources like those men. He'd been paid handsomely to hack three systems—a government agency and two private companies. Hack them and locate six people. Perhaps he'd been naive. He didn't even know who his client had been. Just a dark web contract like hundreds he'd taken on before. No names. No meetings. Just a deal—crypto currency in the bank. A delivery date. Poof. Deliver and get paid. Don't deliver and don't get paid. It was the simplest of contracts.

Whatever his client was after, it had a lot of people very excited. Had they found him out—that he'd double-crossed him and tried to sell his discoveries elsewhere? Had his client sent that strange old man to his Leesburg rambler to retrieve the data files? Was it one of his other targets who sent him? If so, then who sent the men who crashed into his Leesburg house and his apartment last night? No, it couldn't all be the same people. The old man at his Leesburg house came first. The four assassins came later. They couldn't be connected. And the old man wasn't one of the assassins from the Arlington Arms, either. That meant there were at least two somebodies hunting for him.

No. Four. There was Gallo and the Russians, too.

They all wanted him. Him, and something called *Whisper*. All the names he was paid to locate were found in that single computer folder titled "Whisper." That folder was hidden behind cybersecurity he'd never encountered before—layers upon layers. It had taken him days to find a way into the target. In the end, despite the highest levels of security protocols, it had been careless employees who clicked the wrong link on the wrong email that allowed him in. After penetrating his target's outer firewalls, he'd begun scouring the network architecture, searching out vulnerabilities to allow him to penetrate deeper inside. The firewalls and other security protocols were more and more robust with each level of the target's architecture. Each level moved him closer and closer to the treasure chest. When he had found the correct path, that folder—Whisper—contained everything he'd been sent for. The money was his.

His head hurt, trying to understand what was happening now. He sat back against the living room wall, thinking. What would Jack Reacher do? Bond or Mitch Rapp? They were all men of action. Men of superior skills and intellect. Trained and skilled.

Right. Trained and skilled. That was the trouble. They *were* trained. They had the skills.

What did he have?

"Yeah, Billy," he said to the empty room. "What do you have other than a wild imagination and a big gut?"

He pulled Mr. C.'s Vietnam rucksack over and dumped the contents onto the carpet in front of him. Two changes of jeans and pullovers. They were all a size too big, but he could get into them at least. They were certainly better than the grungy clothes he'd had on for almost three days. There were some toiletries in a shaving kit—an old razor and a couple unused blades in a plastic sheath, a toothbrush still in its original wrapping, a tube of toothpaste, and an unused bar of soap. There was also a pair of running shoes a size too big, but they'd work, two pairs of socks and boxer shorts.

"I have to be ready." He lifted the revolver and examined it—four rounds left. From his jeans pocket, he withdrew two shells and reloaded. "I can do this."

Next, he checked Mr. C.'s cell phone—five percent battery remained. Dammit. He'd left it on all night and drained the battery. He didn't have a charger and he needed one fast.

Mistakes like that one would get him killed.

Sitting back, he considered his situation. He had a total of five thousand, two hundred and fifteen dollars in cash. Five thousand from Mr. C. and the rest was all that remained from his stash in the Leesburg basement. It wasn't enough, but it was a start. He needed three things. First, transportation. Public transportation or even rideshares were too dangerous. Rideshares like Uber or Lyft used credit or debit cards. He had neither. Without a driver's license and credit card, he couldn't rent a car. Second, he needed a place to hide. A good place. And third, the most important at that moment, he needed to know if Mr. C. was all right. He couldn't even think straight until he knew if the old vet was alive.

He checked outside again. Of the occasional passerby, no one showed interest in the house. Knowing it was risky, he went to the bathroom at the rear of the house. A shower and clean clothes would make a difference—a big difference—on how he felt. Survival was about attitude more than anything.

After all, Bond never went into action without nice clothes and a shave. Hygiene was important. While he didn't relish putting on Mr. C.'s son's decade-old underwear, it was all he had. Surely, 007 would understand.

* * *

Twenty minutes later, he'd showered, used one of the tee-shirts in the rucksack as a towel, and dried off. He'd shaved, changed, and slipped back through the rear house window. After rechecking his surroundings, he emerged on a side street without so much as a dog barking or police siren in the distance.

At a convenience store three blocks down, he found a cell phone charger that fit Mr. C's phone. He was tempted to purchase one of the pay-as-you-go phones, but money might be tight soon, and he opted to take the risk and keep Mr. C.'s for the time being. At the counter, he purchased a large coffee with three creams and six sugars, three sausage and egg biscuit sandwiches that had been in the warmer days too long, and paid the bright-eyed Asian clerk.

The clerk's television was tuned to local D.C. area news. The lead story flashed across the screen. He only noticed it because the news crew was filming the reporter—a pretty African American woman with big, bright eyes and a serious expression that projected confidence and concern—in front of *his* apartment building. Every synapse in his body cried out. He couldn't hear the story well and dared not ask the store clerk to raise the volume. He didn't want to be remembered. Instead, he stood and watched the ticker at the bottom of the screen. That told him everything he needed to know...

> *...second shooting spree at the Arlington Arms Complex in less than a day. Neighbors reported multiple gunshots just moments ago, the same apartment where eighty-five-year-old Marvin Culpepper, a decorated Vietnam Veteran with two Silver Stars, was critically injured last night by an unidentified assailant. Culpepper was rushed to The Virginia Hospital Center, where he remains in critical condition. Police are searching for a person of interest...*

"Oh, shit. What the hell?"

"Excuse me?" the clerk sneered. "You talkin' to me, boyfriend?"

"No. Sorry."

"Damn, boyfriend, that shootin's just down the street." The clerk snapped off the TV with his remote control from beside the register. "Don't want no bad juju, so I ain't gonna listen."

Billy tried to paint a calm face. "I hear you. Hey, can I charge my phone for a little bit? I'm not from around here and—"

"No, no. Come on." The clerk, a young man wearing bright eyeshadow and long eyelashes, shook his finger at him. "Boyfriend, electricity ain't free. I'd get fired if the boss man caught me giving it away."

"Right, sorry." What a jerk. He wasn't asking for much. "Thanks for nothing."

"Hey, now," the clerk snapped, "no need to cop that with me. Look, there's an outside plug around back for the maintenance dudes. If you plugged in, I'd never know. Hell, boyfriend, I can't be fired for what I didn't know. Boss man be here in an hour, give or take. Better be gone by then. You feel me, baby?"

"Thanks, man." Billy turned, flashed a wave and his best fake smile, and headed around the rear of the store. As he did, the clerk turned the television back on and raised the volume, nearly freezing him in his tracks...

In National News, while Vice President St. Croix's condition has been called a minor event caused by dehydration and exhaustion, rumors are swirling around his future on the national front.

Previously reported, Senator Jameson K. Wain was considered a front-runner for the vice-presidential nod. Wain got his start with the Department of Defense right out of law school. He has never made secret his larger aspirations for the Oval Office. That came to an unexpected end today when he was found dead in his Dirksen Senate Office Building office. The Capitol Police and FBI have released a limited press statement stating no foul play was believed responsible. Sources inside the senator's inner circle report that Senator Wain had secretly suffered from serious depression since his divorce three years ago. He apparently took his own life. He leaves behind a daughter and...

Billy's thoughts erupted. Senator Jameson Wain? Jesus, no. No. No. Wain had been one of the six names his client wanted a dossier on. Two nights ago, after finally breaching that company's highly secure system, he'd found the Whisper folder. Inside it, had been an entire subfolder on Wain. His, and the other targets, too.

Sweet Jesus. Whatever Whisper was, it just killed a US Senator.

Chapter Thirty-Nine

Curran

The Virginia Hospital Center is located not far from Piper's Arlington apartment. It took me no time to drive there. After, that is, I double-checked for a tail to make sure that when I parked, two clumsy thugs in brown uniforms didn't shoot me. Not that they could hit anything. Still, a lucky shot was as deadly as a skilled one.

Having survived the melee, every inch of my body was now screaming at me. I was lucky no bones were broken or protruding where they shouldn't. Well, I assume no bones were broken. I know there were none sticking out. A guy would notice that. A knowledge of anatomy was important.

Once, when I was younger, I was on a foot chase and got hit by a car. I rolled over the hood, landed on my feet, and kept going. Same chase, I had to drop down into an alley from the second floor and did so without even losing stride. Of course, all that ended on the Voula Beach Road. Life changes are hard.

With every bump on the ride over, my bones and muscles cursed me. The only part of me that didn't hurt was my head.

Hey, I was at a hospital. Maybe I should get a fast checkup. I could have a cracked spleen or an upside-down kidney or something. Getting old means your body starts falling apart like a car past its warranty. Funny how there were no people calling to talk about my body warranty. Now, that would be something a telemarketer might get me to listen to.

I parked in one of the outside side parking areas just off 16th Street and took care to check my surroundings. I'd love to say that caution was to ensure Levene and Freedman weren't about to make another delivery. No, it was because I was afraid of the shooting pains that would come as soon as I climbed out of the Jeep and onto the pavement.

Sitting there, I tried to piece together what had just happened at Piper's apartment. Levene and Freedman—obviously *not* delivery guys—were searching Culpepper's apartment. Had they returned to the scene after last night's gunfight with Culpepper and Billy Piper? From the crime scene, someone other than Culpepper had been shot. There had been bloodstains on the carpet and wall and a missing piece of carpet I was sure had been taken by the crime techs. There was always the possibility that Billy Piper had taken a bullet, but the bullet holes in the stairwell entrance suggested he'd escaped, uninjured—there was no blood in the stairwell. Though, he could have been injured.

Levene and Freedman were after Piper, just as I was. One of them mentioned him by name as they came after me. Who were they? Not cops, that was certain. They must be some of the "others" Mr. Nobody warned me about. He also warned me the others wanted Piper dead. Levene and Freedman had enough "want dead" to go around when they tried to shoot me. Lucky me. Just a few hours on this job, I was already getting shot at, chased over a balcony, and beaten up by a rogue US Marshal.

What did the rest of the day have in store?

I slowly climbed out of the Jeep—actually, I turned and half-fell to the ground as delicately as I could. As I touched down, every inch of my body cried in agony. I nearly dropped to the ground, but two pretty hospital staff walked past. I didn't want to embarrass myself. I promised some icepacks and painkillers as soon as I could—for my muscles, not the ladies—and they walked me to the hospital entrance.

My best lead to find Piper had started at the Arlington Arms shootout. Joleen Adams said Billy Piper was involved. He was a close friend of Culpepper. There had been a gunfight, and Culpepper was in the hospital. Hence, if they were such good friends, Piper might show up here to check

200

on him.

See, this detective stuff isn't all that hard.

At the reception counter just inside the hospital entrance, I learned three important things. First, Mr. Culpepper was indeed in the hospital ICU. Second, only family was allowed up. Third, just when I was about to become Culpepper's nephew, the receptionist informed me that the police were with him at the moment. I'd have to wait until they were through. That might be a while. Oh, there was a fourth extremely important thing I learned, too.

The receptionist said, "Mr. Culpepper's grandson went upstairs waiting earlier. You might check with him while you wait."

Grandson? Well, that beat me being a nephew. "Thank you. I'll go find him."

I headed to ICU on the second floor and reconnoitered a little. I might get lucky and find Billy still waiting to see Culpepper. He didn't know me without my old man disguise, so I could get close before he could run. I might be able to talk him down a little and get him out of the hospital quietly. How, I had no idea, but I didn't want a lot of drama.

On the short elevator ride up, I formulated my story. All I needed was one good enough to get him out of the hospital where I could tell him the rest. I had no idea what the "rest" was—*Hello, Mr. Piper. Did you notice people are trying to kill you? I'm here from some other people who aren't trying to kill you. They hired me to protect you. Shall we go?*

Who wouldn't go for that?

The ICU waiting area was empty. No Billy Piper. No cops. No "others" either.

I slumped into a chair where I could see the elevators at one end of the corridor and the stairwell entrance at the other end. The waiting area, an open alcove halfway down the hall, gave me the perfect view. While waiting, I checked in with the two most important people in my life—Tommy Astor and Janey-Lynn.

My call to Tommy went right to voicemail. Not surprising, so I left a message.

"Hey, Tommy, checking in. Your friend, Mr. Nobody, wasn't lying. Things are already getting heated. I have a good lead on my assignment. Soon as you can, call back. I want to know a little more backstory. The Marshals sent that cocky bastard from your office to beat the shit out of me this morning. Then, I was nearly killed falling ten floors off a balcony and almost shot before, during, and after. I figure a few more details couldn't hurt. Thanks."

Yeah, yeah, I only fell two floors. But a good story is important.

My second call connected with Janey-Lynn. "Hey, Janey-Lynn, it's—"

"Lowe? Where the devil are you? I got your message about Agent Evans. I guess that's sort of good news. More or less."

I wasn't so sure. "For now, yeah. If you hear from Evans again, let me know."

Her voice was strained. "Yes, of course. Lowe, there were more men here looking for you. I don't think they're cops or feds. They scared me. I told them to piss off, and they left. I just don't know how far they went."

Crap. "Are you okay?"

"Yes, yes. Bogart gave them the what-for." She paused. "I'm just gonna keep him close with me. Is that okay?"

"Absolutely." I considered how much to tell her. "Hey, about your stepson, Randy—"

"Oh, no." The tone in her voice was nervous, almost jittery. "I'm so sorry about him, Lowe. We need to talk when you get back. Are you okay? What have you gotten yourself into? It has to be bad, Lowe. Charlie's murders were bad enough. But those other men, they're not here about that, I'm sure."

Yeah, it was bad. Bad in that I was both a murder suspect and a target of untold numbers of angry people. They were shooting at me, and now I was balcony-challenged. All this was good, too—kinda. Good as in a boatload of money, good. Assuming, of course, that I lived.

"Don't worry about me, Janey-Lynn. What's the deal with Randy?"

She sighed but said nothing.

"Janey-Lynn?" I jumped into the deep end. "If you don't mind me saying, he's a shithead. What's wrong? I know something is bothering you. I can help."

"No. You don't have time to help right now." Her words were hard and pointed. "You worry about you. I know you're into something dangerous—probably dumb, too. All these men coming around and all. Let me guess—Tommy? You watch yourself, Lowe Curran. You owe me dinner, remember? *And* dessert. Lots and lots of dessert."

Gulp.

She chuckled, and that sent a twinge of discomfort up my spine. "Okay, Janey-Lynn. Are you going to be okay for a while? If those men show up again, call Tommy. If you want, I can send my buddy Stevie Keene down to house sit."

She hesitated for a long moment. "Of course I'm okay. I'm tough. I don't need any babysitter. We'll talk when you can get home. When do you think that will be?"

"Not sure." I checked the elevators and stairwell as I tried to put her off. "It might be a few days."

Oh, crapola.

"Lowe? Are you there?"

Shit. Shit. Shit.

"Gotta go, Janey-Lynn. Take care of Bogart. I'll be back when I can." I hung up and pocketed the phone, letting my other hand slide down to rest on my Kimber beneath my jacket.

Just exiting the stairwell, were my new nemeses, Levene and Freedman. They saw me, too, and froze. One leaned sideways and spoke to the other—who was who, I didn't know. But they were laser-focused on me. Their pace increased down the hall, making a beeline for me. A couple dozen paces away, they stopped and looked past me.

I stood and let them see my hand behind my back. *Careful boys, I don't play well with others.* Then I began to backpedal and glanced over my shoulder to follow their stare.

Emerging from the middle elevator was a short, round, frumpy guy with thinning hair and glasses. He carried a cup of coffee and a bag of food. His

203

cheeks were bulging with something smeared across his mouth.

Billy Piper.

As I turned to head for him, Levene and Freedman broke into a run.

At first, Billy was oblivious to the three of us descending on him. Then, he looked up from a huge, sugary pastry and locked eyes—first with me—then with Levene and Freedman. His face turned to pure terror—eyes wide, mouth open, face blanched. He dropped the coffee where it splattered on the tile floor, stuffed a huge piece of the pastry into his mouth, and backed into the closed elevator door.

"Billy," I shouted, "get back."

As he turned and frantically looked for an escape, the first elevator pinged and opened beside him. He jumped for the doors.

I was nearly airborne when I grabbed him, stuffed him into the elevator cab, and banged away on the close-door button. My legs and arms reminded me I'd recently fallen from the second-floor balcony, but they obeyed my commands under protest. Adrenalin was their master.

As the doors slid closed, Levene and Freedman reached us. One of them gripped the doors and tried to pry them open. Then, a gun slid between the doors at belly height.

"Billy, get back. Get low." I bit those little piggies, prying open the door as hard as I could. The hand jerked back. Then, I kicked at the barrel of the gun and knocked it back through the doors. They finally closed.

"What the hell, man?" Piper cried out, recognition flashing across his face. "You? It's you, isn't it? Damn, old dude. What do you want?"

"I'm Lowe Curran, Piper. I'm on your side."

"What?" Piper's eyeballs nearly popped out. "Did you say..."

"Lowe Curran." Not having a better introduction, I went with, "Billy, people are trying to kill you. Other people sent me to find you and protect you."

He stared, still chewing the pastry. Behind his eyes raged confusion. Those eyes were fixed on me with an intensity—fear—like a convicted murderer facing his sentence.

"Piper?" I grabbed his arm and shook him. "Come with me if you want to live!"—*Sorry, Arnold.*

Chapter Forty

Curran

The brief descent in the elevator was surreal. My left hand was locked around Piper's arm to ensure he wouldn't fight me or try to bolt the moment the elevator doors opened. My right gripped my holstered pistol and readied for what might be on the other side of those doors.

Piper was beyond panic. He stood in the corner of the cab, shaking and sweating with big, wide eyes locked on me. Terror streamed down his face and mixed with pastry filling, forming a glistening cherry ooze across his cheeks.

We rode in silence for those short moments.

When the elevator doors opened, I tugged on his arm. "Stay behind me, Billy. Do exactly what I say, and we might get out of here alive."

"Might?" His eyes bulged again. "I want nothing to do with you."

"Why not? I'm the good guys."

"There's more than just you?"

"No." I peeked out of the cab. "It's an expression."

"You weren't a good guy at my place the other night."

"Sure I was. You're still breathing, aren't you?" Tugging him along as inconspicuously as I could, I moved us through the lobby and out into daylight. "You'll have to trust me, Billy. I'll explain everything later—after we get somewhere safe."

"You almost got me killed before." He tripped several times, trying to keep up. "Let me go. Where will I be safe with you?"

Hell if I knew. I hadn't thought up that part of the plan yet.

I glanced over my shoulder a few times as we approached my Jeep. So far, Freedman and Levene were nowhere. Maybe hospital security caught them. Pulling a gun in the hallway was frowned upon.

Two gunshots split the air. The side window of an oversized pickup truck beside us shattered and rained glass on us. A third shot whistled past my head with only inches to spare and sent me diving for the pavement, pulling Billy down with me.

Son of a bitch!

I tugged out my pistol and chanced a peek over the hood of a car in front of us.

A fourth shot hit the pickup behind us again.

Two men—regrettably not Freedman and Levene—angled across the parking lot near the hospital entrance. Both had their guns up in firing position and neither seemed concerned with using them. I say regrettably not Freedman and Levene because these two made it four assassins coming at us. *Four.*

"Is it them," Billy cried, "from upstairs?"

"No." I shoved him ahead of me, below the hood of the truck. My Jeep was in the next space ahead, and I propelled him toward it. "It's two more of 'them.'"

"What?" He froze. "Two more? Who—"

"How do I know? You've pissed off a lot of people, Piper." I pushed him around the pickup's front fender, triggered my Jeep's remote lock, and yelled, "Get in."

He moved in frozen movements, mumbling something unintelligible—except for cussing me out. Even as I thrust my shoulder under his butt and drove him up and into the Jeep, he resisted. He nearly fell backward onto me.

Back in the day, the State Department provided me cool training about handling crisis situations like this. My favorite was dealing with protectees in said crisis. Sometimes, calm voices and kid gloves had to be abandoned for tough love and force of action. This definitely qualified as one of those situations.

Two more rounds cracked through the air. The shooters were just a few car lengths away now.

Sirens wailed in the distance.

Great. Four hitmen and now the cops. Of all the times I didn't want the cops to show up, this was one.

To slow the shooters, I popped up over my Jeep's hood, fired three rapid shots, and scurried around the vehicle. Another shot their way, and I climbed in behind the wheel. As I did, I heard someone shouting from the hospital entrance.

"Drop your weapons. Hands in the air."

Hospital security had arrived. They immediately engaged the two shooters.

The two assassins turned, fired at the approaching uniformed guards, and fled into the depths of the parking area.

"Keep your head down, Billy. Low as you can."

We were screeching out of the parking spot in a second. Wanting to look back but knowing the move could cause me to crash, I focused on our escape. Two turns later, we skidded out of the hospital compound onto George Mason Drive. Cars were coming—too close—and I braked hard to avoid a collision.

Mistake.

A large, dark SUV slid to a stop in front of us and blocked our path. The driver bound out and bent over its hood, aiming a pistol at us—at me.

Deputy US Marshal Terry Gallo.

Crapola. Was there anyone who didn't want to kill me today?

Billy looked over the dash. "Oh, shit, shit, shit. It's him. That's—"

"I know, Billy. Stay down."

"Turn off the vehicle, Curran," Gallo yelled. "Hands out the window where I can see them. Do it now."

With no options, I complied. Gallo had no sense of humor, and his gun was aimed at me. If he were really in a foul mood—say, not enough coffee this morning—he could put a dozen rounds in me before we got away.

Grant it, we were at a hospital, and I would get really good, fast trauma care. But still...

"Okay, Marshal. You got me." I put my hands out the Jeep window. "I don't know why you got me. But you got me."

He ignored me. "Piper, hands out the side window. Now."

"Do it, Billy. He's not as nice as me."

Billy's face contorted. "I know."

"Look, we can't trust the authorities, Billy." Of course, that's what Mr. Nobody said. For me, not trusting them meant I got the two-hundred grand. "Wait for my signal, and we'll get out of this."

"What signal?"

Gallo called out, "Curran, come out your door. Move slow and get around in front of your vehicle. Move now."

"Gallo, what do you want?" This was not going well. "I haven't done anything."

"You call that shootout at the Arlington Arms nothing?"

Wasn't he well-informed? "That wasn't me. I ran when the shooting started. I—"

"Out, Curran. Now."

I complied. I had no choice, and Gallo's voice didn't sound like he was willing to negotiate. As I moved around my Jeep and turned back to face my windshield, Gallo was on me like a vulture on a bunny carcass. He pressed his pistol into my neck, frisked me with his free hand, and relieved me of my pistol in seconds.

"Okay, Curran. You're coming in with me. I knew you were behind Piper's disappearance."

Me? "I didn't—"

"Forensics will prove you were in that shooting earlier. And now, with Piper, I've got you on federal charges."

Oh, sure, bring up forensics and federal stuff.

He bent me over the Jeep's hood and handcuffed me before I could say,

"Uncle." Then he grabbed the handcuff chain, pulled me backward, and marched me sharply to the rear door of his SUV.

"Hey, now, I thought we worked everything out, Marshal."

He opened the rear door. "Shut up and get in."

I resisted. "Look, I didn't hurt Madison. I stayed with her because she was afraid and left alone. I'm not jerking you around. She—"

"Leave Madi out of this." He shoved me backward into the SUV's rear seat. "Don't ever say her name again."

"She prefers Madison."

Crash...

The SUV jerked violently with the screech of shredding metal on metal. Its nose skidded across the road, and the vehicle rocked sideways. The violent wrenching sent me first backward in the seat and then forward again. I collided with Gallo and we both tumbled onto the pavement.

My Jeep smashed a second time into Gallo's front quarter panel, rammed clean through, and sped away down the street. It was around the next turn and gone before either Gallo or I could get to our feet.

Before driving out of sight, Piper's hand flashed out the driver's window and gave us the finger.

"Gee, Marshal," I said, finding a good laugh amongst the pain shooting through my already aching body. "I think your *protectee* just got away—again. And again, it's not my fault."

"Screw you, Curran."

I snorted another laugh, and it hurt to breathe. "I think you were supposed to have me drop my keys out the window before I got out. Then, you should have secured him before you manhandled me. Or is that too old school for you?"

The growl through his clenched teeth suggested it was not all that old school for him.

Chapter Forty-One

U.C.

From U.C.'s vantage point across 16th Street outside the Virginia Hospital Center, he watched the mayhem unleashed on Curran and Billy Piper—by his men. What should have been a simple snatch-and-grab operation turned into a running gunfight that was sure to bring dozens of law enforcement down on them in minutes. To make matters worse—if that were possible—as he started his four-by-four to insert himself in the battle and try to regain the advantage, Marshal Gallo appeared. In seconds, he'd boxed in Curran and Piper.

He couldn't get Piper first. If Piper returned to federal custody, his mission might fail.

No, there was hope.

As Gallo extracted Curran from his Jeep, he made a fatal flaw. That flaw left Piper in the vehicle alone. Gallo was so focused on Curran that he forgot basic law enforcement tactics. A moment later, Billy Piper escaped.

"You little bastard," U.C. said to himself, grinning. "You might have just saved my ass."

The sounds of police response filled the air from all directions.

Time to go.

He circled the hospital to the north side and watched for his two men to make their escape and head to their predetermined rendezvous.

For fifteen minutes, he weaved through Arlington traffic—three times, he pulled over or double-backed to check for surveillance. Finally, he arrived at the abandoned office building. He waited another five minutes and carefully checked the street and perimeter for any signs of trouble.

Clear.

He found his two men—Hodges and Wang—waiting exactly where he'd directed them to be in the abandoned office building's basement. The area hadn't seen more than rats and the occasional stray dog or cat in months. The only tracks that led to the far corner storage area belonged to his men.

He rapped twice on the old steel door. He waited. Then, he rapped once more before entering the storage area.

Metal racks littered with miscellaneous abandoned scrap and old machinery parts greeted him. Hodges and Wang sat on old, rickety office chairs adjacent to a stack of empty wood crates. Both men held semi-automatic pistols aimed at him as he turned the corner into the storage cavity and approached them. They eased, waved, and holstered their weapons as he stopped a dozen feet away.

"Sort of a mess at the hospital, boss," Wang said in an edgy voice. "Not our fault. Those two clowns came out of nowhere. We were watching them when your boy, Curran, showed."

U.C. glanced lazily around. "I should cut your fees in half for that bullshit. Tell me why I shouldn't."

Hodges smiled confidently. "Because we got the tracker put on Curran's car first, then put one on those other guys' ride. We had just placed it when Curran and Piper came out of the hospital. Two for one."

"I haven't gotten either, yet." U.C. studied them. "Are you sure both trackers are working? Do you know who those other two are?"

Hodges shook his head. "No, but they were at Piper's place earlier. We swung by to recheck the place before going after the old man. Curran and those other two were shooting it out at Piper's place. They lit out the moment the cops showed."

U.C. thought about that. "So, they're not cops or feds. Someone new?"

Both men shrugged.

"Let me see the tracker."

Wang lifted a shoulder bag from beneath his chair. He opened it, extracted a small cell phone-like device, and tossed it to him. "It's GPS. Range isn't an issue. Blue signal is those two clowns. Red is Curran's ride."

U.C. slipped the tracking receiver into his jacket pocket. As he did, his other hand tugged his silenced semi-automatic from his back and easily shot Hodges and Wang where they sat.

They both fell from their chairs, unmoving.

He approached them, did a meticulous search of each man to ensure there was nothing that might betray him, and picked up the shoulder bag.

Before he left the storage area, he put another round in each man's brain to ensure there were no lingering threats.

If you want to keep a secret, don't tell anyone. If you do, kill them.

Chapter Forty-Two

Ambassador McKnight

"Ambassador, I have developments you should hear." R. Bryan Scott walked into the Ambassador's den with a gleeful look on his face. "I've just gotten off the phone with my contact in the West Wing."

The Ambassador lifted his eyes when his aide stopped in front of his large antique desk. For a long moment, he watched the man, trying to decide the gravity of the information simply by Scott's body language. The arrogant, ladder-climbing younger man had proven his worth since joining his team in Athens as a political operative, though his ego and methods often got in the way of the Ambassador's own plans.

"What is it?"

Scott didn't sit. He tried to control a smile from appearing on his face. He failed. "First, as I think you already know, Senator Wain was found dead this morning of an apparent suicide."

"Yes, terrible business." The Ambassador considered him. "A man's death shouldn't give you joy, Bryan."

Scott nodded, but the smile didn't fade. "General Alvarez just left the president. He declined consideration for the vice presidency."

The Ambassador steepled his hands on the desk. "How very coincidental—"

"No coincidence, sir," Scott said. "Not considering your visit yesterday. I'd say Piccolo is eliminating his biggest threats."

"That's a dangerous accusation, Bryan." The Ambassador's eyebrows rose noticeably. "His biggest threats?"

"I meant only that..." Scott's face tightened. "I meant he removed two off the shortlist already. He's waiting on you to make a move. You'll be next."

"Yes. I'm sure he is. Assuming, of course, that it *is* Piccolo. Have you traced that barbarian from yesterday?"

Scott shook his head. "Nothing. Not even a hint. I'm still working on it, sir. Thank you for allowing me to handle this without the authorities."

"Continue on—for now. If you find anything, you will not move until I am informed. Is that clear? I must weigh the consequences of not working with the authorities. I must consider the president in this play."

Scott cocked his head. "Sir? I think you continue to let me handle it and stay clear. I would prefer not to involve you in the day-to-day—"

"No. Sometimes, allowing your adversaries to play their roles—when you know what those roles are—is more powerful a defense than any other."

"Yes, sir." Scott looked at him, then the floor, and finally back at him. "But, at some stage, you'll have to step out of the way and let me protect you."

"I will, Bryan. I will." The Ambassador found his aide's eyes. "Is there anything else?"

Scott's lips parted, but he said nothing.

"Bryan?"

Scott frowned. "About the president, sir, and the authorities. I don't think we should alert them even after we identify who's responsible."

"No? Isn't that a sizable risk?"

"I've got a plan to contain the risk, sir." Scott stepped a little closer to the desk. "The president will demand the FBI or Secret Service be involved. Therefore, I suggest we not tell him."

The Ambassador leaned back. "Explain, Bryan."

Scott contemplated the floor again. When he looked back at the Ambassador, his confidence was chiseled across his face. "Allowing this to play out is our best offense. After all, if you are the president's V.P. replacement, you'll be on your way to the White House in short order.

Playing this situation—"

"Strength and strategy." The Ambassador grinned wryly. "Help uncover the crime and thwart it ourselves? Yes, I see your point, Bryan. Control is power. Excellent suggestion."

Scott allowed himself a broad, prideful smile. "Thank you, sir. From you, that is a compliment. We're agreed? I'll control this from our end. Our own people?"

The Ambassador nodded. "Agreed."

"I've got some private protective agents coming to handle the house. Also, a detail to accompany you outside the residence. They will be very discreet, sir."

The Ambassador considered that. "If you must. Private contractors, Bryan, and not an army. I need my privacy."

Scott cast a confident nod. "Of course, sir. I have contacts—"

"I know full well your reach, Bryan." The Ambassador held up a finger. "Get at least one operative—a female—for Abby when she goes out. I don't want her to be caught up in this. Whatever this is."

A voice from the doorway startled them both. "What is for me when I go out?"

Abby walked into the room with a tray of coffee and sandwiches.

"I'm bringing on additional security," the Ambassador said matter-of-factly. "You'll have someone assigned—"

"Don't be silly, Bradley." She set the tray down on a server near the window. "I've lived and worked in the same dangerous places you have. Longer, too. I can take care of myself. But thank you nonetheless."

The Ambassador rose and walked to her as she poured coffee. "Abby, listen to me. Until we know who and what is coming our way, it's best you allow me—"

"No. That's all there is to it." With that, she turned and strode from the room.

"Sir?" Scott asked in her wake.

The Ambassador blustered a wave after her. "Do it anyway. I'll be damned that woman bests me."

216

"Of course. I think it might be wise if we paid this expense from one of the outside accounts, sir. You know, so the press or authorities don't get wind of it too soon."

The Ambassador turned away, signaling the end of their meeting. R. Bryan Scott was just the man he'd hoped. Thorough. Intelligent. Protective. Above all, shrewd. If things worked out over the next few months, he might just position him in a more senior role in his office. How very coincidental that he had hired Scott away from Jameson Wain so many years ago. But then, political operatives moved through political circles like piranha, looking for lunch.

Chapter Forty-Three

Curran

I'd been sitting in the holding cell at the Marshal's office for over an hour. I thought Gallo would drag me into his Eastern District office in Alexandria. He didn't. Instead, I was in this small field office not far from the hospital. It was in a nondescript office building just off Interstate 395 and Seminary Road. But it had all the comforts of home—underground parking, nice quiet elevators, deluxe accommodations in the three-cell holding area, and a pretty receptionist sitting behind bullet-resistant glass just off the lobby. If I hadn't been in handcuffs, I might have asked her out.

No, really. I would have.

The entire situation confused me, to be honest. Marshals are mostly tasked with protecting the federal judiciary, handling federal prisoners, hunting down fugitives, and of course, WITSEC. Nowhere in my memory banks did it report the Marshals investigated apartment break ins, computer hackers, missing IT nerds, or hospital shootouts. I might have missed that in the Virginia private investigators training program—the one I never took. For now, I had no clue why I was in so much trouble with Gallo. Why he was involved in anything other than locating Piper was a mystery to me. And why was he taking such a keen interest in me? Back at the hospital, he was more interested in grabbing me than Billy Piper—his missing WITSEC protectee. That cost him dearly when Piper escaped.

As far as I knew, I haven't done anything to put me on the Ten Most

Wanted list. Even if Evans thinks I might have. My aging memory did slip from time-to-time—normally as I left one room for another. Still, I'm pretty sure I'd recall committing an international felony or going on a crime spree across the nation.

When a young Deputy Marshal retrieved me from my cell and stuffed me rudely into a chair in a nearby interrogation room, I figured I was about to find out. The room was TV show perfect. A four-by-three-foot table with two chairs on either side of it. There was a microphone and speaker sitting in the middle of the table with the green light already on. On the right-side wall was the observation window made of one-way glass that allowed shy people to observe my meeting with Gallo. In fact, he was probably on the other side of the glass, watching me squirm right then.

"Is someone going to tell me why I'm here?" I said to the junior deputy as he handcuffed me to a security bar affixed to the interrogation table. "I'm the victim in this. Those guys were shooting at me—at us. All I did was try to keep Piper alive. I did it all for you guys. You're welcome."

Facts are facts. They were true. Maybe they weren't all the facts. But they were true, nonetheless—well, most of them.

"Shut up," the deputy spat.

He left, and before the interrogation room door closed, Gallo entered. Odd, too, as he didn't carry the obligatory stack of files that were supposed to intimidate me into confessing to being an international terrorist or something. He didn't bring coffee for me but had a cup for himself. Most strangely, he instantly dropped the interior blinds over the observation window and clicked off the speaker and microphone in the middle of the interrogation table.

That concerned me. Either he was very shy, or he didn't want witnesses to my escape attempt that would leave me dead on the floor. My gut churned, and I concluded my escape was imminent. Gallo wasn't the shy type.

"Look, Gallo—"

"Shut up, Curran." He sat in the chair facing me and leaned back, arms folded across his chest and a dull, sardonic grin escaping his mouth. "I talk. You listen. Got it?"

"Sure, okay."

"You got into a shooting match at the Arlington Arms apartments earlier this morning. Not coincidentally at Billy Piper's place."

Silence was my friend.

"You got into another shootout outside the Virginia Hospital Center with two unidentified gunmen. Billy Piper was involved. Another not-coincidence."

I liked silence.

"Once again, Billy Piper is missing. The common denominator in all this chaos is you."

Silence is important.

"Come on, Curran. Time to own up to it. It's just you and me in here. What the hell are you into?"

I had a little dilemma. Mr. Nobody warned me not to allow the cops or anyone else to know my mission. At the moment, if I didn't come up with a good story, I'd be locked up. Or maybe dead on the interview room floor after my faux attempted escape. If that happened, I'd have trouble finding Piper. No Piper, no two hundred thousand. I thought fast and decided to thread the needle.

"Look, Marshal, I'm the victim—twice. I went to the Arlington Arms to locate Piper. Two shooters came at me, not the other way around. Same thing at the hospital. I went there hoping to interview Culpepper—to find Piper—and two more guys came at me. Both teams tried to kill us."

"What are you doing chasing Piper? He's a federal witness. You have no business—"

"Oh, come on." I put on my best angry face. It was easy. I was pissed. "We both know he hacked TAE. I was sent to find him, remove the ransomware, and retrieve their data. You accused me of killing him. So, the best way to prove my innocence is to prove he's alive."

Oh, shit. Tommy was going to be pissed.

"So, TAE was hacked? You lied to me before. So did Astor."

Crap. "Okay, we weren't exactly forthcoming. I don't think it's a crime to *not* report being a victim, is it? The Feebies weren't really interested in helping, and I'd already gotten the TAE system back from Piper. You guys tried to bully Tommy. What did you expect?"

"Semantics. Games." Gallo's face was apple red. "Don't play me, Curran. If you'd told me the truth—"

"Bullshit. Piper was already missing. We had nothing to do with that."

Gallo leaned back again. He stared bullets through me for a long time. Finally, he said, "Two assailants at the apartment? Two at the hospital. Which ones tried to kill you and Piper at the hospital?"

"Let me explain." If it got any more complicated, I'd ask for a whiteboard and draw some stick figures. "The two guys at the apartment were there at the hospital when Piper showed up—their names were Levene and Freeman. That's all I got about them. At the hospital, we made a run for it. Then, two more shooters—a different two—came at us in the parking lot. So, in truth, four shooters were trying to get us. The two from the apartment and two new ones."

I gave him a physical description of Levene and Freedman. It couldn't hurt, and maybe he could run interference or something.

"Four different assailants?"

I nodded. "Well, technically, two teams of two. But, yeah, four." I considered giving him Clue's Butler, Wadsworth's, 'One plus two plus two plus one,' just to lighten the mood. Naw, I'd save that for another time.

"Why?"

"You tell me." I shrugged. "All I wanted from Piper was to clear my name."

Gallo grinned sarcastically. "About Piper, maybe. You're still a person of interest in the Cantrell murders."

Like I said, well informed. "Yeah, true. Face it, though. Piper is my alibi for Cantrell, too. Not to mention, I'll be cleared shortly. But since you know about me and him meeting at his Leesburg place, you can be my alibi, too."

"Hah, in your dreams. Get back to Piper."

Testy, wasn't he? "You know, I actually saved Piper's life at the hospital. You lost him again, not me. I was on my way to you with him when you stopped us. It's on you that he got away. It's a shame he didn't want to go with you. I wonder why."

Gallo jumped up, cursing and mumbling. Maybe he was chanting my last rites.

"I didn't break any laws, Marshal. All I did was defend myself and your missing witness. We escaped two teams of shooters—the hospital CCTV and any witnesses will prove that. Unfortunately, you let Piper escape. God only knows if the shooters already caught him again."

"You better hope they haven't."

"Why? You saw me saving him. He was alive when he left. If he shows up dead, now, you know I didn't do it. I've been here with you in custody." Facts are important.

Those facts sent him into a deeper, darker mood. He slammed his palms on the table and leaned over it, breathing fire at me. "Those guys could be working with you."

How stupid was that?

"So, they tried to kill me for what? Theater?" When he leaned back and cursed again, I added, "He's probably already dead. What are you gonna charge me with? Refusing to get shot?"

"Screw you, Curran."

Now, it was my turn to lean back and be contemplative. I folded my arms the best I could, given the handcuff holding one to the table. I was winning this debate. "Look, you're my alibi that I had nothing to do with his death or disappearance—whichever it ends up being. Like I said, the hospital will have plenty of witnesses and video that shows me protecting him up to the point you let him escape."

Maybe rubbing his nose in his mistake wasn't the best strategy. Though, it was fun.

"I'll find something to charge you with. Maybe discharging a firearm in the city. Breaking and entering. Interference in a federal investigation. Federal witness tampering." He forced a fake smile. "I'll put you in jail forever."

"What's with you, Gallo?" I thrust myself forward. "I have nothing to do with Piper's situation. He hacked us. Seems like you—his WITSEC handler—should have known that and done something about it. Doesn't that make you a co-conspirator? Maybe you're an accessory? I bet Tommy Astor's lawyer can make hay with that one. Is that why the interview room blinds are down and the recordings off?"

His face darkened, and the words that gushed out were very unflattering. Me. A goat. Unnatural sexual things. You understand. Oh, and murder and obstruction, too.

"I want a lawyer. I'll have Tommy Astor get one for me."

"I'm not afraid of Astor. It's you I want."

"Why? I never heard of you until this started. Since when do Marshals investigate all this crap? You got a beef with me, Gallo. I don't know what it is, but it's deep, and you're going out of your way to tie me up. I'll warn you for free—if you screw with me, you screw with Tommy Astor. Do that, and you'll be a crossing guard in no time."

He actually laughed. "He can't get you off a federal charge of witness tampering. All his friends in high places won't like that one."

Wow, he was reaching. "We both know Piper had video cameras all over his place. Okay, I was there. I was recovering information he hacked from TAE. When I left, he was not only alive but freaking out because someone else was coming for him. That night, I thought he was full of shit. Obviously, he wasn't. I'm sure it's all on tape. How is it you didn't know he was in the hacking business again? Or did you? Were you getting a cut?"

He sat there, staring at me. His eyes never blinked, and I wasn't even sure he was breathing. I think I hit all the right buttons to give him a lot to think about. All facts he already knew, sure. But sometimes, you have to hear what you already know from someone else before you actually know it.

"Curran, I'm going to bury you." His phone buzzed, and he slid it out of his leather jacket pocket. Before he tapped on the screen, he added, "Piper is still missing—he's in trouble. By all accounts, in more trouble than from just me. When I find him, if he says one word that's different than your story, I'll get you the needle."

The needle again. What is it with everyone I know trying to get me lethal injection? "If you want that, you better find him, then. He could already be face down in the Potomac while you piss around bullying me."

Gallo ignored me and finally looked at his cell phone. Whatever the message, it had his full attention. Things didn't seem good. His face blanched, and stared with dead eyes. He paced the cell a couple times and kept reading his phone. He cursed and mumbled as his demeanor descended into rage. Then, he went to the interrogation room door and opened it.

The young deputy was just outside. Gallo said something into his ear. Whatever it was made, the other deputy recoil.

"Are you sure, Marshal Gallo? What about his gun? What about the shooting charges?"

"Release him." Gallo jammed a finger into the younger's shoulder. "Just do it, Aguillo. Now. Put this all on me. I got it all wrong, and we have the wrong guy."

Something was going on, and it was terribly wrong. Was this a trap? Was I about to pretend-escape? There was plenty of water in the Potomac for two bodies, after all.

To Deputy Aguillo, he said, "I'm gone for the rest of the day. Get him outta here." Gallo spun toward me. "Curran, you're free to go. Get your belongings from Aguillo. Get the hell out of here fast before I change my mind."

I wasn't a religious man, but someone was looking out for me. Thank God my old bones were moving good and fast just then.

Chapter Forty-Four

Curran

As I collected my things, astonishingly enough, they included my Kimber and spare magazines from the deputies, I noticed my personal cell phone had a dozen missed calls. All from Tommy Astor. Then, looking at the phone, a realization hit me like a gut punch. My go-bag was in my Jeep. In it was my extra cash, Mr. Nobody's satellite phone, and other fun stuff that I desperately needed. My Jeep, if you haven't been paying attention, was somewhere in the Washington Metro area under the control of Billy Piper. Piper was on the run from at least two sets of bad guys—all killers. He was also avoiding me and Gallo. Not that I blame him. If I was him, I'd run from Gallo, too. Still, without my Jeep and my go-bag, I was screwed.

Two hundred thousand bucks were slipping through my fingers.

As I stood outside the Marshal's office, I contemplated my next move. Since my Mr. Nobody phone was in my Jeep, I couldn't report in. It had been nearly ten hours since I'd last done so. That was six hours too long. I didn't know Mr. Nobody, but I knew he wasn't a patient man. He didn't like to be ignored. However, there was no better way to make him a happy camper than to report in next time that I had Billy Piper in hand.

My big dilemma—or two big dilemmas—might make that tough. I had no vehicle and only about two hundred bucks in cash in my wallet. My credit cards were maxed out. I should have paid them off sooner, but you know, eating and paying for gas for my Jeep to make money cost money, too. Those pesky credit card companies were like shylocks—the vig took up almost as much as I could afford to pay each month. My second problem was that I had no idea where to begin searching for Piper. I had no way of going after him. If I didn't figure it out, Gallo, or the two teams of shooters, might beat me to him and it was all for nothing.

Gallo? What exactly happened inside the Marshal's office just now? He received a message, and he immediately tossed me aside like I wasn't important anymore. Until that message, I'd been the focus of his hatred. Then, bam, he took the rest of the day off. Whatever had been in that message was bad news for him.

I hope it wasn't Piper's body with a big hole in his head.

I had to get a car. I had to find Piper. I had to save my money. *Stat.*

With no options, I pulled out my cell and looked for a cab—at least they still took cash. Uber or one of those other rideshares only worked with credit cards. We already discussed the state of mine. There was only one person to call—Tommy Astor.

"Good God almighty, Lowe," he sputtered. "Why haven't you checked in or answered your sat phone? Our mutual friend is furious."

Damn, they've been trying to find me. "Sorry. I'm running down leads. The sat phone's in my Jeep, and I'm not. I'm checking in with you now."

"Jiminy Cricket, Lowe," he growled. "You're not supposed to check in with me. With him. I wasn't supposed to get involved anymore. Our friend had to call me. I've been waiting for you to return my call. Why are you at the Galleria in Tysons Corners?"

The Galleria? "Tommy, why do you think I'm at the Galleria?"

"Because you are." He flustered a bit. "When you wouldn't answer the satellite phone, I had it traced."

I bet Mr. Nobody traced me. That might be tough to explain later. But still, problem solved. I knew where Billy Piper was. At least, a few minutes ago.

"Sorry about the check-ins. Things got away from me. I'll do better."

"Yes, all right. I'll call our friend and tell him you're working it—hard. Is everything okay? No problems?"

"Too many problems to go into now." No time to waste chatting. "I gotta go, Tommy."

"Lowe," Tommy said in a concerned voice, "I can tell you're in deep shit. Keep your head on a swivel. Watch your back."

Good advice. "Thanks. Am I still at the mall?"

"Yes, why? Aren't you—"

"Gotta go. Thanks, Tommy." I tapped off my call.

I headed for the street corner to find a cab and was nearly flattened by not one, not two, but *three* tour buses rampaging down the boulevard. They were stuffed with tourists headed for D.C., I'm sure. I doubted anyone would have noticed if the bus squished me on the hot pavement except for a ripple in their caramel mocha cashew whipped cream iced lattes.

Surviving that summer ritual assault, an Alexandria taxi rolled by, and I flagged it down.

He had the good manners to skid to a stop a few feet away and nearly back over me as I tried to reach the side door.

Have I mentioned Virginia traffic?

The cabby grunted something when I told him the Galleria and started the meter. He immediately returned to his own cell phone, where he had a rapid conversation with someone in a language I'd never heard. Before we wheeled away from the curb, he was oblivious to me in the back seat, sloshing back and forth as he blindly serpentined through traffic.

As I sloshed sideways in the cab and banged my head on the door window, I wasn't sure who I should fear more—the four gunmen hunting Piper or Mustafa the cabby.

Chapter Forty-Five

Billy Piper

Billy Piper worked on his milkshake with vigor, slurping it through the straw like an eight-year-old. All the while, his eyes darting about, searching the crowds, looking for the next wave of assassins. His burger and fries were gone, and the last of three bags of potato chips was open and nearly empty, too. Most people in life-threatening situations lose their appetites. Not him. His grew exponentially to the situation. He'd probably gained twenty pounds since this whole thing began.

Piper had always wished himself a swashbuckling adventurer. The three-J's—James Bond, Jason Borne, and Jack Reacher—were his idols. He'd read and seen every book and movie about them. He lost himself in those stories, those character's lives. He'd wished—prayed—for a taste of their lives. With few friends and less family, books and movies were his only haven.

And computers.

Until the Russians caught him hacking them. Then, he'd realized that the world of make-believe adventure wasn't as sexy as it seemed. It was scary and dangerous. He'd spent a year hiding under the Marshal's protection. Months feeling anxious every time he'd stepped outside. Every knock on his door or a car stopping nearby. Slowly, over time he realized he was lost among the anonymous, He was safe. It was then that the three-J's called to him—*come on, Billy, do it, you're one of us. Go after it all. Take it. Do it...they'll never find you again. Never.*

Someone did. The Russians? Maybe, but unlikely. It was more assuredly connected to Whisper. Whatever that was, it might cost him his life. He had to find a way to broker what he had into safety.

James, Jason, and Jack could do nothing to save him. He had to do it himself.

Sweat pooled around his eyes, and he wiped it away, glancing around the food court. He sat in the narrow metal chair, his back to the side wall, eyeing everyone who neared him. The Galleria, one of two indoor multi-level malls in Tysons Corner, Virginia, was bustling as always. The Galleria was crushed with shoppers, retirees on their daily indoor walks, and teenagers milling about in their social cliques, accomplishing nothing.

He'd chosen the Galleria for anonymity. He could hide in plain sight until he developed a plan. He'd tucked the old Jeep between two large trucks in the parking garage, hoping it might not be noticed. Then, having searched the vehicle, he discovered that crazy old guy's black backpack. It was full of equipment and personal belongings. None of that was as important as the nearly ten-thousand dollars of cash and the satellite phone. Reason made him strap the backpack on when he entered the mall. It lay between his legs now, with his knees clamped around it.

Ninety-seven hundred dollars would help a lot now. Besides, it was probably part of the money the old man had taken from him, claiming it as a gift. It was not a gift. It was a plea bargain for his life.

The odd guy at the hospital was some kind of spy, for sure. The backpack proved that—ammunition, binoculars, a lockpick kit, survival knife, and other items all spelled spy. Spelled trouble. He was the same old guy who'd found him at his secret Leesburg rambler. His operations center that even Marshal Gallo hadn't discovered. That old man knew subterfuge and was sharp and tough. That other night, he'd entered his house as a doddering, feeble-minded old man. In moments, he'd morphed into a dangerous, exacting operative, trained and focused.

He hadn't had a chance.

That old spy was on his trail again and had caught up to him at the hospital. It might only be a matter of time before he found him a third time. Was he coming to kill him?

The spy claimed he was sent to protect him. He'd fought off those other two assassins at the hospital. He'd fought the two others in the parking lot, too. He wasn't sure, but one of the assassins in the hospital parking lot looked like one of those at his apartment complex last night—one of the men who shot Mr. Culpepper.

"Jesus," Billy muttered to himself, "how many people are trying to kill me?"

He slurped the strawberry shake again and slipped the satellite phone from his pocket. He checked the crowd of teenagers milling everywhere. Around them, mothers chased toddlers around the food court. Nothing seemed awry.

Except for that crazy old man who was not a crazy old man at all. *Curran. He said his name was Lowe Curran.* He knew that name, and that terrified him more than perhaps anything else.

He'd given Curran—when he was a gun-toting old man feigning Alzheimer's—the computer files he'd demanded. They included stolen data, the ransomware unlock codes, and his twenty-five grand. He'd not cheated him at all. Yet now, Curran—as a gun-toting spy—was on his tail. Was Curran after him because he'd hacked information on him and the others? Or was Curran after him because of what the data revealed about *him?*

Sweat poured down his cheeks, and he shook himself. "Come on, Billy. Hold it together."

The phone vibrated in his hand, and he looked at the screen. There were a dozen unread text messages—*You are late checking in, Curran...Report... Report...Where are you, Curran?...What is your status...Report...*on and on. It was the last message, sent just a few moments ago, that sent his blood pressure into the red zone—*Curran, TA provided update. Report immediately. Do you have the target? Target must not be compromised by anyone else. Report immediately.*

Sweet Jesus. Lowe Curran wasn't just *any* spy. He was an assassin. An assassin sent by whoever was on the other end of this satellite phone. The assassins at his apartment. The assassins at the hospital. The target was *him.*

Jesus, Curran's after me.

He reread the messages. Then, without thinking, he typed a response— *Who is this? Why do you want me? I haven't done anything to you.*

He waited and waited. No response. Nothing.

Then, it struck him like a train. In every modern spy movie he'd ever seen, the bad guys traced people using only their cell phones. Even turning it off wouldn't stop them. After he'd sent that text, they knew exactly where he was.

His breath seized as the sweat poured from his brow. He had to wipe his eyes again to allow them to focus.

Dammit, Billy, you just killed yourself.

He dropped the satellite phone onto the floor and crushed it beneath his foot. It took him three heel-stomps before he was satisfied it was truly dead. For good measure, he gathered up the pieces and discarded them in a nearby trash bin.

"Jesus, what am I going to do?" he said aloud. Then his blood chilled. "This was about Whisper. Whisper had to involve the Russians. Semenov found me. Oh, dear God. No. Everyone wants me dead."

"Not everyone, kid," a voice said from behind him. "I'm glad you're still here. I was afraid I missed you."

He spun in the seat, knocked the remains of his shake onto the floor, and nearly screamed.

Oh, shit, shit, shit...him.

Chapter Forty-Six

Curran

"Miss me?" I clamped a tight grip onto Piper's shoulder. "We need to get out of here, Piper. I warned you. There're people trying to kill you. Not me, though. Believe that. I'm here to protect you."

"Damn, you." Piper's eyes were as big as dinner plates and staring at me. "How, ah, how did you find me?"

"Magic."

"Huh?"

"Relax, Billy. I'm on your side. I'm gonna get you outta here. Fast and quiet. Do you understand?"

He shook his head. "What's going on? Why is everyone trying to kill me? Why are you?"

"Truth is, kid, I don't know." I pulled him to his feet and grabbed my go-bag off the floor, shouldered it on my left, and nudged him toward the exit. "Those other men are going to find you if we don't go to ground. You have to trust me."

"Trust you?" Piper stopped moving and twisted to face me. "Are you with Semenov?"

"Who? No. I'm not with whoever that is. Now, shut up. Do as I tell you." I scanned the crowd, looking for threats. "We're moving."

"No." Billy refused my nudge forward and slipped his hand beneath his windbreaker. "Are you—"

"Don't do that, Billy." I dug my fingers into his shoulder and made him wince. "Touch the gun, and I will kill you. I'm here to help you, honest. Trust me, and you'll get outta this. Screw with me and you're dead. It's that simple."

Anger filled his face. "I don't trust you, Curran. Not one bit."

I leaned close and liberated his pistol from him, tucking it into my side waistband.

"Tough. You're coming anyway." I scanned the crowd again, and the most threatening thing was a band of wild teenagers playing grab ass at the food court entrance. "Where's my Jeep?"

He was rigid. "Why should I tell you anything?"

"Don't. You can stay on your own and get shot full of holes." I released his shoulder. "If I was going to kill you, I would have in your basement. I didn't. I saved you earlier. Choose. Me or bullets."

It took him only a second. "Your POS is hidden in the parking garage."

"No shit, which one?"

He gestured deeper into the mall toward the north entrance. "The other side."

"Walk." If I recalled the mall map I'd skimmed on my way in, there was an administration hallway fifty yards or so ahead. Down that hall, was a maintenance door leading into the parking area."

He slowly shuffled forward. "Is Curran your real name?"

"Yeah, why?"

"Oh, shit." His face blanched. "If you gave me your real name, you'll have to kill me. Right?"

"No, you idiot." I nudged him forward faster, taking another grasp of his arm, a half-step behind with my other hand, ready to grab my pistol if trouble found us. "That's only in movies."

"Yeah? Really?"

"No, I lied." I shoved him again. "But like I said, I could have killed you the other night."

He relaxed a bit.

We reached the metal maintenance door at the far end of the administration hall just as a voice called out from behind us.

"Freeze! US Marshal!"

Piper jerked himself free of my grasp and spun to look back.

There, at the hall entrance, stood Marshal Gallo.

"Marshal, help," he yelled. "He's got a gun. He's forcing me to do this."

"You dumbass," I growled.

As Gallo started forward, I kicked the emergency bar and knocked the maintenance door open. Then, I yanked Piper back around and propelled him through the open doors. "Gallo's not one of the good guys, Piper. Let's go."

"Stop and drop your weapon." Gallo was running now. "Stop, Curran. Don't make this worse."

I negotiated Piper around a row of dumpsters and out the walled-in maintenance area to the sidewalk behind the mall. As we approached the roadway, I thrust him forward, almost off his feet.

"My Jeep? Where is it?"

He pointed across the perimeter road separating the mall from the parking structure. "Up...up...second floor near the stairs."

The stair entrance was just ahead. I ran, dragging him behind me, to the stairs and up. As we reached the entrance, Gallo emerged from the walled-in dumpster area.

A large delivery truck pulled up to the sidewalk in front of him and blocked his view.

I shoved him into the stairway and drove him forcefully upward.

As promised, my Jeep was right around the corner from the stairwell. Luckily, Piper had the sense to pull my keys from his pockets and dangled them to me. I grabbed them, stuffed him into the passenger front seat, and ran around to the driver's side.

In a moment, we were screeching out of the parking lot and out into Tysons Corner traffic.

After several blocks and dozens of turns and maneuvers, I sped down the ramp onto the Dulles Access Road and headed west toward the airport.

I constantly checked for Gallo. He was nowhere to be seen.

Luck or divine intervention prevailed. I was going with luck. If there was such a thing as divine intervention, I'm sure I've used my allotment by now.

Chapter Forty-Seven

Curran

"Well, that was easier than I thought," I said to Piper as I wheeled into Katelyn Astor's parking space. "We can't stay long. Gallo will look for us here. But, I need to get a new vehicle."

"Easy?" Piper twisted in the seat. "Are you kidding me? If those assassins don't kill me, your driving will."

Funny, I'd thought the same thing about Mustafa the cabby earlier.

"Stop complaining." I took Piper's arm and steered him toward TAE's entrance. I checked behind me to make sure Gallo hadn't beaten us here. "Listen good, Piper. I'm the only thing keeping you alive. My contract is to do just that. This place is safe long enough for me to get new transportation. Oh, and you owe me a new Jeep."

"New?" He wrinkled up his brow. "That piece of shit was—"

"Shut it. From now on, don't speak. You won't move without me moving you. You won't even pee without permission. Got it?"

"Yeah, yeah." He rolled his eyes. "I've seen the movie. Look, if I have a vote, I don't want anything to do with you—"

"You don't have a vote." I shoved him through the doors into TAE's lobby. "Think of it this way: you're still alive. Be happy."

He nodded.

"Think about that."

"Maybe." He considered that. "Okay, but the day is young."

"I'm not. So cut the cheap movie lines and do as I say."

I nodded to the receptionist who knew me on sight, prodded Piper ahead of me, and made our way down the main corridor to the rear of the building. There, I keyed into the last door on the right and shoved Piper into my office. Well, not truly *my* office, but my office space. Tommy let me use it whenever I needed one. That was often and I needed an address other than my barn loft to conduct business. Our deal since he retained me had been simple. Tommy Astor's needs came before anyone else's needs. After all, he had me on retainer. When I had free time—which was about three weeks a month—I worked for anyone who wasn't a competitor or problem for Tommy. This office gave me an "official" place to do business and to handle Tommy's many little projects.

Truth was, Tommy gave me use of the office to keep track of me and my other clients. He wanted to ensure his investment was safe and that I didn't bring him trouble. While we trusted each other, he kept track of me, and I checked for eavesdropping devices in my office every few months. I've never found any. But that didn't mean things wouldn't change.

Trust by mutual suspicion.

Yes, I'm a bit paranoid. My scars and occasional limp were the reason. Oh, and the dozens of "others" trying to kill me.

"Sit over there." I pushed Piper toward a narrow sofa that doubled as a bed for me when long hours kept me from home. "Don't leave this office. Don't answer the door. Don't—"

"Okay, okay." He threw up his hands. "I get it."

Next, I checked my backpack contents, or the lack of contents. That was a gut punch. "Where's my satellite phone? There's five hundred bucks that's missing from my stash."

Piper glanced around, trying to locate a safe reply.

"Piper?"

He shrugged. "I spent some money trying to hide out. Oh, and on lunch. A big lunch."

Lunch? "How did you spend five hundred bucks on lunch?"

"Screw you, Curran." He grinned an antagonizing grin. "It was probably my money anyway."

I flashed up my hand. "Where's my SAT phone?"

"Ah, yeah." He grinned again—I was already hating that sarcastic, 'screw you' grin. "You got a text. A lot of them. You were late checking in, and they wanted an update. Oh, and they asked if you got *me* yet."

Sweet holy crap. "Where's the damn phone?"

"Gone." He forced a faux giggle. "I answered the texts and smashed it."

My heart stopped. All I could think about was how much this was going to piss off Mr. Nobody. That is, if I ever heard from him again—or my two hundred thousand bucks.

"That was my lifeline. Our lifeline. What the hell were you thinking?"

"Are you kidding me?" He jumped up. "You're toxic, man. Toxic. First, you break into my place. You robbed me. Then, you chased me. Those hitmen chased me—"

"I'm not a hitman." Though at the moment, it was tempting. "I'm who's keeping you alive."

He shrugged indifferently. "Everyone wants me dead. You got to me first. That text asked if you had me and that I was not to be taken by anyone else. It sounds like I am dead either way. They can trace you by cell phone. If the Russian mob…"

Russian mob? "Look, Piper. I don't think the Russian mob is after you. Well, maybe they are. But I'm not them. Those texts you saw are from the people paying me to keep you alive."

"I don't believe you." He dropped back onto the couch. "I'm dead. That's all that matters. I smashed your phone to keep them from finding me. Except, you found me."

I hope Mr. Nobody wasn't going to deduct that satellite phone from my pay. Those things are expensive.

Something struck him, and he snapped his arms folded. "Look, Curran. I gave you everything you asked for the other night. Everything. You took my money—"

"You gifted it to me."

"Whatever." He rolled his eyes. "I did everything you asked. You still tied me up and shot at me."

He had me there. "But I didn't kill you. Did I? I was making a point not to follow me. Get over it. I left you alive."

"You almost got me killed." His eyes were telling me he wasn't lying. "I no sooner got out of there when those other guys showed up and busted down my back door. They were there to kill me."

Boy, was he fixated on dying.

To change the subject, I asked, "Hey, by the way, how'd you get out of my flex cuffs?"

"A trick I saw on the internet. It works, too." He self-consciously rubbed his wrists. "Hurt like hell, dude. I almost dislocated my thumb."

"Sorry, *dude*." I wasn't, but it was the thought that counted. "If I'd known I was going to be paid to save your butt today, I'd have just taken you with me."

He cocked his head. "Who's paying you? Why?"

Really good questions. Wish I had the answers.

"Don't worry about that." For a long time, I watched him watching me. Oddly enough, I felt a little sorry for the fat little geek—angry, arrogant, and smart-mouthed as he was. "All that's important is that I'm here to keep you alive. You're worth a boatload of money to me—alive. Dead isn't an option."

"Well, I feel so much better."

"You might lose the attitude with me." I went over and lowered the window blinds. Then, I removed the cord from the phone and stuffed it into my pocket. Finally, after surveying the room for anything that might cause a problem, I squared off on him. "Strip."

His face screwed up. "What?"

"Strip. Down to your mighty whites."

"Are you nuts?"

I grabbed him by the arm and tugged him to his feet. "I've gotta check your clothes for tracking devices. Strip."

That resonated. In a moment, he was down to his blue boxers with little flags and his holey green socks. He tossed me his pants, shirt, and jacket,

239

which I immediately rolled together in a big ball and tucked under my arm.

"Now, stay put."

He looked like he was going to have a meltdown when I went to the door and opened it.

"Hey, you said you were going to check them for bugs."

"I lied." Did he really expect anything else? "I'll take these with me. I doubt you'll run off naked. If you do, you're stupider than I think. You'd be dead in an hour."

Before he could spit out the string of expletives that followed me out the door, I headed for Tommy's second-floor office.

Tommy sat in his office chair, feet on his desk as usual, talking on his cell phone. When he saw me bust in, he quickly begged off the call and stood.

"What in Jiminy Cricket are you doing here, Lowe?"

I dropped into one of the ladderback wood chairs around his conference table. "I got trouble, and I need your help."

"Help? Sweet God-A-Mighty, you gotta do your job, man—alone." His arms snapped closed across his chest. "I can't help. You can't screw with these people, Lowe. Now, get your butt outta here and go find—"

"I found him." My eyes met his. "He's downstairs in my office."

"What? Here?" His eyes snapped shut as his hands flew to his face, covering it. "Are you out of your rabid-ass mind? You can't do this, Lowe. You can't involve me."

Was he kidding? "Tommy, you brought them to me."

"Stop. Don't say it. Don't even think it." He came around his desk and stood over me. "You listen to me, boy scout. You get your friend outta here. Fast. Quick fast. Like your life depends on it."

What the hell was wrong with him? I asked him that, and added, "I need wheels, and I need time to regroup. Things got very heated earlier and—"

His desk phone speaker chirped that someone wanted him. He called out, "Yes, what is it?"

"Tommy, that US Marshal is in reception. He says it's urgent."

Oh, crapola. Triple dipper crapola.

"Oh, sweet cornbread." Tommy's eyes lasered onto me. "Tell him I'll be right there. Don't let him out of reception."

"Sir, he's very agitated." A long pause, then, "He's shouting at me to get you down there. He says if Curran is here, he wants him, too. Please, sir."

"Good God, almighty." Tommy threw me an aggravated glance. "I'll be right there."

The phone speaker clicked off.

"Listen, you silly shit," Tommy snapped and threw a thumb over his shoulder. "Take my private entrance down. Get your friend, and get the hell out of here. I'll buy you a few minutes. Don't come back here, Lowe. Not until things are right again. And you were never here. Got me?"

I quickly explained about Mr. Nobody's cell phone. Then, "What about transportation? At least to get me somewhere where I can get my own."

His face twisted. "Sweet Jesus, Lowe. Anything else? You want maybe I should be your personal chauffeur?"

"Sorry, Tommy. You got me into this. I took the assignment after you promised me I wasn't doing anything that I was actually doing. Get me going again, and I won't be back until Mr. Nobody says it's all good."

Tommy's door burst open with a loud bang.

Katelyn Astor stormed in, red-faced and spitting expletives that would sink the Seventh Fleet.

"You sonofabitch, Curran. Who the hell is sitting in your office? Why is he naked?"

"Naked? Oh, holy Jezebel." Tommy's eyes rose to the ceiling, and then he grinned, turning toward Katelyn. "Sweetheart, which company car do you have?"

"None. I've got my personal Range Rover. Why?"

Tommy went to her and spoke softly so I couldn't hear. Her eyes fired bullets at me, and Satan welled up in them. When he was done, he turned back to me.

"Get outta here, Lowe. Katelyn will meet you around back with her Rover. She'll take you somewhere to get transportation. Then you're gone. Do you get me, Lowe? Gone. Call me with a burner phone in two hours. I'll have new contact info for you with our mutual associate."

"Thanks, Tommy. I'll figure a way to buy a junker or something for cash. Untraceable."

Katelyn chopped the air viciously at Tommy. "Are you kidding me? Really? Why go to all the trouble of making him take care of himself? Why don't I just *give* him the damn Rover."

When Tommy chuckled and winked at me, I realized just how much I loved him.

Chapter Forty-Eight

Curran

"A re you ever going to explain all this?" Piper demanded for the millionth time. "Who's paying you? What do they want? When—"

"Enough." I jumped on the Range Rover's brakes. This expensive ride handled so much better than my old Jeep, yet still we barely made the off-ramp on Route 66. We careened down the short ramp, skidded around the right onto a side road, and ended up in a parking spot outside a gas station bathroom. "I've explained it a million times, Piper. You know what I know. And I don't know shit."

His face contorted, half from the dramatic exit off the highway and half from my grasp of his collar that lifted him sideways from his seat. His seatbelt cut his circulation off, and his face turned deep red.

"All you need to know is that I was first sent to retrieve what you hacked from my clients. Their names aren't important. Then, they sent me to find and protect you. I found you. I'm going to protect you. End of story."

"Okay, okay," he gasped. "Let me go. I'm cool. Honest. Cool."

I released him, and he grabbed his door handle. He would have opened the door and made a break for it had my Kimber .45 not dissuaded him. Silly boy.

"I'm not going to hurt you unless you force me to. But understand this," I said, waiting for him to release the passenger door. "No one else is getting you."

"What's that mean?"

Was he dim or what? "If I can't have you, no one will."

His face blanched and he turned around in the seat and went rigid. "I knew it. You're a hitman."

"I'm no hitman." Though, I sort of liked the sound of that. "I'm the opposite. I protect people. People like you. But if you keep trying to escape, I can't do my job. If one of those other groups—you remember the nice men at the apartment last night and at the hospital earlier?—if any of them find you, you'll be worm food. So, cooperate and graduate, Piper."

For the longest time, he sat contemplating his kneecaps. Finally, he took a long, protracted breath, and faced me again.

"Curran, was it the same people who sent you to my house dressed as an old crotchety man the same ones who sent you to find me and protect me?"

Truth was, I wasn't totally sure. Maybe.

"More or less. We'll call him Mr. Nobody. He hired me to find you. I've never seen or heard of him before. He's paying me to keep you in one piece. I don't know anything about him other than my friend said he was okay."

Piper processed this. "Then how do you know Mr. Nobody isn't the one who sent those hitmen after me? You know, like have you find me so they could kill me? Or maybe kill both of us?"

"Well, because, ah, well..." Damn if he didn't have a great point. I thought long and hard on that one. The answer was easy. Easy, but it didn't really comfort me. "The guy who sent me to you the first time and hooked me up with Mr. Nobody. That guy is a good friend. A great friend. Long time one, too. He wouldn't screw me like that."

"Did Mr. Nobody tell you someone might try to kill me?"

"More or less."

"You were okay with that?"

No, but I was okay with two hundred grand. "It's the job, Piper. Find and protect. I've done this sort of thing in the past—for many years. I'm good at it. I don't think Mr. Nobody sent me to find you just to have someone else kill you."

That settled him a little. "Did he ever suggest you kill me?"

I was about to answer when the words stuck in my throat. No, he actually didn't ask me to. But then, I told him right off the bat that I wouldn't do anything like that. Surely, Tommy Astor knew that, too.

"Did he?"

I shook my head. Better that Piper didn't know we were in a gray area on that one. After all, when I told Mr. Nobody that I wouldn't kill anyone, or that I wouldn't hunt down witnesses, and so on, both he and Tommy flat out lied to me and said that wasn't it. Except, Piper *was* a government witness. And I *was* sent to hunt him down. If they could lie to me about that part, they sure could have used me to find Piper, so someone else could kill him. Convoluted, sure. Plausible, definitely.

The flaw in all this speculation was that it might require Tommy Astor to play a roll. No way. Tommy was on Team Curran. He wouldn't do something like that.

Would he?

Billy settled back in the seat. "Okay, Curran, what's the plan?"

Billy Piper was a short, pudgy, pain-in-the-ass hacker who seemed to whine or antagonize me about everything. He hated dogs—Bogart was evidence—and lived by screwing other people out of their information and money. But he was still a pretty smart guy who asked pretty good questions.

Yes, Marlowe S. Curran, what's the plan?

* * *

I am resourceful if I'm anything. Truly.

My plan was simple. It was safe. Above all, it was easy. All it called for was a trustworthy old buddy and a remote hunting cabin deep in West Virginian's Appalachian Mountain range.

West Virginia is a beautiful state. Its rolling mountains, rivers, and forests made it an outdoor paradise like no other. You can drive for miles and miles through the Appalachians and never see houses or communities, or a flying saucer. Okay, maybe not a flying saucer, but maybe a Big Foot.

That's why my brilliant plan was so, well, brilliant.

Except as resourceful as I can be, I am also rather forgetful. Like forgetting to call ahead when executing one of my simple, safe, genius plans.

"Get out of the vehicle, boys," Stevie Keene called, leveling a 12-gauge pump shotgun at us from his front porch. "Slow. Hands where I can see them. You know the drill, I'm sure you watch T.V."

Stevie obviously couldn't see me behind the wheel. Probably the sun's reflection or something. That was it. That was why he hadn't lowered the shotgun or put a big welcoming smile on his face. It had to be the glare. Stevie loved me. Really.

"Out." He lifted the 12-gauge and pointed it at my side of the Range Rover. "You damn tourists get lost?"

Tourists? They'd have to be pretty dumb tourists.

I opened my door—slowly so as not to cause his finger to twitch. "Stevie, it's me—Lowe Curran."

His face twisted a little. "Pappa?"

Jesus, he just saw me a few hours ago. Was he that drunk he didn't remember?

His face lit up. "Well, hell, man, why didn't you call first? I didn't recognize you in that fancy Rover. You normally can barely make it up this mountain in your piece of shit Jeep."

See, it was the glare.

"Come out, Piper." I waved him out of the passenger side. "Put the bazooka away, Stevie. I come in peace."

Even with his many flaws—none of which were his fault—Stevie was your quintessential chameleon. Put him in a Brookes Brothers suit and tie, comb his hair, and he can pass for a Wall Street money man. As long as you don't let him talk. Now, though, he was the other face of the chameleon. He was dressed in dirty jeans, a sweatshirt with its sleeve cut off above the elbow, and barefoot. Thankfully, he'd showered and cleaned up since yesterday. There was no sign of another bender, either. Good thing, too. I needed him steady.

"Feeling better, Stevie?" I asked. "Get some sleep?"

"Huh?" His face twisted again. "Wha...oh. Yeah. I saw you yesterday morning, right? Damn, brother. I thought I was hallucinating again. Yeah, I'm good."

Hallucinating? *Again?* Maybe this wasn't my best plan after all.

"Look, if you're not feeling good—for real—I'll be out of your hair in a day."

"No, no, brother. I owe you big so many times over. I'm good. Really." He lowered the shotgun and walked down the porch steps to the front of the Rover. He eyed Billy up and down like he was about to bid on a horse at auction. "What's your story, kid?"

"Stevie?" Piper glanced at me and turned back to Stevie. "I'm Billy Piper. I'm a computer technician, and—"

"Zip it. I don't care." Stevie headed for the stairs. "You're in trouble again, Pappa. You've got one of those damn lost causes with you. Now you need my help. I hope you know what you're doing."

About Piper or about asking him for help? I asked Stevie that.

"Both, brother. I'm not at my best, and this kid smells of '*oh shit.*'"

Did I mention that Stevie Keene was incredibly intuitive? And, of course, he knew me all too well.

Chapter Forty-Nine

Curran

"Stevie, how steady are you?" It was a question that might piss him off. Still, the image of him lying drunk on the hood of his Blazer made it fair game. "You were pretty shaky yesterday."

Stevie snapped his eyes from Piper to me. In that instant, I wondered if I'd made another mistake. His stare penetrated me like a slow-burning laser. With each unspoken moment, my doubt doubled. Maybe he wasn't ready for intrigue and adventure. He'd gone from drunk and disoriented yesterday morning, to worried about hallucinations and paranoia. Maybe this plan of mine, brilliant as it sounded, was flawed.

"Stevie?"

"It's Stephen. Not Stevie." He turned and headed into his cabin, offering a lackluster wave for us to follow. "Haven't you learned anything all these years?"

Wow, that was new. Stephen? Really?

I shoved Piper into the house. "Inside."

"Wait," he said, turning. "Stevie? Stevie, who?"

"Keene. Why? You want to send a thank you note?"

Piper's face twisted a little. "Stevie Keene? No. No notes. I don't want to be here. Got another plan? Let's go."

"No." I shoved him again.

Inside, the cabin was more of a hunting lodge ready for city-folk guests hoping to bag big game. The main room—like a grand hall—had two-story log ceilings. The walls were log, of course, and the staircase rose from the side of the room up to a balcony that ran the entire width of the cabin. His main bedroom and four or five guest rooms lay beyond, off the balcony. The kitchen and dining room were open from the grand hall and ran to the rear of the cabin. There were one or two amenities off the rear that visitors were rarely invited to see. I was an exception. That'll come later.

Oddly, for a hunting lodge, there were no deer or moose heads anywhere. No bear rugs or hunting trophies adorned the walls. Just a few hand-painted mountain paintings, some of a nearby river, and an attempt at an old Blue Tick hound resting near a fireplace.

Stevie was the, er, artist. He sucked, but he tried. Honesty is important.

Those paintings were bad. Real bad. But he was my friend, and older than me, he could probably kick my butt one-handed. Even in his worst days, drifting in and out of lucidity. So, I loved them. Every poorly stroked, mis-colored one. Some, like Ranger, the Blue Tick, was my favorite. If you looked at Ranger just right, you could almost see the real dog in there. Or so I've told Stevie.

"I'm sorry, Pappa. It's been a rough few weeks. I know I blew it the other night for you. Is this your target from Leesburg?"

I nodded. "Indirectly, yeah."

"He's trouble. You sure it isn't that hottie grandma that's the real issue?"

Huh? "What?"

Stevie huffed something and slumped into an old, worn leather chair near the fireplace. "She doesn't want you to whack another relative, does she, Pappa?"

What did he just say?

Piper looked at me with a smartass grin. "Pappa?"

"Don't call me that, Piper—ever." I flashed up a hand to silence him and pointed at Stevie. "I did not kill Janey-Lynn's husband. You know that."

He grunted. "If you say so."

"And don't call me Pappa."

Another grunt. His face was awash in a fight between normalcy and the malaise I'd seen in him since we reconnected years ago. For my sake, and Piper's, I hoped the old Stevie Keene would win the battle.

"Who painted this stuff?" Piper had been staring at Stevie. "They're—"

"Stevie did them. Now sit and be quiet." I reached him in two strides, grabbed an arm, and roughly guided him into a straight-back chair against the wall. "Open your mouth again, and I'll gag you. Your benefactors said I had to find and protect you. They didn't say I had to listen to you."

He pulled free of my grasp. "I was just gonna say how much I liked the work. Jesus, dude, I'm not a child. I can talk when I want. This stuff is great. Is it for sale?"

Unbelievable. "Stop talking, Piper."

"Now, hold on, there, Pappa." Stevie looked up and rubbed his eyes a bit. Then, he stood and headed for a pine-board bar in the corner of the room. "The boy can talk when he wants."

Great. What Stevie didn't need was more booze or a fanboy. "Look, Stevie. I have a deal for you. But only if you're on your feet solid and ready."

"A deal? If you're dealing, it's bad news." To my surprise, he manipulated another of those alien peapod coffee makers aside from the bar and made himself a coffee. He waited there, watching it drip. "If you're sure about me, Pappa. I'll listen. But don't tell me anything you'll regret if you don't think I'm up for it."

Was he? "It's simple. You got your head on enough to help me babysit this guy for a few weeks? Can you stay clearheaded that long?"

Stevie's face tightened at first. I'd insulted him. Then, he drained the coffee cup—steaming all the way—and started another. When he turned back to me, his eyes had softened and he watched me with an intensity—an understanding—I'd not seen since our days in Greece.

"Look, Pappa, I don't know." He looked at the wood floor at nothing. "I wanna do this. I have to do it. I owe you. You got a mess on your hands or you wouldn't be here. So, if you'll give me this one last chance. I won't screw up. I promise. I'll stay straight."

If I could have planned his delivery of that speech, I would have only missed it by the intensity of his words. I'd heard it before. Most times, he stayed clear enough for me to use him—only on the periphery. At least enough to put some money in his pocket and give him some lost dignity. This was different. This was already a rough assignment. An assignment that might be made or lost on a missed signal, a misguided decision, or a simple stupid move. Any of those could get us killed. It was, as we used to say, a Turkey Shoot—gobble, gobble.

Mr. Nobody's soliloquy at my loft the night I met him told me that much. That and the flying lead over the last twelve hours.

Still, this was Stevie. He'd had my back for years, and he was the only option I had. If he was nothing, he was loyal. I needed someone loyal. Someone to sit on Piper when I had to step away. After all, Janey-Lynn and I were still murder suspects. I had to keep an iron in that fire, too. I couldn't drag Piper back and forth to her place without raising too many questions. The bottom line was, I had no choice.

I waited for him to sip his second coffee and walked to him. "I've already done the hard part—I found Piper. I'll cut you in for fifteen percent on the rest. It's simple protection work, Stevie. If you can stay straight—on your meds and sober—it'll be easy work."

"Fifteen percent?" He sipped his coffee and refused to look up at me. "Fifteen percent of what? How much trouble you expecting? Can't be a lot if you're willing to use me."

I so wish that were true. "You're cut could be as much as thirty-Gs. I don't know what to expect. I already got into shootin' matches twice today." I told him about the Arlington Arms Apartments and our adventure at the hospital. "Whoever's after him isn't shy—or low on ammo."

"No shit?" He did some mental math. "You're starting at two hundred grand?"

Wow, for a guy with a traumatic brain injury that kept him isolated and challenged most of the time, he sure could do math fast.

"Twenty percent," he said curtly. "No less."

He emptied his coffee mug and turned to brew another alien-pod cup. "Talk. But same rules. Don't tell me anything you honestly don't think you can trust me with. You have to judge that. Not me."

I did. I told him everything. All the painstaking details about my hunt for Piper and how we landed on his front porch. To his credit, it was like me talking to the old Stevie Keene. The one before the Voula Beach Road. He listened, asked good questions, and absorbed it all in stride.

Some people in my situation might have lied and candy-coated the dark spots. I wasn't one of those. Stevie and I had seen the real fight—many times—and we ended our winning streak on the Voula Beach Road. I wasn't going to ask him to back me up with half the truth. It was all in or nothing.

After an hour discussing it, he returned to his leather chair and dropped into it with a huff. He stared into the coffee like he was looking for answers. He closed his eyes, laid his head back for a long time, and mumbled to himself. When he finally lifted his head again, his eyes seemed clear and his tone low and crisp.

"Two sets of shooters? Two teams, at least. Unknown origin?"

I nodded. "So far."

"And a US Marshal?"

Another nod.

His gears ground away. If there was one thing Stevie loved more than his remote cabin and booze, it was a challenge. This one pulled the old Stevie from the gloom and darkness that had been his world for so many years. He sipped his coffee and contemplated me across the room.

"The Marshal's the biggest problem. I don't mind getting into it with some shooters. Shooting back is fair play—fun even. And yeah, Pappa. I'm up to that."

"Good."

He lifted a finger in the air. "But dancing around with a fed is another thing. Especially since, well, I'll point out the obvious, you've been obstructing justice, and you've kidnapped a federal witness."

That was harsh. "Piper came with me—voluntarily. Didn't you, Piper?"

Piper was lost somewhere on my story hour and had dozed off in a chair.

"Hey, Piper?" I aimed a gun finger at him. "It's us or them. Pick."

"Huh?" He shook himself back to the now. Glancing between Stevie and me, he stood and went to the bar to help himself to a drink. "I don't want anything to do with either of you. But I guess I don't have a choice."

Well, that was better than asking for a lawyer. "See, Stevie. We're clean with the Marshal."

"Uh, huh." Stevie stayed in his chair, contemplating everything I'd told him. His eyes closed again, and for a long time, I thought he'd fallen asleep until he suddenly stood and went straight to Piper, who was still standing at the bar. "Look here, hacker-boy. I don't know what Curran has told you, but I don't suffer fools. I also don't plan on getting shot for a measly forty-G's."

Piper's face blanched. "Okay."

"You do as you're told. When you're told—"

"Yeah, yeah." Piper rolled his eyes. "Curran already gave me the speech. I get it."

Stevie jammed his finger so deep into Piper's temple I thought it would come out the other side. "Look, shithead, I'm not auditioning for some dipshit movie. I'm making sure we understand each other. This isn't a gameshow. It's not TV. You've pissed off a lot of people and have feds chasing your fat ass. Why, we don't really know, do we? But if all these pissed-off people are sending shooters after you, it's a big deal. What do you have, and where is it?"

Piper shrugged. "I don't have anything anymore. He's got it all."

Stevie looked taken aback. "Then why the hell, Pappa, are we worried about him at all? If you've got the goods, let's vamoose. Just the two of us."

The real Stevie Keene was definitely making a comeback. Maybe those alien pea pod coffee gadgets had promise.

"He's the key to it all, Stevie." I let that sink in. "I've got some copies for emergencies—just in case I need to negotiate. The real package is him and the stuff I've got. One requires the other."

Stevie glanced at Piper, scowled, and returned to me. "So, we need both? Okay, do what you gotta do to get the copies of whatever. I'll sit on this dumbass until you get back."

Piper started to speak, but Stevie's hand flashed up. "Quiet."

"One more thing." I made Stevie's eyebrows raise. "A little factoid you should know before you jump in."

"Whatever it is," he snorted, "it can't be as bad as what you've already told me."

Guess again. "He was in WITSEC because he hacked the Russian mob. He stole a few million of their hard-earned rubles. They, of course, are not happy."

Piper, to his credit, stayed quiet.

"Well, ain't that special? You've gone and pissed off mass murderers." He shook a finger at Piper, but turned to me with a big, wide, 'gotcha' grin. The hazy, challenged Stevie Keene was gone, and the old, hardcore Stevie Keen was back. At least, for now. "Then my fees are seventy-five-Gs. Ninety if I get shot again. Ten up front. You pay rent if we're using my place as a safe house."

"Don't push it."

He drilled steady eyes into me. "Look, brother, no jokes. Drop this. Toss this little computer nerd somewhere far away and forget him. This thing has disaster all over it. More trouble than we've seen in a long time."

He was right, but that didn't matter. "I know, Stevie. But I took the job, and I need the money."

"You can't spend money if you're dead." He turned away. "Walk away, man. Just walk away. We're not kids anymore."

"I can't."

"Then we're both screwed."

Chapter Fifty

Curran

The mark of a true friend is someone that you can show up unannounced and ask a life-threatening favor and get a "yes." Seventy-five grand helped a lot, too. That's what true friends are for. Cash for favors.

After cementing our deal with a few ground rules and a one-way negotiation on the rent I had to pay, I got Piper settled into his second-floor guest room. Then, I jumped back into my new Range Rover—people just bestow gifts on me all the time—and headed home. I had to collect more cash and the backup USB drive of Piper's hacking from my loft. I'd need both for the long haul ahead safeguarding Piper.

Too many people showed up to my loft—uninvited—who might stumble upon my bounty.

The ride back was peaceful. No jabbering Billy Piper. And the music was great. Katelyn Astor also had a great collection of classic rock loaded into the sound system—classic as in sixties and seventies. Once back on real hardtop roads, I put on some Creedence and enjoyed the ride.

As I rolled down the long country road to my loft, my pissed-off-o-meter reached eight on a scale of ten—and climbing. I normally stay around three just for security purposes, and during my recent exploits, it had reached a ten-point-nine. So, all things considered, eight was a simply heightened state of alertness.

For good reason.

Randy Cantrell's hooptie sat in front of my barn loft stairs.

What did he want now?

I parked, slid from the Rover, and eased toward the stairs. I know he was Janey-Lynn's kin and all, but if I shot him real fast and put a kitchen knife in one hand and my coffee pot in the other, even Agent Evans might consider it self-defense. If Evans knew him, he'd consider it a gift to society.

Maybe.

Lights were on inside my loft as I climbed the stairs to my front door.

My door was locked. Worse, my house key, strategically positioned in a crack between two of the porch wallboards, didn't work. I tried three times. Nothing.

Did Mr. Manbun actually change my locks?

As I was about to give the door a good kick, the inside lock jiggled, and the front door opened. Randy Cantrell stood there. He'd improved his appearance, too. He was wearing a blue kimono robe, no shirt, and shorts.

What a stud.

"Old dude?" He flipped on the front stoop light. "What'd ya want now? I told you this was my place."

"And I told you I rent…" Janey-Lynn came into focus as she scurried from the kitchen to the door. "Janey-Lynn, what's going on?"

She stood by him. "Randy, it's okay. It's—"

"I know." He smiled a greasy smile. "It's Scooby Doo."

"Lowe Curran," I said in a slow delivery. "I know it's tough to remember. Try real hard."

Janey-Lynn tried to ease Randy back into the apartment, but he wouldn't budge. "Randy, be civil. Let Lowe in, and we can talk."

"Nothing to talk about, mommy dearest." The sneer in his voice sent irritation boiling through my veins. "I've moved back into *my* apartment until you sign over the house and the farm. Your boy toy is out. Hell, he can bunk with you until we get the papers settled."

Papers?

"Janey-Lynn?" My face must have been as shocked as my voice because

Mr. Manbun laughed raucously. I ignored him the best I could, but the urge to snap his scrawny neck was almost overwhelming. "Randy, we've already discussed this apartment. I've paid rent."

"Lowe, we have to talk." Janey-Lynn's face was ash. "Come in."

Randy held up his hand. "Nope. He murdered my father, and he's not coming in."

This was not going to end well.

"Sure, I'll come in." I stepped into Randy's hand and pushed him backward through the front door. There was no resistance. As expected, he was about as tough as Mr. Chicken. He stumbled back, tripped over his own feet, and fell onto the floor. "Oops. Sorry. I hope you didn't get any booboos."

He was up on his feet and slicing the air between us with his silly, skinny karate chops. "I'll sue your ass, PI. I'll have you arrested for assault."

Janey-Lynn stepped between us. "Enough, Randy. Calm down."

"Actually," I said, peeking around Janey-Lynn, "that was an accident. Maybe battery, but not assault. Battery is the unlawful touching part. Assault is, oh hell, never mind. Tell me what's going on."

Randy stabbed the air. "I don't have to say anything to you, PI."

"Shut it, Randy." PI was better than old dude. "Janey-Lynn?"

She retreated a few steps across the room. "Lowe, I don't know what to tell you. But for now, at least—maybe a few days until I can get this sorted—you better move into my house. I've already taken most of your things up to my guest room."

"Guest room? That's funny." Randy smeared on a sophomoric grin. "He'll be bedding in your room—excuse me—my dad's room, by midnight. Soon, it'll be my room, though. Without you in it."

Nope. Not going to end well.

I stepped into him so our noses nearly touched. Actually, his gnarly, outrageous beard touched me, and I nearly sneezed. As he backpedaled again, I followed and kept the pressure close and personal. When he collided with a chair and couldn't retreat any further, I jammed my finger into his chin and brought him to his tiptoes like Stevie had done to Billy Piper a couple hours ago.

"Listen to me, you little shit." My voice was calm and steady. Fear was often more achievable that way. "Janey-Lynn isn't like that. Neither am I." Okay, she isn't, but on occasion, I am. "I don't know what's going on, but you better take a deep breath and cut your mouth. I'm not in the mood to suffer your juvenile insults."

His eyes teared, and he held his breath. He didn't say a word. He was like a kindergartner who got caught peeing his pants.

I went on. "I didn't kill your father. Though he deserved it. Funny, too, because that's crossing my mind with you."

His entire body shivered, but he put on a brave face. A quiet one, but brave. He tried to give me the tough-guy stare but had to blink a few times. When I laughed at him and walked away, I thought his tears would flow. They didn't. He stopped them with a wipe of his eyes.

"Well, *mommy*? Are you gonna explain things to your boytoy, or am I?"

Janey-Lynn stood across the room, looking out the window. When she turned, her tears were flowing—pent-up anger and rage. I'd never seen her so ready to blow a gasket as at that moment. I'd also never seen her take crap from anyone. Randy has something over her—some kind of power I didn't understand.

"Lowe, can I speak with you outside?"

Randy snorted. "Yeah, explain how you stole my money and farm. Except you're not going to get away with it."

What?

I followed Janey-Lynn outside onto the stair landing. "What's going on, Janey-Lynn? Tell me."

The porch light was dim, but still couldn't conceal her angst. She dropped her head, and her voice was a mere whisper. "Charlie cut Randy from his will years ago. As you can see, he's a piece of work."

"He's a piece of something. Go on."

That made her smile. It lasted a parsec. "He showed up this morning at my house right after the police left the cottage. He demanded I sign over the house, property, and Charlie's bank accounts to him."

"Based on what?"

"Lowe, let me handle this. Okay?"

"No."

"Please? It's very personal, and I know you've more important things at stake. Let me deal with Randy. I know I can. I'll find a compromise."

Compromise? "Why? Just let me toss him out. If he's out of the will, he's out. You don't owe him anything."

"It's not that simple. It's not." She cried big tears and retreated when I reached for her shoulder. "Charlie hated the little pissant. He was an illegitimate child from a fling Charlie had before we were married. He lived with us a short time, many years ago. The bastard stole tens of thousands from us. He stole several pieces of jewelry of mine, too, including some family heirlooms I inherited from my first husband. Now, he's come for the rest."

Coming for and getting were two different things.

"Janey-Lynn," I said, lifting her chin and giving her my famous confidence-building wink. Well, famous in some places. "What's he claiming? A fake will? What?"

She shook her head. "Stay at my place or go do whatever you're doing. I know that's important. I know you're in something very deep. More men came looking for you today. So, go. Handle that. I'll handle him. Please. You might make things worse if you don't."

She had a point. There was no way I could handle Randy tonight. Not unless it entailed a shovel and a deep hole out in the back pasture. I had to get back to Stevie and Piper. Still, seeing the anguish on Janey-Lynn's face was tearing me apart. For a moment, I was back in my twenties and standing in Carli's front yard. I had to go overseas on short notice. She was devastated. There was something she needed to talk about, but I was late for my flight. I promised to return soon and work whatever it was out. Though, I wasn't good at working things out. Time was forever against me. I made those promises far too often—to her—and we both knew they were likely not for the keeping.

I had chosen poorly that evening. I returned eight weeks later. Not a phone call or email from her in all that time. Someone new lived in her apartment. No forwarding address. No nothing.

Carli was gone.

To this day, I live with that pain and regret. I also live with the "what if" and "what happened." I had no answers and, of course, feared what they might be anyway.

Looking into Janey-Lynn's face, I saw that same desperation. That same aloneness. What was I to do? Piper's life was in danger. Stevie was pinch-hitting for me. My entire professional future lay between them.

"Janey-Lynn, I do have to go. But I'll be back in a day or two." I recited my pay-as-you-go phone number for her. "Call if you need me. I wish I could stay. I'll get back here as fast as I can."

My famous wink did it.

"Lowe, what you have to do is more important. I can handle Randy." She smiled a faint smile and touched my hand still on her shoulder. "It's gonna take time, though. I'll get the rest of your things moved up to the house in the morning."

"Will you be okay without me here?"

She nodded confidently. "I'll kick his scrawny ass if he tries anything."

There was my Janey-Lynn. I kissed her cheek and turned to Randy as he appeared in the doorway. "You're in luck. I've got plans. Janey-Lynn will keep me informed. If you so much as don't lower the toilet seat, I'll be back. Whatever's going on, I suggest you work it out without all the snarky comments and innuendo. You know, Randy, like a big boy."

He glared hate at me.

Something struck me. Well, two somethings. First, I had a bunch of money and a computer drive hidden in the apartment. I wasn't taking any chances on him finding them. Second...

"Janey-Lynn, where's Bogart?"

Before she could answer, Randy's mouth brightened into a big, malicious smile. "That stupid mutt? He was prowling around the barn, barking and snarling at me. I shot his ass with my dad's old shotgun."

Redline...danger Lowe Curran...danger.

I spun subconsciously and landed a right hook into his jaw, so powerful it sent him backward into the apartment. Somehow, he kept his footing. I followed him through the door and landed a second that sent him over a chair, into the kerosene hearth, and down on his back. Before he hit the brick, I was on him and rearing back to finish the job.

"Lowe, no. Bogart's fine." Jane-Lynn ran in, grabbed my arm, and pulled me clear. "He missed by a mile. Bogart's up at my place. He's unhurt. I promise."

Well, it was the thought that counts. I grabbed Randy by his manbun and pulled him to his feet, sunk a boilermaker into his gut that doubled him over with a loud grunt. Then, I tossed him back across the room onto the sofa like the sack of shit that he was.

Wow, for an old, decrepit man, I was doing okay.

"Randy, let's understand one another." I reached him again and had his manbun in my grip, holding his head up high for another jaw-breaking punch. "Threatening animals and friends—especially my dog and Janey-Lynn—is unacceptable. Just trying to hurt my dog is bad. Second, lying to me about it is bad. And third…" I twisted his manbun so tightly he cried out, and tears parachuted down his cheeks. "That means you can't be trusted around Janey-Lynn while I'm away. That leaves me no choice."

His eyes were red and swollen. His face was tear-stained. His body quivered, and his jaw showed the impact zone in a red, swelling knuckle pattern.

"I wouldn't shoot him," he mumbled, unable to hold my eyes. "I wanted to scare him off. Honest. He tried to bite me. I didn't know he was your mutt. I thought—"

"Stop." I twisted his hair again, and he cried out. "I'm calling my buddy at the BCI to come on around—a lot. Then, I'm calling a friend who'll send someone to keep Janey-Lynn company until I get back. You will be a good boy, Randy. You will."

He started to object when Janey-Lynn took my arm and bade me release him and step away. Then, she helped him to sit upright on the sofa.

"He will be, Lowe. I'll be fine. Just go. Randy and I will sort this out ourselves. No need for all this. I don't need the police."

"I'm still calling Tommy." When I told him this story, he'd be out here with a couple bodyguards in a flash. By bodyguards, I mean the kind that earns commission based on broken bones. "You handle the legal things as you want. I'll handle the other things the way I want."

Randy straightened up. "What do you mean by that?"

"That means, Randy, that I've killed nicer assholes than you." I forced a laugh. "And the guy I'm calling won't like what he hears. If you think I'm a prick, wait until you meet Tommy. He makes me look like a boy scout."

Janey-Lynn's face blossomed into a smile that she couldn't tamp down. She headed for the front door. "Come on, Lowe. I'll walk you out."

I started to go but stopped. "Janey-Lynn, I gotta get a few things. Can you take little sonny-boy outside while I pull it all together?"

"Sure, okay." She cocked her head and gave me a quizzical look. "Come on, Randy. We can wait outside for him to leave."

They made it three steps before lights flashed through the front window, and a car door slammed outside. A second later, heavy footfalls on the outside stairs and a hammer fist nearly knocked the apartment door down.

"Come out here, Curran," Marshal Gallo bellowed. "Come on out, or I'm coming in."

Holy crap on a popsicle stick. It just wasn't my night.

Chapter Fifty-One

Curran

Gallo stood in the open loft door with his Glock aimed at me. I hoped the safety was on, but as luck has it, Glocks have no traditional safeties. So, his finger on the trigger was about five pounds of pressure away from blowing my head off. You can imagine I was very, very careful not to move. Or breathe. Or blink.

"Easy, Marshal," I said. "You released me. Remember?"

Janey-Lynn stepped away from me. "Lowe? What's going on?"

"I'm not sure. The bigger story is too complicated."

She faced Gallo. "Marshal?"

"Hands up, Curran," he commanded. "Mrs. Cantrell, you stay right there."

Not wanting to give him any reason to shoot me—and I know that was a low bar to set—I lifted my hands. He grabbed my shoulder, pulled me out the door onto the landing, and down the stairs.

"Okay, Gallo. Easy."

Janey-Lynn followed us down the stairs as Randy appeared on the landing behind her.

Great. Just what I needed. An audience.

At the foot of the stairs, Gallo kicked my legs out and forced me to my knees. In a few expert movements, he handcuffed me. From there, he lifted me by the cuffs to my feet again—almost dislocating my shoulders—and forced me facedown over the hood of his SUV as he had earlier.

"You're coming with me, Curran."

Ah, shit. "Come on, Gallo. You released me a few hours ago. What now?"

"We're leaving." His voice was hard as granite, and his delivery cold. His face was awash with worry or fear or something. Whatever it was, he wasn't doing a great job hiding it. "In the vehicle."

"Relax. I'm going." As I started to lean back off the SUV, he grabbed my pistol from the holster behind my back. "That's a legal—"

"Quiet." He tucked my .45 into his waistband and gave me a fast pat down. "Anymore 'legal' stuff?"

"Nope." I hoped he wouldn't find the switchblade tucked into my hiking boots or the anti-aircraft gun in my underwear. "Tell me what's going on."

Janey-Lynn was there now. "Marshal?"

"Stand back, Mrs. Cantrell," Gallo snapped. "You're already in enough trouble with a murder investigation going on."

That was uncalled for. "Janey-Lynn, take Randy and deal with him. I'll be fine. It's a misunderstanding."

"No, it's not." Gallo scoffed. "The misunderstanding was releasing you before. I won't make that mistake twice."

Before I could argue, he stuffed me sideways into his rear seat. Then, he seat-belted me in place and rolled down the window. Finally, he shut the door.

"Keep quiet. I'll explain everything soon."

"Gee, thanks." This was not an official visit. Of that, I was sure. "I can't wait to hear."

Outside the SUV, Janey-Lynn was arguing with Randy as he descended the stairs. She yelled at him to leave with her and let Gallo do what he had to do. Randy laughed and wanted a front-row seat to my demise. When Gallo opened his driver's door, Janey-Lynn grabbed Randy by the arm and tried to pull him away.

Randy spun around, shoved her backward, and slapped her violently across the face.

She went down, stunned.

"Oh, shit, I—" he stammered.

"Janey-Lynn," I yelled, but I couldn't finish my sentence.

Gallo, much to his credit, charged over and grabbed Randy by the shoulder, shoved him away, and onto the ground. "Stay down, mister."

"Stop, Marshal," Janey-Lynn yelled, getting to her feet. "It's all right. I'm okay. He just lost his temper."

Gallo grabbed Randy by the shirt and lifted him into a seating position. "I don't know who you are, asshole, but hitting her was a huge mistake."

Randy's face reddened, but his smart mouth stayed clenched.

"If I didn't have Curran to deal with," Gallo said, shaking Randy. "I'd run your ass in for assault and battery."

Randy nodded as his eyeballs burst into tears.

Sure. I tried to explain assault and battery to him before, and he wouldn't listen. Now, he'll listen to Gallo. I get no respect.

"Marshal, please." Janey-Lynn ran to Gallo and tugged at his arm. "This isn't necessary. It was a mistake."

Gallo's face lightened, and he looked at Janey-Lynn as though seeing her for the first time. He released Randy and shoved him backward onto the ground again. Then, he retreated to the SUV, where I waited.

"All right, Ms. Cantrell. If he—"

"He won't," she promised. Just then, I think Randy would agree.

Janey-Lynn went to Randy's side and helped him to his feet. I guess her maternal instincts outweighed her loathing for him. As she did, more vehicle lights came down the farm road and turned into the barn drive.

Evans and another plainclothes BCI agent—Kershaw if I recalled— climbed out of Evan's unmarked cruiser and approached us.

"Who are you?" Evans demanded of Gallo. "What's your business here?" This was getting interesting.

Gallo eyed both BCI men and swept back his leather jacket. I couldn't see but I'm sure it was the old "here's my badge" move so famous in cop shows.

"I'm Deputy US Marshal Gallo. My business is my business. Move your car, officer, I'm leaving."

"I'm Special Agent Evans, BCI. This is Agent Kershaw. No one's going anywhere until I get answers."

"To what?" Gallo growled. "I'm federal. You're *just* staties. Move."

Evans glanced over at Randy just getting to his feet. Then, he looked at Janey-Lynn and finally at me sitting in Gallo's SUV.

"Lowe?" Evans asked. "I got a warrant to search your apartment. What did you do to get this fed involved?"

"Don't worry about that." Gallo nodded. "Execute your warrant. I'm taking him with me."

"Not so fast," Evans said, walking toward me. "I checked NCIC en route here, and there's nothing but my warrant concerning him."

Why didn't that comfort me?

Gallo outstretched his arm and blocked Evans from my door. "Marshal business."

"Oh, Marshal business? Why didn't you say so." Evans cast a wry glance at Kershaw and pushed Gallo's arm away. "Got a Marshal-biz warrant?"

"On its way." Gallo stepped in front of him now, escalating the confrontation. "I have a verbal from the Circuit Court. I'm leaving with him. You can have that shit bird over there." He tossed a thumb over his shoulder at Randy. "Assault and battery on Ms. Cantrell. I'll swear out a statement later."

Evans waved to Kershaw, who immediately ascended the barn stairs and disappeared into my apartment. I didn't like where this was headed and wanted to read that warrant.

I called out the SUV window, "Vernon, what's with your warrant?"

"We're looking for cash and any evidence related to the Cantrell murders."

"Cash?" Uh, oh. "Based on what?"

"It's all in the warrant," he said and brushed past Gallo to toss the folded court document onto the seat beside me. "Read it when you can."

"Gee, thanks."

He faced Janey-Lynn. "What's the Marshal saying about assault?"

"It's nothing." She refused to look up. "I'm fine."

"Humor me."

After a glance at me—and my nod—she gave him a summary of what happened. To her credit, her story was pretty close. She tried to make

Randy a little less guilty and tried not to suggest Gallo had gone apoplectic. All she did was leave Evans more confused.

"What am I to do with this?" Evans looked at me again. "Curran? You're a shit magnet."

See, I told you so.

I considered my best strategy, and I delivered it. "I got nothing, Vernon. I have no idea what Gallo has on me. I have no idea why you're searching my apartment, either. Just take care of Janey-Lynn. Her stepson is trouble. He might hurt her after we all leave."

"Oh, I can handle that one." Evans scowled at Randy. "You and I need to chat."

"No." Randy was unsteady on his feet. "That Marshal attacked me."

"He started beating on Janey-Lynn," I said. "Marshal Gallo interceded. But feel free to take him in for questioning so I can get out of these cuffs."

As Evans contemplated Gallo, Agent Kershaw appeared at the top of the stairs. He waved to him, and in a moment, Evans joined him on the upper landing. They chatted for a few minutes, and Kershaw had two plastic evidence bags. I could feel the noose around my neck tighten when Evans looked down at me—or perhaps it was the needle pricking my arm. Whatever they had, it was big.

Oh, shit. I know what they had.

Both agents came down the stairs and faced off with Gallo again. Evans threw a thumb toward Randy and Janey-Lynn, who were standing side-by-side.

"Kershaw, take that one into custody." He gestured at Janey-Lynn. "Then call in the crime techs."

"Okay, boss." Kershaw moved quickly and handcuffed her.

"Sorry, Janey-Lynn," Evans said with little enthusiasm. "I got a warrant for your arrest, too—murder."

"Murder?" I asked. "Vernon, have you lost your mind?"

"No." Evans slapped the roof of the SUV. "Those video files aren't helping as much as I'd hoped. There's more evidence, too. I'll save that for later."

I said, "More evidence that can't exist because neither of us did anything."

"Yeah?" Evans jutted a finger first toward me, then Janey-Lynn. "Both your alibis are bullshit. You've been lying."

Well, he got me there. I had an alibi, but I couldn't really use it. "Come on, Vernon. What changed since we talked last?"

"Well, first, Lowe," he said, "we just found twenty-five grand hidden in your apartment. Care to explain?"

No, not really. "I don't trust banks. That's my life savings."

"Sure it is." He turned to Janey-Lynn. "How coincidental that you withdrew that same amount from your business account two days before your husband's murder."

"No, I didn't." Janey-Lynn's voice was almost shrill. "That's not true, Agent Evans."

"We just found these in your loft, Curran." Evans held up the second evidence bag. In it were two pistols—one affixed with a silencer. "Money says one of these is the murder weapon."

What the hell was going on? Yes, the pistol with the silencer was mine—not legally, but still mine. "Vernon, one of them is mine. The other isn't. I have no idea how that one got in my place. Did someone send you looking for it here? Like maybe in a particular place?"

Evans aimed a finger at me. "As a matter of fact—"

"Enough." Gallo cut the air with his hand. "I couldn't care less about your murder case, Evans. I'm taking Curran. Federal trumps state. When I'm done with him, you can have him. Not until. So, do whatever you want with this mess here, but we're leaving."

Why was that suddenly making me feel better?

"That might be, Marshal." Evans wasn't intimidated. "I still want to see your warrant before you leave. Get someone of authority on the horn for me to talk to."

I'd almost forgotten about Randy Cantrell. He got put down moments ago. Now, he was enjoying himself. His mouth was agape, and his eyeballs couldn't get bigger. He had a smile pasted on his ugly mug that I so desperately wanted to bitch-slap off.

"Vernon, I can explain the cash," I said. "I can't explain the second pistol.

CHAPTER FIFTY-ONE

It's not what you think."

"It never is." He held up a hand to shut me down. "For your own damn good, be quiet, Lowe. Twenty-five grand is steep money for a hit around here. Your mistake was that cash and her withdrawal connect the dots right to Charlie Cantrell's murder. How stupid to keep the gun—or was it arrogance?"

Really? He thinks Janey-Lynn paid me twenty-five grand to kill Charlie? I would have killed the bastard for free if I could have gotten away with it. Not that I had, mind you. Just doing the math. He did have one good point: why would I keep the murder weapon in my loft? That would be tantamount to the stupidest thing I'd ever done. And that says a lot.

"Vernon, you know this is all wrong."

"I don't care." Gallo slammed my side passenger door. "I'll call my office and have the Senior Marshal call you, Agent Evans." He climbed into the SUV, pulled his cell phone from the holder on the dash, and dialed. "Marty, it's Gallo. I need Marshal Carver to get on the horn to the Virginia State Police ASAP. He'll know what it's about. Thanks."

Janey-Lynn struggled against Kershaw's grip on her arm. "This is all crazy. I didn't withdraw any money. I had nothing to do with Charlie's death. I want my lawyer. Now."

"Soon as we process you," Evans said. "You had me fooled, Janey-Lynn. Curran made me look like an ass, too. But I got you both, now. Though I have to say, it pains me."

Gallo hung his head out the open window. "Agent Evans, it'll be a couple minutes before Senior Marshal Carver can call. He'll explain everything."

Without another word, Gallo hit the gas and drove around Evan's car, nearly taking the front fender with him. A few moments later, we were gone.

"Gallo," I said, leaning as far forward in the seat as the belt would allow. "What's really going on?"

Gallo floored the SUV and we skidded out of the county road onto Route 50 a few miles away from the farm.

"How about a hint?"

We weaved around several cars and almost went off the road. As soon as he straightened the vehicle out, I realized we were heading west, not east toward his office. A sick, gnawing feeling consumed me. We were heading into lonely, sparsely populated western Virginia.

"Gallo, murder is—"

"Shut it, Curran." He drove an elbow backward into my face to push me back. "The bastards have Madi. They want Piper. You're going to give him to me."

Chapter Fifty-Two

Ambassador McKnight

"Mr. President, I'm gratified at your confidence." The Ambassador glanced over his speaker phone on his desk at his aide and winked slyly. "I'm humbled by the offer. If that is what it is."

"It is. The truth is, Brad, Emilio Alvarez asked to be withdrawn from consideration. He was a shoo-in. Party leaders thought he'd make a great first Latino president, too. After all, the vice presidency is just a first step. At the end of this term, whoever is vice president will be the party's next candidate for president."

The words 'candidate for president' rippled through him. In all his years, this was the path he'd been on. He'd taken some extreme chances. Executed extraordinary tactics. Steps few would be willing to take. Yet, he had. Now, it was coming to fruition.

"Chris, I am deeply honored." He paused and pushed the last button of what he already knew. "May I ask what the rush is? Has something else happened to the vice president?"

"Yes. It's time to act now." A long, empty silence before the president cleared his throat. "This is all between us, Brad?"

"Of course. It goes without saying."

"Grayson is not well. He has a brain tumor." The silence returned but only momentarily. "The tabloids—hell, even the mainstream media—knows.

The tumor is inoperable and was discovered mid-campaign. Back then, we couldn't rock the boat. Things were too close as it was. He's tried to fight it quietly. Regrettably, well, you've seen his performance. He simply can't continue. You are aware of his collapse at the Kennedy Center during the ending days of the campaign. Yesterday, his Secret Service detail brought him to Walter Reed when he passed out in his limo. The news is all over it. It's time to get past this, Brad. As soon as I have a clear replacement and Grayson can prepare some initiatives for me, he'll resign. It's already dicey, and I must be poised to move extremely fast."

"I'm sorry to hear all that."

The president lowered his voice. "Our Middle East initiatives are going to shit, Brad. Grayson has been working his contacts from home to try and get some cooperation from The Kingdom and Tel Aviv. The Kingdom is pushing its oil weight around, and the Israelis don't trust a move we make. Can't say as I blame them after the past few years. Hell, we've been speaking out of both sides of our mouth with them, the Iranians, and even with the Syrian crisis. Although I'd like to give Grayson time to glue this back together, I'm not sure he has the time or ability to do that. I've engaged my old pal, Frank Feld to try and keep things together, but I'm not sure even he can do it alone. We need a better plan."

The Ambassador smiled. One of the few people Abby respected in the ranks of so-called Mid-East experts. If the president could only hear Abby pontificate about the ills of the Middle East and her plans to fix them with lofty ideals. If she had her way, it could all be done now—right now. And, most importantly, not the way the West wished it to be. Hers was a more "stay out of the Middle East's business" approach that Western allies didn't care for. Strange, too, considering her Mediterranean blood and the region' need for Western support.

"I understand, sir. What can I do to help Grayson?"

The president grunted. "Be ready on a moment's notice. If he can't glue this together enough, you'll have to try. Have a plan. Be ready to execute. Can you do that?"

A moment's notice? He'd worked his ass off for over thirty years. Now, it was down to moments.

"Yes." The Ambassador changed direction. "What about Emilio Alvarez? Does he know?"

"Yes. But with him, I just don't get it. He owes me a better explanation. What he told me was pure bullshit. He suggested some deep-seated health concerns. Bullshit, I tell you. He's running scared of something—"

"Or someone." The Ambassador hesitated, adding, "I'm sorry, sir, that was inappropriate of me. Pure speculation."

"No, we're on the same page, Brad. Jesus, I wish it weren't so." The president sighed loudly. "Can you please cut the bullshit when it's just us? For once? You weren't at the top of my list. You know that. Now you are it."

"I heard about Senator Wain, too, Mr., er, Chris. I'm so sorry. What a tragedy." He noticed Scott didn't conceal that same grin he'd had before when discussing Wain. He quickly tapped the call to mute, saying, "Bryan, that's enough."

Scott nodded solemnly just as the president spoke again. "Now look, Brad. I'm not making any announcements or signals outside the key leadership. Grayson knows, of course. He is fully on board. I can't afford for his condition to get in the way of the entire Mid East initiatives. Not after how far we've come."

The Ambassador knew it was time to strike and tapped the call off mute. "Chris, what if I began working with the vice president? As an advisor, I could help guide his strategy and perhaps even open some doors for him. Then, when the time comes, it will be an easier transition, and the region will already understand my involvement."

The president went silent. One, two, three minutes with only the occasional sigh or cough to signal he was still there. Finally, "I couldn't ask for a better plan, Brad. That's exactly what we're going to do. A Special Assistant. It might make his situation less noticeable to the press, too."

Yes, and put my name in the headlines.

The president continued. "I'd like you to meet with some senior folks on the hill first. I need to make sure they're on board before I jump in the deep

273

end. Understand?"

"Of course. Understandable. Send me your wish list. Though, I'm sure I can guess. I'll begin as soon as you like."

"Good. Oh, and Brad, there is one thing—perhaps two."

The Ambassador knew those two things. "Senator Piccolo and Governor Hersh?"

"Yes." Silence. A long, awkward silence. "Give me a day or so to speak with them. Both are exceptional men—exceptional candidates. I don't think either of them has the experience to lead the ticket in a few years. And there have been some rumors around town, too—ugly rumors."

Scott leaned forward and scribbled something on a pad of paper and turned it for him to see, mouthing, "Even he thinks Piccolo or Hersh are behind Wain and Alvarez."

"Chris?" The Ambassador frowned and shoved the paper away. "You're not thinking either of them pushed General Alvarez out, are you? This isn't some Tj O'Connor thriller. Do you really believe—"

"I don't want to, Brad. What are the chances? Wain takes his own life—presumably. Alvarez pulls out without a damn good reason knowing the job is his, for a nod. You had a visitor the other day—"

"What?" The Ambassador's eyes flashed at Scott. Their eyes locked, and ice formed between them. "I'd like to know how you came by that information, Chris."

Scott threw his hands in the air, shaking his head. "Wasn't me, boss. Honest."

The president sighed. "That's not important. I know. And you should know that I'm sending a Secret Service liaison to meet with your people. Non-negotiable. I can't have another 'oops.' One more 'oops' and the entire nation—maybe the world—will start screaming conspiracy. I can't have that kind of scandal going on. Not now. Not ever."

"I understand." The Ambassador broke his stare with Scott. "I'll do whatever you ask, Chris. You can count on me."

As soon as the call ended, the Ambassador turned and looked across his den to Abby sitting in a tall-back leather chair near the window. She hung up the phone extension and had on a wide, devilish smile.

"Well, my dear," the Ambassador said, steepling his hands above his desk. "You may say it now."

She stood and came to him. "I told you so." Then, ignoring Scott across the desk from them, she pushed the Ambassador's chair back and slipped onto his lap like a schoolgirl. "And it's about time. I am so proud of you, Bradley. I've known all along you were destined for greater things than simply an ambassadorship. All those years ago in Athens—I knew."

His lips found hers for a long kiss. Then, he said, "I could not have done this without you, Abby. I hope you know that. Since our younger days, you've been the voice guiding me along."

She hugged him tightly.

"I think an engagement is in order." He leaned back from her, and his face softened. "No?"

"Sir, let's not get ahead of ourselves." Scott stood abruptly. "We need to be careful about that one, sir. There are other threads to pull—"

"We're done here, Bryan," The Ambassador said. "We can reconvene in the morning."

Scott didn't budge. "But sir. We have to begin planning—"

"In the morning." The Ambassador dismissed him with a hasty wave of his hand. "I have other plans this evening."

Chapter Fifty-Three

Curran

"Who's got Madison?" My thoughts swirled—was it Mr. Nobody's 'others?' "Tell me what happened. Tell me *everything.*"

Gallo swerved violently again as he passed a slow-moving pickup hauling something in a homemade trailer. "They called today when I had you in lockup. They have her. They wanted you released to find Piper. They want me to bring Piper to them. If I don't make it all happen..."

"Right." The bastards. "You're certain it's legit? Not just a veiled threat?"

Madi's green eyes were in front of me, now. Normally pretty and friendly, they were fearful now. That tore me up inside and began swirling rage around my brain. In the short hour we'd spent playing checkers—and me losing money—something strange had happened. We, well, bonded. How was that possible? I had stayed in her house out of a strange, unfamiliar need to protect her while her wayward babysitter was gone. It was a one-off, a passing exercise in compassion.

Where the hell had that all come from?

"She's gone, asshole. Someone took her out of school. They flashed a badge and claimed to be a Marshal that I sent for her."

Whoever "they" are, they'd thought of everything. Mr. Nobody warned me of others hunting for Piper. Tommy Astor got twitchy talking about them. I'd considered bad guys trying to keep me from my two-hundred grand. I'd never considered the lengths they'd go to for Piper. I hadn't considered any ploy like kidnapping Madison Gallo. I'm not sure I ever would have thought of that one.

"Gallo," I choked on the words as they came out of my mouth. "Proof of life?"

He jammed on the brakes, and I bounced off the front seat and bobbled around the back. He slid the SUV into a convenience store parking lot and rolled around the side where no cars were parked. He spun in the seat and aimed his Glock at my face.

"You son-of-a-bitch," he snarled. "Don't even think that. Where's Piper?"

"Gallo, I'm on your side. You know who I am and what I used to be—"

"Yeah?" He jutted the gun into my face a bit closer. "I know more than that."

"Then you know we both understand the risks here. We both know the M.O. of people like this. Are you sure Madison—"

"Yes, God dammit. Yes." He sat there, raging hate at me as his hand started to quiver. Then, he retracted his gun and settled back in the seat. "They sent me a video. She was reading a book, sitting with some woman. The news was on in the background. It was this afternoon's broadcast. I'm sure it's today, and she's okay."

My blood pressure settled. I had no idea about being a dad. Other than what I'd seen on TV and movies, I could only guess what he was going through. I'm not saying sticking guns in my face and threatening my life was okay. But I understood the need to do whatever it took to save someone you love. I had an opportunity to do that once. I blew it.

Thirty years ago, I'd left the military after being recruited by Dark Creek. Why, I can't recall, but they offered me some grand scheme to go adventuring around the world and make big money. Up until I departed on my first Dark Creek mission, I thought all that adventuring would include Carli. It didn't, and she wasn't there when I returned. She vanished. No trace. No tracks. No forwarding address. Gone. I should have tried harder to find her. At the time, I thought I did. In hindsight, I didn't do enough. Maybe I was relieved I was free. Maybe I was still pumped on bravado and bullshit. I convinced myself we were both better off. She for not having to always be waiting for me to come home. Me for not having to worry about her being alone. I thought it was the noble thing to do. Truth is, I was an ass and blew the one chance I'd had to have a woman like her—to have *her*. I know that despite the many women since, there was never anyone like Carli. I never married. Never considered it. Regret had been my mistress all these years. I was okay with paying this penance. Thirty years ago…well, thirty years, six months, and a few days ago. But who's counting? I'd lost Carli to pride, distance, and stupidity. Two of the three were very dangerous excuses. They are like gasoline and matches. The stupidity was one-hundred-proof me, and it's followed me my entire life.

The look on Gallo's face—the loss, the fear, the helplessness—were as real to me as they were to him. Just different years. Different people. Different circumstances. The only common denominator was, well, *me*.

"Gallo, I have Piper."

"I know." He faced me across the seat again. "I know what I'm demanding is wrong. It's illegal. It's—"

"It's okay with me. Drive." I told him where Stevie's mountain complex was, and off we went. I asked him to remove my handcuffs. He refused. "Nothing's going to happen to that little girl, Gallo. Nothing. They can have the little twerp and whatever else they want."

As we sped onto Route 50 heading west, he stewed in some kind of self-deprecating trance. I guess all fathers—parents—feel responsible and terrified when their kid is in trouble. Those that don't, probably don't deserve them to begin with.

As we crossed into West Virginia, he began to speak again.

"Curran, who sent you for him?"

I shrugged. "You're not going to believe this, but I'm not sure." I explained my weird rendezvous with Tommy Astor and Mr. Nobody. I felt bad admitting Tommy's involvement. But there was a nine-year-old little girl—terrified and waiting for her dad to save her. Tommy could deal if things got ugly. "It's about the money for me. It all sort of made sense as it was happening. I trust Tommy."

"You've become a mercenary?" He watched me in the rearview mirror. "All this time I thought you were just some schmuck PI."

All this time? What the hell did that mean? I asked him that.

For a minute, a very long, tense minute, he stared straight ahead as we made the climb into the Appalachian Mountains headed west. He was debating something inside. Something he might tell me. Maybe.

I asked him again.

"Let's just say I know more about you than anyone in the world, Curran. At least, I know the things they don't. Maybe I know the things you don't know, too."

The things I don't?

"I don't trust you, Curran. Not at all. For all I know, you're leading me into an ambush, knowing that I can't bring backup. Maybe you and Piper are in this together. You both smell money. Know this—I'm not letting you screw me and get Madi killed. I'm not losing her, too."

Gallo played more word games than any game show. Just when I thought he'd start his word salad again, he drove off Route 50 into a driveway that led a quarter mile off the highway to an old stone church. The area was secluded. I hadn't seen a house or gas station or another car for miles. We were totally isolated.

My mouth went dry. The handcuffs dug into me and reminded me that I couldn't defend myself. Whatever Gallo was about to do, I couldn't do a damn thing about it.

He wheeled us to a stop and climbed out of the SUV. Then, with silence and his pistol jammed into my side, he dragged me from the rear seat and shoved me face-first over the SUV's hood again. He'd uncuffed me and dropped them on the hood—right beside his Glock.

As I slowly turned to face him, my stomach twisted.

"What now, Gallo?"

He stared at me—through me. "That little girl is all I have, Curran. I'll do anything for her. I'll give up my badge, my gun—my life. Nothing can get in my way. Still, I can't do it without you—and I don't trust you."

If that was supposed to be a surprise, it wasn't. "I told you I'll help. I'm bringing you to Piper. You have my word."

He scoffed at me. "And once we're all cozy together, you might screw me. Just because you played chess with Madi doesn't mean I can trust you not to toss her away, too. You're good at that."

Jesus, how deep did he dig into me?

"Gallo, it's Madison, it was checkers, and she cheats."

For a second, I thought he might crack a smile. That thought dissipated when he cursed and glared hard, cold anger at me.

I said, "Look, I may be a lot of things, not all good either. But I won't let anyone hurt that little girl. You have to trust me."

"Yes, I do have to." He took a step back. "Pick up my pistol, Curran."

Ah, what? I turned sideways and glanced at his Glock sitting on the SUV's hood within easy reach. "Why? So you can pull a backup piece and kill me in self-defense?"

"Pick it up."

I did and lowered it to my side.

The starlight glistened on the sweat beading around his eyes. "You have the gun. Go if you want to. Go and do whatever you're going to do. I'm going after Madison. You have the gun. Keys are in the ignition."

What kind of low life did he think me? Jesus, whatever old files he read about me, I had to have Piper hack into and delete.

"No." I lifted the Glock, and, with my thumb, dropped the magazine onto the ground. Then, slowly, I snapped the slide back and ejected the nine-millimeter round from the chamber, catching it in the air. I tossed him the pistol. "I'm not who you think I am, Gallo. I might not be the best guy in the world. But I'm not what you think."

I stooped and picked up the magazine, and handed it over with the ejected round. Then, I backed away.

He stared unbelieving at me. For a long time—a weird, deja vu time—he watched me. Then, he hit me with the hardest punch he could possibly throw from five feet away.

"You don't know me either, Curran." He reloaded his Glock, jacked a round into the chamber to have it fire-ready, and holstered it. "Madison's mom and I were married very young. We were still in college when Madison was born."

I didn't know where this was going, but it unnerved me.

"Madison's mom, my wife, Renae, died of a very rare cancer—Li-Fraumeni syndrome. LFS itself doesn't really kill you. It opens the door to different serious cancers. They kill you. Madison was only three. She barely remembers her—wouldn't at all except for the photos I have."

"I'm sorry, but what's this—"

"Renae's mom—Madison's grandma—died of the same cancer. It's hereditary." His eyes flooded, and his voice was just above a whisper. The pain in his words shuttered me to the bone as he turned away. "Madison's mom was *Renae Trevino.*"

Trevino? Is he saying...oh, shit. *No. No. No.*

Now, my face was awash. I knew what was coming before he spoke the words, and it hit me like a boxer's gut punch.

"Madi's grandma was Carli Renae Trevino." His voice was gone now, just choked words and broken syllables. "She died of that cancer in nineteen ninety-six. It took her just three weeks after her doctor found it. But not before she gave birth to Renae. All this happened while Madison's grandfather was off chasing his tail overseas."

Sweet Jesus, no. No. Carli had been pregnant. That's what she had tried to tell me the night before I left for my first Dark Creek mission. I'd been so self-absorbed that I didn't want anything getting in my way of the adventure. I hadn't given her the chance to tell me. She took that for rejection. *Jesus, no.*

As though I'd seen her just last night, the emotions flooded in. The pain. The anguish. The loss. I lost Carli twice—first to my own arrogance—then to cancer. Yet, I'd not known. I'd not been with her. Never said goodbye. She died alone. And she left behind my...daughter.

"Carli was pregnant? When I got home, I looked—"

"Not hard enough." Gallo wiped his face and cleared the moonlit shimmy from his cheeks. "When you left, she gave up on you. She went away and hid to have the baby. She'd planned on telling you after Renae was born. The cancer took her too fast, and she had no family left."

Carli hid from me? *Damn me to hell.* I pushed her away, and she hid from me. I lost her to a disease I never knew she had. I lost her before I knew of…oh, God.

I looked at him, and our eyes met. They locked onto the truth that he'd kept for years and that I never knew.

He said it at the same moment it hit me with a lightning bolt through my heart.

"Curran, I married your daughter, Renae. Madison is your granddaughter."

Chapter Fifty-Four

Curran

Granddaughter? Well, now I know how she cheats so well at checkers. It's hereditary.

A spear of shame struck my heart. A rush of regret and embarrassment consumed me. Sitting in Gallo's kitchen, playing checkers, an odd familiarity found me each time I looked at the green-eyed little girl. Now, I didn't see Madi's cute, smiling face. I saw Carli. Her eyes. Her infectious grin. Her mischievous glances here and there just when she was about to take one of my checkers. A giggle of triumph when it was a king. Why hadn't I seen that? Why hadn't I seen Carli in that sweet, beautiful child's face?

"Gallo, does Madison know who I am?" The words felt like someone had their fingers around my throat. "Anything?"

"No. I knew your name but fought the urge to find you. I've been on this assignment working Piper when you popped up. Then there's the Cantrell murders."

Yeah, and you wanted to frame me. I said as much, and that reddened his face.

"Do you blame me? You ran out on Madi's grandmother and left my wife—only a baby—alone. You're a class-A prick, Curran. Hell, yes. I wanted you to be guilty so I could lock you up."

He didn't candy coat it, did he? "Okay, I guess from your perspective—"

"My perspective?" He wheeled around, and I thought he was going to throw a punch. He didn't, but his face turned stone cold. "Which part is just perspective? The part where you ran out on Carli or the part where Renae grew up and died without a father?"

I wish he'd punched me. Stomped me. Kicked my guts in. No, I wish he'd shoot me.

"I didn't know, dammit." The words cracked out. "She didn't tell me. I looked for her for weeks. No one knew where she went. No forwarding address. Nothing. I tried. I didn't know."

He was on me—sudden and direct. He grabbed my shirt and shoved me back so hard into the side of his SUV that he knocked the wind out of me. I didn't fight back. I didn't want to. He lifted me by my shirt and slammed me back again—once, twice, three times. Each time, the ferocity grew, and his face darkened into a place that scared me.

"You should have known. Damn you to hell, Curran." He slammed me a fourth time and then shoved me sideways off the SUV and away from him. "I read her letters. Renae had a few left behind that her mom wrote to her. The adoption family kept them for her until she was eighteen—just before we met. Carli tried to tell you, but you left. She didn't want you staying just for the baby, so she ran away, had Renae, and planned to tell you later. She didn't want you to feel trapped. Imagine that. She was protecting you. You bastard."

Tears rained down, and my breath wouldn't come. So many years had passed. So many dreams and memories and every day wondering what happened to her. She just vanished off the face of the earth. Not too many years ago, just after I'd gotten back on my feet from Voula Beach, I tried to find her again on the internet. Nothing. Not a damn thing after nineteen ninety-six. Poof. Gone.

I wiped my eyes. "Did the letters say anything else?"

"Screw you, Curran." He backstepped, opening the distance from me. I guess he was either fighting the urge to kick my ass some more or getting clear of the powder burns when he shot me. "You don't get anymore. You live with it as I have. Live with losing her and knowing it's your fault."

Yes, it was my fault. But...*wait a damn minute.* "I didn't kill her, Gallo. I didn't leave her either. Things were fine—at least, I thought they were. I took a good job. One that would take better care of us than the Army. I left for my first field operation, and when I got home—"

"Six weeks late," he snapped. "A month and a half later."

"Yes, okay. I told her three weeks. The op ran long." I tried to recall just where and why that had been, but it was hidden from me in a veil of pain and remorse—guilt. "I sent letters once or twice—there was almost no email back then. That's all I could. I was on the move. When I got back, she was gone. No trace. If I'd known about Renae—"

"What?" He stabbed the air between us with an icy finger. "You'd what, Curran? Stay? Be a father? You're telling me you would have stayed home?"

Would I? "I don't know, Gallo. I don't. But I would have made sure she knew I was coming back. That I'd be there for them. Of that, I'm sure. I didn't leave her, Gallo. She left me. And she never gave me a choice about Renae."

Those words hit him with as much force as his pummeling me moments before. He blinked a few times as the anger drained from his eyes, down his cheeks, and disappeared. Maybe it was gone. Maybe it went into timeout.

"Maybe," he said in a soft, almost sympathetic voice. "That doesn't change the fact that Madison has been taken, and it's your fault."

That was up for debate, too. But at that moment, I'd take that responsibility.

"Then let's get her back." I gestured to his Glock holstered on his side. "I'm gonna need my pistol."

Our eyes locked together with an energy that was hot and raging—anger, fear, trepidation. Suddenly, though neither of us had thought about it until that moment, we were family. The bond between us—a little nine-year-old girl who was somewhere, scared and alone—was in danger. Wherever she was, she was praying her daddy would rescue her.

Little did she know that her grandfather—*Pappa*—was coming, too. And God help those sorry bastards who took her.

"I guess that's in the cards." He eyed me sideways. "Don't make me regret

285

this, Curran. I'll shoot you—family or not."

I can't remember what having family was about. Not since I was a kid. Now, after him stalking me and gunning for me, we were suddenly that.

"I need you to promise me something, Gallo."

"Really? A promise?" He walked to the SUV, leaned in, and withdrew my Kimber and spare magazines. He tossed them to me. "I just gave you your life back—and your gun. Don't push it."

"Don't get in the way when we find the bastards who took Madison."

He never hesitated. "I promise."

The drive to Stevie's compound was surreal. It was also very quiet. We drove west on Route 50 into the mountains and then south on some West Virginia roads in total silence. I don't know if it was that neither of us knew what to say, or neither of us wanted to be the first to speak. Gallo knew for some time who I was. I had no clue about him or Madison. He must have planned what he'd say to me when we finally met. Or maybe he didn't. Maybe he never planned on finding me. Maybe he didn't want Madison to know anything about me.

At that moment, the thought of never knowing Madison was painful and heartbreaking. I'd only spent an hour with that little girl in her entire life. I'd stayed to look after her because of her rogue babysitter. We'd played checkers, and I'd lost my wallet to her. How had that happened? Was that some kind of ethereal family bond that drew us together? I'd gone there to get dirt on Gallo. Dirt to force him to leave me alone. Instead, I found a little nine-year-old who needed me—perhaps just for an hour—but she needed me.

Really, Curran? Ethereal bond? Get a grip.

As we pulled off the two-lane and onto the long dirt trail that led to Stevie's compound, I turned in the seat to face Gallo.

"Look, Gallo," I said in the sincerest tone I could muster. "I just didn't know. If I had, I never would have let Renae grow up alone. Never. You have to believe me. But that's in the past. Madison is now."

He nodded almost imperceivably.

"I promise you this," I said, and turned forward again as my fingers touched my Kimber on my hip. "I'm going to get Madison back to you—to us. I don't care who has her or where she is. I'm going to get her back—safely."

"Then what?" he asked coldly. "Are you going to—"

"I'm going to end this. Whatever it is. I'm going to end it."

Chapter Fifty-Five

Curran

I knew we had a big problem the moment we pulled up to Stevie's cabin. It wasn't that he was waiting with a machine gun to cut unwanted strangers into shreds, either. It was simpler than that. It was that Stevie Keene didn't respond at all to our arrival.

I would have felt better if I'd been ducking buckshot.

Instincts made me slip my pistol out as I opened the passenger door. "Take the back, Gallo. Watch out for Stevie." I described him carefully. "He might come at you. If he does, don't kill him. He's on our side, and we're going to need every friend we can get."

"I thought you said he was reliable?"

"He can be a little, er, unstable."

We'd discussed Stevie on the last hour of the drive. I'd explained virtually everything that had happened to me since my dressing up as Methuselah and talking my way into Piper's Leesburg lair a few nights ago. In turn, he said nothing. Not quite quid pro quo, no.

"I never said reliable." I joined him at the driver's side of his SUV. "I said unpredictable. He's good in a fight. Trust me. He saved my ass in Greece."

He eyed me through the dark. "You got your butt shot off in Greece."

Damn if he didn't have a point. "I did. But I'd be dead if Stevie hadn't been there. The last memory I have is him standing over me, fighting off those bastards. He took a bullet or two trying to get me clear."

He shrugged and studied the cabin.

Stevie's entire compound—the cabin, two out-buildings where he had a woodworking shop, a barn for a couple horses, and a bunk house for hunting guests—was dark. No lights. No sound. No signs of life.

That shouldn't be.

"I'll go in the front." I gestured toward the side of the cabin. "Take the back. Stay out until I call for you."

He shook his head. "I'm a US Marshal. You're a nobody. I'll go in the front. I have authority. You have nothing."

As he started forward, I grabbed his arm. "Gallo, you *were* a Marshal. Since you grabbed me earlier tonight, you stopped being one. I know what I'm doing. I might be getting old, but I know what I'm doing. Now, go around back."

He glared at me but relented and headed around the side of the cabin.

I crept up the wooden porch stairs. All the while, I kept an eye on the windows to make sure a gun barrel didn't suddenly protrude to blow me to pieces. Stevie wasn't always careful to know who he was shooting at before he pulled the trigger. At the front door, I peeked in the window but saw only more darkness.

"Stevie? Hey, it's me. It's Curran."

Nothing.

"Okay, I'm coming in. Don't shoot, stab, or mutilate me, brother."

I turned the knob and pushed the door open with my foot, keeping my body behind the thick log walls. Half-expecting a shotgun blast, I cringed.

To my delight, no gunfire.

"Stevie?" I slipped around the doorway. "Stevie?"

Crickets.

Floorboards creaked down the hall from the grand hall where I'd entered. I lifted my pistol and prepared for whatever might come.

"Stevie?" I called again. "It's Curran."

"Nothing here, Curran," Gallo called back as he walked out of the dark hall. "Rear of the house is empty."

Damn him. "I told you—"

"I don't take orders."

"You should. I could have shot you. That's why I told you to stay put in the back."

Oddly enough, he shrugged. "Yeah, you're right. I wasn't thinking. Where's your friend? More importantly, where's Piper?"

Exactly my questions.

"I'll check upstairs," I said. "You clear down here."

He turned to go and stopped to face me again. "Another order?"

Sweet Jesus. "How about a suggestion? Just do it."

I was about to climb the wood-railed staircase when a bang—something heavy on light wood—turned me around. The sound repeated three times by the time I'd followed it to a pine door in the far rear of the room.

"Gallo, in here." I waited for him to join me. It was too late to start sneaking around silently. If there was bad news in this cabin, it already knew we were there. I gestured to the door and lifted my pistol, holding up three fingers.

He nodded and counted down with his left hand. His right held his Glock. On three, he yanked open the door.

Inside was a deep, dark room—a junk room filled with hunting clothing, animal traps, fishing gear, and several gun safes. Except for one item in the rear of the ten-foot-deep storeroom.

Billy Piper—bound at the ankles and wrists with duct tape wrapped haphazardly around him. A thick piece of tape was across his mouth with a small slit cut to give him room to breathe through his mouth if he wanted.

I dragged Piper from the room and rolled him onto his butt while Gallo climbed the stairs and cleared the rest of the cabin. In a few moments, he'd returned, but I wasn't finished cutting the tape from Piper's extremities.

"What happened, Billy?" Gallo demanded, ripping the tape from his lips so violently that it took skin and whiskers with it. "Where's Keene?"

Piper spit and rubbed his mouth and cheeks as soon as I freed his hands. "Dammit, that hurt, Marshal. Couldn't you be easy?"

"No." Gallo grunted. "You're getting what you deserve for running off on me. What happened here?"

CHAPTER FIFTY-FIVE

"Easy, Gallo," I said, freeing Piper's feet. "Get him some water."

"After he talks."

Piper wiped some blood dripping from the torn flesh on the corners of his mouth. "All right, all right. Your buddy, Stevie, started drinking after you left, Curran. He ranted about nothing. Then he tied me up, rolled me into that closet, and left."

"What was he ranting about?" I helped him to the couch near the fireplace. "Where'd he go?"

"I don't know. He got pissed off at the world." Piper rubbed his wrists and ankles. "He went through a half bottle of booze within a half hour of you leaving. Last thing I saw was him grabbing up a fresh bottle and slamming the closet door on me. What a jerk. First, he interrogated me like I was some perp—"

"Well," I said, "you are."

Piper's face twisted angrily. "Whatever. Anyway, first, he interrogated me as he got drunker and drunker. Then off he went."

As much as I hated to admit it, this was exactly what I feared he'd do—the getting drunk part, not the rest. He'd done it before. Many times. But the allure of big money and repaying me for the other night had given me hope he'd stay sober for a few days. I'd been wrong.

"Any idea where he went?" Gallo asked, dropping into an overstuffed leather chair facing the couch. "His POS Blazer is in the front yard."

Piper shrugged. "I was in the closet. I couldn't see or hear anything. I'm starving and want something to drink. And I don't mean water. I've about had it with you guys."

Gallo jumped from the chair and descended on Piper like a cat on its prey. He grabbed him by the shirt as he had me earlier and hoisted him to his feet.

"Listen, you stupid bastard," he roared. "You were running an illegal hacking operation out of an unapproved house while in WITSEC. You probably cost me my career. Then you ran and God only knows what all this is going to cost me. You're not in a position to whine and complain."

"Come on, Marshal—"

"Shut up." Gallo tossed the fat little man backward and nearly toppled him over the couch. "One more unhelpful word, and I'm getting a shovel—there's a lot of forest to bury things in."

Piper's eyes were big as plates, and he glanced from me to Gallo, back to me, and finally settled on the floor. "I don't know where Stevie went. But he couldn't have gotten far. He was drunk as hell."

The shotgun blast behind us shattered two light globes on the wagon wheel chandelier overhead and sent us all diving for cover.

Chapter Fifty-Six

U.C.

"Are you gonna hurt my daddy when he comes?"

U.C. stared at little Madison Gallo lying on the small folding cot across the room. "Aren't you worried about yourself?"

She shook her head. "You look like a mean man, but you don't look like you'd hurt me. Not really."

U.C. laughed out loud. *Gutsy kid.* "I tell you what, kid. If your daddy does what he's told, everyone goes home just fine. Him, too."

"Promise?" Madison eyed him suspiciously. "You gotta swear."

"Sure, I swear." *Precocious, too.* "You're pretty brave for a little girl."

"Daddy says it's just him and me." Madison blinked a few times. "I gotta be brave and strong. That, and I'm on my own a lot."

"He leaves you alone?"

She shook her head. "No. I just am sometimes."

"Too bad, kid." U.C. felt bad for her. He didn't want to include her in all this, but he'd had no choice. He had his orders. "Get to sleep."

Madison started to speak again, then changed her mind and laid her head down on the rolled blanket, acting as a pillow. She didn't take her eyes off him.

"To sleep," U.C. ordered.

She closed her eyes, but he doubted she would sleep for a while, if at all. Kids have an amazing ability to just drop off to sleep sometimes. But now, fear had control, and the kid might still cry herself to sleep. He wasn't ready for that.

For an hour, U.C. sat in the dark, watching her lying on the cot. There were no windows and only one door, and he positioned himself adjacent to it in case anyone but one of his two men outside entered. If the door opened, he would have time to put several bullets through any intruder before they could locate him.

Just as he began to nod off, his cell phone vibrated in his pocket. He slipped it out, noted the blocked warning, and tapped on the call.

"Do you have the child?" the Controller asked.

"I do."

"Marshal Gallo?"

Perhaps he should play things closer with the Controller than he had been. They were coming down to the wire, and he had no idea what was in store for him when it was over. The Controller had begun eliminating loose ends in the past few days. Every thread connecting back to Greece. Within hours, there might be only one connection left—him. While he had served the Controller well over the years, the endgame was close. Well, an endgame. There could be others. The question was, was he part of those plans, or was he the last loose end?

"He hasn't made any moves yet. He has Curran. I confirmed that a couple hours ago. I'll contact him shortly. Once I have Piper and the data, I'll report in."

The Controller was silent for a long time. Then, "I'll trust your plan. However, one way or the other, this ends in twenty-four hours."

"What's your endgame?"

"I don't understand the question."

"There's more people involved than just Piper and Curran."

Silence.

"You can't expect me to—"

"I do." The Controller's voice was sharp and direct. "Once you have Piper and the data, eliminate everyone. No traces. Maintain Piper until we know for certain what copies may exist and who possesses them. Then, he is no longer of value."

"Everyone?" U.C. glanced at Madison. He accepted that Curran and Piper were necessary. But killing a US Marshal and a couple rich country people wasn't in his plan. And Madison Gallo? "I'm not killing the kid."

Silence.

"There has to be another way."

Silence.

"I'm not doing it."

Silence, a sigh, then, "Then you will simply leave the child behind. I will arrange to do what has to be done."

God, no. "There has to be—"

"I'm very disappointed in you, U.C. Very."

The call ended.

U.C. glanced at the now sleeping little nine-year-old. He didn't necessarily like children. He just didn't like the Controller's orders. There was almost no point in killing her father or the farm people—but he understood precautions. Madison Gallo was totally without reason. Killing a nine-year-old would tarnish his ability—his reputation—for assignments in the future. After this, after killing young Madison Gallo, he'd be left with only that class of work.

The Controller was disappointed in him? *Yeah, me, too.* But the Controller's disappointment meant one thing. When this mission was over, there would be someone waiting for him. His only option was to complete the Controller's orders. To the letter. Each one. *All* of them.

That was no option at all.

Chapter Fifty-Seven

Curran

The shotgun roared behind us. I hit the floor behind one of the overstuffed chairs and tugged my pistol out, looking for a target. There wasn't one. That's because Stevie Keene's veins were filled with straight Kentucky bourbon and not American red cells. Whether it was accidental or a drunken misfire, the recoil from the twelve-gauge pump gun knocked him off balance and onto his butt. He lay on his back, staring blindly at the ceiling. The shotgun lay three feet beside him. The wagon wheel chandelier swung back and forth and threatened to crash to the floor.

Piper was face-down behind the sofa next to me, hands clamped over his head and neck as though in an air raid drill.

Gallo was already up on one knee with his Glock trained on Stevie, ready for a kill shot if needed.

"Gallo, no." I jumped up and secured the shotgun. "Stevie, it's me—Curran."

Gallo didn't budge. "If he twitches, I'm shooting."

I eased over to Gallo and pushed his pistol down at an angle to the floor. "I got this. Trust me."

"That's asking a lot. This is your partner?"

I regrettably confirmed that. Then, I knelt beside Stevie and shook him. His eyes were open wide, staring dully at the beamed ceiling. He was breathing irregularly, and he reeked of booze. Piper had been right. He'd drank a bottle of hooch or more. How he could walk was beyond me. How he was alive, I didn't know. But then, over the last few months, I'd witnessed Stevie descend into this condition often. He'd been fine for years before. Then, without reason, the monster returned and took control of him. Since then, he was sober fewer days than not.

Of all days to falter, this wasn't a good one.

"Stevie, you okay?" I shook him again. "Can you get up?"

He mumbled something and rolled onto his side, gagged a little, and nearly retched on me. He took him several tries before he finally reached a kneeling position. He slowly regained cognition and surveyed the room. He locked onto Piper, seemingly oblivious to Gallo and me.

"Who let you out, boy?" He tried to get to his feet but fell back onto his butt. "Who—"

"Me, Stevie." I grabbed his arm, dragged him onto his feet, and strong-armed him into a ladder-back wooden chair. "You almost killed us all, brother."

For a long time, he stared at me, blinked, and gagged. Then, a light went on somewhere beyond the distillation process, and he looked up at the still-unsettled chandelier.

"Curran? Ah, crap. Sorry. I heard voices. Thought you were those bad guys you're worried about." He gestured to the wagon wheel overhead. "Did I do that?"

Gallo descended on him, kicking the side of the chair and knocking him out of it onto the floor again. "You almost killed us."

"Huh?" Stevie eyed Gallo from the floor. With painful, slow movements, he returned to the chair. This time, standing behind it and holding it for balance. "Who are you?"

"Deputy US Marshal Gallo." Gallo stabbed the air in Stevie's face. "I ought to arrest you right here and now."

"Oh, you're that stick-up-your-ass-Marshal I've heard about." Stevie glanced from me to Gallo. "Arrest me for what?"

"Discharging a firearm in public."

"It's my house, not public." Stevie belched loudly. "Screw you."

"Attempted murder," Gallo added.

Another belch. "Seems I shot at the wagon wheel, not you."

Gallo's face reddened, and he spun on me. "I'm not working with this derelict. We go it alone."

At that moment, I was in his camp of reason. Stevie wasn't operational material. Other than his witty comebacks against Gallo's threats, he was unsteady and untrustworthy. Both things could get me killed. They might also get Madison killed.

I took Stevie's arm. "Come on, brother. Let's get you to bed. Some sleep and tomorrow some food. Gallo's right. You're not on this one."

Stevie tried to resist but nearly toppled over doing so. Instead, he threw a chin toward Piper. "This is on you, boy. You and that damn Whisper thing."

Whisper thing? I shot a glance at Piper who rolled his eyes and plopped himself down on the couch.

I said, "We're going to have a long talk soon as I get back, Piper."

"Whatever." Piper lay back on the couch, rubbing his eyes. "I need some sleep, too. You guys are crazy."

It took me five minutes, with Gallo's help, to negotiate Stevie up the stairs to his bed. There, we dropped him on his side and braced pillows behind him so if he vomited during the night—and I'm sure he was going to—he wouldn't choke to death.

Back in the grand hall, Gallo went in search of food as I confronted Billy Piper, sitting in an overstuffed leather chair.

"All right, Piper, give. What's so important in that data you hacked to cause this? And what's 'that Whisper thing?'"

He yawned. "I don't know."

"Bullshit." I kicked his feet a little. "It's all connected. The murder of a local rich farmer—Charlie Cantrell, and his girlfriend. The gunfight with your neighbor, Mr. Culpepper. Everyone chasing you. Everyone shooting at me. Now, the kidnapping of a nine-year-old little girl."

"What? No." Piper thrust himself up to a sitting position. "What are you talking about, Pappa?"

He didn't just call me that again. I kicked his feet again and, this time, made him wince.

"I told you not to call me that." Then I threw a thumb over my shoulder toward the kitchen where Gallo was milling around. "Someone took Marshal Gallo's daughter. Whoever is after you, kidnapped her to get you. Tell me what's so important about that data."

"Oh, shit." Piper's eyes darted around and finally fixed on the floor at his feet. "I'm not sure, Pa…Curran. I don't know what it all means."

Gallo walked in carrying an ancient glass Mr. Coffee carafe with steaming coffee in it in one hand, three dirty coffee mugs in the other. "Anything?"

I nodded, deep down elated to see an actual coffee pot. "Piper was about to explain."

"Good." Gallo's eyes locked onto Piper as the anger radiated out and across the room. "Get to it, Piper."

"Look, I'm sorry," Piper blurted. "Someone paid me to get information. That's all. I got it and was, well, trolling around for other stuff—a little side project—when Curran found me. I didn't know anything about your daughter. I didn't know you had a daughter."

In the few seconds it took Piper to deliver that alibi, I moved between him and Gallo. You know, just in case, Gallo swapped his coffee pot for his Glock. Gallo handled it all in stride. His face was still angry. His eyes were sad and scared for Madison. But his brain was working right, and I didn't see any signs of murder simmering.

"Start at the beginning, Piper." I took the coffee mugs and the pot from Gallo. I filled the three mugs and handed them out. "Don't leave anything out. We'll decide what's important."

He did, and it took nearly two hours.

Piper, for all his amazing computer skills, was not strong on communication. His story might have taken only an hour, but he drifted from facts, to speculation, and to fantasy. Gallo and I had to drag him back to center several times. In the end, his story was not what I expected. Though it explained a lot.

What he didn't want to discuss was how he got into this mess while still in Witness Protection. He was supposed to be hiding from the Russian mob. Yet, there he was, hacking into big corporations and big-name politicians all over the Washington Beltway. Not exactly the way to keep out of sight of people who are trying to rearrange your anatomy.

It started a few weeks ago. Billy, being the upstanding citizen that he was, had been perusing the dark web for paying clients. That is, searching for people to hack. While he was hunting his next victim, he found a dark web site where someone was looking for his form of talent—hackers. He was careful at first, but after a few chats here and there, the anonymous benefactor gave him a test run—a hack into a beltway bandit. It took him only hours, and boom—he retrieved the files this mysterious benefactor wanted. Needless to say, he made a new friend, and he agreed on a larger contract with a sizable, fifty-thousand-dollar payday.

The deal was simple. Hack three targets and locate files on six people. Grab whatever data the targets had on each, find any other links surrounding those targets, and send the results to a secure site. If he accomplished all that within ten days, fifty-g's would be his. If he failed, or if he told anyone about his assignment, there would be consequences. Like, they'd kill him.

It had taken him a week to identify and retrieve the data this benefactor contracted for. But he succeeded. Almost.

"Okay, now details." I sipped my coffee and eyed Piper suspiciously. "What were the three targets, and who were the six names?"

"No." He sat upright and defiant. "I want some assurances—"

"Assurances?" Gallo pounced. He grabbed Piper and lifted him onto his tiptoes. "I'll give you an assurance, shithead. Someone has my daughter. They want you. The only way I'm going to find—"

"*We* are going to find," I corrected.

"Right." He nodded toward me. "The only way *we're* going to find her is to know what you know. Get talking."

Piper didn't see or hear me. He dangled in Gallo's grasp, trying to outstare him. Finally, he relented. "Okay, okay."

Gallo dropped him back onto the chair. "Talk."

"Okay, okay." Piper raised his hands in surrender. "The three targets were the Department of State, McKnight Enterprises, and Si-Int. The first two targets didn't have much."

I took it all in. "I never heard of McKnight Enterprises or Si-Int."

"Explain," Gallo demanded.

Piper did. "State had records on three of the six names. Ambassador T. Bradley McKnight, former Deputy Secretary until he retired a few years ago. North Carolina Senator Jameson Wain. And the retired Vice Chairman of the Joint Chiefs, Emilio Alvarez. I got their personnel records. Not much more. Long careers and all, but nothing that stood out."

"Okay, I knew of Ambassador McKnight in Greece, as a matter of fact. He was the US Ambassador when we got clipped on the Voula Beach Road. So, he has a company now?" I was getting a little twitchy waiting on his delivery. "Keep going."

"McKnight Enterprises was a shell company—no brick and mortar." Piper looked from me to Gallo. "But they had a computer system and one weird thing."

"What?" Gallo asked.

"Give me a minute," Piper snapped. "I tried three times to get into McKnight, but each time, I got blocked, and weird probes began pinging me. I'd never seen anything like it. The probes were back-tracing me and were running off satellites."

"Satellites?" I asked. "Why would an empty shell company with no connections to anything have satellite security links?"

Piper shrugged. "You tell me. But there was something about that firm that almost got me killed."

"You earned it," Gallo smirked. "What about the other names?"

The words were poison to him. "Well, Si-Int had all six names in one file. It was buried deep behind multiple firewalls and the best cyber protections I'd ever seen."

"Who's Si-Int?" I asked.

"You're kidding me, right?" Gallo looked at me. "Si-Int are old associates of yours, Curran. A Beltway Bandit. Private intelligence company of former somebodies and special ops types."

Si-Int didn't ring any bells. "Associates of mine?"

"Dark Creek," Gallo said. "A few years back, they screwed up bad and all hell rained down on them from the government—very publicly. Instead of just going away to lick their wounds, they changed names, fired a bunch of big shots at the top, and reemerged as Silhouette Intelligence, Inc.—Si-Int. I learned all that checking them out once."

A few years back? Was he talking about the Voula Beach Road? And how in the hell did Tommy Astor and Mr. Nobody figure into all this? They sent me after Piper and all his hacked data from them. Was it for Si-Int? McKnight Enterprises? Or something else?

"So, Dark Creek, AKA Si-Int, had a file on everyone?" I asked.

Piper nodded. "All six names were in a computer file folder named 'Whisper.'"

"Whisper's a file?" A very bad churning began in my guts. "You mentioned McKnight, Wain, and General Alvarez. Who are the other three?"

Piper sat there for a long time, contemplating Gallo and me. "McKnight's personal aide, a guy named Bryan Scott. A nobody."

Gallo kicked Piper's chair. "That's four."

"The last two," he said, staring at me, "were your crazy buddy, Stevie Keene, and, well—*you*."

Chapter Fifty-Eight

Curran

Stevie and me?

I found myself staring out the window into the darkness at nothing. What did I have to do with any of this? Dark Creek? That's so long ago...*Oh, shit*...I spun to Gallo and Piper. "It's all about Greece—Voula Beach. It's about Khaled Hafez Kalani. It has to be."

Gallo's brow furrowed. "What do you and Keene have to do with the other four people, Curran?"

The only connection I knew was Greece. I gave them the short version of how I came to be an old man with an occasional limp and metal screws all over my body. After the soliloquy, I put some gray matter to use.

I said, "Before Dark Creek became Si-Int, I worked overseas for them. McKnight was the US Ambassador to Greece during my op protecting Kalani—name two. If I recall, General Alvarez—name three—was the Director of Defense Intelligence before he moved up to the Joint Chiefs. He would have signed off on my mission with Kalani. I have no idea how Senator Wain fits in. I don't know anything about him and don't recall his name over there. I never heard of R. Bryan Scott or Whisper, either. But Stevie and I were at the Voula Beach Road. We were lucky to get out alive."

"Jesus," Gallo said. "McKnight, Alvarez, and Wain? Can't be."

"Can't be what?" I asked.

"Ask me later," Gallo said, eyeing Piper. "What else?"

Piper aimed a finger at me. "If I remember the file data, I think you're right about Greece. Part of my contract was to prepare dossiers on all six of you. I started to but didn't finish. I got to Wain, though. He got his start as a DOD legal officer out of law school. His first post was at the American Embassy in Greece between 2004 and 2010. I have no idea what Whisper is, but it's the name of the big file with all of you in it."

"That's five of the six connected to the Kalani Voula Beach mission in Greece," I said. "That has to be the connection."

"I'd bet Scott, too," Gallo added, "He's McKnight's aide? Then maybe he was his aide in Greece."

"Right." That made sense. "Now the question is, what's it all mean?"

The entire list of six were all involved in something called Whisper. At least McKnight, Wain, Stevie, and I were in Athens during the Voula Beach Road operation. It made sense that Scott might be there as well. And Alvarez was involved, too, somehow. Whatever Whisper was, or is, would unlock it all.

I said as much to Gallo and Piper. Both stood there, looking at me like they just learned I had Ebola, as I coughed on them.

Gallo's eyes locked onto mine. "This is all great. But I really don't care. I just want Madison back unharmed. How does any of this help with that?"

Madison. Yes. She was all that mattered.

Billy retreated to the fireplace and stared into its emptiness. "I didn't know they'd do this, Marshal Gallo. I didn't. I know I'm a jerk sometimes, but I wouldn't do anything to a kid."

"They who?" Gallo walked to the fireplace, grabbed Piper's shoulder, and spun him around. "What haven't you told us, Piper?"

"Nothing." Piper couldn't look at him. "I didn't know anyone would go after your kid. You weren't even involved."

No, that wasn't it. It was something else. "Billy, there's something you're not telling us. Get to it."

He lifted his eyes and looked between Gallo and me several times.

"Piper," Gallo growled, "someone took my daughter."

"McKnight," Piper said with his eyes going big and scared. "The day

304

before you found me, Curran, I called McKnight's offices. I didn't have the files from Si-Int yet, but I figured they had to be worth money to him. I told them I was paid to get information and asked them what it was worth to give it back to him instead."

What the hell? "You tried to blackmail Ambassador McKnight?"

"Yeah." Piper's face paled. "I figured if the information was worth hacking, it was worth selling. Worth more to him to keep it secret."

"You dumbass." Gallo walked across the room, shaking his head. "McKnight got scared and decided to hide behind my daughter. I ought to shoot you right here."

Piper held up his hands. "I didn't know. I never should have tried to deal with his aide—"

"With Scott?" I asked. "You didn't talk to McKnight?"

He shook his head. "No, I got a hold of that R. Bryan Scott guy. When I demanded to speak with McKnight and told them I knew about him and McKnight Enterprises, Scott brushed me off. Scott acted like he never heard of McKnight Enterprises. The next thing I knew, you—Curran—were pointing a gun at me."

Gallo and I exchanged glances. When our eyes met, we both knew exactly what the plan was.

Gallo said it first. "We're going to visit McKnight in the morning. Sleep a few hours and then we go. We need to be fresh. Sneaking in at night might get us shot by the Secret Service."

Huh? "Why the Secret Service?"

"You don't read the news, Curran?"

No, it was depressing. And who these days believed them, anyway?

"That's what I was going to tell you before. There were five people on a shortlist as potential vice president replacements. Alvarez, Wain, and McKnight were the top three. There was also Senator Vincent Piccolo of Iowa and Virginia Governor Hersh. It was all over the news."

Well, in my defense, I've been busy. You know, as a murder suspect— excuse me, person of interest—and hunting down Piper. Oh, and dodging bullets and rescuing dogs.

305

"Alvarez withdrew from consideration for medical reasons." Gallo held up five fingers and lowered one. "Wain committed suicide yesterday." He lowered a second. "Piccolo and Hersh were very low on the list and—"

"McKnight?" I watched him lower two more fingers. "You think McKnight is knocking off his rivals?"

He nodded. "Maybe. Doesn't matter. But after Alvarez and Wain, the Secret Service will be protecting McKnight."

"Great. First, McKnight was involved with the Voula Beach Road. Now, vice presidential candidates are dropping off around him. Next, someone kidnaps Madison. The common denominator is him—McKnight."

Chapter Fifty-Nine

Curran

T*he sizzle of charring lamb...gunfire...Hezbollah inside the compound. An explosion. Another. It rocked me into the wall. Blood bathed me. Confusion. Gunfire. More explosions.*

"Stevie," I called out, "Rogue Two report."

I played the peeking game, and a Hezbollah terrorist shot me in the shoulder, sending me down hard.

Light. Darkness. Light. Darkness. Light.

I fought for control.

The gunfire quieted. The English voices—calls for support and directing fire— were silent. Angry, loud Arabic replaced them.

Someone in the doorway...a checkered keffiyeh...his dark eyes—he lifted his AK-47 for the kill shot...

I turned my eyes up—not in prayer but in resistance.

*Carli was there now, standing just a few feet away. She shook her head defiantly and pointed toward the terrorist readying to kill me. Her lips moved—*No, Lowe. No. It is not what you think. Go on. Stay here—*she turned and pointed again toward the terrorist.*

I followed her gesture. Stevie Keene lay nearby. He rose to one knee, bleeding and disheveled. In one smooth movement, he rose, pivoted, and shot the Hezbollah fighter just as the man squeezed his own trigger. The rounds chattered across the ground. One struck me in the thigh. The rest went wide.

Carli stood over me and began to fade into nothing. She tried to say something, but I couldn't understand.

Stevie replaced her, leaning on his rifle for support, oblivious to the carnage still around us. "Not this time, brother. Not this time. I'm not letting them."

Mistakes, mistakes.

"Carli," I cried out and sat upright on the couch across from the fireplace. "Carli? Stevie?"

The nightmare had visited me again.

Someone bound down the stairs toward me. "Curran? What's wrong?"

I rolled my legs over the couch edge and looked at Stevie. My face was bathed in sweat, and my hands still quivered. I wasn't in the dusty Voula Beach villa. I wasn't bleeding from the head, shoulder, and thigh. I wasn't a trigger-squeeze away from death. Stevie was there, looking down at me, but it was here, not there. Carli was gone—gone from somewhere she'd never been.

The nightmare.

"Jesus, Curran," Stevie said, lowering the pistol I hadn't seen him with before. "I thought you were in trouble, brother. I heard you calling for Carli again. Same nightmare?"

I nodded. "Yeah. We gotta get going. Where's Gallo?"

"Gone." He slid his pistol into his waistband. "So's Piper."

"What?" I jumped up. "Are you flippin' kidding me?"

"No." He thrust a thumb over his shoulder. "They must have left during the early morning."

Gallo was going rogue. "That sonofabitch."

Stevie eyed me. "Are you thinking what I'm thinking?"

"Yes, he's going to try and rescue Madison alone—give up Piper to make a deal." My gut knotted up. "Either way, all he'll do is get everyone killed."

"What's the plan, brother?" Stevie asked, looking and sounding steadier than he had in months. "We going to visit Ambassador McKnight?"

"Yes, but we gotta make a stop first. Gallo may have Piper. But I have the rest of what McKnight wants. It's worth a whole lot more than that chubby little weasel. We might still save Madison."

"The backup computer files?" Stevie headed for the stairs. "I smell like ass and booze—in that order. Make us something to eat. I'll grab a shower. Then we'll get that kid back."

Chapter Sixty

Curran

I t's amazing what a shower, pot of coffee, and clean clothes can do for you.

Stevie Keene took the pot of coffee into the bathroom earlier, spent a half-hour in the shower, and even shaved. Not much. Just enough to appear presentable. Which for him, was lightyears from his former self.

"If I'm going to die today, I want clean clothes and brushed teeth," he'd said. "In that order."

I was all for his improved hygiene.

We drove to Janey-Lynn's farm, planning our strategy. For the first thirty minutes, I filled him in on all we'd figured out last night while he slept off his bender. In a nutshell, our best guess was that Whisper was a codenamed file concerning the Voula Beach Road. That incident was linked to at least three powerbrokers in the running for vice presidency and later, perhaps the Oval Office. One of them quit. One committed suicide—*right*. And one of them was behind it all. The pieces fell into place, and the picture was terrifying.

Stevie listened and drained coffee from a dirty travel mug the size of a toaster. He nodded occasionally and swore loudly at each "ah ha" moment I delivered.

"McKnight is behind all this?" he asked. "All the way back to Voula?"

"I think so. I just don't know what Voula has to do with the rest of it. And

I still don't know what Whisper is for sure."

That sent his brain—fried as it might be—simmering. "Who cares? Right now, it's only about the little girl."

He was never more succinct in his life. "Exactly."

Our master plan was to get my USB backup drive of Piper's information from my stash, confront McKnight with it, secure the release of Madison Gallo, and get out alive. Easy peasy.

There were a million details missing. In fact, all the details were missing. I'm better with the big picture stuff and Stevie is better with, well, something else. We kept our plan simple and open-ended enough that we could wing the details, and we'd still be on plan.

It all went to shit the moment we reached my barn loft apartment.

A large, black SUV was parked in front of the barn. What was it about big, black SUVs? The government used them. The bad guys used them. Rich executives used them. How was someone like me to know who was who?

"Get ready, brother." Stevie checked his pistol tucked behind his back. "I don't like this."

Me either. "Stay put. I'll go up. And Stevie, remember Madison—be steady."

"Me? I'm clean, sober, and steady. What could go wrong?"

At the top of the landing, I took my Kimber .45 out. My door was ajar, so I nudged it open and eased inside.

The place had been ransacked again. This time, I was pretty certain it wasn't by Gallo—though it might be by his colleagues. I knew it wasn't him because as I walked into the carnage that used to be my apartment—broken chairs, shredded cushions, toppled bookshelves with books askew, and every possible item anywhere strewn about—two men stepped out of my spare room to greet me.

"Don't move, Curran," a heavy-set guy said. "Hands where—"

"I know the drill." I held my hands away from my body so as not to draw gunfire from the silenced H & K Mp-5 submachine guns they carried. I let my Kimber dangle by the trigger guard off my finger.

The thinner guy angled around, so they had me in their crossfire. "Then you know to drop your weapon on the floor."

Both men were casually dressed in tan cargo pants, pullovers, and military-style black field jackets. They had tactical body armor and "mercenary" stamped on their foreheads.

"Who are you?"

"Doesn't matter," the thin merc said. "Drop the piece."

I slowly laid my pistol down on the coffee table and took a step back so as not to give them any reason to blast me into submission.

"What do you want?" Not that I expected an honest answer, but maybe playing dumb would disarm them a bit. "How about a hint?"

One of them held a volume of my Encyclopedia Cash-ola in his hand. He let it flop open, revealing the carved-out hiding place where my twenty-five grand used to be. Joke's on them—it was now in the Loudoun County evidence locker awaiting my execution.

"Okay, Curran," the heavier merc said, "Where is it?"

Speaking of missing things, I asked, "Hey, where's Bogart?"

The heavier merc glanced at the other. "Bogart?"

"My dog."

The thinner lifted his subgun. "He's at the main house with your girlfriend and the loudmouth. Don't worry. We don't hurt dogs."

Phew, that was a relief. "What about—"

"Focus, Curran," the heavier one said. "Where's the backup drive? And don't say 'what backup drive?' Your dumb game is already getting old."

Okay, I'll go with the lying strategy. "Well, it used to be in those books. Obviously, someone stole my money and the drive."

The thin merc took two giant steps forward—without saying 'may I'—and drove the silenced barrel of the subgun into my gut. It doubled me over and onto the floor.

"Drag him along." The heavy merc scooped up my pistol. "U.C. will decide what's next."

A gunshot rang out from outside.

Both mercs were startled. The heavy one recovered, threw a chin toward the door, and said to his partner, "Go check."

"Got it." The thin merc left the loft and went down the outer stairs. A few moments later, he turned. "Your buddy took one for the team. Learn from that."

Jesus, no—Stevie? After all we've been through, he ended like this? A million regrets ran through me and took what little wind I had left right out of me. Not Stevie? Jesus. We'd been through hell together, and while I recovered from my physical wounds, he never did from the mental ones. I never should have brought him into this mess. It was my fault. All of it. Madison. Stevie. God knows what else. It was all on me.

"You killed him?" The look on the thin one's face answered me. "You bastards. He could barely function on his own. He wasn't a threat."

"You really didn't know him, did you, Curran?" The thin merc gestured to the other. "I sure hope U.C. won't mind."

U.C.? Nothing rang any bells, but my head wasn't quite settled just then. I tried to conceal the pain lingering inside. I did a bad job, and my old bones and body parts rebelled as the thin merc shoved me out the loft door. There, I froze, looking down at Stevie's body lying at the rear of the dark SUV. A single merc, short and wiry with tight, curly black hair, knelt, searching his body.

"You bastards," I repeated over and over.

The heavy merc gave me a shove that nearly sent me head-over-heels down the stairs. I managed to keep my balance and reached the bottom of my feet. The curly-haired merc—Lenny—moved away from Stevie's body and grabbed me.

"Why are you so broken up, Curran?" Lenny sneered. "Your pal did you in Greece, right?"

What? "What does that mean?"

"What a dumb shit." Lenny shoved me hard. "You didn't know? Keene sold you out, Curran. You and your whole damn team. Made a mint, and all he had to do was take a couple of bullets to make things look right."

Stevie was the mole inside my team? Impossible. We were brothers. All these years?

"You're full of shit," I spat. "Stevie—"

"Gave you up like an unwanted dog." Lenny threw his head back and laughed. "He's been feeding us info on you all along."

Anger. Hate. Betrayal. All those emotions welled inside me like a burning rage about to burst out. My brother. My brother, whom I'd spent years helping and protecting—he sold me out? No, I didn't believe it.

I considered moving on Lenny and making a play for escape. Then, Madi's young, green eyes popped into my mind. It was all about her, now. It had to be. I had to learn from these mercenaries what they knew about her and where she was. That's the only play I had.

"You're lying," I spat again. But as the words came out, I knew he was not. "If he was one of you, why'd you kill him?"

"Loose ends." Lenny laughed again. "A lot of that going on today."

The heavy merc said, "Lenny, get that body out of here. Clean up behind us. We're going to the main house."

Lenny nodded.

On the brief drive to Janey-Lynn's main house, I thought about Stevie. He'd done a lot of bad things over the years, but nothing as deeply painful as selling me out. He saved me in Voula, but why? If he'd sold the operation to Hezbollah, then why let me live? And all these years, I believed in him and was there when he needed—a meal, some money, a sober-up bed. This morning, he'd agreed to a foolhardy—and sparse—plan to save a little girl he didn't know. To think that was part of his charade almost made me retch.

Damn, brother. You?

At Janey-Lynn's, they dragged me from the SUV, gave me a couple cheap shots in the gut to keep me compliant, and forced me through the front door into her great room.

Janey-Lynn sat in an old leather recliner near the fireplace. She was still dressed in her nightgown. Her face was bruised, and dried blood showed on the corners of her mouth. When I appeared, she tried to stand, but another merc, this one bulky with muscle and steroids, stood behind her and shoved her back into the chair.

"Keep your paws off me, boy," she snapped. "I warned you not to touch me."

I looked at her. "Are you okay? Who did this to you?"

"I'm good." She eyed me strangely. "Don't do anything stupid, Lowe. No heroics."

Heroics were not on my mind just then. Living through the next little while was.

I said, "I thought Evans arrested you last night?"

"He did." She looked away. "I had a few favors due. I'm out on bond. Now, though, I wish I wasn't."

Somewhere in the back of the house, Bogart barked up a storm. He carried on howling to warn me he was trapped somewhere.

I looked at her, worried, "Is Bogart—"

"He's locked up in the pantry, Lowe," Janey-Lynn said. "He's fine. We're both fine."

"Who did that to you, Janey-Lynn?" I pointed to her face.

For a long time, she said nothing. Then, she looked from one merc to the other and shook her head. "It's not important."

"Enough, Curran." The heavy merc shoved me toward a straight-back chair against the wall opposite Janey-Lynn. "We didn't lay a hand on her. But we will if you don't give us that computer drive."

"I told you—"

"He's a lying shit," a voice said from the main hall adjacent to us. "Shoot him right now."

I turned as Randy Cantrell walked unhindered into the room.

Chapter Sixty-One

Curran

I didn't see this one coming. I should have, though. Randy Cantrell was a snake and a self-centered jackass. If anyone was going to screw up my grand plan, it was him. I just didn't think he was stupid enough to be in bed with mercenaries. That never ended well for the "smartest guy in the room." Just ask Ellis from Die Hard. He got killed for kissing ass—deservedly so.

"I misjudged you, Randy," I said. "Playing with the big boys."

"Screw you, Private Dick," he sneered.

Behind him, a balding, strong-framed man with a narrow, dangerous face followed. He wore an expensive suit with no tie and highly buffed shoes.

No. It couldn't be.

"Get over there by mommy, Cantrell," the well-dressed man said, gesturing to Janey-Lynn. "Keep quiet until this is over."

"I told you I can help…for a price." Randy moved behind Janey-Lynn's chair. "Just pay up."

Stupid bastard. What had he done? If he'd made a deal with these mercs, he was as good as dead. Though that wasn't such a bad thing—was it?

"Quiet," the suited man ordered and turned to me. "Hello, Curran. Long time, brother."

How was he here? He was dead a long time ago.

"Wally Volesky," I said, "why aren't you dead?"

"U.C.?" The heavy merc looked at Volesky. "You know this guy?"

"U.C.?" I asked. "Oh, yeah—"

"Up close." Volesky—Rogue Five from Voula Beach. "After Voula, I needed a change of persona, brother. You understand."

No, I didn't, but I was beginning to. "You and Stevie sold us out? You two set us up with the Hezbollah? For what?"

"Stupid question, even from you." U.C. threw his head back and laughed raucously. "You don't know shit, do you? Everything is about money, brother. Everything. That's why we worked for Dark Creek. Wasn't it? Then I found someone who paid better. I only needed a little help—Keene was all about helping. For the right price."

I jumped up and took a step toward him. When the thin merc grabbed my arm, I drove a heel into the side of his knee and heard a loud "snap" that sent him crumpling to the old carpet.

"Dammit." He grabbed his dislocated knee, screaming, "I'm going to kill you."

"Stop, Ernie," U.C. barked. "I warned you about him."

I continued to within a couple steps of Volesky, aka U.C. "You two got my team killed. You nearly got me killed, too. Your grunts finished Stevie a few minutes ago. What's this all about, Wally? You owe me that much."

The heavy merc and the one behind Janey-Lynn descended on me, pulled both my arms behind my back, and drove me to my knees.

"Stevie?" U.C. cocked his head and narrowed his eyes on Ernie. "What about Keene?"

I said, "Loose ends."

"He did his part," the heavy merc said. "I figured—"

"Yeah, you figured right." U.C. stared impassively at me. "He was a washed-up nut case anyway. For old time's sake, Pappa, if you give me the backup drive, I'll let the old lady and you live. Without that drive, you got nothing on anyone. You're no threat."

"Liar." I'd seen all the movies with this plot. In each one, the bad guys made promises they didn't keep. "It was hidden in my loft, and now it's gone. I'll get it back. I just want the little girl. I'll do whatever it takes to get her."

Janey-Lynn leaned forward. "Little girl, Lowe?"

"Yeah." I tried to hide my emotions, but they crackled my voice. "Gallo's daughter. They took her to get their hands on Piper, the hacker, and the backup drives he stole. Gallo disappeared with Piper this morning. Now the backups are gone. My guess is he has them, too."

"He doesn't," she said and looked over her shoulder at Randy. "Does he, Randy?"

All eyes fell on Randy Cantrell. He stood behind Janey-Lynn, grinning like the cat in the birdcage. Except this cat was a weaselly little bastard with a manbun and too-tight pants halfway down his butt.

"What have you done, Randy?" I demanded. "If you've made some kind of deal, it won't go the way you think."

U.C. walked to him. Lightning fast, he snatched Randy by the throat and dragged him around Janey-Lynn's chair like a ragdoll. Without effort, he lifted Randy up on his tiptoes and suspended him there, gasping for breath.

"Mr. Cantrell, do I understand you've had my backup drive all this time?" U.C. shook him, making him gurgle for air. "You've not been negotiating in good faith. That's disturbing."

Randy's eyes bulged, and his feet and arms dangled like an untethered marionette. "I just...want...a deal. I can...help."

"Randy, no." I stood again. "He'll kill you either way. There's a little girl out there—"

"Screw...you...PI," Randy croaked, gasping for breath between words. To U.C., he managed, "I've got...it."

U.C. glanced at me, winked, and tossed Randy against the fireplace like the bag of shit he was.

Randy hit with a crunch and slid down onto his side, facing the rest of us. "A deal man. A deal."

"Stop this." Janey-Lynn stood and pointed a stone-cold finger at Randy. "Randy Cantrell, for once, think of someone else. That little girl needs help. You can free her."

"Not my problem." Randy moaned, stood, and caressed his throat. "All I want is some money. Fifty grand should cover it."

U.C. pulled a small pistol from his suit coat. He continued chuckling to himself as he walked up to Randy and smashed him across the face with the pistol.

Randy fell to the floor again as blood gushed from his mouth.

"Now, Mr. Cantrell," U.C. said, exchanging his pistol for something from his pants pocket. He flipped open a knife. "Give me my backup drive. If you don't, my first cut will leave you unable to have children. From what I see of you, that's no loss."

Damn if U.C. Volesky didn't have redeeming qualities after all.

"Ah...ah...okay, okay," Randy cried and quivered, getting to his knees. "I can show you. I hid it outside—please, no more."

U.C. turned to the heavy merc. "Handle this."

The merc nodded, grabbed Randy by the arm, and lifted him to his feet. "Move."

Janey-Lynn went to Randy. "Are you all right?"

Are you kidding me?

"Get away from me." He pulled away from her and grumbled something that caused her to retreat to me.

"I'm so sorry, Lowe." Her eyes showed embarrassment. "He doesn't know better."

U.C. said, "Really, Mrs. Cantrell? This piece of shit beat on you. Now, he's selling you out. You're worried about him? You're an extraordinary woman."

Beat on her? "Janey-Lynn? Randy did that to your face?"

She ignored me. "Was this all necessary? He's a fool. You needn't hurt him anymore. It's unnecessary."

"Oh, I assure you, it was necessary," U.C. said. "He'll give me what I want. Doing so, he might even save you."

I walked to Randy and jammed a finger into his forehead.

"I tried to warn you, Randy. So did Janey-Lynn. They'll kill you."

Randy blustered. "Screw you."

"I'm sorry, Lowe." Tears filled Janey-Lynn's eyes. "Let him do what he will."

If not for Madison, I'd have agreed. "U.C., what about the little girl? If Randy gives you what you want, let her go."

"You don't have any negotiating room, Pappa." U.C. grabbed me by the arm and pulled me across the room. "The kid is safe for now. Backup drive or not, I still want Piper. Bring him to me. I'll ensure the kid is unhurt and goes free. Deal?"

Was he kidding? "I guess stone-cold traitors don't watch much television, eh, Wally?"

He cocked his head. "What's that mean?"

"I don't trust you."

"You don't have a choice."

He had me there. "Okay, I'll find Piper—again. The kid goes free before I turn him over. Janey-Lynn, too."

U.C. smiled a big, wry smile. "You're gutsy as ever, Curran. Gutsy enough to take me on. Good for you. And Keene said you were turning soft—getting too old."

That stung. It was bad enough Stevie Keene informed on me to the likes of U.C., but to belittle me at the same time? Jesus, how did I not know?

I swallowed bile and disappointment. "Piper for the others—deal?"

"Sure, okay." He nodded. "But to keep you honest, I'm sending Lenny along. He'll be your new best friend until you find Piper. That way, you don't go to the cops and don't get any silly ideas for some grand scheme."

Was he a mind reader?

"Okay by me."

"We'll take Mr. Cantrell with us to retrieve my computer drive. We'll keep him until we get Piper back. You better hurry before my patience wears anymore." U.C. ordered the heavy merc and his sidekick to take Randy out and followed them to the door. Before he left, he turned and found my eyes. "Curran, you get Voula Beach—don't you? All of it, now?"

"Yeah, I get it. You and Stevie sold us out to the Hezbollah."

"Hezbollah? So, you don't know. Voula Beach was just the beginning." He turned and headed out. "Find Piper, Curran. Madison Gallo is a sweetie."

Chapter Sixty-Two

Curran

After U.C. and his merry band of mercenaries left the farmhouse, the short, wiry merc named Lenny came inside. He had my Kimber tucked in his pants and stood in the doorway holding a silenced MP-5 subgun on us. His swagger was palpable, and I so wanted to punch him in his face.

"Shame about Keene," he taunted. "He sure played you, though. Played you like a bitch fool."

True enough.

From behind Lenny down the hall, Bogart howled up a storm. Even from the far end of the house, we could hear him scratching and clawing at the pantry door.

"Lenny," I said, throwing a thumb toward the hall. "Janey-Lynn's dog needs water. He's not well. How about you let me get him water."

"Oh, like I haven't seen that movie." He grinned. "I let you do that, and you sick him on me."

Janey-Lynn picked up the thread, calling out to Bogart, "Bogart, be quiet, or I'll get my hose."

Bogart instantly began whining and crying, moaning a death moan, and when she called his name again, he went dead silent.

"Please, Lenny, he's really old and in bad health. He needs water—now." Janey-Lynn put on a frantic, worried face. "He's got diabetes. He's dying.

I'll do anything you want. Anything. Just some water."

Lenny seductively—or more to the point, disgustingly—looked her over. "Anything? Well, you're pretty damn hot for an old broad. We can work something out, I guess. Go ahead, but if that dog even shows his face, I'll blast him and then you—but you *after*."

I patted the air. "He's like me, Lenny. He's old and worn out."

"That's what I heard, Curran—from your best pal." Lenny laughed. "Okay, we're all going together. Anything goes down I don't like, everyone dies."

"Hold on, boy," I called into the hall.

Bogart stayed silent.

Lenny lifted his MP-5 and threw a chin toward the hall. "Go."

"Thank you." Janey-Lynn smiled the best she could and walked down the hall with me a couple steps behind. Lenny trailed six feet back.

Very smart, Lenny. Not too close to catch a kick or punch. Not too far that you can't control us.

Janey-Lynn filled a big ceramic bowl with water from the kitchen sink and went to the pantry door. She opened it and slid the bowl in quickly, leaned in, patting and consoling Bogart.

"Be a good boy, Bogart. Stay quiet for mommy." She closed and latched the door. To Lenny, she said, "Thank you. He wouldn't last very long in his shape. Can I let him out to pee?"

"Don't push it, sweetheart." Lenny took a step back and lifted his subgun. "Now, we'll all get back to the living room. No bullshit."

I glanced at Janey-Lynn. "Is Bogart okay in there?"

"He's scared and lying down." She started back down the hall, saying loudly, "Bogart, I'm right here. Be good."

The door halfway down the hall rattled. Something scratched and pushed on it.

Lenny stopped behind us three steps from the living room. "What the hell is that?"

"It's just a bathroom," Janey-Lynn said. "It's an old house. Things make noise."

"Bullshit, it makes noise." He lifted the subgun and pointed it at me. "Sit right on the floor, Curran. Don't move. Lady, come here."

"Yessir." She raised her hands shoulder-high and moved beside him. He took her arm and pressed the subgun barrel against her side. "It's nothing, honest."

"Right. I've seen that movie, too." Lenny pressed the subgun into Janey-Lynn with one hand. With the other, he grasped the bathroom door and turned the knob. "I'm watching you both."

He should have thought that one through.

The moment he opened the door, Janey-Lynn yelled, "Bogart, out!"

The big Lab exploded through the open door and struck Lenny full force in the chest, knocking him off balance. Bogart's mouth clamped down around Lenny's gun wrist and wrenched it to the side, forcing the weapon away and drawing a deep gush of blood.

Lenny screamed and tried to shake him off.

He might have succeeded if I hadn't gotten to my feet and kicked him squarely in the groin. I followed through with a hammer punch to his face and snatched the subgun from his dwindling grasp.

As Bogart thrashed Lenny's arm back and forth, Lenny buckled from my assault and was down. He hit the hardwood hall floor with an "oof" and raised his free hand—holding my Kimber, trying to twist it around to shoot Bogart.

"No," Janey-Lynn cried out. "Don't."

I swiveled the MP-5 around and fired a single shot just above Bogart's gnashing teeth and head. The bullet struck Lenny in the chest, just above his heart and slightly off-center. His eyes flashed surprise, and the pistol fell away. He gurgled a couple times and was gone.

Bogart stopped thrashing and released Lenny's dead wrist. He turned to me, wagged, and ran to Janey-Lynn, moaning.

Oh, sure, go for the woman. I just saved you.

"Good boy, good boy." She wrapped her arms around him and hugged him close. "You saved your mamma."

His mamma? When did my stolen dog—excuse me, rescued dog—become her child dog? I asked her that as I rooted through Lenny's pockets.

"When you abandoned him yesterday," she quipped. "What a dumbass. He actually believed Bogart was in the pantry."

Yeah, well, I believed her, too. I guess I was a dumbass deep down. Dumb enough to have been betrayed and lied to by Stevie Keene for years. Thinking about it just then, I wish I'd put the bullet in him myself.

In Lenny's inside pockets of his field jacket, I found two thirty-round magazines of nine-millimeter for the MP-5 subgun. His wallet was cash only with no IDs or leads. I retrieved my Kimber, holstered it, and stood above his body.

I said, "I'm not sure what's going to happen to Randy, Janey-Lynn."

"Maybe I'm a terrible person, but he deserves what he gets." She looked away, embarrassed. "He wants the farm. All of it. Charlie didn't want him to have it. That's why he cut him from the will. But there's a clause that says if anyone in the line of inheritance is a felon or guilty of moral turpitude, they can't inherit anything."

Wow, tough rules. "You've got neither problem, Janey-Lynn."

Tears welled in her eyes again. "Yes, I do. I'm out on bond right now—murder charges. Tommy pulled strings to get me released. Randy framed me, I just know it. That twenty-five thousand out of the farm accounts looks like I paid you. I didn't withdraw the money, Lowe, but Evans can't explain it any other way after finding that cash in your loft. We both look guilty as sin."

"That's why you've been so timid about him?"

She nodded. "I didn't want to do or say anything to rile him. I tried to make a deal, too."

"You should have told me."

"Looks like he's going to win."

Maybe. But as they say, it ain't over until the fat lady sings. See, not all my lady friends are gorgeous. Most of them, sure—but not all.

"It'll work itself out, Janey-Lynn. U.C. may eventually solve this."

"No." She walked over and stood by the window, staring out. "We have to stop that. Even Randy doesn't deserve that."

There it was. She just soothed any lingering doubts I had that she had arranged Charlie's murder.

"Janey-Lynn, we're screwed either way." I headed into the living room to the bar. There, I poured us both a hefty bourbon—sure, it was barely nine a.m. "They've got Randy and my backup drive. I have no idea where to start looking for Piper and Gallo. These mercenaries are pros, and Gallo is no match for them—not alone, and he can't call in help. I'm not sure I'm up to it anymore, either. But I'm all Madison has."

Janey-Lynn dropped onto the couch with her drink and pulled Bogart onto her lap. She loved on him for a few moments before knocking back the bourbon.

"Go to Tommy, Lowe," she said in a small voice. "There's more he hasn't told you."

"What's Tommy got to do with these mercenaries? I knew he was somewhere in this mess—after all, he referred me to Mr. Nobody. But mercs?"

"Lowe, he didn't find you back in the day by accident." She stroked Bogart as the big dog moaned in pleasure. "You didn't find me by accident, either."

What was she saying? "Janey-Lynn, this all started back on the Voula Beach Road. Greece and Dark Creek—who became some private CIA called Si-Int. How's Tommy figure into this? It's so far in the past."

"No," she said calmly. "Not as far as you think. U.C.'s not Si-Int."

"You know about Si-Int?"

She scratched Bogart's ears. "Who do you think Tommy Astor is?"

Chapter Sixty-Three

Curran

Tommy Astor is with Si-Int?

That thought baffled me the entire drive to TAE.

I knew he was a killer in the boardroom—a master player in business. He wheeled and dealt with the most powerful people I could think of—like "Uncle Shelly Rawlins and the Honorable Jay Thomas Carello. You know, the guys I hang with on the weekends—*not*. But Si-Int? Tommy was many things but a spy wasn't one of them.

Or was he?

I brushed past Tommy's receptionist and made my way to his office. As I barged in unannounced, I realized pretty fast I wasn't unannounced.

Tommy sat behind his desk, feet propped up in their usual "the boss can do what he wants" position. He toyed with his Colt Python as always. The look on his face made me wonder if it was unloaded this time. Katelyn sat across from him at the small conference table and was flanked by someone I didn't recognize—though he seemed oddly familiar. He was average height, lean but appeared very fit. He was completely bald with a thin mustache, goatee, and piercing, dark eyes.

"Good morning, Mr. Curran." The stranger stood and extended his hand in either a customary greeting or a ploy to keep my gun hand occupied. "You have not kept in touch as directed. Now see the mess you've created?"

Holy shit on a peanut butter sandwich—that voice—*Mr. Nobody*.

Somebody cheated and warned him I was coming.

As I stepped into the room and refused his handshake, the door closed behind me. Two large, suited men blocked any retreat. I hoped I didn't need one.

"Mr. Nobody, we finally meet." I eased sideways to get the bodyguards into my peripheral vision. "I guess Janey-Lynn warned you I was coming. What's all this about?"

Mr. Nobody waved a hand and sent his men out of the room. Though, I'm sure that if I lost my manners, they'd bust in and crush my bones into dust.

I faced Katelyn. "Katie, all this time and you knew what was happening behind the scenes?"

"Some," she said, looking pleased with herself. "It has been fun watching you making a fool of yourself."

Ouch. "Flirting won't earn my forgiveness."

Tommy cleared his throat. "Katelyn, please excuse us. It's that time where I need someone left with plausible deniability."

"For my murder?" I was only half-kidding as Katelyn smiled wryly and left the room. "Tommy, we gotta make this quick."

"Mr. Curran, I will allow some explanation at this juncture. You've earned it." Mr. Nobody eyed a chair at the small conference table and waited for me to take a hint and sit. "I am Carmen Vulcano, Chairman and CEO of Si-Int. You know it as the former—"

"Dark Creek." I kept my right hand below the table near my Kimber. I wasn't sure Si-Int were the good guys or bad guys. "My old employer."

"Actually," Tommy said, "your past and *current* employer, ole' buddy."

Past and current? What did that mean? "I'm listening."

Mr. Nobody, who was now Mr. Vulcano, continued. "After Voula Beach, Dark Creek had to reorganize and transform to remain relevant. Our primary benefactors insisted. The Board of Directors installed me as its new CEO and, ultimately, Chairman. It cost many millions to undig from that disaster. I wanted that money—and our market position—back. I wanted resolution."

"Revenge, too." I winked. "Right?"

"Yes. Revenge." Vulcano took a long breath, glanced at Tommy, and back to me. "I'll cut to the details. Your operation with Khaled Hafez Kalani was thwarted from the start. Some very powerful people didn't want him telling DIA what he knew. They had resources and people in place to ensure that did not happen. They had money. Money begot betrayal. Betrayal begot the Voula Beach Road."

I figured all that recently. "Who did all the begoting?"

"May I?" Tommy raised a finger to interject. Vulcano nodded his approval. Funny, I'd never seen Tommy ask permission to do anything. "Kalani was going to reveal—for his freedom and a hefty payday—an Iranian operation to infiltrate the US government at the highest levels."

Ah, what? "Iranian?" I said. "They had spies at the embassy in Athens, and they hit us on the Voula Beach Road to cover it up?"

"Yes." Tommy gave me one clap. "A most important spy."

Vulcano raised a hand and quieted Tommy like a light switch, turning him off. "The Iranians compromised members of your team at the Voula Beach Road—they worked with Hezbollah—"

"Yeah, I know. Stevie Keene and a punk named U.C.—Wally Volesky." Just saying their names made me sick. "I'll explain later."

Vulcano eyed me. "The Iranian CIA, its Ministry of Intelligence & Security—MOIS—had their spy arrange for Hezbollah to raid the safehouse and kill Khalani. Killing Khalani ensured no one ever learned the identity of the Iranian spy in the embassy."

Years of nightmares grabbed hold of me and shook me to the bone. All this time, it wasn't my failure. It was a setup from the start. Hearing what Piper had found already gave me a clue about Voula Beach. Hearing Tommy and Vulcano confirm it just drove the knife in deeper.

Hold on. Something wasn't right. "So the Iranians killed Khalani just to shut him up? They did that. Why's this all happening now?"

The two exchanged awkward looks. Tommy answered me after a nod from Vulcano.

"It's complicated. The Iranian spy—code-named Whisper—was deep in the American Embassy in Athens. We believe Whisper was recruited in Egypt years before and had a very long-term mission in play. Kalani knew this and would have provided the information to DIA. Whisper had him killed along with your team. Loose ends just in case he gave any information to you."

This story sounded like the Manchurian Candidate—*The Tehran Candidate*. I considered what Piper had found. I gave them my take on General Alvarez and Senator Wain. "Confirm or deny, fast. I got a little girl to rescue."

"Yes, of course," Tommy said, frowning. "Listen for a few more minutes, and we'll get Madison Gallo back."

Oh? "*We* will?"

Vulcano did the light switch thing again. "You are correct about Alvarez. He ran DIA at the time. He signed off on the original deal with Kalani—money and a new life for intelligence. We think he already knew there was a spy in the Athens embassy but couldn't prove it."

I jumped in. "Wain was a DOD lawyer at the Greek embassy. Let me guess, he was working the deal with Kalani for DIA? Funny how the government wants lawyers involved in spy operations. If you want to screw someone, bring in the lawyers."

"Very good, yes." Vulcano raised his chin. "McKnight, Alvarez, and Wain were all there before, during, but not after the Voula Beach Road debacle. We assume they were all compromised—all involved in the Voula Beach Road."

"Since then, two of them have been killed." My guts churned, and I told them about Stevie and his betrayal in Greece. "Oh, and I met Wally Volesky this morning at my place—he was reported killed in Voula. He and Stevie Keen were the rats inside my team. He killed Stevie this morning to start cleaning up loose ends. Actually, one of his thugs, Lenny, did. I killed Lenny. I'm going to kill Volesky next. I'm on a roll and don't want to slow down."

Vulcano and Tommy had a silent conversation and watched me tearing up over-explaining Stevie Keene's involvement.

Vulcano continued. "There is someone else involved now, too. Someone engaged Billy Piper to search for intelligence at McKnight's and the other targets. It's why that escapes us—and who."

"I think you already know McKnight is Whisper, Lowe," Tommy said. "McKnight was the only person with the position and information necessary to orchestrate the Voula Beach incident."

Loose ends. Yeah, I know about those. "Yeah, McKnight. I sort of reached that same conclusion—with Billy Piper's help." I explained about finding, then losing, Piper. They were not amused. "A senior American diplomat working for the Iranians and killing Americans to cover it up. Jesus, what a mess. And hey, maybe he'll be the next vice president. Wouldn't that be fun?"

"Yes, it certainly would," Vulcano said, raising a finger. "We must get to the bottom of it fast. Recover the evidence Billy Piper found and clean up. We must stop McKnight and the Iranians."

"Why not bring in the FBI and CIA?" I asked, and I instantly felt stupid. "Can't trust them, either. They might want to turn this into a "them" game or might even be penetrated by Iran, too. That would get us all killed."

Vulcano nodded slowly. "There are other reasons, too. However, we are equipped to handle this. You must believe me."

I didn't, but that didn't matter either.

"Billy Piper has to be located." Tommy stood and walked over to the table. "That's why we sent you to retrieve our Whisper dossier and get Piper back. He has other information from McKnight Enterprises. The other question is, who paid him to hack Si-Int, McKnight, and our State Department? Who's involved here, how, and why?"

"McKnight Enterprises was a dry hole. Piper told me he got everything from *your* files—Si-Int's. So—"

"Piper lied to you, Lowe." Tommy leaned back and aimed a finger at me. "There was far more there than he admitted to."

Something still bugged me. "Why didn't you have me grab Piper when I found him the first time? We could have stopped a lot of this chaos."

They had another long, detailed telepathic conversation.

The answer struck me. Brilliance often does. "You didn't know what he found—not in Si-Int, but McKnight and State. Not until I brought you those stolen files. You found out someone sent him to get all the intelligence on Whisper, and you need to know who and why."

"Yes—at the time, we didn't know what we didn't know," Vulcano grunted. Brilliant.

Vulcano's voice was sullen and cold. "We want Piper—not just the files—*him*. We had to know what else he learned. More importantly, when he hacked McKnight Enterprises, he tripped an Israeli satellite surveillance trap. Why they were surveilling McKnight, we don't know."

Okay, story hour was over, and I stood. "This has been fun, really. But my little green-eyed granddaughter is a hostage and scared to death. I've gotta save her. I could use some help, Mr. Nobody and Mr. Liar—" I stabbed a finger at Tommy. "It'll get messy."

Tommy moved to me and took my shoulder like a dad about to bestow manhood lessons. "Lowe, when you left Dark Creek, they didn't abandon you. When Mr. Vulcano took over, he came to me to be a conduit to you. It's Si-Int who has paid your retainer all these years. They wanted to keep you close until we could solve the Voula Beach Road incident. You owe them."

"Owe them?" I pulled free of his grasp. "Bullshit. I got my ass shot up and nearly killed. I learned my best friend betrayed me just after he was killed today. Before that, I lost the love of my life. I never knew I had a kid or grandkid. All this time, I've been living like a pauper on your measly retainer—out of *guilt*. Since taking this assignment, I almost got killed a half-dozen times. I owe them?"

"Yes." Vulcano folded his arms abruptly. "There is much more you don't know, Mr. Curran. But you're right. It's time to stop talking and act. My two men outside—Poole and Vassey—are two of my best. They will assist you."

"Thanks for sharing all this, guys." The distaste in my mouth oozed out. "You could have told me all this years ago, though."

Tommy said, "I know. There were reasons. You'll have to trust us."

Yeah, right. *Trust...nope.*

331

"You must retrieve Piper *alive*." Vulcano aimed a rigid finger at me. "You must retrieve the backup drive and any copies."

I shrugged. "After I save Madison Gallo."

Both men agreed.

"Lowe," Tommy said, "There's no wiggle room on this, ole boy. Understand?"

"Mr. Curran, there can be no mistakes." Vulcano's hand flashed up again. "Despite what Piper told you, there was evidence at McKnight Enterprises. We must have it. He played you."

I'm shocked, I tell you, shocked. "You all played me. You might be playing me even now."

"No. Not this time, Mr. Curran." Vulcano lowered his voice and handed a folded slip of paper to me. "This is an address we believe will assist you. We must have Whisper—McKnight—alive, too."

"Alive?" Well, that was a kick in the ass. "What if I trip and accidentally shoot him? Like, maybe ten times?"

Vulcano came up to me and stopped close enough I could smell his toothpaste. "Then you'll forfeit the half-million dollars I've put on reserve for you."

A half-million dollars? That's a lot more than the two hundred K he promised before. Why didn't he lead with that?

Chapter Sixty-Four

Curran

J ust after noon, me and my two Si-Int operatives-for-rent rolled off Route 193 onto a sideroad. I pulled over.

Poole sat in the passenger front seat. In the back seat sat the other operative, Vassey. They'd changed from their suits into black tactical pants, boots, and tops and were loaded for bear. That is, if hunting bear required M4 carbines with the latest laser and holographic sight packages and tactical vests full of toys that go boom in the night.

They'd given me similar gear. I declined the M4 rifle, as I preferred my Kimber up close. We each also had tiny earwigs affixed to a transceiver on the vest. If I was going to get killed today, at least I could talk to someone on my way out.

I turned in the seat and eyed them both. "You know Vulcano's rules?"

They both nodded.

Vassey said, "Do you?"

"They're more guidelines than rules." Sorry, Captain Sparrow. "I have one mission—to rescue my granddaughter. Nothing else matters. If we get an opportunity to grab Whisper, great. If not, I'm leaving with Madison and you two can play it how you like."

Poole glanced back at Vassey, then at me. "Mr. Vulcano won't like that."

"Nine-year-olds trump old vendettas."

Vassey leaned forward. "I don't blame you, Curran. But we got our orders, too."

"I get that. We all do what we have to. Just don't shoot me in the crossfire." I thought for a second. "Or on purpose."

Poole laughed, oddly enough. "That goes for you, too, Pappa."

Pappa? "Do I know you guys?" They were way too young to have been around me in my day.

"Nope. But we know you."

Great, my fan club.

Without further ado, signing autographs, or doing fan selfies, I pulled my Range Rover—excuse me, Katelyn's Range Rover—far off the side road behind some trees. We all climbed out.

Poole worked a small tablet that he'd been studying on the ride over. He turned it around to show me. It was an aerial satellite map of the area we were in, and in the center with an X was McKnight's estate.

"Is that NSA Satcom?"

Vassey grinned. "No, it's Google Maps."

I knew that.

"Vassey, take the north approach." Poole gestured on the tablet. "I'll come in the south. You—"

"I'm going up east." I checked my Kimber and double-checked the four magazines on my belt. "Look, boys, they know I'm coming. They might or might not guess I've got friends. Let's just cut the Green Beret drama and go get my granddaughter."

They agreed and geared up.

I said, "And boys, the next one who calls me Pappa gets shot."

They were gone.

I climbed into the Range Rover and did something no one—especially Poole and Vassey—would ever expect. I'm good for strategy like that. I drove right up the paved driveway to the grand Tudor home at the end.

Who would ever think I'd be that dumb?

Upon my arrival, there was nothing—and that unnerved me.

There was no security waiting. No mercenaries. No Secret Service. No one. I pulled up to the front, around the circular drive, and stopped. I waited for the arrival of the security forces.

None came.

Well, my devious plan might just work. Only a fool on a mission like this would go through the front door. Surely, McKnight had his men watching the side and rear access points—the blind spots. I sure would.

Out of the Range Rover, I walked to the front door and did the peeking game—yeah, I know, it didn't work well in Voula. I glimpsed through the side panels of his front door. Inside was a grand foyer with no one around. A long, wide hall extended deeper into the house and ended in a room beyond. There were two doorways on my end of the hall and two at the far end that I could see.

As silly as it seemed, I walked in the front door. Surprise was mine.

My radio crackled in my ear. Vassey said, "Curran, I've got two Secret Service agents down out here. They're tied up and gagged in the gardener's shed. Alive. Watch yourself."

Good plan.

Voices rumbled from the room at the far end of the hallway. I stalked toward them, following my Kimber. At the end of the hall, I flattened myself against the wall and leaned around with my pistol ready. My pulse was breakdancing, and my nerves were dancing on needles.

The room was a lavish great room with a two-story ceiling and walls of books and mementos. There were four people in the room—I knew two of them.

A middle-aged woman with dark Mediterranean features sat on a large leather sofa on the far side of the room. She was stone-faced and staring at the floor. Beside her was the aged, well-dressed Ambassador McKnight I'd seen in press reports—yeah, I do watch the news sometimes. He had a full head of silver hair and had striking features. He stared across the room at the other two people. One of them was the troublesome cherub, Billy Piper. Though, he sat on the floor rather uncomfortably, handcuffed and gagged. The last person was Marshal Gallo.

Gallo held his Glock out, aimed at McKnight.

"I'm going to give you three more seconds, McKnight." Gallo lifted his

Glock into a shooting stance. "Give me my daughter, or I'll shoot."

"I've told you, sir, I do not know what you're talking about. I have no idea who you are or who Madison is. If you will just explain—"

"Whisper." I stepped into the room, catching Gallo's eye and patting the air to keep him from shooting me. "We're here for Whisper."

When Gallo temporarily turned his Glock toward me in surprise, McKnight jumped to his feet and tried to make a move toward a large bookcase on the near wall. Gallo spun back around and fired a single shot ahead of him. The bullet kicked up a cloud of paper and debris from the books not two feet ahead of McKnight.

"Back up, McKnight," Gallo warned. "Next one is all you."

"I'd do that, Whisper," I said. "Where's Madison?"

McKnight stood rigid. "I don't know who that is. I don't know who you are. But I know you're in big damn trouble, gentlemen. My Secret Service—"

"Forget them," I said. "They're busy elsewhere. I figure we have about thirty minutes before anyone notices they're not responding to the radio."

McKnight slowly turned to face me. "And you are?"

"Lowe Curran." I moved closer and went eyeball-to-eyeball with him. "You probably don't remember me. You ordered my team and me murdered on the Voula Beach Road many years ago. I lived. My partner did, too. Well, until earlier today when your minions killed to clean up loose ends."

McKnight was a master statesman and negotiator, for sure. Just as he had been with our country's enemies over the years—"Yes, Mr. Karzai, we will always love you"—he looked squarely at me and lied.

"Voula Beach? If you're referring to that DIA failure to handle a simple Hezbollah terrorist, then you're a fool."

I closed the distance and grabbed McKnight by the throat, forced him backward and down onto the overstuffed chair nearby. I pressed him deep into the cushion and nearly through it.

"You ignorant, corrupt bastard." I dug my fingers into his throat as hard as I could without crushing his windpipe. "Madison Gallo is my granddaughter. Get her to us, or I'll snap your neck."

The Mediterranean woman behind me jumped up, ignored Gallo's wavering Glock, and grabbed my arm. She tried heartedly to pull me away but couldn't. Her fear was not as powerful as what drove me—saving Madison.

"Leave him alone. It's not him you want. It's…it's not him."

The words took their time getting into my brain, but eventually, I released the lying bastard and stepped back.

"Who are you?" Gallo demanded of the woman.

"I am Abigail Angelos." The woman helped McKnight to a sitting position and waited while he caught his breath. "I am his fiancé. Whatever you believe Bradley has done, you are mistaken. It was not him."

Gallo and I exchanged glances—*and the government is here to help.*

"Ideas, Gallo?" I asked. When he shrugged, I added, "Did you search the place?"

He shook his head. "I was about to. Let's tie them up. You take the basement up, I'll start—"

"Nowhere," said a calm voice from the doorway behind us. "Everyone stay still. Drop your guns on the coffee table, gentlemen. Step away and put your hands behind your head."

As I slowly—*very slowly*—turned, I locked eyes on a man I'd never seen before. He was strapping, with light-brown hair, and wearing an Oxford shirt and khakis. He held a heavy revolver in both hands, aiming it right at me.

"Ambassador? Abby? Are you all right?" he asked.

"Yes, Bryan." Abby slumped down on the arm of the chair beside McKnight. "Thank God you've arrived. I was afraid they'd found you out."

Chapter Sixty-Five

Curran

So, this was R. Bryan Scott, McKnight's trusted aide-de-camp. One of the names Billy Piper was paid to locate.

"Ambassador, the Secret Service men are gone," Scott said.

"Gone?" McKnight turned an angry glare at me. "Your doing?"

"Me? No." Something was off. Why would a deep-cover Iranian agent be upset that his Secret Service detail was gone. Wouldn't they just get in the way of killing us?

I wasn't the only one seeing the plot hole. Gallo did, too.

Gallo said, "Ambassador, yesterday, someone kidnapped my daughter, Madison. That someone is responsible for the deaths of more than a dozen good people—starting in Greece and others more recently. They might also be responsible for General Alvarez withdrawing from the president's consideration for vice president and Senator Wain's so-called suicide. Up until this moment, we believed you were responsible."

I tipped my chin toward Gallo. "Ah, there's more, but I'll save it for later."

"Are you mad?" McKnight did his Academy Award performance of being shocked to win. "I've known Alvarez and Wain for decades. I would never be involved in such treason."

Yeah, neither would Mr. Arnold—the Revolutionary traitor, not the actor and former governor.

I said, "Si-Int is onto you, Whisper. I had a second backup of Billy Piper's hacked data you want so bad—including the data he stole from McKnight Enterprises. Si-Int knows about Embassy Athens and Kalani—about the plan to infiltrate the White House. Everything. It'll get you the needle, McKnight." Finally, I got to threaten someone with the needle. It felt good.

I'd almost forgotten about Piper sitting on the floor, seeing he was gagged and not making any noise for a change.

"Isn't that right, Billy?" I glanced over at him on the floor. "Your data backups will prove all this?"

He grunted something, and I took that as a yes.

McKnight's face screwed up. He glared at me, then Piper, and back to me. "You're insane. I have no idea what Whisper is. There is no McKnight Enterprises. If Si-Int thinks they have something on me, have them confront me—"

"Don't respond to them, Bradley." Abigail moved to Bryan and took his pistol. "Bryan, go into the den and call the authorities. I will watch them."

Bryan nodded. "Yes, good. I'll call the Secret Service first."

The moment Bryan turned toward the door, Abigail smashed the pistol onto the back of his head. He dropped to the floor with a large, bloody gash behind his right ear—out.

The room did a collective gasp—me included—and Gallo and I backpedaled while we tried to find a place to duck lead.

Abigail turned and fired at Piper in a hasty shot. It hit the floor beside him. "You're coming with me, Piper. Hesitate, and I'll kill you right here."

Holy plot twist. I didn't see this coming.

Piper's eyes were big, round, and terrified. Even with his gagged mouth, he managed a muted "Yeah, yeah, okay."

"Ab...Abi...what..." McKnight stuttered. "Abigail, what's happening?"

"Shut up, Bradley. For Christ's sake, just shut up."

McKnight's face paled from so many questions. "It's not you?"

"Really?" Abigail gestured at him with her gun. "You'd still be a lonely foreign service nobody if it weren't for me. You could have been president. And I, well, if not for Si-Int and this fool here," she aimed her pistol at Piper, "I would have been running this country. Imagine that."

McKnight opened his mouth, but no words came out.

"I'm leaving." She grabbed Piper by the arm and yanked him to his feet. Then, she backed toward the doorway using Piper as a shield. "If anything stops me from getting out of the country today, little Madison will never be found."

My stomach knotted, and I fought the growing rage. Anger swirled in my brain so fast it made me dizzy. I fought for control of my emotions. To fail that, I'd never save Madison.

Plan B.

I dove for my Kimber on the coffee table.

Abigail jerked a shot at me and ran from the room.

The bullet hit my lower arm, and I lost balance and fell to the floor.

Dammit, I knew I was going to get shot.

Chapter Sixty-Six

Curran

Abigail Angelos—*not* Ambassador McKnight—was Whisper. She was responsible for the massacre on the Voula Beach Road, my occasional limp, and Stevie Keene's betrayal and violent death. Not Ambassador McKnight. She was the Iranian spy trying to infiltrate the White House and control the future. Not Ambassador McKnight. Most importantly, she was responsible for kidnapping Madison. Not Ambassador McKnight.

I was going to kill her. Not Ambassador McKnight.

How in hell did everyone—Si-Int and me—get this so wrong?

Now, she had Billy Piper, the only good witness to the madness, and Randy Cantrell. Okay, so I could do without him. I'm just keeping score.

Yikes. I'd almost snapped the Ambassador's neck moments ago. I hope Tommy and Vulcano have good lawyers.

There was gunfire out front, and the chatter in my earwig said Poole got a bullet in the leg trying to stop Abigail.

Things were a blur for a while as Vassey put his combat first aid to work. He stabilized Poole outside and joined us inside to patch up the bullet hole in me in no time.

"It's a graze," he told me.

"Well, I still got shot." Okay, so it was barely a scratch.

"Get on your feet," Poole said, giving me a hand. "We can still find

Whisper."

Gallo moved Scott to a chair. He tried to bring him around but couldn't. Vassey declared Scott would live for sure, but he'd need a hospital soon.

"Any ideas, Gallo?" I ditched my body armor. "Madison could be anywhere."

His face was grim. "No. But, Christ, we gotta come up with something."

McKnight sat at a writing desk facing the windows, staring out at nothing. His face was awash in a recipe of grief and shock. Maybe a little guilt, too— or at least responsibility. Finally, he turned to us.

"I cannot believe you thought me an Iranian agent," he said in a strained, but agitated voice. "But then, with the facts before me, I understand. I have been duped for decades by the love of my life. So many lives. It's my fault—all of it. Please, if you believe anything, believe that I had no hand in your daughter's plight, Marshal Gallo. What can I do?'

Great question. "Think, Ambassador. Where might Abigail go?"

He did. He contemplated each of us for a long time. Then, reason took hold. "She still maintains a Greek passport. Perhaps the Greek Embassy in Washington—"

"No, she won't go there," a man said from behind us. "Abigail Angelos is, in truth, Ariana Abbasi. She is not Greek. She is Iranian. And we at Mossad wish to find her, too."

I twisted around as Gallo did the same. We both lifted our pistols and took quick aim at two men entering the room, each holding silenced Uzi machine guns.

Jesus, another plot twist. I recognized the two men entering the room. I'd first met them at Billy Piper's apartment when they tried to kill me. Later, they came at us at the Virginia Hospital Center. Both times, they had not been pleasant.

I kept my pistol poised. "You're Freedman and Levene. You tried to kill me. You're Mossad? Why is Mossad trying to kill me?"

Footnote here. Mossad is the Israeli CIA, more or less. They have an international reputation as very successful badasses. Among their many, many effective operations over the years were the elimination of Black

342

September terrorists for killing Israeli Olympians during the Munich Olympics in 1972 and, most recently, by blowing up a bunch of Hezbollah terrorists using only their pagers. Pretty ingenious bunch.

"I am Levene." The older man gestured to his partner. "He is Freedman."

I didn't take my Kimber off him. The lights were finally going on in my brain. "Mossad—you guys—guys paid Piper to hack everyone looking for intelligence on Whisper. Why?"

"We spy. You spy." Freedman shrugged. "You see, Mr. Curran, many years ago, we ran an asset in Egypt—a low-level Greek diplomatic officer. Her name was Abigail Angelos. She was very helpful there. Soon, she met McKnight and became his mistress. Rather fortuitously, she went with him to Athens and became both his lover and his assistant at your embassy. While perhaps we should have withdrawn, we did not. We continued running her as our asset. We had no idea she was a double agent for the Iranians all that time."

"And you still ran her and never told us." I eyed the two Mossad agents. "How very Jonathan Pollard of you."

For those of you not in the know, Pollard was a former US Navy intelligence officer who was also an Israeli spy. You know, spy vs. spy. In this case, Mossad vs. the US. He spent thirty years in prison for espionage. If I had my way, Whisper was going to do forever in the dirt.

Levene continued. "After the disaster on the Voula Beach Road, we realized there was a problem in your embassy—Hezbollah was receiving intelligence, and there were many American and Israeli operations thwarted. Then, McKnight and Angelos left for the US. The intelligence leaks stopped. Thus, we believed, as you did, that McKnight was Whisper. Recently, with McKnight's rise in your presidential politics, Mr. Piper was engaged to try and find intelligence against McKnight. We needed proof before falling on our sword with your government. They would take a dim view of us having an asset inside your state department—let alone one running for the White House. But that ire would be blunted with information on McKnight."

"But it wasn't McKnight," I said, eyeing them. "It was Abigail Angelos—his mistress."

"Yes, but she was actually Ariana Abbasi, a MOIS agent," Freedman said. "The files Mr. Piper discovered would have led us to her."

I shrugged. "So why try to kill me? If we're all allies and such. Seems—"

"We did not try to kill you, Mr. Curran. Just scare you off—to keep you from finding Piper first and keeping the information from us. Please believe me."

"Believe you? Hah." I wavered my Kimber between them. "Why should I believe you?"

"It doesn't matter." Levene moved carefully into the room and glanced at Scott. "We must hurry, or we'll lose Whisper."

Hurry? Yeah, hurry, but I'm not getting shot in the back. "Give me one reason to believe you're not going to shoot us the first opportunity you get."

Freedman exchanged glances with Levene.

Levene extracted his cell phone and dialed a number. "Sir, this is Agent Levene. I believe you were expecting my call. Yes, he is here. I'll put him on the phone."

He extended the phone to me, and I took it and read the number—Tommy Astor's private line. *What the hell?*

"Tommy?"

"Trust them, Lowe ol' boy." Tommy's voice was sharp and direct. "A lot happened after you left. I'll explain everything later. Just get on with it and get little Madison back safe." He hung up before I could respond.

I gestured to Gallo to lower his gun. "For now, we're on the same team."

"Bullshit," Gallo sneered. "But if it gets Madi back, I'll play along."

Freeman threw a thumb over his shoulder. "Leave one of your people to secure the premises. Call for others immediately. I doubt Whisper will return, but prepare nonetheless."

Iranian spies. American spies. Israeli spies—MOIS, Mossad, Si-Int. What in hell had Tommy gotten me into? I sat back on the couch and put my head in my hands. Everything we'd learned over the past few days— perhaps everything Si-Int learned since the Voula Beach Road—was wrong. McKnight, Whisper, Stevie Keene, Mossad hunting Iranian agents using Iranian agents—everything. I didn't know whether to laugh at Iran's brilliance and cunning or cry at their brilliance and cunning.

I just wanted it over. I wanted Madison safe. I wanted to put a bullet in Abigail Angelos Abbasi's brain. If I got these things, I'd never ask for anything for Christmas again.

"How could I be so stupid?" McKnight had been listening and stood. Tears drained down his face, and his eyes were big and red—anger and grief fighting for control. Something struck him. "Wait...as you know, there has been no Iranian diplomatic presence in the US since 1980. But there is a high-ranking Iranian official—Hamid Taheri—who works within the Pakistani embassy in Washington. He has an estate buried deep in the woods outside Poolesville. It's remote. Abigail might go there."

Freedman was already moving. "If not, we're going to cause big problems for no reason."

"Good." I eyed the two Mossad agents who'd nearly killed me before becoming my dear friends. "I have a burning desire to cause an international incident. It's been fifteen years since my last one."

Chapter Sixty-Seven

Curran

Hamid Taheri's estate was indeed buried miles from nowhere and surrounded by creeks and trees. Poolesville, Maryland, was a rich and charming community in Western Montgomery County. The estate bordered the Montgomery County Agricultural Reserve, where farmland and rural sprawl were protected from the likes of property developers. It also spawned the rich and famous to maintain estates that looked like settings for some lavish "how the rich lived" magazine. Taheri's estate could be the poster child for one.

Isolated and surrounded by dense woods and rolling acres of farmland, it was perfect to hide hostages and spies and fend off any attempted attack without anyone hearing or knowing.

That seclusion worked both ways.

Freedman and Levene already knew the details of the compound. I guess that was the product of being Mossad agents in Washington, D.C. Their intel was important—and good. The property was set back into the woods and secluded. The main house was a three-story mansion that resembled one of those British manor houses in a PBS mystery. It had more guards and dogs and security cameras than the White House. There was also a ten-foot high steel fence around fifteen acres and roving foot patrols along the fence. The guards seemed pumped and animated, too.

Either the Ayatollah was having a sleepover, or the MOIS had someone very important hiding inside.

Like an Iranian spy and Madison Gallo.

One of them was coming home with me today. The other was going home in a body bag. Yeah, that might irritate Tommy and Vulcano, but hey, I don't see them anywhere around me at the moment.

It took us an hour to mobilize. Vassey called Vulcano for reinforcements. They arrived by helicopter and sat at McKnight's place before we left. They provided us with tactical gear and more rules from Vulcano. We were back airborne in minutes.

Like all Vulcano's previous rules, I ignored them. In my defense, my brain was overloaded. It tossed out the stuff I didn't care about. I lost the last six months' worth of overdue bills and the last three seasons of The Bachelor, too. No, I didn't watch The Bachelor. It was a symbolic reference.

"Are you sure about this, Curran?" Gallo asked. "We're gambling with Madison's life."

"No." That was a gut punch I didn't need. "Got any better plans?"

"Why not let me call in federal backup?"

"Impossible." Vassey sat nearby listening. "The feds will want to negotiate diplomatically. The next time you'd see Madison—if—she'd be in college."

Gallo swallowed that. "Right."

My earbud buzzed with signals from the rest of the team. The plan was in play.

Two minutes later, my Range Rover went careening up the long driveway at top speed and crashed through the steel gates at the estate's entrance. The vehicle made it ten feet before a hail of bullets stopped it. Armed guards erupted from every direction and rained gunfire into the vehicle, shredding it to a pulp. The moment it exploded—not from the gunfire but a small charge Vassey had placed under the seat—the rest of hell opened up.

Having drawn out the guards, Vulcano's marksmen opened fire from outside the fence and put eight of them down. None of them dead. Vulcano didn't want a mass shooting incident on an Iranian estate. The teams carried high-powered tranquilizer guns.

Me, I had my Kimber. I'm a rule breaker. Sue me.

The helicopter Gallo, Levene, Freedman, and I were in took off moments before the remote-controlled Range Rover began its trek up the driveway. By the time we slipped over the trees and down onto the Iranian compound, there was no outside resistance left. We were out, and the helicopter regained altitude in seconds.

Si-Int—read that Vulcano and Tommy Astor—gave us thirty minutes. They would not allow their operatives to enter the mansion. Their men would secure the grounds and perimeter. This was the epitome of plausible deniability. That left the two Mossad agents, Gallo, and me to go in. If we couldn't rescue Madison in thirty minutes, all was lost.

We reached a side entrance—locked.

A little sticky explosive goo here and there, and boom. No more locks.

We crashed through the doors, tranqued three armed guards inside, and continued deeper into the estate. Okay, I lied. I had a tranq pistol, which I reloaded, and my Kimber holstered on my hip. I didn't want to be the one to start a war with Iran, so killing was out of the question unless I had no choice.

The mansion was massive. It would take hours to search. We had twenty minutes. Levene and Freedman split from us at the main hall. They continued to the left, deeper into the mansion. Gallo and I went right toward a large, arched entrance to the ballroom.

The moment we turned the corner into the opulent room—a crystal chandelier, gold inlaid crown molding, and pristine marble flooring—we scored.

Abigail Angelos Ariana Abbasi—alias Whisper—stood with her back to the wall across the room. She held Madison around the neck with one hand and pressed a small pistol against her temple with the other.

Randy Cantrell and Billy Piper were nowhere.

"Daddy?" Madison's face was pure terror, but somehow, she wasn't crying. There was angst and uncertainty in her eyes, but they held strong and focused. "I knew you'd come, Daddy."

"Madi!" Gallo yelled, raising his pistol, looking for a shot. "Are you all right? Are you hurt?"

To Whisper, I said, "Abigail Angelos? Ariana Abbasi? Or do we just call you Whisper?"

"I have not heard the name Abbasi for many years." She actually laughed. "Please, use it. And this little one is fine. Unharmed. Stay back."

As Gallo and I closed the distance to Abbasi and Madison, my heart ached in my chest. Every synapse in my being wanted to attack—common sense and the remnants of past training focused me.

This was the time for thoughtful strategy, not anger and vengeance.

"Don't hurt her," Gallo said, almost begging. "We want her. Not you."

Abbasi forced a laugh. "I am to trust you? No, I think."

"You know how this works, Abbasi." I stepped closer. "Walk away. Give us Madison and the others, and go. I don't give a crap about your spy games or politics, lady."

"How noble." She laughed and shook Madison. "You have invaded Iranian property. It is you who must retreat or start a war."

"Well, I had nothing else to do today," I sneered. "Give us the kid. Neither Gallo nor I give a damn about your Whisper operation."

"Really?" She grinned when movement from our left spun us around. "Think again."

U.C. stood across the room holding a silenced MP-5 subgun. It was leveled at Gallo and me. He had us flanked and cold. A touch of his finger and we'd be cut to pieces.

People sneaking up on me was getting old.

U.C. wasn't the only surprise. The big surprise took the wind, and the fight, right out of me.

"You're outgunned, brother." Stevie Keene walked in behind U.C. He aimed a Beretta pistol at me. As we locked eyes, he grinned. "Surprised?"

"What in the flying monkeys?" I glanced at Gallo and then Stevie. "You're dead, you treacherous, lying, betraying bastard."

"No, brother. All part of the ruse." He winked. "Why couldn't you just go away?"

I lowered my tranq pistol as the heat rose in my face. Gallo's expression mirrored mine.

We'd been had.

Gallo said, "Curran, what the hell is going on? You said—"

"Yet here I am." Stevie let go a dry laugh. "Drop your guns—all of them—and kick them away. You know, like in the movies you love, Curran."

We did, and the weapons skidded away.

"Keene?" U.C. pointed a chin for Stevie to flank us. "Are you up for this?"

Stevie said nothing.

"Keene?" U.C. repeated. "You've had three chances to end him, man. This is your last one."

"I got this, U.C.," Stevie grunted. "Do your shit, I'll do mine."

"Christ, Stevie, you've been lying to me for years." A sickening, bitter taste filled my mouth. "The booze—PTSD—all an act? Just to cover up you selling out in Greece."

He grinned, though it was meek and shameful. "Oh, I took a couple bullets—well placed by U.C. Things really were tough for a long time, brother—"

"Brother? Screw you," My whole body vibrated with the rage building inside. "You're no brother."

He shrugged. "Okay, I deserve that. Look, bro... Pappa, they wanted you dead in Voula. I couldn't do it. We were tight—for real. I promised to keep you out of their way. Hell, they didn't expect you to ever leave the hospital. When you did, I watched you for years until that damn computer geek stirred things up."

Billy Piper found what no one else could—Whisper.

"Screw you." I turned to Abbasi, still clutching Madison. "Keep me. Let Madison and her dad go. We'll call back the chopper. They'll take you wherever. You have my word."

U.C. snorted. "Sure, right. You never were a good liar, Pappa."

"Screw you, *Wally*." God, it irked me that these bastards were calling me Pappa and Brother like they hadn't betrayed me and killed so many people. "You're traitors. Worse."

Madison twisted against Abbasi's grip and loosened herself a little. "Daddy?"

CHAPTER SIXTY-SEVEN

"Be calm, Madi," Gallo said. To Abbasi, he added, "Please, leave her."

"Stop it, kid." Abbasi tightened her grip. "Quit fighting me, or I'll kill your daddy and your granddaddy."

Madison stilled. She looked across the room at me like she saw me for the first time. Fear melted from her eyes—replaced by recognition and understanding. From behind the wash of fright, she smiled.

Abbasi shook her again. "U.C., get over here and take this kid. You know what you have to do."

"No." Gallo stepped toward Abbasi, hands patting the air. "Please. Anything else. Me. Curran. Both of us. Not her."

Abbasi leveled her pistol at him. "Back up."

He didn't budge.

"Come on, kid." U.C. moved and took Madison's hand. He led her toward the door. There, he turned and jutted a warning finger at Abbasi. "I'm not killing no kid, lady. I'll get her out of here. You do what you gotta do. No one touches this kid."

Abbasi lifted her pistol and shot him neatly in the forehead. He dropped where he stood.

Madison screamed and stepped away. She dropped to the floor, crawled behind a big silver serving cart, and hid out of sight.

Jesus, just an opening...please.

"Get back here, brat." Abbasi turned the pistol on Stevie. "I guess it's up to you, Keene. You've failed me. Redeem yourself."

"The kid?" Stevie looked from U.C.'s lifeless body to Abbasi. "Are you insane?"

Gallo lunged for Abbasi's gun. She got off a quick shot that hit him in the abdomen and put him down hard. He hit the marble floor, moaning.

Madison screamed and crawled from cover over to him, sobbing. "Daddy, daddy, daddy, please don't die."

Enough.

"Everyone go easy," I yelled. It was bullshit, but I had to slow the tempo and find a way out. "Abbasi, tell me what it'll take to end this."

"You dying." She lifted her pistol just as a big red dot formed on her

351

forehead. She sensed the danger and dove onto the floor near Gallo just as a sniper shot shattered the ballroom windows. It missed her and smacked into the wall instead.

I leaped sideways. I hit the floor with an *umph*, scooped up my Kimber, and rolled onto a kneeling position.

Before I could fire, Stevie grabbed Madison and backed toward the side door.

"Stop, Stevie." I took aim at him. "Don't make me kill you."

Abbasi had the same plan as Stevie and ran to them. She smashed her pistol across Stevie's face and snatched Madison away, lifting her as a shield.

"Put her down, Abbasi." I aimed my pistol at her face. A shot was precarious with Madison in her grasp. An inch either way, and I might kill Madison. At this distance, the muzzle flash and expanding gunpowder might seriously injure her, too. I lowered my Kimber ever-so-slightly. "Put her down and go."

Madison's eyes flashed big and tearful. She quivered and looked from her dad's fallen body to me. Then, strangely, she calmed. Her eyes settled on me with a confidence I didn't understand.

Madison said, "You're my grandpa?"

"Yes, Madison. I am." My heart shattered into a million pieces of regret. My hands trembled—part from my thunderous pulse and part from the fear of letting her down again. "Play like you play checkers, okay?"

"Checkers?" She grinned. "Yes, like checkers. Save my daddy and me, Pappa."

Pappa? Like the Grinch before me, my heart—and confidence—grew three sizes that day. I snapped my pistol up just as Madison twisted violently and bit Abbasi in the arm wrapped around her shoulder. The split-second Abbasi relaxed her grip, cried out, and let Madison slip sideways, I shot Whisper in the right shoulder to disarm her. Her pistol dropped away. My second shot struck her right thigh. Not an inch too far left. Not an inch too far right.

It was just right. Accuracy is important.

Abbasi erupted with a guttural scream and went down.

I lunged forward and grabbed Madison before Abbasi hit the floor. I kicked her gun away and crushed Madison into me. She clung to me, wrapped her arms around my neck, and hugged me with all her might. She shook and quivered. Sobbed and smiled meekly all at once.

"You're my pappa."

"I am. It's gonna be okay, kid." I hugged her and leaned down to face Abbasi. "You're done, Whisper."

Abbasi's right arm dangled limply, bleeding. She tried to stem the flow of red life pouring out of her thigh with her good hand. "Bastard. You—"

"Quiet." I kicked her leg and made her cry out. "My granddaughter is right here."

"Daddy?" Madison asked. "My daddy?"

"I'll get him help, Madison. I'll—"

"Don't move, brother," Stevie Keene said, rising to his feet. "I don't want to hurt either of you. But I gotta get out of this."

Dammit. Will this day ever go my way?

Chapter Sixty-Eight

Curran

"Go, Stevie." I set Madison down and moved her behind me. "I won't stop you."

He stood in the doorway with U.C.'s silenced pistol on us. "You gotta understand, Lowe, she paid me seriously big money. She wanted me to end you in Voula. Then, after you surprised everyone by walking away from that hospital, she wanted me to finish you then, too. I convinced her to let me keep track of you instead—told them your death would draw too much suspicion after Voula. But you just wouldn't stop."

"Stop what?"

"You just kept coming. After fifteen years, you started after all of us all over again."

"No, I didn't. Piper hacked into that. It wasn't me. It was him and Si-Int. I was on the outside of this mess. I didn't know how any of this fit into Voula until a few hours ago. I wasn't after you—just Piper. Then you kidnapped Madison. You forced my hand."

That seemed to throw him, and he lowered his pistol a little. "A couple weeks ago, when somebody started sticking their noses in Abbasi's files at McKnight Enterprises—and he didn't know shit about all this—your name popped up. Abbasi sent me to that cottage to end you right then."

Oh, crap. "You killed Charlie Cantrell by mistake?"

"Mistake?" He laughed. "Hell no. I didn't want to kill you, man. Not you.

I figured if I framed you for that louse's murder, you'd at least be alive."

Stevie killed Charlie Cantrell to save me? I didn't see this one coming—that's like four times this week I didn't see trouble coming. I was slipping.

"You stuck me with a double-murder rap?"

"I figured you'd worried more about that than Whisper, brother. Then, none of this would have happened. If only—"

"Don't call me brother, Stevie. Never again."

"Sure, I got that coming." He stepped back. "Look, you gotta know—they'll hunt you down. They won't use me again, but they'll come for you."

That had my attention. "The Iranians?"

"More than them, Pappa." He laughed awkwardly. "Watch your back."

"Go." I pointed to the door. "We're even, Stevie. If I see you again—"

"Yeah, we watched those movies together. Don't be cliché." He backed up again. "I'll do you a solid, Pappa. You'll owe me again. You'll see."

"Do what?"

He turned and was gone.

I went to Abbasi and knelt, searched her, and found the backup USB that would clinch my payday with Tommy and Vulcano. All this chaos over files on this drive. It didn't seem right. Yet, those files could ignite a war, might ruin an alliance, and had already killed dozens of people.

And terrorized an almost-nine-year-old little girl—my granddaughter.

Crunching glass turned me around, and I lifted my Kimber and shielded Madison. Only a friendly face kept me from shooting.

Vassey. He eased in through the shattered rear window.

"Gallo and Abbasi need a medic," I yelled to Vassey. "Get to work."

Vassey pulled out a medical kit from a backpack over his shoulder, knelt, and went to work on Gallo. Madison slipped from behind me and went to them, sitting beside her daddy and watching Vassey saving his life. She kept looking to me for comfort and back to Gallo. Tears finally played free and trickled down her face.

I knelt beside her—painfully—and put my arm around her like grandfathers do. It didn't seem odd or mechanical. It seemed so very familiar to hold her and console her. For a moment, I felt Carli beside me, too. This little girl had Carli in her—me, too, oddly enough. That very bond seemed so very real now. To think that Madi and my connection began over a few games of checkers and thirty dollars in gambling losses.

The best thirty bucks I'd ever spent. Of course, I let her win.

"He'll be okay, kid," Vassey assured her. "Trust me. I've seen worse." Then he moved to Abigail Angelos, alias Ariana Abbasi, alias Whisper. He pulled out a combat dressing and wrapped it tightly around her thigh to stop the bleeding. Then, he injected her with two syringes and spared no effort on her comfort. "She'll make it. We gotta go now, though."

I hugged Madison tighter. "You okay, Madison? Scary, I know—"

"I knew you'd come." She crushed into me again and kissed my cheek. It seared through me like fire. "I prayed you and my daddy would come. I didn't know you were my pappa then, but as soon as I did, I knew these bad people were in trouble."

My granddaughter, wasn't she brilliant?

When I stood, Madison stayed beside me, holding my hand. A feeling I'd never felt washed over me like a wave and warmed me to the bone. Damn, is this what I missed all these years?

Freedman and Levene came into the ballroom. They tugged two former hostages along with them—Billy "Chip Magnet" Piper, and Mr. manbun himself, Randy Cantrell.

"These two belong to you, Curran?" Freedman called.

Jesus, I guess they did. "Yeah, guilty."

Piper and Randy had been worked over badly—bruises and blood covered their faces. Piper had probably talked too much. Randy, well, he was just one of those guys you wanted to beat the crap out of anyway.

"You two all right?" I asked.

"Screw you, PI-man," Randy blustered. "This is your fault."

Piper started cursing and muttering, and I flashed up a hand to shut him up. Then, a very interesting idea hit me. Odd time, mind you, but my brain works like that.

"Piper, come here." I walked him across the room. "I saved your life like three times this week."

CHAPTER SIXTY-EIGHT

He nodded. "So? You almost got me killed five times."

"Maybe." I told him how he was going to repay me in order to get my help in staying in WITSEC. When I was done, he shot looks from Randy to me, to the two Mossad operatives, and back to me.

"Child's play. I just need a computer or cell phone. And maybe thirty minutes. You gonna square this with the Marshals, right?"

I slapped him on the back. "I'll get you a tablet on the way home."

"Done. And I want my twenty-five g's back."

Indian giver. "Fine, but I'm keeping Bogart."

"Who?"

"Rufus."

I looked at Levene and Freedman as the thump-thump-thump of helicopters—at least two—filled the air. "It's been great, guys. But I gotta get Whisper home. It's past her jail time, and I gotta get paid."

"No, Curran." Freedman held up a hand. "We're taking Abbasi. You're going home with the others."

Ah, what? "Nope. I got a lot riding—"

"Stand down, Pappa," Vassey said, moving between me and the Mossad agents. "Mr. Vulcano's orders. They get Whisper."

Screwed again. I wonder if Vulcano was secretly a lawyer.

Freedman extended his hand to me—palm up. "That includes the data drive. It's not on her; you must have it. It's part of our deal with Si-Int."

Of course, it was. Reluctantly, I tossed it to him. "You have no idea how much this is costing me."

"Sorry, Curran. It's just how it is."

It's like it always is. They get what they want, and I get shot and screwed.

He and Levene exchanged thanks with me and carried Abbasi out of the ballroom onto the rear estate grounds toward the helicopters.

"Ready, kid?" I took Madison's hand and watched my fortune loaded onto the closest chopper. "For the record, we're not betting on checkers anymore."

Chapter Sixty-Nine

Curran

It's nice to have friends like Carmen Vulcano and Tommy Astor. They gave us a nice helicopter ride away from the carnage at Hamid Taheri's mansion. First, they delivered Gallo, Madison, and Piper to a nearby hospital. I walked Madi to her room, holding her hand all the way. We were surrounded by four of Vulcano's best-armed Si-Int operatives. No one would be getting close to any of them other than doctors and nurses.

Madi had a tear in her eye when I kissed her cheek and assured her daddy would be all right. She wanted me to stay, but this time, I had to leave.

"I'll be back later, Madi," I said, hugging her tightly. "I have to finish with the bad men. Then, I'll come back. I'll bring the best ice cream you ever ate."

She giggled. "And checkers?"

"Sure. Checkers." Ah, crap, I better add some cash to that list.

I left the hospital in tears and the chopper brought Cantrell and I to TAE. I embarrassed myself the entire flight.

Damn, I didn't know he had a helipad on his roof.

Tommy was waiting. "I'll get you home shortly, Lowe, ole buddy. We should talk."

"Oh, yeah, we should."

He led me away from the humming rotors and left an armed operative watching over Randy Cantrell in the helicopter behind us.

"Lowe, you did good."

Awe, shucks. "Thanks, Tommy. I wish you'd given me the whole story from the beginning. It might have been easier."

"Which beginning?"

Good point. "The one where Dark Creek became Si-Int, and they've had me on retainer for years. And that you were using me as bait to find Whisper."

His face screwed up until it gave way to one of his famous used car salesman grins. "Yeah, well, I guess that's what we did. You did great. You saved Madison. You saved her dad, and you got Piper and Whisper. Jiminy Crickets, if McKnight made it into the White House with her on his arm, it would be a shitshow for decades."

Yeah, no kidding. A real Iranian spy in the White House. At least it wasn't the Russians this time. How many movies and news shows have made that a cause celebre over the years? Surprise on them.

"Tommy, there's a little matter of my money." I watched to see if the used car guy would morph into an IRS agent. "You and Vulcano said Whisper had to be delivered to you alive. Well, she would have been—"

"Relax, Lowe." He gestured to the aircraft. "After you left to go to Taheri's after Madi, Mossad contacted us. Don't repeat this, but Mr. Vulcano has some contacts there. Anyway, Si-Int made a deal with them. A very lucrative deal to hide their shenanigans. See, Whisper knows about other Mossad games in the Med and Middle East. They'll get her talking and will share with us."

"Shenanigans? That's very kind of you. They're an ally who was spying on us. Don't forget that."

"Yes, siree. We spy on them. They spy on us. It's just business."

"Business?"

He winked. "Look, Lowe. They look as stupid as we do. Long story. They pledged Si-Int future intelligence and support in the Middle East. They get Whisper. If we turned her over to the US government, they'd make a similar deal. Why shouldn't we get something? We did the hard work. Everyone wins."

Not me. "I'm out a lot of money. I need it—now more than ever."

"It's in the chopper." Tommy slapped me on the back like all used car salesmen. "Minus the cost of a new Range Rover to replace Katelyn's since you it blew up."

"Doesn't Katelyn have insurance?"

"We're self-insured." He stepped back to let me go. "Oh, and my friend, Si-Int, still wants you on retainer. Somebody has to find Keene."

Yeah, someone should. I wasn't so sure it was me, though.

"Okay, Tommy." I headed for the chopper. "But my retainer—and fees—just went up."

"Sure. Sure. And Lowe?" Tommy leveled a finger at me. "Don't lose Mr. Cantrell out the door at ten-thousand feet. Someone will notice."

Damn, he read my mind.

* * *

When we sat in the field adjacent to Janey-Lynn's farmhouse, the brave and manly Mr. manbun couldn't get out of the helicopter fast enough to vomit. I guess he's never been on a whirly-bird before—other than a carnival ride.

"Let it all out, Randy." I headed for the house. "Then brush your teeth."

In the front yard, I knew my trouble wasn't over.

Evans and his partner, BCI Agent Kershaw, pulled up behind me just as Janey-Lynn and one of Vulcano's Si-Int operatives came out of the house. She ran down the stairs to me. The operative took a position on the porch in overwatch, eyeing the lawmen intently.

Janey-Lynn wrapped herself around me with a force I'd never had from her before. She laughed and cried and shuttered all over. She held me there for a long time, not saying a word.

"Janey-Lynn?" I pried loose and stepped back. "I'm not sure what's about to happen. Don't worry, though. I have a plan."

"A plan?" Evans called to me, snorting a few times. "Why Marlowe S. Curran, your plans are always bad. Where's Randy Cantrell?"

Randy, on cue, emerged from the field, wiping spittle from his face. He saw Evans and Kershaw, and that pale, ugly, airsick face turned gleeful.

"You worthless cops, it's about time," he cawed. "Arrest her. Him, too."

Kershaw walked up to him. "For what, Mr. Cantrell?"

Still a little leery, I said, "Vernon, I have information for you. It'll be tough to prove, but—"

"Save it, Lowe." He aimed a finger at Randy. "Mr. Cantrell, what would you like to have me make an arrest over?"

Randy jutted a snake-jaw at Janey-Lynn and me. "She paid him twenty-five thousand bucks to kill my dad. That's murder—a felony or more than one. Arrest them."

Kershaw looked at me and winked. "Mr. Cantrell, do you know what falsifying evidence is? What obstruction of justice is? Providing false testimony?"

"Sure, I guess." The questions confused him. "Are you charging them with those, too?"

"We certainly will be making those charges, Mr. Cantrell." Kershaw took Randy's arms, twisted them behind him, and handcuffed him in seconds. "Mr. Cantrell, you're under arrest for all those very things—oh, and forgery and fraud, too." He recited Miranda.

"Got it all?" Evans moved up nose-to-nose with him. "Odd things have been happening, Mr. Cantrell."

Randy's face blanched. "Huh?"

"Like bank video footage of you withdrawing money at the Middleburg Bank a few days before your daddy's murder."

Randy's eyes darted around like a snake, looking for escape. "So? I can use the bank if I want."

"We received banking records—anonymously," Evans added, "proving you withdrew twenty-five thousand from the Cantrell farm accounts that day. You failed to tell us that, Randy. You lied and obstructed our investigation. And you didn't have authorization to access that money."

"But-but you found the murder weapon in Curran's loft," Randy cried. "What about that?"

"Yeah, we did." Evans glanced at me. "Funny, too, that a muffled voice—an anonymous voice—gave us a tip. That wasn't you, was it?"

"No. But I can explain the bank—"

"Good." Kershaw leaned into him. "The records also indicate you falsified the signatures to withdraw the money from your father's account. Now, we'll have to verify all this since the records came from a hacker. Our warrants should have the evidence in a few hours."

Randy nearly fainted. He looked at Janey-Lynn and me and let fly a string of expletives that made me blush. Well, not really, but they could have.

I said, "Vernon, about Charlie's murder—"

"Hold that thought, Lowe." He faced Janey-Lynn and me. "Janey-Lynn, please excuse us. Lowe, let's take a walk."

Janey-Lynn politely stepped back to the porch as I followed Evans out of earshot of everyone.

"Aside from the email with the bank video, we got another email from someone calling himself "Whisper." This Whisper fella confessed to killing Charlie Cantrell and his mistress. He had enough details that we haven't publicized to convince us he's the real deal. He also confessed to planting the murder weapon in your loft. Between that and Randy Cantrell's bullshit, we're dropping all charges on you and Janey-Lynn."

I knew where the video and bank records came from—a pudgy little hacker I knew. Indian giver that he was. Now, the confession? Could it be that Stevie Keene did me that solid he promised?

"What details did Whisper have?"

"He knew exactly where the pistol was in your loft. He also knew what day and time he called us with that anonymous tip on its location." Evans glanced back at Randy, who was vomiting again. "Oh, and there was the thing about the ring."

"Ring?"

He nodded. "The killer took Charlie Cantrell's wedding ring off his body and shoved it down his lover's throat—post-mortem. It was supposed to send a message that this was all about his cheating. You know, to frame you and Janey-Lynn. Maybe a cheaters-on-cheaters thing."

I recoiled a bit. "Vernon, I've told you, Janey-Lynn and I aren't having an affair."

"Uh, huh." He waved toward Randy. "It's gonna make my day slamming that shitbird in a cell. He'll do time for the charges he racked up—couple felonies, a few misdemeanors."

Felonies and charges of moral turpitude. How nice.

"Thanks, Vernon. I owe you."

He shook his head. "Nope, I owe you. I almost had the needle in your arm, Curran. You didn't deserve that."

No, I didn't. "Comes with the job."

He followed me back to Randy and Janey-Lynn standing with Kershaw.

"What, PI-man?" Randy tried to be a tough guy again, but the spittle on his face blunted his delivery. "I might have some problems, but you and mommy-dearest are homeless. When I get done—"

"Ah, no, Randy." I patted his face like a schoolboy. "Your dad's will says felonies and charges of moral turpitude bar any inheritance. Isn't that why you were framing Janey-Lynn? If she were convicted of murder, you'd get it all?"

His face washed over with *oh-shit.* One light at a time came on, and he nearly dropped.

"You bastard." He tried to kick me, but Kershaw yanked him backward. "This is your fault. This place is mine."

Janey-Lynn pulled me back a step. "I'm sorry for you, Randy. I am. If you go to jail or whatever happens, come and see me after. I'll give you some help to move on. I promise."

Are you kidding me? This worm-bag beat on her, tried to frame her for murder, and tried to steal what was hers a dozen times over. And she wants to help him?

I said all that and kept my eyes on Mr. manbun with disdain he felt slap him.

"Randy, you don't deserve her. So, if you show your face around here without Janey-Lynn's okay, they'll never find your bones."

Randy started to bite back but his eyes filled with tears that escaped down his face. Instead of blustering, he dropped his head to his chin and wept.

Kershaw perp-walked him to their unmarked cruiser and jammed him into the rear seat.

Evans faced Janey-Lynn. "You're an amazing woman, Janey-Lynn. Just saying."

"Hey, what about me?" I asked. "I saved the day. I saved the country, too."

"Oh, yeah?" Evans walked to the cruiser. "I don't know what you're talking about, Curran. Joyriding in on a fancy helicopter don't mean shit to me."

As the BCI men drove off, Bogart bound from the house and leapt up on Janey-Lynn, licking her face and moaning.

"Traitor." I rubbed his ears. "I saved you from Piper. I gave you dog treats. I—"

"He sleeps with me, Lowe," Janey-Lynn said. "And I sleep naked."

Gulp.

I looked around for a good reason to vacate but found only the big duffle bag near the front porch that Tommy Astor left in the chopper for me. "I gotta go to Keene's place and see if I can find some leads on him. Can I leave that with you?"

She looked down at the bag. "What is it?"

"A half million bucks." I had talked Tommy out of me paying for Katelyn's Range Rover. After all, I was nearly killed doing his bidding. "Cash."

She snorted. "Sure, it is, Lowe."

I opened the bag and showed her the bundles of greenbacks. Then, I gave her a snippet about how I earned it. For her part, Tommy had beat me to the punch and filled her in on the past few hours while I was airborne en route there. "I need that money, Janey-Lynn."

"You going to buy yourself a place? The barn loft's not good enough for you now?"

"No, I'll stay there if it's okay." I shook my head. "My Carli died of a rare cancer. So did our daughter, Renae—Madi's mom. It's hereditary."

"Oh, no. I'm so sorry, Lowe." Janey-Lynn's eyes were bright with a few tears filling them. Worry and compassion accented her words. "You're giving this to Gallo for Madi?"

CHAPTER SIXTY-NINE

Yes, I was. I turned away so she wouldn't see my weakness.

For a long time, I looked out over the farm field where Janey-Lynn's horses grazed. A warm summer breeze carried scents of cedar and summer hay to me. The sky seemed welcoming as it darkened, swaddling me with a calm, enveloping embrace—something I cannot ever remember since losing Carli so many years ago.

Something—someone—was there, out in the veil of early evening.

Two figures watched me from atop the corral fence—Carli and a younger version of herself—Renae. I knew that somehow. It doesn't take a genius to know my heart had conjured them back. At least, for a short time. They sat there, smiling like everything was going to be all right. I wish I was as sure.

They weren't there, of course. Though, I wish I was—sitting between them like I should be. Could they ever forgive me? Could I ever forgive myself?

Oddly enough, Bogart sat next to me, leaned on my leg, and stared at the corral fence. He woofed a couple times, wagged, and looked up at me.

"Yeah, boy. I know."

I had a hard time keeping my emotions in—all that I'd screwed up and how much I'd failed them. In time, later, when the lights went out and me and Jack Daniels commiserated about life, I'd let it out. For now, I wanted them to know I was going to do what I should have done all those years ago—stay close.

After all, I was Madison's pappa.

Janey-Lynn slid her arm around me but said nothing.

"Janey-Lynn, I owe them. I failed Carli when she needed me most. I just didn't know it. I never met my daughter, Renae, and almost lost Madison. I won't lose her to some damn disease. I figure half a million will get a lot of good doctors on this. She's going to live. I won't accept anything else. Tommy has some friends ready to start research—pro bono. They owe him—and finally—he owes me."

"Damn, you, Marlowe S. Curran." Janey-Lynn crushed herself into me again with her country-girl bearhug. After a long moment, she kissed my cheek seductively and stepped back, holding my shoulders.

"If you gotta go to Keene's, Lowe, take my truck. Try not to blow it up or anything. Find clues if you must. But don't go after him yet. You owe me dinner."

Gulp. "Yeah, I do."

She winked. "With double dessert."

Acknowledgements

I always fear I'll miss acknowledging someone who gave me help and somehow slipped from my memory. One thing is for sure, the usual suspects are still right here with me. This time around, I've added some, too. First and foremost, thank you to Kimberley Cameron, my illustrious agent who has stayed with me through everything. You are the best. Then there's Shawn Reilly Simmons and Level Best Books for offering me a new home for my old works and Lowe Curran and his adventures, too. I hope this is a long, long dance. Special thanks to Gina H for helping promote my work and get my name out there. It's a slog. A battle. But it's better with you pushing me on. As always, I have to thank my editors and beta team—Jean, Nicci, and newcomer, Susan. You keep me straight and make me kill characters I love—for the best, I'm sure.

There are those who chipped in to help in many ways, some of which they don't even know:

Wayne L—for his brilliant IT consultation and cyber guidance. I promise not to use it nefariously! Mike K—the real deal in the art of war. Greg O for friendship and kicking me now and then. And Tom Sloan, author and pal, who understands we work alone, but we're still all in this together. Thank you all so much for your advice, head slaps, and friendship.

There're also the grands who keep me young—tired, but young. My wife, Laurie, who reminds me I'm not. And my writing companions, Annie Rose, Sawyer, Jax, Tuck and Angel. Yes, my pets. Deal with it! Sadly, I know as always that I'm missing a few people. It'll come back to me the day after this is published. I'll make it up to you, I promise!

Thank you all—known and unknown—and I hope you love Curran, Tommy, Janey-Lynn, and of course, Bogart as much as I do.

367

About the Author

Tj O'Connor is an award-winning author of mysteries and thrillers. He's an international security consultant specializing in anti-terrorism, investigations, and threat analysis—life experiences that drive his novels. With his former life as a government agent and years as a consultant, he has lived and worked around the world in places like Greece, Turkey, Italy, Germany, the United Kingdom, and throughout the Americas—among others. In his spare time, he's a Harley Davidson pilot, a man-about-dogs (and now cats), and a lover of adventure, cooking, and good spirits (both kinds). He was raised in New York's Hudson Valley and lives with his wife, Labs, and Maine Coon companions in Virginia where they raised five children who are supplying a growing tribe of grands.

Tj's work has been recognized by: The American Legacy Awards; the American Fiction Awards; the Independent Publishers Book Awards (IPPY); the Military Writer's Society of America; and others.

AUTHOR WEBSITE:
www.tjoconnor.com

SOCIAL MEDIA HANDLES:
Web Site: www.tjoconnor.com
Facebook: https://www.facebook.com/tjoconnor.author2
Blog: http://tjoconnor.com/blog/

Twitter/X:@tjoconnorauthor
Instagram: https://www.instagram.com/tjoconnorauthor/
Amazon: https://www.amazon.com/author/tjoconnor
Goodreads:
https://www.goodreads.com/author/show/7148441.T_J_O_Connor
Youtube Channel: @tjoconnorauthor3905
Bookbub: https://www.bookbub.com/profile/tj-o-connor

Also by Tj O'Connor

Dying to Know

Dying For the Past

Dying to Tell

New Sins for Old Scores

The Consultant

The Hemingway Deception